THE CRITICS LOVE

Hunter's Moon

"HEAVENLY! MS. ROBARDS WRITES WITH A GRACEFUL FLAIR! *Hunter's Moon* is exciting! A real thriller and the most wonderful love story!"

—*The Literary Times*

"AN ENGROSSING TALE of passion, intrigue, and murder. Fans of Robards' previous works will not be disappointed."—*Booklist*

"THE ENDING IS SO SHOCKING IT'LL KNOCK THE READER BACK WITH SURPRISE . . . the story line will send shivers down the spine. All of this and steamy passion leaves the reader riveted with action-packed suspense and heartwarming emotions."

—*Rendezvous*

"THE SEX IS UNBRIDLED, UNHARNESSED, and UNSTOPPABLE."—*Kirkus Reviews*

"Karen Robards has surpassed her own high standards with *Hunter's Moon*. Whodunit remains a puzzling mystery until the riveting and surprising climax."

—*Gothic Journal*

"ENTERTAINING."—*Minneapolis Star-Tribune*

By Karen Robards

Ghost Moon
The Midnight Hour
The Senator's Wife
Heartbreaker
Hunter's Moon
Walking After Midnight
Maggy's Child
One Summer
Nobody's Angel
This Side of Heaven
Forbidden Love
Sea Fire
Island Flame

HUNTER'S MOON

KAREN ROBARDS

DELL
NEW YORK

Hunter's Moon is a work of fiction. Names, characters, places, and incidents are the products of the author's imagination or are used fictitiously. Any resemblance to actual events, locales, or persons, living or dead, is entirely coincidental.

2011 Dell Mass Market Edition

Published in the United States by Dell, an imprint of The Random House Publishing Group, a division of Random House, Inc., New York.

DELL is a registered trademark of Random House, Inc. and the colophon is a trademark of Random House, Inc.

Originally published in hardcover in the United States by Delacorte Press, an imprint of The Random House Publishing Group, a division of Random House, Inc., in 1996.

This book contains an excerpt from *Heartbreaker* by Karen Robards. This excerpt has been set for this edition only and may not reflect the final content of the published book.

ISBN 978-0-345-52684-7

Printed in the United States of America

www.bantamdell.com

9 8 7 6 5 4 3 2 1

This book is dedicated, as always, with love to my sons, Peter and Christopher, and my husband, Doug. It also commemorates the births of my niece, Samantha Spicer, on February 28, 1994, and my nephew, Austin Johnson, on February 24, 1995.

PROLOGUE

November 15, 1982

At approximately 7:10 p.m., twelve-year-old Libby Coleman, freshly released from the rigors of her cotillion dance class, slides out of the backseat of a navy blue Lincoln Town Car. With youthful exuberance, she slams the door behind her before turning to grin at the occupants. Madeline Weintraub, driver of the car and mother of Libby's best friend, winces at the force of the slam, fearing for the continued integrity of the vehicle's trim. Her husband prizes the car, which is new.

"I'll call you when I get home!" Allison Weintraub rolls down the rear window to tell Libby.

"Go on in, Libby. I don't want to leave until you're inside," Madeline rolls down her own window to instruct. The warm air, scented with just mowed hay, caresses her face. It is a beautiful night, Madeline thinks, admiring the vast rolling lawn, like jade velvet in the darkness, and the neatly clipped lines of the boxwood hedge that shelters the stone path from driveway to porch. A huge yellow ball of a moon, which she has learned the locals call a Hunter's Moon, hangs low over the horizon. A few stars blink against the midnight silk of the sky.

"Okay, Mrs. Weintraub. Hey, Allie, did I tell you what you-know-who said after you danced with him?" Libby's grin broadens in anticipation.

"Russell Thompson? What did he *say*?" Allison squeals excitedly.

"Libby can tell you when you call her," Madeline says, beginning to roll up both windows with the master control switch as a way of terminating the chatter between the girls, which she knows from experience can go on all night.

"Mo-o-om!" Allison wails.

"We have to pick up Andrew, remember?" Madeline reminds her. "Go *inside*, Libby."

"I'm going. 'Night, Allie. Thanks for bringing me home, Mrs. Weintraub."

Libby waves, then turns and trots for the house. It is a large house, a mansion in fact, because Libby Coleman is the daughter of one of the premier horse farm–owning families in Kentucky's Bluegrass region. Madeline Weintraub, a relative newcomer to the area, feels fortunate that Libby has chosen Allison to be her best friend. She congratulates herself yet again for persuading her husband to enroll their only daughter in the expensive private school she and Libby attend. Libby's friendship is a social coup for Allison. Madeline expects to reap increasingly important benefits from it as the girls grow older. For the sake of those benefits, she is glad to act as chauffeur, and prepared to wince in silence over a few slammed car doors.

"Who is Russell Thompson?" Madeline asks her daughter over her shoulder, watching with half an eye as Libby starts up the wide stone steps that lead to the six-columned front porch. Really, she thinks, to anyone who didn't know their pedigrees, slender, blond-haired Allison would appear the old-moneyed blue blood. Chunky, rosy-cheeked Libby, with her satin bow askew in her untidy brown hair and her white, beruffled party dress splotched with orange Hi-C, certainly does not look to the manner born.

Allison giggles, and clambers over the seat back to plop down beside Madeline.

"He likes me," she confides, then wrinkles her nose. "*Libby* says. But sometimes I think he's kind of gross."

"Oh, yes?" Madeline murmurs encouragingly, hoping her daughter will continue. Allison's preadolescent view of the world is a source of never-ending interest to her. It is hard to remember ever being that young herself. Certainly she was never that carefree.

"When he laughs and drinks at the same time, Hi-C shoots out his nose." Allison shakes her head with disgust. "Can we *go*, Mom?"

Having watched Libby gain the safety of the lamp-lit porch, Madeline nods and shifts the car into reverse. Her last impression of Libby is of her bouncing dress, bouncing curls, bouncing hairbow as she skips toward the front door.

Though Madeline doesn't realize it as she backs down the long driveway, this image will be seared on her consciousness forevermore. She will resurrect it countless times, for Libby's family, for the police, for half a dozen private detectives, for an army of newspaper reporters, neighbors, and friends.

Because that view of Libby Coleman skipping happily across her own front porch is the last anyone will ever have of her.

From there, she simply vanishes.

Despite a massive search, public pleas by her frantic family, and offers of a huge and continually growing reward for information as to her whereabouts, Libby Coleman is never seen again.

1

October 11, 1995

"Hey, Will! Will! Would you look at that?"

Will Lyman responded to his partner's urgent whisper by opening his eyes a slit and glancing up at the monitor installed in the ceiling of the van. He was slightly groggy, and it took him a second to remember where he was: parked outside a barn at Keeneland Race Course in Lexington, Kentucky, charged with bringing to justice a gang of the pettiest crooks it had ever been his displeasure to chase. He, who had pursued big-time names from Michael Milken to O. J. Simpson and worked on big-time cases from the Hillside Strangler to the Oklahoma City bombing, had been assigned to get the goods on a gang of has-been horsemen who had taken to supplementing their income by substituting fleeter-footed "ringers" for the broken-down Thoroughbreds they were scheduled to race.

How the mighty are fallen!

It was just before 4:00 a.m., and dark as the inside of a grave in the van. The gray glow of the monitor's screen provided the only illumination. The picture was grainy, old black-and-white TV quality, but the image it conveyed was unmistakable: a slender young woman in skintight jeans had entered the previously empty tack room in the barn they had had under surveillance since dark. Back to the camera, she was in the act of bending over the bait: a large burlap feed bag stuffed with five thousand dollars in cash.

When Wyland Farm manager Don Simpson took it home with him, they had him. Case closed.

Only this girl was not, by any stretch of the imagination, Don Simpson.

"Who the hell is she?" Wide-awake now, Will shot off the dilapidated couch that filled one side of the lawn service van that was their cover to stand staring in disbelief at the monitor. "Do we have a file on her? Lawrence never mentioned a girl. He said Simpson would pick up the money himself."

"Nice ass," Murphy said, staring at the screen. The comment was detached. Murphy, fifty-two-year-old father of five, had been more or less happily married for thirty-some years. When it came to female flesh, he was looking, not buying.

"We got anything on her? Do you know who she is?" Irritated that Murphy had forced him to notice the small, firm, unmistakably feminine butt that was thrust almost in his face as the girl bent at the waist, backside toward the camera, Will spoke with an edge to his voice.

"Nope. Never seen her before in my life."

"Well, don't go into a panic over it." Will spared a second to glare at his partner. Murphy never hurried, never worried, never got into a state about anything. The trait was about to drive Will insane.

"Okay, okay." With a grin, Murphy swiveled sideways in his chair, turned on the computer that rested on the narrow work station built into the wall opposite the couch, and started punching computer keys. "Caucasian, female, between, oh, twenty and twenty-five years old, five feet seven, wouldn't you say, and maybe a hundred fifteen, hundred twenty pounds. . . . What color's her hair?"

"How the hell should I know? The damn picture's in black and white." With an effort, Will controlled his irritation and took a closer look. "Dark. Not blond."

"Brown," Murphy decided, typing it in.

"She's opening the bag!"

The clicking of the computer keys ceased as Murphy swung around to watch too. The girl on the monitor now crouched in front of the sack, which rested on the speckled linoleum floor in the corner directly opposite the hidden camera. Her hands were busy untying the frayed piece of hemp that was wrapped tightly around the sack's twisted neck. Her back was still to the camera, but at least her butt was down. A thick curtain of shoulder blade–length hair kept Will from getting a look at her face. Though her butt was certainly memorable enough for him to be able to pick it out of a lineup if he ever had to.

"Can you get me something on her, please?" Perilously controlled annoyance at both himself for noticing and Murphy for existing tightened his lips.

Murphy turned back to the computer.

"She's found the money." Will hadn't really meant to say it aloud, because he didn't want Murphy distracted. But the circumstances were so damned unexpected that his mind was not operating with its usual efficiency. He needed an ID, pronto. To decide what to do, he had to know who she was. Did the girl, who sank back on her heels to stare at the bundles of cash she had uncovered, work for the target of their investigation, or did she not?

The clicking stopped as Murphy, as expected, glanced around at the monitor. Will shot him a look that should have singed his eyeballs. Murphy hunched a shoulder guiltily, and started typing again. The girl reached into the sack to finger first one then another rubber band–bound bundle of twenties.

"Nothing . . . nothing . . . nothing," Murphy grunted as the screen blinked a couple of times, then shone a maddeningly blank fluorescent green. "No woman fitting her description in the files. Unless I've done something wrong."

That cheerful admission made Will want to tear out his hair. For a quick-talking, quick-thinking, quick-acting type A personality like himself, being teamed with a laid-back kind of guy like Murphy was a penance. Which was probably just what Dave Hallum had in mind when he paired the two of them up. Will's boss was still mad over the loss of his cabin cruiser. Hell, Will couldn't help it if the crooks he'd been chasing had thought the damned thing belonged to him, and decided to blow it up.

Hallum always had been one to hold a grudge.

Clearly this assignment, complete with Murphy, signaled payback time.

"She's taking the money!" Will watched as the unidentified girl, after retying the sack and casting a quick glance around that afforded him the merest glimpse of her profile, stood up with their bait in her arms. Then she turned, finally facing the camera, and walked straight toward them. Her face, Will discovered to his disgust, was as memorable as her butt: fine-boned and beautiful. He blinked in pure self-defense, and in that brief time she—and the Bureau's money—were out of camera range, and presumably out the door.

Murphy, leaning back in his chair, wolf-whistled appreciatively. "Whoa! Fox-y lady!"

Ignoring him, Will pressed a button beneath the monitor, and waited for the second camera panning the barn itself to pick up the action. All he got was a screenful of snow.

"Doesn't look like it's working," Murphy observed as Will frantically twirled dials and pressed buttons.

No kidding. Will gritted his teeth, abandoned the monitor, and with a dagger-glance at his partner snatched up the phone.

2

The burlap bag held place of honor in the center of the picnic table that served her ramshackle family as a kitchen gathering place. Molly felt queasy every time she glanced at it. She had stolen *five thousand dollars* from Barn 15's tack room. Had anyone missed the money yet?

Dumb question. It was just after noon, and she'd walked out of that barn before 4:00 a.m. Of course someone had missed the money. Who in his right mind wouldn't miss five thousand dollars?

The question was, how long ago had they called the police?

If she got caught, she could go to prison for years.

Or worse.

She wasn't stupid. That much money stuffed in a burlap feed bag and left sitting around in a corner of a deserted tack room in the middle of the night sure wasn't a bank deposit. It almost had to be somebody's ill-gotten gains. But whose? For months there'd been rumors around the stable that something dirty was going down. But what? Drugs? Illegal gambling? Fixing races? Who knew? Molly didn't *want* to know.

If that money *was* dirty, whoever it belonged to wouldn't—couldn't—call the police. What was the alternative? Visions of hired hit men on her trail made Molly feel light-headed.

But no one had any way of knowing that *she* had taken the money. She no longer groomed for Wyland Farm. Four days ago she had quit, in a fit of fiery temper that fifteen minutes later she remembered she and her family simply could not afford. Even if Thornton Wyland, obnoxious college-boy grandson of the stable owner, *had* grabbed her butt.

Last night—or rather this morning—she'd arrived at the barn to pick up her last check. Which Don Simpson would make her beg for, she knew, and might not even give to her though he owed her two weeks pay. He didn't like people quitting on him, and he had a vindictive streak a mile wide.

She'd thought maybe she might even screw up her courage to the point of asking for her job back. Not that it was likely to do any good. As he often said, Don Simpson didn't believe in second chances.

She should never have lost her temper. The thing to have done in such circumstances was simply knock away the hand groping the back of her jeans, and laugh the whole incident off.

Not punch the farm owner's grandson in the gut, and threaten to render him genderless if he ever touched her again.

And then tell her boss what he could do with himself and his job when Simpson, ignoring Thornton Wyland completely, snarled at *her* for yelling in the barn and spooking the horses.

Temper, temper. It had gotten her in trouble before, and no doubt it would do so again. But this time she should have thought about the consequences before she shot off her big mouth.

Not thinking before she acted was something she did too often. Just like she hadn't thought it through before taking the money from that tack room.

The question was, what did she do now?

Except for the horses, and a gimlet-eyed cat, the barn had been deserted when Molly entered it. Simpson always arrived for work at 4:00 a.m. sharp, and it was a good half-hour earlier than that. The groom who was supposed to be on duty throughout the night was nowhere around. She had seen no one. No one had seen her. No one knew she had been in that barn. No one knew she had the money.

Should she take it back?

Yeah, right, a little voice inside her head sneered. Just wait till 3:45 a.m. tomorrow, sneak back inside the barn with the money, and leave it where you found it. Like no one's even missed it yet. Like they won't even notice it's been gone.

What if they caught her taking it back? Molly shuddered at the thought. That would be the same as being caught stealing it. The consequences didn't bear thinking about.

Besides, she couldn't take it back. She had already spent one of the twenties. Unable to help herself, entranced by the fact that she actually had that rarity, real cash money that wasn't already earmarked for rent or food or something, in her possession, she had stopped by the Dunkin' Donuts on Versailles Road on the way home. The kids had woken up to fresh doughnuts and milk. What a treat! All of them, even fourteen-year-old

Mike, who lately had been way too cool to show enthusiasm for anything, had reacted with delight.

Whatever happened, even if she did end up going to prison—or worse—Molly just couldn't regret those doughnuts.

Anyway, they needed the money. It was wrong to steal, but it was better than starving, especially since they would soon be kicked out of their house, which came with her job at a reduced rent of a hundred and fifty dollars a month. The job had been all that kept the roof over their heads and food on the table for herself and four kids—and she didn't have that job anymore.

What she did have was five thousand dollars, cash.

But she sure didn't want to go to jail. Or worse. What would the kids do then?

Footsteps on the wooden boards of the ramshackle porch brought Molly's head around. Firm footsteps. I-mean-business footsteps. Not one of the kids playing hooky. Not a utility company man, come to collect what they owed or turn off the electricity or gas. Not a social worker, or a truant officer, nosing around about the kids. From bitter experience, Molly knew what all those footsteps sounded like.

These sounded serious.

She jumped up from the picnic table bench from which she had been nervously eyeing the evidence of her guilt and snatched the burlap bag off the table. She barely had time to stuff it in the cabinet under the sink and grab the shotgun that was kept on the far side of the refrigerator before the knock sounded on the door.

The gun wasn't loaded—she was afraid to keep a loaded gun around the kids, so she hid the shells in a hole in the underside of the mattress in her bedroom—but whoever was at the door wouldn't know that. Anyway, intimidation was what she had in mind, not murder.

Creaking springs and a ferocious burst of barking announced that Pork Chop had heard the knock too. A huge animal, part German shepherd and part who-knew-what, Pork Chop was ferocious-looking enough to freeze the devil himself in his tracks. Black and tan, with a long, springy coat that added inches of bulk to his already impressive size, Pork Chop was in reality as harmless as a kitten.

But whoever was at the door wouldn't know that.

Toenails scrabbling on the linoleum, Pork Chop almost knocked Molly down in his mad dash for the door. His hackles were up and he was making enough noise to wake the dead.

Ox, Molly accused him silently as she moved to stand beside him. Then, the gun butt snuggled firmly under her armpit, she opened the flimsy wooden door and grabbed Pork Chop by the collar as if she was scared he'd devour whoever was on the other side of the still-latched screen if she let go.

The spicy scents of perfect Indian summer weather greeted her. Ordinarily the sheer beauty of the day would have gone a long way toward soothing any agitation she might be feeling. She loved October, loved the way the bright sunlight looked spilling over the carpet of red and gold leaves covering the yard, loved the mild temperature, loved the smell of woodsmoke that tinged the air. But the agitation she was suffering at that particular moment was far from ordinary, and so she barely noticed what would on most days have given her a great deal of pleasure.

There was a man on the other side of the screen

door. Making no move to open it, Molly held firmly on to Pork Chop's collar as he lunged at the barrier of fine black mesh. The dog's huge jaws parted as he threatened the visitor, revealing rows of teeth that would not have been out of place on a *Tyrannosaurus rex.* Eyes widening, the man on the porch took a single look at Pork Chop, then stepped back a pace.

A glance told Molly that she'd never seen the man before. Fortyish, of average height and lean build, he had sandy hair cut ruthlessly short, a deep tan, and piercing blue eyes. He wore a dark suit and tie and looked grim. A hit man? She let go of Pork Chop's collar and leveled the shotgun at the man's belt buckle. Pork Chop barked hysterically.

"What can I do for you, mister?" Her greeting was hostile.

"Miss Butler?" He had to raise his voice to be heard over Pork Chop's ear-shattering din. Molly battled the urge to tell Pork Chop to shut up. The animal was deafening her—but he was also clearly worrying the man on the other side of the screen. On balance, it was worth it.

"Nope." He wasn't looking for her. Or the kids. As she registered that the person he asked for was unknown to her, Molly relaxed. With her knee she shoved Pork Chop back from the screen, preparing to shut the door in the stranger's face.

"Miss Molly Butler?"

Molly froze. The name was close. Too close. He *was* looking for her. He just had the name a little wrong. Molly fixed him with a wary gaze, her fingers tightening around the barrel of the gun. Without waiting for her to say anything more, he reached into an inside pocket of his jacket and produced a leather wallet.

"Will Lyman, FBI," he said, opening the wallet to flash a badge and some sort of identification card at her. "I need to talk to you, Miss Butler. Could you please put down the gun, and call off your dog?"

She might have tried—he was with the *FBI*, after all—but calling off Pork Chop was easier said than done. Anyway, it was too late. Pork Chop's attention suddenly found an object worthy of focus. Molly's only warning came when the volley of barking ended in a high-pitched yelp. With that the dog leaped right through the screen, his hundred-pound body as deadly as a missile to the flimsy mesh. Landing clumsily on four huge, bunched paws, now in full cry, he leaped skyward again, exploding past the unwelcome visitor in a frenzied bound. Knocked clean off his feet, the FBI man went down with a yell and a crash. His head just missed the rusting metal glider.

The neighborhood cat that had inspired such passion took one look at the behemoth tearing up the ground behind her, and swarmed up the gnarled trunk of a huge oak.

At the foot of the tree, Pork Chop leaped and snapped at the intruder, who calmly settled herself on a lower branch and proceeded to wash a calico paw, twitching her black-tipped tail with disdain. A single leaf, turned gold by autumn, fluttered down to land on Pork Chop's nose. He shook it off, and went mad at the indignity of it all.

"Shut up, Pork Chop!" Molly yelled. For all the good it did, she might as well have saved her breath.

The screen door, never very solid (she had put it up herself), had been knocked awry by Pork Chop's assault. It was open now, the wooden frame hanging lopsidedly from its hinges, stopped from closing by its low-dipping front corner, which was snagged on a board protruding from the uneven porch floor.

She would have to get Mike to help her fix the door when he got home from school, she thought distractedly. Mike would complain as he did about almost everything nowadays, but he could hold the door up while she tightened the hinge screws. And she would have to buy new mesh.

Thank goodness for the five thousand dollars. Without it, the mesh would have to wait.

But she couldn't think about that right now. Her first priority was to get rid of the man sprawled on her porch.

Molly looked him over assessingly. He lay flat on his back, eyes closed, arms outflung, unmoving, utterly silent. It occurred to her that perhaps he was seriously hurt, even dead. A squiggle of fear invaded her consciousness at the latter possibility. What would she do with a dead FBI man on her porch? Under the circumstances, she didn't dare call the police. She sure didn't want to draw attention to herself with five thousand stolen dollars concealed under her sink.

The FBI man opened his eyes, blinking up at the porch ceiling, and that particular fear was laid to rest. Molly could almost see the instant when he regained complete awareness, because the muscles underlying his face tightened visibly. He sat up, scowling. Warily she watched as he ran the fingers of his right hand through his close-cropped hair. His wallet with the badge and ID lay open against the worn boards about two feet from his left hand. He saw the wallet, reached for it, and got to his feet clutching it, brushing off his suit with his other hand. His tie was crooked. It was navy with a tasteful maroon paisley pattern, Molly noted. The shirt was expensive-looking white cotton, now adorned with a streak of dirt.

His gaze collided with hers through the intact mesh of the upper half of the screen door. His expression, hard before, turned downright stony.

Molly couldn't help herself. She grinned.

Clearly he didn't like being the object of her amusement. His mouth tightened as he restored the wallet to his jacket pocket and moved toward her.

"Miss Butler, I should tell you that we know you took five thousand dollars in cash from a barn at Keeneland Race Course this morning. Now may I come in?"

Without waiting for an answer, he stepped past the damaged screen door, curled a hand around the barrel of the shotgun, and jerked it from her grasp with complete disregard for whether or not it might go off. Tucking the weapon beneath one arm, he walked past her into the house.

Or maybe, Molly thought, *stalked* was a better word.

3

Rendered speechless by the bombshell he had just dropped, Molly swiveled to find the FBI man in her kitchen with his back to her, looking down the open barrel of her shotgun. Having ascertained that it was unloaded, he snapped the gun closed and set it down against the far wall. Then he turned, ignoring her as he glanced around the room.

It was clean, but that was about all that could be said in its favor, Molly realized as she imagined seeing the kitchen through his eyes. The old linoleum was an indeterminate color, somewhere between brown and gray. The walls were mustard yellow and the countertops were nicked green laminate. A hodgepodge of washed breakfast dishes air-dried in a plastic rack beside the sink. A pair of hand-sewn, green-checked kitchen towels served as curtains for the one small window. The cabinets were dark brown wood veneer. The gas stove, chipped white enamel, contrasted with the newer refrigerator, which was Harvest Gold. The picnic table that they had long ago hijacked from a nearby park because they couldn't afford to buy furniture stood in the center of the room, painted white. One of its pair of benches jutted out at an angle where Molly had jumped to her feet at his approach. A broom, dustpan, and mop took up the narrow space between the refrigerator and the far wall. The "pantry," a freestanding unit of metal industrial shelving painted white to match the table, held what was left of the jars of tomatoes and green beans and corn that Flora Atkinson, a neighboring farmer's wife, had given Molly for helping to get her house ready for her daughter's wedding last spring. Three pounds of weeks-old hamburger, excavated from the depths of the freezer before Molly had left for Keeneland that morning, thawed in the sink for supper. A covered metal trash can, also painted white but badly chipped from much use, stood in the far corner next to the pantry. Nobody viewing the room could doubt for a minute that the people who lived in it were poor.

Which was just fine, Molly decided with a lift of her chin. Being poor was nothing to be ashamed of. A lot of real fine people were poor. The Ballards included.

"Come in, Miss Butler. And shut the door." The FBI man was unsmiling. Deep lines, probably from too much sun, bracketed his mouth. Crow's feet radiated from the corners of his eyes. Probably it was the way they contrasted with his tanned skin that made their blueness seem so unsettling.

He *couldn't* know about the money. Nobody had been in that barn. Nobody. Not even the groom. Just the horses, and a cat.

But somehow he did know.

Molly shivered. For an instant she toyed with the idea of darting out the door and just taking off running as fast as she could. *He* would never catch her. She was as fleet-footed as they came, and he was a stodgy old man in a suit. But then she thought of the kids and the thousand and one other ties that bound her to this place and realized that there could be no running away. She had to face him down, to do her best to convince him that he was wrong.

But the FBI? Talk about sending a tank to swat a fly! She'd expected the police or even a hit man if she was found out, but not a federal agent! The butterflies in her stomach took wing.

"I don't know what you're talking about," she said, crossing her arms over her chest and not taking so much as a step closer. "Anyway, if you're looking for a Miss Butler, you've got the wrong person. That's not my name."

"What is your name, then?" He had the quick, clipped speech of somebody from the North. He sure wasn't from around there.

"*You're* the one who's supposed to be from the FBI. You tell me."

"You took the money."

"I told you, I don't know what you're talking about."

His eyes narrowed. "Don't play games with me, Miss Butler. I don't have the patience for it right now."

"Oh, my, did Mr. FBI man fall down and go boom? And did it make him cranky? I wonder what hurts more, your dignity or your bum?"

He didn't like that, Molly could tell. Instead of replying directly to her defiance, he reached into his coat pocket and pulled out a cellular phone, which he held up in a fashion that was clearly meant to be a threat.

"If you're not going to cooperate with me, Miss Butler, you leave me no choice but to have you placed under arrest. All it takes is one phone call."

Molly almost hooted. "You guys pack *phones* now? At least on *Hawaii Five-O*, the FBI agents carried guns."

His mouth tightened. "Are you going to cooperate?"

"How do I even know you're really with the FBI? Anybody can get a fake ID."

"In the circles you run with, that's probably true. But my ID happens to be the real thing. If you want to, you can call the Bureau and check. I'll give you the number."

Molly pursed her lips, then took the two steps it took to convey her to the kitchen phone. "I think I'll call the police instead," she said sweetly, looking at him as she brandished the receiver.

"Go ahead." He returned his phone to his pocket, crossed his arms over his chest, and fixed her with a steady gaze, clearly waiting.

Her bluff called, Molly hesitated. What now? He saw it, too, the quick flash of panic in her eyes before she could school her expression. No way was she going to drag the local cops into this if she could help it. First of all, there was the small matter of the burlap bag full of cash stashed on top of the cleaning supplies in her cabinet. Then there was the fact that her friendly neighborhood police department would be all too ready to believe the worst of her—of any of the Ballards. She'd had run-ins with them before, mostly over the kids. Just this past summer they had caught the eleven-year-old twins throwing eggs at passing cars, and last Christmas, Mike had been arrested for shoplifting a Pearl Jam tape. Only the kindness of the music store owner had saved him from prosecution. Versailles was a small town, where everybody knew everything about everybody else. Everybody fit into a category, and the category that she and her family occupied was troublesome poor white trash.

No, she definitely didn't want to call the local cops in on this. Left to their tender mercies, she'd be in jail before she could sneeze, and the kids whisked off into foster homes. Again.

"Well?"

Molly had the uneasy sensation that he could read her mind. The notion made her nervous. She hung up the phone.

"All right, so maybe you are from the FBI, but I tell you you've got the wrong person. My name is not Butler."

"You got a VCR?"

"What?" The question was so unexpected, it threw Molly. He repeated it.

"What if I do?"

Actually, Mike had a VCR. Last June he'd worked helping old Mr. Higdon set out his tobacco, and the used VCR had been part of his payment. Working for something, as Molly had tried her best to impress on him, was a whole lot better than shoplifting it. They didn't put you in jail for working.

How was she ever going to be able to take the high moral ground with Mike now, with that five thousand dollars hanging over her head? Unless, she thought, she was going to serve as a living example of the wages of sin by spending the next few years of her life behind bars.

Those butterflies in her stomach did flips.

"Where is it?" Impatient with waiting for an answer, he turned and walked through the narrow rectangular doorway that opened into the living room. Not wanting to let him out of her sight, Molly followed.

The downstairs of the dilapidated clapboard farmhouse consisted of three rooms: the kitchen and the living room, side by side in front, and Molly's bedroom in back. The one bathroom was in a shedlike addition stuck onto the kitchen as an obvious afterthought; the remains of the outhouse still stood some little distance up a slope in back.

The living room was as haphazardly put together as the kitchen. Time-darkened hardwood floors were covered in the center by a worn, oval-shaped braided rug in shades that had once been brown, green, and rust. A tweedy orange couch with a sagging middle, rescued from a Salvation Army donation bin, sat against one fake-wood paneled wall. Flanking it were an ancient brown Naugahyde recliner, the rips on both arms repaired with black electrical tape, and a brown-painted Adirondack chair with floral cushions Molly had made from pillowcases. Two mismatched battered wood tables were topped by cheap white bean-pot lamps. Faded gold drapes, opened wide to let as much light as possible into the dark room, adorned the single large window. A nonworking fireplace fronted by a black wood-burning stove on a round brick pedestal was built into the far wall.

The TV with the VCR claiming pride of place on top was impossible to miss. It was placed against the short wall the living room shared with the kitchen. When Molly reluctantly appeared in the living room doorway, the FBI man had already found it, and was in the act of pulling a tape from an inside jacket pocket. Sending a quick glance her way, he continued with what he was doing. He pressed a button on the VCR, popped the tape into the machine, pressed another button and turned on the TV. Then he crooked a finger at her. Molly took a couple of unwilling steps forward, into the room, as the screen, for those first few seconds, showed nothing but gray snow. A moment later, to her horror, the picture appeared in vivid detail. Molly stood transfixed, watching speechlessly as her video self found and made off with a burlap feed sack containing bundles of cash.

Somehow he'd gotten the whole thing on tape!

He watched her as she watched the screen, and as soon as he saw he'd made his point he turned it off.

"Well?" he said again, straightening to look at her.

Molly clamped her shock-parted lips together, crossed her arms over her chest, and tried to ignore the icy cold that crept along her limbs. Her gaze met his. He had her and they both knew it. How could she deny what was right there on tape? Claim she had an evil twin?

4

"Okay," Molly said at last. "So maybe I did take the money."

"I don't think there's any *maybe* about it."

Molly said nothing.

"Where is it?" he asked.

Without a word Molly turned and walked into the kitchen. Pausing only to remove the tape from the machine—she could hear the funny little noise the VCR made when it ejected a tape—he followed. Of course he wouldn't be stupid enough to forget the evidence. Tape in hand, he watched from the living room doorway as Molly retrieved the burlap sack from beneath the sink, and with poor grace plopped it onto the center of the table. Restoring the tape to his coat pocket and joining her at the table, the FBI man untied the sack and glanced inside, as if to make sure the money was still there. Then, apparently satisfied, he twisted the neck into a knot.

"Why'd you take it?"

That was such a stupid question that it angered Molly. "For fun," she said, hugging herself. "For kicks. Why else would a rich girl like me steal a bag full of money?"

His lips compressed. "I'd cut the sarcasm if I were you, Miss Butler. You're in big trouble here."

"Are you going to make that call and have me arrested now?" The question was pure bravado. As she waited for the answer Molly felt sick with fear.

"What you did is a felony offense," he said. "You're looking at big-time time here. Maybe fifteen, twenty years."

Oh, God. Molly felt light-headed. With the best will in the world not to let him see how scared she was, she couldn't keep her body from reacting. Her knees gave out, and she sank bonelessly down on the bench where she'd been sitting when she had heard him coming. Lips parting, she drew in a great, shuddering breath.

"Maybe," he said slowly, watching her, "I could get them to go easy on you—if you cooperate. I need to know who sent you to pick up the money."

Molly glanced up at him in surprise. He was intent, frowning at her and leaning forward on one strong brown hand that rested on the table. She could see the black strap of a wristwatch peeking from beneath the crisp white cuff of his shirt. His watchband was leather, the watch's face rimmed in gold. His suit was fine wool. His tie was silk. His clothing, like his whole demeanor, proclaimed that he was part of the privileged establishment. No way would he be able to understand what it was like to be her, to be young and poor and caught up in a daily life-or-death battle just to put food on the table.

No way would he be able to understand what it was like to be her now, looking up at him, scared to death.

His eyes burned brightly blue at her. Meeting their

gaze, Molly decided that any further attempt at lying about what she had done was a waste of time and energy. With that tape, he had her cold.

"Nobody sent me," she said.

"I can't help you if you won't tell me the truth."

"That *is* the truth. I took the money because we—I—needed it. Nobody told me to."

"What were you doing in that barn at three forty-five in the morning?" He hurled the question at her as if it were a brick.

"I—I work there, for Wyland Farm. At least I did."

"What do you mean, you did?"

"A few days ago, I got mad about something and quit. I went by the barn this morning to pick up my last check."

"What did you get mad at?"

To Molly's fury, embarrassed heat crept up her face. "A guy grabbed me, and I didn't like it."

"Who? Don Simpson?"

"No, not Mr. Simpson. Thornton Wyland. His people own the stable."

He took a minute to digest that, then began again on another tack. "So you went to the barn to pick up your last check *at three forty-five a.m.*?"

"I always start—started—work at five. Three forty-five is not real early in the horse business."

"Who were you supposed to pick up the check from?"

"Mr. Simpson."

"He wasn't there."

"He usually gets there around four. He likes to be the first one to arrive. I came a little early because I didn't want to miss him. I needed—need—that check."

"So you arrived early. What time? Who did you see? Who was in the barn?"

"I guess I got there about three-thirty. I didn't see anyone. There's usually a groom on duty all night, but if he was there I didn't see him."

"So, tell me, Miss Butler, what did you do in a deserted barn between three-thirty and the time you entered that tack room?"

"I checked on the horses, and talked to Ophelia." There didn't seem much point in correcting him about her name again. Besides, she thought it might be a good idea to allow him to retain that small area of ignorance. She didn't quite see how at the moment, but it was always possible that his misapprehension about her name might be turned to her advantage.

"Talked to *who*?"

"Ophelia. She's a burro. She was hurt not too long ago and she's been nervous of people ever since. She trusts me. I wanted to make sure she was all right." Actually, Ophelia had been the victim of a vicious attack about two months before. While loose in the Wyland Farm fields one night, she had been slashed numerous times across the hindquarters with what, from the size and shape of the wounds, appeared to have been a straight razor. The attacker had not been identified. Security had been stepped up around the farm, though concern was blunted by Ophelia's lack of value. She was not a Thoroughbred, after all. The burro was only permitted at Keeneland because she had a calming effect on Tabasco Sauce, Wyland Farm's great bay hope. Ophelia was his best buddy.

"What do you—did you—do for Wyland Farm?"

"I'm a groom."

"You said Don Simpson is your boss. Is that all?

What kind of personal relationship do you have with him?"

Molly didn't like the implication of that. She looked him straight in the eye. "We don't have anything going on, if that's what you're asking me."

He didn't even have the grace to look abashed. "So you don't have any kind of personal relationship with Simpson, is that what you're telling me?"

"That's what I'm telling you."

"Anybody else?"

"What?" Her eyes widened.

"Are you—dating—anybody else?"

"I don't think that's any of your business. If you're thinking about asking me out, the answer's no." He wasn't, and she knew it. She just couldn't seem to resist the urge to be smart-mouthed.

"I'm not planning to ask you out, Miss Butler, believe me. I'm merely asking a question: Who do you see socially? Who do you date? Who's your boyfriend?"

"What do you want to know that for?"

He frowned. "Miss Butler, if you want to stay out of jail, you're going to answer any questions I ask you. Truthfully. Got that?"

She scowled right back at him. He apparently took her expression as an affirmative answer to his last question, which in fact it was. "Boyfriends? Dates? Male social acquaintances?"

"I go out with Jimmy Miller sometimes. His dad owns Miller's Garage in town. And Tom Atkinson. He's a neighbor. And some others, when they ask and I'm free."

"Do you have any personal involvement with Bernie Caudill?"

"Bernie Caudill?" The name sounded familiar, but Molly couldn't quite place it.

"He identifies the horses running at Keeneland."

"Oh, you mean the fat old guy who checks the horses' mouth tattoos?"

"That's him."

"No. I barely know him."

"Tim Harden? Jason Breen? Howard Lawrence?"

To each name, local trainers all, Molly responded with a negative shake of the head.

The FBI man was silent for a minute. "So what you're telling me is that you were in that barn at three forty-five in the morning for no other reason than because you wanted to pick up your paycheck."

"That's right."

"So what were you doing in the tack room? Seems a strange place to visit at that time of day."

"I was going to get a handful of sweet feed for Ophelia. She loves it."

"Ophel—oh, yes, the donkey."

"She's a burro."

He dismissed that distinction with an impatient twitch of his mouth. "You had no idea the money was there, who it was for, or anything. You just saw it and took it because you needed it, is that right?"

"That's right."

"So tell me something else: Why did you look in the feed sack?"

"Because it wasn't the right brand. We always use Southern Farms. The sack was Bentons' brand, which is an inferior feed. It wasn't supposed to be fed to our horses, which means it had no business being in our tack room, because somebody might use it by mistake. The wrong feed upsets the horses' digestive tracts.

With Thoroughbreds, you have to be careful. I was going to get it out of there just to be safe, but when I picked the sack up I knew immediately that it didn't have feed in it. So I looked inside."

"Were you surprised to find money in there?"

That was the understatement of the decade. "Oh, yeah."

He was silent for a moment, his expression pensive. His gaze moved over her face and down as much of her slim, blue jean–clad body as he could see with her sitting down on the opposite side of the table. It was clear to Molly that he was weighing her words, trying to decide if she was telling the truth.

"How old are you?" he asked abruptly.

"Twenty-four."

"You live here with your brothers and sisters, is that right? You have several of them?"

"Four. Two brothers, two sisters."

"And you're the oldest."

"What did you do, check me out before you came? Of course you did. You're the FBI, right?" Resentment laced the words. "In that case, you already know I'm the oldest, so why ask?"

Her bristling clearly had no effect on him. His next question was, "Where are your parents?"

Molly stiffened. This was going too far, into the realm of the personal, where she never allowed anyone to penetrate. "Look, do you really care? Where my parents are doesn't have anything to do with this."

"I want to know."

Well, she wanted a lot of things, like for him to go away. But she wasn't going to get it, not since he had that tape and she couldn't order him out of her house. That tape gave him the upper hand—and the right to demand answers, no matter how sensitive the questions. "My mom's dead. My dad took off into the sunset when I was a baby. Okay?"

He regarded her without speaking for a moment. Then his mouth twisted wryly. "Today is your lucky day, Miss Butler. I'm going to believe you're telling me the truth, the whole truth, and nothing but the truth. I'm going to take the money and go away and forget you ever stole it. Unless I find out you lied to me. In that case, I'll be back."

He picked up the bag of money by its knotted neck, inclined his head toward her, and started walking. Unable to believe that she was really about to be let off the hook just like that, Molly swiveled on the bench to watch as he headed out the damaged screen door.

"Have a nice day, Miss Butler," he called back over his shoulder, just as if theirs had been the friendliest of casual encounters. Though vaguely peeved at the jauntiness of his farewell, Molly's overwhelming emotion as she watched him go was a flood of relief. She was not going to go to jail after all.

Though he still didn't know about the missing twenty.

Even as she entertained the thought, the FBI man came to an abrupt halt some two feet shy of the steps. Had he changed his mind? she wondered in a sudden panic. Could he read *her* mind? Was he coming back?

Her question was answered as Pork Chop walked stiff-legged into view, neck fur bristling, gleaming white teeth exposed. Apparently the dog had been napping on the porch.

To his credit, the FBI man stood his ground. He held out a hand and let the huge animal sniff his fingers, saying something that Molly couldn't quite decipher in a quiet, soothing voice. At the attention, Pork Chop melted like the marshmallow-hearted idiot he was. He wagged his tail—clearly now that the man had let him sniff his fingers he must be a friend—and got his head patted for his pains.

Finally the FBI man stopped patting her traitorous animal, stepped off the porch, and walked out of sight. And, Molly devoutly hoped, out of her life.

5

The news that greeted Will when he called Murphy from a pay phone at the 7-Eleven on Versailles Road was bad: Howard Lawrence was dead. Lawrence was the trainer for Cloverlot Stables, and their stool pigeon. He was the one who had confirmed the details of the scam for Will, who had fingered Don Simpson and the others, and who had left the bag of cash, supposedly a payoff on a ringer run in a previous race, in Barn 15's tack room. At this point, Howard Lawrence *was* their case. Thanks to the interference of the sexy little number to whom Will had just, to his own disgust, given a major break, they had not yet managed to secure a shred of evidence against anybody else.

"What do you mean, dead?" Will demanded, outraged, when Murphy broke the news.

"You know, as in kicked the bucket, deceased, dearly departed?"

"He's *dead*?"

"That's what I said."

"How in the name of all that's holy did that happen?"

"He killed himself."

"He killed himself?"

"Yup." Murphy sounded glum.

"You were supposed to have him under surveillance!"

"I did. I was following him, and he pulled in for a burger, went through the drive-in window, then stopped in the parking lot to eat. He looked like he was fixed there for a little bit, so I drove up behind the building and ran inside to use the bathroom. When I pulled around again, he was still in his car. I could see him clear across the parking lot. He was kinda leaning back in the seat with his eyes closed, but I didn't think anything about it. I thought he was just taking it easy for a minute! How was I supposed to know he'd blown his brains out, right there at Dairy Queen?" Murphy was clearly aggrieved at being blamed.

"Shit!"

"That's what *I* said."

"Damn it to hell, Murphy, you shouldn't have let it happen!"

"What could I do? There wasn't anything I could do!"

"Shit!" Will said again.

"Man, I'm sorry."

Will could almost see Murphy's apologetic shrug over the phone. He ground his teeth.

"I suppose the local yokels are on top of it?"

"Oh, yeah. Fact is, one of the girls who works at the place found him. She was carrying out a special order and when she walked past his car she dropped the food and started screaming. Police were there in under five minutes."

"You talk to them?"

"Naw. Once the girl started screaming, I never got out of the car. When the cops got there, I drove away. Didn't want to tip them off that we had an interest in Lawrence."

"Are you sure—*positively* sure—he's dead?"

"Yeah."

"If you never got out of the car after the girl started screaming, how can you be sure?" Will's patience was being sorely tried. Damn Hallum for saddling him with this bonehead!

"I saw the whole thing on *The News at Noon.* It was their big story: local horseman commits suicide at Dairy Queen. Believe me, he's dead. Funeral arrangements are pending."

"It was on TV? Christ!"

"At least nobody knows he was connected to us." Murphy sounded as if he was offering comfort. "Anyway, he already told us everything he knew. We still got a case."

Will closed his eyes briefly. "You're wrong, Murphy. We don't 'still got a case.' We had the goods on Lawrence, but he's dead. Without his testimony, we've got nothing on any of the others. Nothing, do you understand that? No witness, no evidence, nothing. Nothing on *no*body, except a lot of hearsay." Which translates to a whole heck of a lot of hard work straight down the drain, he thought savagely.

"Maybe we can scare one of the others into confessing or something. Bring them in, and tell them that Lawrence told all before he died."

"And if they don't confess, which they won't if they've got the sense God gave a goose, we have nothing. Except egg on our faces, and a big-ass expense account bill with nothing to show for it. Plus we'll have tipped them off that their little scheme has been found out, which means they will immediately knock it off. Leaving us with nothing again."

"At least they won't be committing any more crimes."

"Oh, I'll tell Hallum that. Maybe he'll put us up for Citizens of the Year."

"Nothing we can do to change anything now." Again Will could almost hear Murphy's shrug.

Will did not speak for a moment. He couldn't. Traffic whizzed past on the four-lane highway not far from where he stood. A couple of rubes in overalls came out of the 7-Eleven and climbed into a beat-up pickup, revving the engine loudly as they drove off. A vapor trail of malodorous exhaust wafted toward Will's nostrils. He leaned back, out of its way.

Overhead, the sky was a gorgeous cerulean blue with fluffy white clouds floating across it. Unseasonably warm air caressed his face. In downtown Chicago toward the middle of October it would have been twenty degrees cooler, the air crisp like it was supposed to be in autumn. The streets would have been crowded with people bustling about real business. Wind would have whistled through the canyons created by the skyscrapers . . .

"Etheline, don't forget my cigarettes! You hear?" A fat woman in an idling Chevy shouted the admonition at her equally large teenage daughter, who was walking into the convenience store and who answered her with a dismissive wave. In Chicago, nobody smoked anymore. Here, the damned state motto might as well have been *Tobacco is a vegetable.* Half the population lit up. God, he wished he were back in civilization again!

His idea of hell was to be stuck here for the rest of his life.

"You sure it was suicide?" he asked Murphy desperately.

"*The News at Noon* said the gun was found inside the car with Lawrence's fingerprints all over it. No one was with him. What else could it be?"

What else indeed? Just because Lawrence's death was awfully convenient for the men he was ratting on didn't mean it was murder. But still . . . "You copy down the license numbers of the cars in the lot?"

"No." Murphy sounded surprised. "Should I have? I didn't think about that, with it being a suicide and all."

You didn't think, period, Will growled, but he didn't say it aloud.

"You recover the money?" Murphy asked.

"Yeah." Deep in thought, Will responded with scarcely more than a grunt.

"Uh, Will . . ." There was a pause.

"What?" That pause caught Will's attention. He could feel more bad news heading his way.

"The girl's name is Ballard, not Butler. Molly Ballard. I guess I read it wrong." Murphy sounded sheepish.

"Thanks for telling me." Will's voice was dry. With Murphy, he was becoming inured to screwups. At least the girl had been telling the truth when she had insisted she wasn't Miss Butler. Will grimaced as he remembered. He hated being made to look a fool. Thinking that, he had an abrupt vision of himself lying flat on his back on her porch.

In the looking-foolish sweepstakes, getting his suspect's name wrong paled in comparison.

"You got the money back, so I guess it didn't matter," Murphy said hopefully.

Will lifted the receiver from his ear and contemplated it for an instant. Then he replaced it and said carefully, "No, I guess when you look at it that way it didn't."

"You want me to make some calls and try to get the coroner's report on Lawrence, or anything?"

"No," Will said, feeling a sensation close to panic at the idea of Murphy's doing anything more. "Stay put. I'll be there in twenty minutes."

Without giving Murphy a chance to reply, he hung up.

As he started back to his car, Will discovered to his disgust that there was gum stuck to the bottom of his shoe. A big, fat, grimy pink globe, with long, slimy strings stretching from his expensive leather sole to the remnants of the goo left on the asphalt. He wasn't even surprised. Just about all the locals who didn't smoke chewed gum, and spat it out wherever it suited them.

This day had gone wrong right from the beginning, from the moment the girl made off with the bag of cash that was to provide their filmed evidence of Don Simpson receiving a payoff. From there, though Will wouldn't have believed it possible, events had spiraled rapidly downhill. And now he had gum on his shoe.

As the saying goes, sometimes you eat the bear, and sometimes the bear eats you.

Or as Will more succinctly expressed it to himself, sometimes life sucks.

He scraped the gum off onto the raised edge of the sidewalk as well as he could, walked to the nondescript, company-sanctioned white Ford Taurus that in his mind stood out like a sore thumb precisely because it was so bland, and headed toward Lexington, some ten miles away.

A sudden craving for a glass of cold milk, a bagel, and a copy of the *Chicago Tribune* hit him. Since he'd given up caffeine in deference to the ulcer that intermittently plagued him, fifteen minutes with milk, a bagel, and the paper had become his method of choice for handling stress.

It beat pounding on walls.

These people had never even heard of bagels. When he had tried to order one, in a variety of local delis and restaurants, what he got most often was a blank stare. His favorite response came from the clown who told him to check in the pet shop up the street. Bagels, beagles, get it, ha-ha.

The locals sure had a great sense of humor. He'd better be careful or he'd die laughing.

He had been in the sticks just a little over a week, and he could already feel his blood pressure shooting through the roof. Big-city life was in his genes, he'd decided days ago. "Fresh" country air—actually it was ripe with more than a hint of manure—nauseated him. Give him a couple of lungfuls of smog anytime.

It was bad enough that he was suffering so on behalf of a two-bit horse race–fixing ring that nobody would have given a damn about if Senator Charles Paxton, D-Ky., and his buddies hadn't lost a bundle at the local track last spring, but it was much worse that the investigation now seemed to be thoroughly blown. If he couldn't salvage something from the wreckage, he was going to have a black mark on his record. His career would be damaged, and all over a nothing case that wasn't even important enough to merit an "official" investigation. He and Murphy were checking out the scam strictly as a favor to the senator. Nobody but Dave Hallum knew they were there.

Driving toward Lexington, Will turned the case over in his mind, desperately looking for a fresh angle from which to approach it. The facts were these: Senator Paxton, quite rightly as it turned out, had suspected that something was rotten in Thoroughbredland when he kept losing where he usually won. He had asked George Rees, Hallum's boss at the Bureau and Paxton's close friend, to check it out. Rees had in turn passed the ball to Hallum, who had, with malice in his heart and a wicked grin, lobbed it to Will, who'd been on his shit list at the time because of the splintered cabin cruiser.

When Will had protested that agents from the field office in Louisville were the ones to handle the case, he was informed that he was mistaken: Everybody knew everybody else down there, including the local FBI agents. Under those circumstances it would be almost impossible to keep secret an investigation involving the region's most famous horse-breeding operations.

What was needed was an outsider—namely, Will. He would be assisted by John Murphy, a recent transferee to the Chicago office from West Virginia, where he'd spent the past fifteen years coasting by on the occasional marijuana bust, from what Will could gather.

Will hadn't liked the assignment, or his new partner, but that was life with the Bureau. Accompanied by Murphy, he'd flown down, set up shop in the nearest Executive Suites hotel, and promised himself he would have the whole mess sorted out by the time

Keeneland's three-week racing season ended on October 29.

He would have made his self-imposed deadline too. It hadn't required a lot of brains to focus on the track's recent consistent winners as the preliminary targets of his investigation. A little electronic surveillance, a little sifting through trash at Keeneland and various stables associated with it, and he had a rough idea of what was going on, along with a quintet of suspects. What he lacked was proof, as well as some way of busting all five and making the charges stick.

The background checks he did on the targets yielded pay dirt: One of his prime suspects, Howard Lawrence, was sleeping with an underage girl. That was all the leverage he needed. He visited Lawrence, terrifying him with the specter of being charged with statutory rape and transporting a minor across state lines for immoral purposes (the idiot had taken the girl with him on a jaunt to Nashville a month previously). He then revived him with the possibility of avoiding that fate and being financially well rewarded for his cooperation in an ongoing investigation, and promised him both protection from reprisals by his fellow conspirators and immunity from prosecution for his part in the scheme. Lawrence was intelligent enough to recognize that under the circumstances his choices were limited. He spilled everything he knew, and agreed to help set the others up.

The scheme was strictly penny-ante stuff, designed not to make anybody rich but just to supplement the salaries of those involved. Its mechanics were simple: Four local horse trainers—Lawrence, Don Simpson of Wyland Farm, Tim Harden of Greenglow Stables, and Jason Breen of Sweet Meadow Stud—had formed an unholy alliance with identifier Bernie Caudill, whose job it was to match the lip tattoo identifying each racehorse with the Thoroughbred's registration papers. This was the process by which bettors were assured that the horse that was supposed to run in a particular race was the horse that actually ran. The trainers were using "ringers," substituting Thoroughbreds that outclassed the competition and running them at long odds intended for the lesser horses supposedly entered in the race. The horsemen then bet heavily on their animals, won big, and split the profits.

Leaving everybody happy. Except Senator Paxton, who took losing personally.

Will winced as he pictured himself calling Hallum and telling him that the investigation initiated by George Rees as a personal favor to his friend the senator had been derailed because the witness they were supposed to be both watching and protecting had committed suicide. He would look bad. Hallum would look bad. George Rees would look bad. And that wasn't good. He'd be on Hallum's shit list for the next twenty years.

Hallum's paybacks were notorious. Knowing how much Will hated the sticks, Hallum would probably assign him to Podunk permanently. He'd be stuck in this endless *Green Acres* rerun until retirement.

He had to come up with some way of salvaging the situation. But what?

Suddenly the very pretty face and form of Miss Molly Butler—uh, Ballard—popped into his mind.

She was an insider. And, as long as he had the tape of her little venture into grand theft in his possession, she was *his*. Signed, sealed, delivered.

The question was, how best to use her?

6

Molly and her family were in the middle of supper when someone knocked on the door. Four of the Ballards looked up immediately. The fifth, seventeen-year-old Ashley, her nose in a book as usual, had a slower response time. But when Pork Chop erupted from beneath the table with a scrabble of toenails and a frenzy of yelps, Ashley surfaced as well, glancing around inquiringly at her siblings before looking toward the door.

"I'll get it." Mike scrambled up from his place at the table, abandoning his meal without a visible sign of regret. Hamburger Helper for the third time in a week made him want to puke, as he had informed the whole family when they sat down. Thin as a bone and, at fourteen, already taller than Molly, Mike wore the ubiquitous teenage uniform of jeans, sneakers, and an open flannel shirt over a white T-shirt. His shoulder-length hair was pulled back in a ponytail at the nape of his neck, and a small gold hoop pierced one ear.

Molly wasn't wild about his hairstyle or his earring, but if she had learned one thing in the course of parenting this group, it was don't sweat the small stuff. Shoplifting was worth fighting about; earrings weren't.

"You can't do anything or go anywhere until you do your homework," Molly warned him, assuming, as did Mike, that the visitor would be one of the teenager's many friends.

"I already told you, I did it at school."

"Yeah, right," eleven-year-old Sam snorted. He echoed Molly's sentiments exactly. Mike was bad about homework, and getting worse. Molly had tried nagging, bribery, and threats without much success. Mike just didn't care about school right now. Though she was trying hard, Molly couldn't figure out quite what to do about it.

"I did *my* homework right after I got home from school. So did Sam," Susan said virtuously. Molly smiled at Susan with affection. Mike shot her a dirty look.

The twins looked a great deal alike. Both were fine-boned, pale-skinned children with the large, densely lashed brown eyes that all five of the Ballard siblings had inherited from their mother. Unlike Molly herself and Mike, both of whom also had their mother's luxuriant coffee-brown hair, the twins had silky blond hair, which on Sam was cut to just above his ears and on Susan reached her shoulders. They looked delicate, which they weren't, and angelic, which they weren't either.

What Ballard was? Molly asked herself dryly just as Mike opened the door. Well, maybe Ashley qualified.

"Hi," said the visitor from the other side of the screen door, which Molly had managed to shimmy closed but had not yet had the time or money to fix. The porch was dark, and with the still-intact upper mesh panel obscuring the caller's features it was impossible to ascertain anything other than that he was an adult male. "Is your sister home?"

"Which one?" Mike's back stiffened. His surprise and suspicion were clear: It was unusual to have a strange man come by the house in the evening, especially asking for one of his sisters. In an impatient aside to the barking dog pushing against his legs, he added, "Shut up, Pork Chop."

Pork Chop, of course, continued to bark—but he was wagging his tail. Whoever was at the door was clearly known to him. The animal stuck his nose through the hole in the bottom screen, sniffing a pair of dark dress trousers. A tan, long-fingered hand complete with white cuff and a glimpse of gold-rimmed wristwatch came into view, patting the dog on the head.

"Molly," said the owner of that hand.

The four Ballards remaining at the table ceased all activity, their eyes now riveted on the door. The three younger ones knew that if a stranger was at the house asking for Molly, one of the Ballards was probably in trouble. Molly, having recognized with a flash of fear the trousers, the hand, and the voice, knew just which Ballard that was.

"Yes, I'm here," she croaked, getting to her feet and moving toward the door as fast as her weakening knees would allow. Whatever the FBI man had to say to her, she did not want to hear it in front of the kids.

Though she had a pretty good idea. He must have discovered that missing twenty.

Oh, God, did that mean that she was going to be arrested after all?

Her siblings stared at her. Mike even shifted his protective position at the door to watch her approach.

"Move, Pork Chop," Molly said to the enormous animal, whose wriggling body stood between her and the door. Pork Chop obligingly stepped right through the hole he had created in the lower mesh panel to wait with his new friend on the porch. Brushing past Mike, consciously avoiding looking at him, Molly jiggled the latch and pushed open the screen door.

The door immediately sagged downward, but she managed to get it open by gripping the handle and lifting, holding the dipping front corner inches above the uneven porch floorboards.

"Hi," said the FBI man when they were face-to-face at last. "Did you forget our date?"

The light from the kitchen spilled over him. Bright blue eyes gleamed a warning at her. Surprise rendered Molly momentarily mute. What on earth was he talking about? She met his gaze with trepidation. He smiled at her, a quick stretching of his lips that brought no corresponding warmth to his eyes. He wanted something, that much was clear, but she didn't think he was here to arrest her. If he was, he wouldn't be spouting that nonsense about a date.

"Hi," she managed, hideously conscious of Mike beside her and the others at the table listening to every word. "I—guess I must have."

Seeing her difficulty with the door, he reached out to grasp the frame, relieving her of its weight. Molly let go of the handle, sank back on her heels, and wrapped her arms around her, never glancing away from his face.

"Not meaning to stand me up, are you?" His tone was light, teasing almost, but his eyes were not. They were narrowed with purpose, a purpose that Molly dared not ignore.

"No, of course not," she said. "Let me just . . ." She glanced sideways at Mike, who was staring at their visitor. It was an effort even to think, so nervous was she. But she clearly couldn't just walk out the door without saying anything to her family.

"Go do whatever you need to do." The FBI man sounded indulgent, although she knew the affability he projected was a sham. "I'll wait."

With that he moved forward, crowding into her space until she was forced to step back from the threshold, admitting him to the house. Mike stepped back, too, looking from Molly to their guest with a frown. The FBI man closed the screen door carefully behind him. Pork Chop wriggled through the hole in the screen to stand next to him, tail wagging.

Dead silence hung in the air.

The FBI man shot Molly a glance that was at definite odds with the smile on his face, recalling her to a sense of their audience. She realized that she had been staring at him, probably with horror, ever since he had walked through the door. She only hoped that her family had been themselves so busy ogling him that they had not noticed her expression.

"This—this is my brother Mike," she said hurriedly, then panicked as she realized that she could not recall the FBI man's name.

Seeming to sense her dilemma, he stepped in, holding out his hand to the teenager.

"Will Lyman," he said, shaking Mike's hand while Molly breathed an inward sigh of relief. If he was her "date," she would know his name at the very least.

"This is Ashley, and Susan, and Sam." Molly gestured to the trio at the table.

"Hi." He nodded at them as they echoed his greeting. All three were as wide-eyed as if he were an alien, Molly saw with rising hysteria, while Mike still frowned as he looked their guest up and down, his arms crossed over his chest for all the world as if he were a suspicious father giving his daughter's date the once-over.

Their astonishment was not without grounds, Molly had to admit. For one thing, she never dated on a weeknight, and for another she had never, ever dated anyone remotely like him. First, he looked about forty. The guys she went out with were generally within just a few years of her own age. Too, it was quite obvious from even the few clipped words he had spoken that he was not a local. And he was dressed all wrong. Although some of her dates had arrived wearing suits when the event called for it, for them it had been an occasional mode of dress: they had seemed self-conscious in their Sunday best. The FBI man was clearly at ease in the dark blue suit he still wore. Although he had removed his tie and his white shirt was unbuttoned at the neck, the effect was far from casual. Black leather shoes gleamed beneath well-pressed trousers. A black belt with a discreet silver buckle circled his waist. The accessories were expensive. So was the suit, and he looked as if he wore one like it every day. Moreover, there was an air about him that said he was at home in a world far removed from the farms and small towns of central Kentucky. Molly had definitely never dated anyone like that.

But he had chosen to present himself as her date, and she was not in any position to contradict him. She was only thankful that whatever he wanted of her, he was willing to wait to reveal it until they were alone.

Because if he was not her date, then the inevitable next question the kids would ask was, who was he? That was the one she didn't want to have to answer. Not unless she had to.

Molly hugged herself, and tried to marshal her thoughts. The children had to be her first concern. "Uh, Sam and Susan, tonight is your night for the dishes, remember. Then you can watch TV until bedtime, if you want—as long as your homework is all done. Mike, *do your homework* before you do anything else, and if you go out be home by nine-thirty, please. Ash—"

"I'll make sure everything gets done, don't worry," Ashley said, standing up and coming around the table toward them. Her tortoiseshell glasses had slipped down her nose, and she pushed them into place as she spoke. "Will you be out late?"

Molly opened her mouth. Then, realizing she had no answer for that, she slanted a desperate glance over her shoulder at the man behind her. He shook his head.

"No, not late," she said to Ashley, then turned to him. "I'm ready. Let's go."

"Molly—" Ashley, tall and thin like the rest of them, still wore the tan corduroys and oatmeal sweater she had worn to school. Her caramel-colored hair curled wildly around her head, and as she looked at her sister she tugged at one shoulder-length strand. It was something she often did when she was troubled.

"What?" It was hard to keep the strain out of her voice. Molly fought to project an image of normalcy until she could get herself and the FBI man out the door. Ashley, no fool for all her frequent absentmindedness, clearly sensed that something was amiss. Her expression was beginning to show signs of concern as she and Mike, who still stood near the open door, arms crossed over his chest, exchanged glances.

"Your shoes."

Following the direction of Ashley's gaze, Molly looked down at her bare feet. Everyone else in the kitchen, the FBI man included, looked down too. Her unpainted toes curled self-consciously against the cool linoleum.

"Oh." The single syllable sounded lame, but under the circumstances it was the best Molly could do. She had been ready to walk out into the crisp autumn night barefoot. On what was supposed to be a date, yet. It must be obvious to Ashley and Mike, at least, that she was seriously rattled. But they didn't know why, and if she could help it they weren't going to find out. What she had to do was get a grip on herself, and hope they believed that she was flustered because the man waiting for her was so different from the usual run of her boyfriends, and she had forgotten their date.

The sight of her bare feet recalled her to a sense of her other deficiencies of dress. She was wearing ancient jeans that had faded almost to the point of colorlessness and an equally faded gray-and-blue-plaid flannel shirt of Mike's. Her face was devoid of makeup, and her hair was caught in a ponytail at the nape of her neck by a plain old brown rubber band.

Never, under any conditions, would she have gone on a date looking the way she did. Especially not with a man like him: an older, sophisticated stranger in a suit.

Ashley knew it. So, probably, did Mike.

"I should change," Molly said with a forced little laugh and an upward glance at her "date."

He shook his head. That non-smile of his appeared again, for the children's benefit, Molly assumed.

"You look great. Anyway, you're just going to be showing me around the area, remember? We probably won't even get out of the car. So grab your shoes and let's go."

His tone was light and easy. The look that accompanied his words galvanized her. She glanced around the floor. Her sneakers—old, cracked leather ones that had once been Mike's before they had started looking so bad that he refused to wear them to school—were in front of the sink. Molly found them, thrust her feet into them, tied the laces, and straightened.

"Are you sure you don't mind me going like this?" she asked her "date" with an attempt at a bright smile. The question, and the smile, were strictly for her siblings' benefit. Ashley was frowning as she looked from her sister to the FBI man and back. Mike's expression was closer to a scowl.

"Like I said, you look great. Let's go." The FBI man swung the screen door open. Molly walked toward him.

"Molly—" Mike stopped her with a hand on her arm as she was about to pass him. He looked, and sounded, worried.

"Do your homework," she ordered in her sternest voice, then, smiling, gave his nose an affectionate tweak. He did not appear completely reassured, but he released her arm.

"I told you, I did it at school."

Molly grimaced at that familiar refrain, and grimacing, went out the door. The night was cool and still, with only the faintest rustle from the leaves of the big oak suggesting the presence of a breeze. The FBI man caught up with her at the edge of the porch. She had to make a conscious effort not to pull away as his hand curled around her elbow.

Mike and Ashley stood in the doorway with Susan and Sam peeking around them. Molly felt the weight of their combined stares as, under escort, she descended the steps and crossed the lawn to the white car parked just behind their own ancient blue Plymouth.

The FBI man reached around her to open the passenger side door. Molly glanced up at his face, which was impassive in the faint light spilling from inside the house.

"Get in," he said.

She did, and he shut the door behind her.

Molly managed a wave for her family, and took deep breaths to calm herself as the FBI man walked around the hood, his shoes crunching in the gravel driveway.

7

Pork Chop barked from the porch as the car, tires rattling over the gravel, backed down the drive. Molly stared at the familiar outlines of the ramshackle house and at the dark figures of her family silhouetted in the doorway until the car reached the road. A quick shift of gears and they were moving forward. Her home and family were left behind.

She finally dared a glance at the man beside her. Seen in profile, he had nice features. His forehead was high, his nose straight and not overlarge, his mouth firm and unsmiling, his chin masculine. Everything was in proportion. To a woman in her thirties, sophisticated in pearls and mink, Molly supposed he would seem handsome.

To her twenty-four-year-old, jeans-and-sneakers-clad self, he seemed downright scary.

His attention was on the road, which was narrow and twisty. Although it was only a little past seven, full night had fallen. The moon had not yet risen. The car's headlights provided the only illumination. The bright beams cut through the darkness, reflecting off the gritty surface of the blacktop and revealing the century-old rock fence that outlined the twelve hundred acres belonging to Wyland Farm. The farm's Big House, where the family lived, was located more than a mile distant across vast rolling fields of rich grass. With its white-painted brick, Greek revival facade, the sprawling twenty-two-room mansion could have been the prototype for Tara. A ten-room guest house was a miniature of the Big House, and even the half-dozen barns echoed the elegant style. But the farm's heyday had been in the seventies and early eighties, when Arab oil money had pushed the price paid for yearlings at Keeneland's annual July auction into the eight-figure stratosphere. Shortly thereafter the Arabs had gone south along with their oil money, and the farm, like the Thoroughbred business in general, had begun to deteriorate. By the time the Ballards had come to live on the property almost seven years before, Wyland Farm was starting a long downhill slide. From a mid-seventies high of forty racehorses in training, forty-seven broodmares, fifty-eight weanlings and colts, and four valuable stallions, the farm currently had fifteen racehorses, just nine broodmares, eleven weanlings and colts, and one proven stallion, who was unfortunately getting on in years. The farm's private veterinary hospital was no longer operational; neither was the canteen for the farmworkers. The equine swimming pool, once equipped with underwater treadmills and Jacuzzis for the rehabilitation of racehorses with strains and sprains, was empty of water and equipment, and filled with leaves and other debris. The stallion barn, with only one occupant, did double duty as the farm office. The remaining barns needed various repairs, and a fresh coat of white paint. Even the jaunty cupolas that topped them were no longer the once brilliant emerald that was one of the farm's racing colors. Time and neglect had faded the cupolas to a soft, mossy green. Molly's house, one of several tenant dwellings dotted about the property, had once sported the same fresh white and brilliant green. Now the white paint was peeling off in long strips, and the trim could more properly be described as gray.

Despite this reversal of fortune, the name Wyland Farm still retained a degree of local magic. This was horse country, Bluegrass country, an oasis of manors and manners plunked down in the midst of the rural South. The human population was thin. The people who lived on this rolling savannah were, by and large, native to the region. They lived there because their grandpappy and their grandpappy's grandpappy had lived there. A few folks, the owners of the big horse farms, were as rich as any in the world, and had been so for generations. But the majority of the population was not. They existed to meet the needs of the property owners, who were the region's de facto rulers privileged with an unacknowledged but very real droit du seigneur.

The whiskey gentry, as they were called by the less reverent in reference to the fabled sour mash that, along with racehorses, was the region's lifeblood, were every bit as aristocratic as the titled lords and ladies of England. In fact, Great Britain's Queen Elizabeth II visited often on the quiet, and was said to be very much at home among the local blue bloods. Movie stars, magnates, and foreign-born billionaires celebrated international success by moving into the region, hoping to acquire for themselves the patina of gentility that, over time, transforms new money into old. The soft southern hospitality and languid drawls that greeted newcomers were deceptive, however. The Bluegrass assessed its people just as it assessed its horses: by pedigree. A foundation of cold steel underlay the welcoming velvet, and the establishment could be ruthless in turning its collective back on those who, in their estimation, did not measure up.

Molly had not been lucky enough to be born into one of the landed families. Her people had never been more than a tiny, unimportant cog in the vast human machinery that served the rich. To her knowledge, her kin had never owned a piece of property, never progressed educationally beyond high school. Faceless and nameless except to their small group of relatives and friends, her family had lived and died in obscurity in a place where bloodlines meant everything.

As a result, she had had to battle all her life against the trap of feeling small and worthless. She fought the sensation anew as she was borne away into the night by a man who had her very much in his power.

"So, do you get most of your dates by blackmail?" Molly was unable to stand the silence a moment longer. Bravado kept her chin up, her voice tart. To ward off the chill that seemed to be attacking her very bones, she folded her arms tightly across her chest.

"No, but then, most of my dates aren't with thieves." His reply was cool, his glance at her brief.

To be called a thief stung. Molly abandoned bravado for outright hostility. "What do you want with me?"

"We'll talk about it over supper."

"I've eaten."

"I haven't."

There seemed to be no reply Molly could make to that. The obvious implication was that she would do as he wished. Under the circumstances, he was right. Molly, who had been sitting rigidly erect, slumped a little in her seat, defeated by the realization.

"If this is about the twenty dollars . . ."

"Twenty dollars?" He cast her a narrow-eyed glance.

"I spent it on doughnuts and milk for the kids, okay? I'll pay it back."

There was a pause. He glanced at her again. "You took a twenty from the five thousand in the feed bag to buy doughnuts and milk for your brothers and sisters?"

"You hadn't missed it," she said, chagrined. His tone told her that.

"No."

"Then what do you want from me?"

"All in good time."

The car paused at a stop sign, then turned onto old Frankfort Pike. Molly realized that they must be headed toward Lexington. Rural, agrarian Woodford County, where Wyland Farm was located, offered little in the way of restaurants. But it was only a brief drive away from Lexington, the small but busy city that was known as the Heart of the Bluegrass.

"What are you doing for money, now that you've lost your job?" he asked, breaking the silence.

"Is that any of your business?"

"Yes," he said. "I think it is."

The unspoken message was plain: He had the right to ask her anything, and if she knew what was good for her, she'd better answer.

"I have almost two weeks pay coming from Don Simpson. Then I suppose I'll look for another job." Not for anything was she going to let on about how truly desperate she was. Having quit one stable, she was unlikely to be taken on by another. The local horsemen stuck together.

"Your phone's been disconnected," he said.

Molly stiffened. It had only happened that morning, after less than a week's notice that the cutoff was pending. Southern Bell, long used to dealing with the impecunious Ballards, no longer cut them much slack. "How do you know?"

"I tried to call before I came. I thought you might appreciate some warning."

"You're right, I would have." Sudden, acute antipathy toward him sharpened her voice. Molly welcomed its presence. It helped to blunt the edge of an embarrassment so painful that it made her want to squirm in her seat. Having the phone—or the electricity, or the gas—disconnected was nothing new, but she still hated anyone to know when it happened. Especially him.

"Forget to pay your bill?"

"I didn't have the money, all right?" A perverse kind of pride kept Molly from lying. Besides, what was she going to say that he would believe? The family had been on vacation and they'd forgotten to send in the check before they left? She'd tried that one in sixth grade, and gotten laughed right out of school.

"I suppose some of the five thousand dollars was going to go to get your phone turned back on."

"Yes, it was."

He said nothing more for a moment. Then, "How much did you make, working for Wyland Farm?"

None of your business was the reply that sprang to Molly's lips, but she didn't bother to say it. He would get the answer out of her anyway. Grudgingly she named a figure that made his brows lift.

"Not much," he commented.

"Enough to get by on."

"Is that your sole income? Do you get money from any other source?"

"You mean like a million-dollar trust fund? No, my folks never quite got around to setting something like that up."

"Some kind of state payments for your brothers and sisters, maybe," he asked, ignoring her sarcasm.

"No."

"Why not?"

"Because I just don't, okay?"

"I should think you'd be eligible . . ."

"Well, we're not," she said shortly.

"No one elsc in the family works?"

"Sam and Susan are eleven years old. No, they don't work. Mike's fourteen; sometimes he'll help some of the neighbors in their fields, but there's not a lot of jobs around here for a kid his age. And Ashley's busy with school."

"She couldn't get a job in the afternoons? She looks old enough."

"She's seventeen. A senior in high school this year. With a straight-A average. If she can keep it up until graduation, she'll get a full college scholarship. *That's* her ticket out of here, not some dead-end minimum-wage job flipping burgers or checking out groceries. So no, Ashley doesn't work. She knows I'd skin her if she tried."

To Molly's relief, he let the subject drop. As the silence lengthened, Molly gradually relaxed in her seat. Wind whooshed past the windows in a soothing whisper. Gently swaying treetops were dark against the night sky. A single star appeared on the horizon, to be followed by another, then another as the cloud cover that had darkened the sky to pitch-black passed to the west without disgorging so much as a single drop of rain. The car lurched unexpectedly as its right front tire hit a pothole left from the previous harsh winter. Another car approached, its headlamps as it passed briefly lighting up the interior of the Taurus. Glancing at the man beside her, Molly saw that he appeared deep in thought.

The car crested a rise, and suddenly small, picturesque Lexington was spread out before them like an illuminated Christmas village. Home of the University of Kentucky, Lexington bustled at 7:30 p.m. during the school year, even on a Wednesday night. Still, the traffic heading into the downtown area was extraordinarily heavy. The Taurus slowed as it became caught up in the congestion.

They turned right on Limestone, and as they drove past the Civic Center Molly saw the reason for the unusual amount of traffic. The marquee advertised *Indigo Girls Tonight at 8:00.*

Of course. She'd read about the show weeks ago, only she'd forgotten it was tonight. There'd been no reason to remember. Though she and Ashley were both huge fans of the Indigo Girls, there was no way they could have afforded to attend. Not that she minded, not really. Such luxuries had never been a part of her life, and she didn't expect them to be.

"You like the Indigo Girls?" he asked. Molly supposed she had been gazing hungrily at the crowd streaming under the marquee, and immediately got herself in hand.

"They're okay." Her shrug was indifferent.

"I like them," he said, surprising her. Molly didn't reply.

A few minutes later they pulled into the parking lot of Joe Balogna's, a popular Italian restaurant. She had expected him to stop at something like a McDonald's or a Kentucky Fried Chicken. Not at a place like this, which was one of the nicer eateries around. As he parked the car, Molly looked down at herself with renewed dismay.

"You don't really expect me to go in there like this, do you?" she asked.

"Why not?" Turning off the engine, he removed the keys from the ignition and pocketed them.

"Because it's a fancy place, and I'm not dressed for it," Molly said through her teeth. Not that it did any good. He was out of the car before she had stopped talking.

When the passenger door opened, Molly, arms crossed over her chest, face averted, stayed stubbornly seated. He looked down at her for a moment without speaking.

"I cannot go in there dressed like this," Molly said at last, unnerved by his silence. She cast him a quick upward glance. "When we left the house, you said I wouldn't have to get out of the car."

"Look," he said, "I missed lunch. I'm starving. I'm going to eat here because it's the closest I can get to real Italian food in this backwater, and I feel like Italian. And you're going in with me because I want to talk to you. I don't care what you look like. Anyway, this close to campus, half the people inside will be wearing jeans, so you'll fit right in."

"It's not just the jeans, it's my hair, and I'm not

wearing any makeup, and this shirt belongs to Mike and—I won't do it."

"Get out of the car, Molly."

Implicit in the words was the fact that she had no choice but to obey. Clamping her lips together, Molly hesitated—and then got out of the car. She went past him without acknowledging his presence by so much as a glance, and heard rather than saw him close the car door behind her. As she walked she tugged the rubber band from her ponytail, wincing at the sting of a random wisp caught by the tenacious circle. Quickly she fluffed the thick, dark strands with her fingers, hoping to restore the naturally wavy mass to some semblance of a style. How successful she was she couldn't tell without a mirror, but without a brush or comb her makeshift effort was the best she could do.

"You've been here before, I take it." He followed her up the steps to the restaurant's front entrance.

"Yes." Precisely once, on a date. She'd been wearing a sundress of Ashley's and her one pair of good heels, with her hair and makeup carefully done. Not like tonight. Confronting polished oak doors and stained-glass sidelights, Molly took a deep breath, squared her shoulders, and reached for the ornate brass knob. If she had to go into a place as nice as this looking as she did, at least she wasn't going to let anyone else know that she wanted to sink into the floor with every step.

His hand beat hers to the knob. Pulling the door open, he allowed her to precede him.

"What a gentleman," she cooed over her shoulder with a glittering faux smile.

"I try," he said imperturbably, following her inside.

Head high, Molly walked into the dimly lit vestibule and up a pair of stairs to where a chicly clad hostess of about her own age stood behind an oak podium. As Molly approached, the hostess looked up. A superior smile appeared as her eyes slid over Molly. Despite her best intentions, Molly felt the scalding heat of humiliation steal up her neck.

"May I help you?" the hostess asked.

"Two for dinner, please." The FBI man spoke from behind Molly.

"Did you have reservations?" A lightning glance at him, and the hostess's attitude was suddenly much more respectful.

"Not tonight." He smiled at her.

"You're lucky the concert crowd has gone, or we wouldn't have room. As it is . . ." She looked down at her chart and then reached for a pair of menus. "I think we can fit you in. Follow me, please."

With a smile for the FBI man and a quick, curious glance for Molly, the hostess led them into the restaurant, which was a place of golden candlelight and stained-glass partitions and burgundy-leather booths. As she slid into the indicated booth, Molly was reminded of nothing so much as the inner sanctum of a church.

"Can I get you anything to drink? Whiskey sours are on special tonight." The hostess handed them menus.

"No," said the FBI man before Molly could reply. His refusal was clearly meant for both of them. Molly wasn't much of a drinker anyway, and certainly didn't feel like anything alcoholic under the circumstances, but his assumption of authority rankled.

"I'll have a whiskey sour," Molly said. Her glance at her companion was a challenge. She almost expected him to countermand her order. But he did not. Instead he opened his menu.

"Gene will be right out with your drink," the hostess promised. With a last smile at the FBI man, she left them alone. Molly watched her miniskirted form twitch down the aisle, and almost wished her back again. She was nervous about being left alone with her companion.

"You like Italian?" He looked up from the menu he was scanning to pin her with those piercing blue eyes.

"I've never eaten anything Italian." Antagonism frosted her voice as she picked up her own menu. He could command her presence, but that was all. She would eat, drink, and say what she pleased. Casting surreptitious glances at the diners around them, Molly confirmed that everybody, even the people wearing jeans, was well groomed. She looked like a bag lady in comparison, she decided. Mortification made her toes curl in Mike's old shoes, but she only held her head a notch higher.

"You said you'd been here before. If you didn't eat Italian, what did you eat?"

"Steak."

"Not too adventurous, are you?"

"No."

"You've never eaten pizza?"

"Oh, pizza," Molly said dismissively.

"You like pizza?"

"Of course I like pizza. Who doesn't like pizza?"

"Then you like Italian. Try lasagna. I never met anyone who didn't like lasagna."

"I told you, I've already eaten."

He shrugged, his attention already back on the menu. "Suit yourself."

"Hi, I'm Gene, and I'll be your waiter." Two glasses of water and Molly's whiskey sour were plunked down on the table. Gene, a college student from the look of him, beamed at them over the round tray he held. "Do you need a little time?"

"We're ready," the FBI man said. Gene looked at Molly expectantly.

"Nothing, thanks," she said, feeling a twinge of regret that she wouldn't at least get a meal out of this encounter. Restaurant visits were few and far between in her life, and the steak she had enjoyed before at Jimmy Miller's expense had been mouthwateringly good. But having declared herself not hungry, she was not going to give him the satisfaction of suddenly changing her mind.

The FBI man ordered lasagna, with soup to start and salad, and milk to drink with the meal.

When the waiter left, the FBI man leaned back in his scat. His fingertips drummed lightly on the tabletop as he looked at Molly. His expression made her nervous all over again.

"Now," he said softly. "Let's talk about what I want from you."

8

"You want me to check the mouth tattoos of every horse that runs at Keeneland, before and after each race?" Molly asked, disbelieving.

"Just the ones that you don't personally know by sight. Just the ones that are long shots, running in a field of claimers. I'll let you know which horses I'm interested in." The FBI man looked at her intently. The conversation was interrupted as the waiter arrived with a bowl of steaming minestrone, which he set down along with a basket of garlic bread. After asking if there was anything else they needed and receiving a negative reply, the waiter left them alone again.

"I can't do that." Molly watched as he tucked into his soup. To make sure there would be enough to go around, the portion of Hamburger Helper she had served herself at supper had been small, and she'd consumed only about half of that. Still, it had filled her up, or so she had thought. But watching him eat with such gusto awakened a pang in the region of her stomach. Molly took another sip of her drink to compensate.

"Why not?" He reached for a piece of bread. With a shake of her head Molly declined the basket he proffered. Hunger pangs or no, her pride would not allow her to accept what she had previously refused.

"First of all, I no longer work for Wyland Farm, remember? I quit. I don't have free access to the backstretch anymore."

"So get your job back." He took a gigantic bite of bread, then returned to his soup.

Molly shook her head, and took another sip of her drink. The whiskey sour was really pretty good, she decided. "It's not that easy. Don Simpson doesn't give people second chances. And in the heat of the moment I think I may have told him to go screw himself."

"So apologize. Tell him it will never happen again. Tell him you need the money."

"What happens if he tells me to get lost?"

His gaze ran over her. "You're a good-looking girl. Use it."

Molly stiffened. "What do you mean by that?"

"Bat your eyelashes at him. Wiggle your fanny. Cry. Do whatever it is women do to soften men up. But get your job back."

The waiter arrived to whisk away the FBI man's now empty soup bowl, replacing it with a salad. Molly looked at the small mountain of greens, at the heaped-on croutons and bacon bits, at the bits of cheese and glistening crown of vinaigrette dressing, and took another envious sip of her drink.

"Suppose," she said, watching him enthusiastically down a chunk of tomato, "just for a minute, that I do manage to get my job back. I'll have my own horses to take care of. I can't go running around the backstretch looking into umpteen horses' mouths. First of all, I won't have time. Second, it'll look pretty suspicious."

"There won't be *umpteen* horses. Maybe four, five, six a week. You can manage that."

"What happens if I get caught? Is this dangerous?"

He looked steadily at her over a forkful of salad. "I won't kid you. It could be."

"Great." She took another sip of whiskey sour, discovered that the glass was down to the last dregs, and regretfully drained it. "In that case, Mr. FBI man, I think you should do it yourself."

"I can't. You can."

"And if I say no?"

"Maybe you'll get lucky and get put in the federal pen right here in Lexington. It's a pretty cushy place as far as jails go. I hear Leona Helmsley loved it." The FBI man speared an errant piece of lettuce with his fork and consumed it. "Your brothers and sisters could visit."

"That's blackmail."

"You got yourself into this by stealing that five thousand, remember? You're lucky I'm willing to cut you a deal." He finished his salad.

"Would you like another drink, miss?" The waiter reappeared, replacing the empty salad plate with a bubbling, cheese-encrusted casserole smelling strongly of pizza. Hunger pangs assaulted Molly anew.

"Yes," she said, at the exact second her dining companion answered *no.*

The waiter looked from one to the other of them.

"Yes," Molly said again, silently challenging the FBI man to countermand her order. He met her gaze for an instant, then gave a slight shrug, declining to debate the issue. The waiter disappeared, presumably to fetch Molly's drink.

"Think of it this way: You'll be working for the federal government for a few weeks. We pay good." He started in on his lasagna.

"You pay? Me?" Molly perked up. The waiter returned, set her second whiskey sour on the table, and departed.

"You said you'd pay me?" she prompted when they were alone again.

"How does five thousand dollars sound?"

"You're joking, right?"

He shook his head. "Nope."

"Let me get this straight: You'll pay me five thousand dollars just to check horse mouth tattoos?"

"Beats going to jail, doesn't it?"

"When do I get the money?"

The sound he made was midway between a snort and a laugh. His eyes glinted with sudden, genuine amusement at her over a suspended forkful of lasagna. "When the job's done."

"And then I'll never see you again, or hear another thing about the money I—took?"

"You help me with this, and the slate's wiped clean. I'll burn the tape—or give it to you. You can burn it yourself."

Molly thought for a minute, sipping reflectively at her drink, while he applied himself to his meal. "No one will ever know that I was involved?"

"No one but you. And me."

"I have to live here. If anyone finds out that I did this, I won't ever be able to work in the horse industry again. We'd probably have to move clean out of Kentucky."

"If that were to happen, which it won't if you're careful, the Bureau would take care of things. You wouldn't be left high and dry, you have my word on it."

Molly looked at him measuringly. "I don't mean to hurt your feelings, Mr. FBI man, but your word doesn't mean a whole heck of a lot to me. I don't even know you."

"You'll just have to trust me."

Molly grimaced. "Great."

"Take it or leave it."

"I don't really have a choice, do I? If I do what you want, I get paid and you go away. If I don't, I could go to jail."

"I'd say that pretty much sums it up." He finished his lasagna, touched his mouth with a napkin, and placed the napkin on the table. The waiter materialized as if from nowhere. Molly, who'd been nursing her drink throughout the conversation, was surprised to find that her glass was empty. She set it down.

"Dessert?" the waiter asked with a smile, looking from one to the other of them. "Or an after-dinner drink?"

The FBI man shook his head to both, and declined coffee, too, as did Molly, who no longer felt like being defiant just to annoy him. They sat in silence while the waiter cleared the table and left the check.

"Next time we come here you really ought to try the lasagna," the FBI man said, removing a couple of bills from his wallet, and laying them atop the check on the small plastic tray. He stood up. "Live dangerously."

"What do you mean, the next time we come here?" Molly asked, sliding out of the booth. With a gesture indicating that she should precede him, he followed her toward the door. Molly was very conscious of him at her back. He made her feel claustrophobic, as though she were literally, as well as figuratively, his prisoner.

"Good night, come back," the hostess called as they passed her. Molly smiled automatically. The FBI man lifted a hand in reply.

Outside in the parking lot, Molly repeated her question.

"Just what I said. I've been in the area eight days, and I've eaten here almost every day, so I imagine I'll be back. Lexington doesn't offer a wide variety of Italian. I'm partial to Italian." He opened her car door for her, and Molly automatically sat. Closing the door, he walked around the car to slide in himself.

"But what do you mean, *we*?" she asked as he started the car.

"You're going to be seeing a lot of me until this is over, and that will probably include me taking you out to meals." The car pulled out into the street. "Trying to meet an informant secretly is a mistake, I've learned to my cost. Someone always sees the two of you together and the deal gets blown. It's better to meet openly. You know, the old hide-in-plain-sight strategy."

"Oh, right. The old hide-in-plain-sight strategy. I must have been absent the day they taught that in Spying 101." Molly sank lower in her seat.

He shot her a glance, then continued: "It would also make things easier for me if I could stop by the barns at Keeneland when I need to without people starting to wonder who I am and why I'm there. *You're* going to be my reason. For the duration of this investigation, I'm your new boyfriend."

Molly was speechless for a moment. She stared at him, taking in his close-cropped sandy hair, his hard-boned, taut-skinned face, his broad-shouldered, leanly muscular body in the elegant conservative suit.

"Nobody will ever believe it," she said with conviction.

He glanced at her then, his eyes gleaming at her through the darkness.

"We'll just have to make them believe it," he said.

9

"You're too old for me," Molly pointed out. "And too . . ."

Her voice trailed off, not because she was too polite to say what she meant but because she couldn't quite find the words she sought.

"Too what?" he inquired.

"Too stuffy," was what she settled for with a scowl.

"Maybe people will think you've found yourself a sugar daddy."

"That's horrible!" Molly sat up straight, indignant at the idea.

"I've got a fair amount of flexibility with my expense account. I could buy you some new clothes, give you an allowance, maybe lease you a car. . . ."

"No way!"

"Then you'll just have to be convincing enough to make people think you're seeing me for love, not money." Something about his expression made Molly suspect he was teasing her a little. If a man as humorless as he appeared to be ever did tease, which upon reflection she tended to doubt.

"Anyway, I haven't said I'll do it yet," she reminded him, subsiding. Her head was buzzing, and she had a terrible feeling that she wasn't thinking as clearly as she might be. When she considered doing what he asked, a vague sense of unease warned her that in agreeing she might be making a mistake. He would be gone in a few weeks at most, while she would still be living and working at Wyland Farm, among people she had betrayed. People who, given a reason, might even be dangerous. Everyone who had ever worked in the horse business knew the rumors: horses drugged by their own or rival stables to enhance or inhibit performance, horses killed for insurance, barns burnt to the ground just in time to save their owners from bankruptcy, public officials bribed to look the other way. Witnesses to the mayhem who expressed a willingness to talk tended to meet unfortunate ends. The surface glamor of the industry had an ugly underside, and she wanted no part of it.

"But you will," he said with calm certainty.

"You're pretty sure of yourself, aren't you?" The car was headed for Woodford County, and as it dipped and rose over the hills and bends in the road Molly felt increasingly queasy.

"Like you said, you don't really have a choice."

"You could be bluffing, about having me arrested."

"Try me."

Molly glanced sideways at him. He looked cool, composed—and about as merciful as an executioner. She didn't want to "try him."

"Okay. I'll do it." Her capitulation was ungracious. A thousand bees swarmed in her head, and her stomach roiled. It occurred to her that downing two whiskey sours without any food to mute their effect might have been a mistake. She was not used to drinking alcohol.

"Good girl." He smiled at her. Molly realized it was the first time she had seen him smile. Really smile, that is. Not the false, humorless grins that she had been treated to before. It made him look younger.

She rested her head back against the seat as the car whooshed through the night. The moon was up, a pale crescent floating over the undulating countryside. In the fields beside the road horses and cattle grazed peacefully.

"If anyone asks, I'm a Chicago businessman down here on vacation," he told her. "We met at Keeneland when I came by early this morning to watch the horses exercise. You were standing at the rail. I asked you out, we hit it off. We see a lot of each other for the next few weeks, and then, regrettably, I have to return to Chicago. End of romance. Sound okay to you?"

"Fine," Molly said, eyes closing.

"Repeat what I just said."

"Don't worry, I'll remember. Could you slow down?"

"It's important that we both tell the same story. . . ."

The car sailed over a rise. Molly's stomach sailed with it. She gritted her teeth, pressed her palms hard into the soft velour upholstery, and tried to will the rising nausea back. Beside her, her companion kept talking. She didn't register a word.

"Mr. FBI man, I think you'd better pull over," she said at last, opening her eyes.

"What?" He glanced at her.

"Pull over," she said through her teeth, because the

matter was now extremely urgent and there was no time to be lost.

He did. The car had no sooner stopped than Molly half rolled, half stumbled out the door and away. She fell to her knees in a dark patch of weeds by the side of the road, and was thoroughly, humiliatingly sick.

When Molly could summon the strength, she got to her feet and walked back toward the car, which was parked some twelve feet behind her. Without surprise she discovered that the FBI man was out of the car, too, leaning against the trunk, watching her. Of course he wouldn't have the decency to let her be sick in private.

"Want some water?" he asked as she approached, and held something out to her. "I keep some in the car. Beats pop."

"Thanks." She took the object, which turned out to be a green plastic bottle of Evian, with a rush of gratitude. Retreating a few steps, she turned her back to him and rinsed the horrible yucky taste out of her mouth. The water was warm, but it did the job. She sluiced her face with it, and rinsed her hands.

"Need a towel?" He was behind her. She nodded, and accepted the soft wad of cloth he passed her. As she dried her face and hands, she discovered that her towel was in reality a man's T-shirt. His, she assumed.

"Are you always this prepared?" she asked, swinging her hair back from her face and straightening her shoulders as she turned to face him. She was embarrassed, horribly, burningly embarrassed, but she wasn't going to let him know that. Whatever else she might lack, she had her pride.

"I used to be a Boy Scout." He took the T-shirt from her, retrieved the empty water bottle from the roadside where she had dropped it, and returned them both to the trunk. Closing the lid softly, he leaned back against it again, his arms folding over his chest. There was the merest quirk of a smile on his face as he looked her over. Like the serene beauty of the meadowlands around them, he was washed in silver moonlight. Unfortunately, that made his aggravating smile all too easy to see.

"Not much of a drinker, are you?" he observed.

"I'm just getting over the flu," Molly lied, bristling. Admitting to a weakness left one vulnerable, she had learned long ago. "My stomach's been upset off and on for a week."

"Oh," he said, and his smile broadened.

"Can we go?" Molly asked, turning a cold shoulder on him to walk to the passenger-side door.

"Sure you're up to it?" He was behind her, reaching around her for the door handle before she could open it herself.

"Yes." Molly sank into the passenger seat with relief. She was still a little weak, but she did feel better. Emptying her stomach and breathing fresh air had helped.

"Put your seat belt on." He closed the passenger door. While he walked around the car, Molly complied.

"We can sit here a minute if you want to," he offered, getting in beside her.

"I'm fine," Molly said with a hint of a snap. He shrugged and started the car. As they resumed their journey Molly was both relieved and chagrined to realize that the car's pace was considerably slower.

"Did you catch anything that I was saying to you

earlier?" Remnants of a smile still curved his mouth as he glanced at her.

Molly hesitated, tempted by that superior smirk to lie, then shook her head. "Not much."

"I didn't think so." Patiently he repeated the story he had concocted to explain their relationship. It sounded lame to Molly, but she wasn't going to argue about it.

"Anything you say, Mr. FBI man," she said with a hint of insolence when he had finished. She was feeling pretty limp, but she didn't think he could tell.

He glanced at her again. Molly was pleased to note that his smile was gone.

"Molly, listen to me: If you call me that, even once, where anyone can hear you, my cover's blown. *Our* cover's blown. The operation is wrecked, and it is very possible that one or both of us might be endangered. I'm your new boyfriend, remember? My name is Will. You call me Will. You think of me as Will. Got it?"

"Anything you say, *Will,*" Molly amended with a superior smirk of her own. Privately, she found it hard to imagine herself calling him by his given name, and as for thinking of him as Will—he would always be the FBI man to her.

They turned off Old Frankfort Pike and headed down the narrow road that led to Molly's house. The moon was in front of them, its soft light glowing through the windshield.

"What time is it?" Molly asked.

"A few minutes after ten," the FBI man—no, Will, she must remember to think of him as Will—answered. Molly was surprised to learn that they had been gone so long. Over three hours—the twins would be in bed. Mike and Ashley would be watching TV and doing homework, respectively. If Mike had not gone out. He had a nine-thirty curfew on school nights, but half the time it was ten or after before he got home.

Mike was going through a difficult phase. It was hard to know what to do for the best.

Rounding a bend brought the farmhouse into view. The first thing Molly noticed was that the house was lit up like a Christmas tree.

The second was that a police car with flashing blue lights was parked in the drive.

"Oh, my God!" she gasped, a thousand and one hideous possibilities running through her mind.

With a quick glance at her, Will sped up. Within seconds they were pulling in behind the police car. A uniformed officer was just stepping onto the lighted porch, having exited the house through the kitchen door. Pork Chop, at his heels, looked up to see the newly arrived vehicle, and bounded toward it barking.

"Molly!"

Ashley, Susan, and Sam scrambled off the porch, heading for Molly as she jumped out of the car. A lightning once-over for the three of them, and she concluded that they were unhurt. Pork Chop, having sniffed her in passing, moved on. She spared no more than a glance for his friendly overtures to Will as she rushed toward her sisters and brother.

She reached them, or they reached her—actually it was a kind of mutual coming-together. Susan and Sam hugged her waist, and Molly wrapped an arm around each of their narrow shoulders as she searched Ashley's face. Ashley, she was alarmed to see, looked wide-eyed and pale even in the yellowish glow of the porch light. It took a lot to discompose Ashley.

"What's happened?" Molly croaked.

"Mike . . ." Ashley said at the same time.

"Miz Ballard?" The cop from the porch came toward them. A second cop got out of the squad car. Molly hadn't even realized it was occupied.

"Has something happened to Mike?" Molly asked Ashley urgently.

"He's in trouble."

"Where is he?"

"He went out, and he hasn't come home yet," Ashley breathed as the policemen converged on them. One was stocky, with heavy jowls and a beer gut that rode proudly above his low-slung belt. The other was taller, lanky and bald. Both wore the brown uniforms of the Woodford County Sheriff's Department, with silver deputy badges gleaming on their breast pockets.

"What's the problem, Officers?" Molly did not recognize either man, though she was familiar with many of the law enforcement personnel in the area. Thanks largely to her mother, and the kids.

"We need to talk to your brother Mike. When do you expect him back?" The deputy was courteous, if not friendly.

"Why do you want to talk to him?" Hostility edged Molly's reply. Releasing the twins, she squared her shoulders and faced the men with her chin up. She had dealt with cops before, and in her experience they were inevitably bad news.

The deputies glanced at each other. The stockier one spoke: "About an hour ago, we got a report that some teenagers were trespassing in a barn over at Sweet Meadow Stud. When we got there, half a dozen kids ran out the back of the barn. We looked around, found beer cans and the remains of a couple of marijuana cigarettes. We think your brother was one of those kids."

"What makes you think that?" The hostility in Molly's voice was pronounced now. It was her way of dealing with her own fear. If Mike was involved with drugs—what would she do?

"One of the boys was wearing a Woodford County High jacket. We showed some yearbook pictures to a witness. The witness identified one of the boys as your brother."

"I don't believe it!" Molly said stoutly, though she harbored a terrible fear that it might be true.

"Are you your brother's legal guardian, Miz Ballard?" the taller cop asked.

"Yes!" She wasn't, though. Their living arrangements were strictly unofficial. For years she had cared for her siblings like a parent, but she had never even tried to make the arrangement legal. She was afraid to. Now another, second fear for her family joined her fear for Mike. If they found out that the younger ones were not legally under her care, what would they do?

"If all this happened just an hour ago, like you said, it would have been dark. How could the witness have seen anyone clearly enough to identify him in the dark?" Ashley questioned with admirable levelheadedness. Molly spared her sister a grateful glance. At seventeen, Ashley was as mature as a thirty-year-old. Molly sometimes wondered how she would manage when Ashley went off to college.

"The witness was driving home, and the boys were running down the side of the road. Her headlights illuminated them. She got a good look at your brother's face." The deputy glanced from Molly to Ashley and back.

"She says," Molly countered, girding up for a fight.

"She says," Ashley echoed, and the twins nodded vigorously.

The taller cop looked the four of them over for a moment in silence. "Does your brother smoke pot, Miz Ballard?" he asked.

"No, of course he doesn't!"

"To get caught now might be the best thing for him, you know. Straighten him out before he slides into more dangerous drugs. You don't want that to happen, do you?"

"I don't believe Mike was in that barn," Molly said, though to her own ears her voice sounded strained. She did believe it, or at least she was hideously afraid it might be true. The idea of Mike being involved with drugs terrified her.

The lanky deputy's lips tightened. "We need to talk to your brother, Miz Ballard. When do you expect him home?"

Molly had a dreadful flash of imagination picturing Mike choosing that moment to stagger up the driveway drunk or stoned, or both, and being hauled off to jail there and then.

"I'm not sure." Her voice was cold.

"In any case, I don't imagine Miss Ballard will allow you to talk to her brother without an attorney being present." Will spoke from behind Molly. Molly was so upset she hadn't even realized he was still standing there. She glanced around at him. His gaze held hers for the briefest of moments. "Will you, Molly?"

"No." She looked back at the deputies. The idea of getting a lawyer before permitting Mike to talk to the cops would never have occurred to her. Hiring a lawyer was not something the Ballards ordinarily did. For one thing, it cost too much. For another, she didn't know any lawyers. But she would worry about that later. For right now, she would grab at any straw that floated her way. With some surprise, she realized she felt better knowing Will, for whatever unlikely reason, was on her—and Mike's—side. A whole lot better.

"If you don't mind my asking, sir, who are you?" the shorter deputy asked, looking past Molly at Will.

"A friend of Miss Ballard's." The lie came out smooth as instant pudding. He was good at telling lies, Molly noted, and vowed to remember that.

"I see." The deputy glanced back at Molly. "Miz Ballard, you don't really want to drag a lawyer into this, do you? Wouldn't it be easier if we could just talk with Mike, find out what he has to say for himself, and take it from there? You know, keep this whole thing kind of informal, if we can?"

Yeah, right. Molly wasn't buying that. "If you want to talk to my brother, we want to have a lawyer present."

The mere threat seemed to annoy the cops, and that was good enough for her. The cops were the enemy, always had been.

"I see." The deputies exchanged looks. The taller one spoke: "Then there's no point in us waiting around, is there? Will you give us a call tomorrow, and arrange a time to bring Mike in to talk to us? With his lawyer, of course." He pulled a card from his pocket, scribbled something on the back of it, and handed it to Molly. She took it without even glancing at it, and tucked it in the pocket of her jeans.

"You *will* call us, won't you?" The stocky cop made it sound more like an order than a question.

"Of course," Molly said, feeling curiously hollow. By tomorrow, she was going to have to come up with a lawyer. And the money to pay him.

"Until we get this resolved, we suggest you keep a close eye on your brother, Miz Ballard. *We* will be," the taller cop said. With a nod for Molly and the others, he turned and headed for the patrol car, followed by his fellow deputy. In just a few minutes they were gone, their car backing down the driveway with a noisy burst of gravel. Molly watched in silence as the taillights shrank to tiny points of red in the darkness before disappearing.

Then she turned back to the others. Ashley and the twins stood close by Will. Even Pork Chop panted trustingly at his feet.

Molly's lip curled as she realized how foolish they were, all of them, herself included, to count as an ally a man none of them had laid eyes on before today. He was only there by accident, and only helping them because she had something he wanted. That help could be withdrawn at any time. And would be, as soon as he no longer needed her assistance.

Molly met Will's gaze through the haze of yellow light thrown off from the house.

"We don't have the money to pay for a lawyer," she told him abruptly, rubbing her upper arms to ward off the chill.

He shrugged, and stuck his hands in his trouser pockets. "Don't worry about it."

"Don't worry—" Molly began, her voice rising, then broke off as something moved in the shadows near the back of the house. A dark form sidled into view, then hesitated. Following her arrested gaze, Will and the children turned to watch as the figure began walking toward them.

"What did *they* want?" Mike asked when he was close enough.

10

"Just your hide," Molly said too pleasantly. She eyed her errant brother up and down. A hooded, quilted black vest had been added to his jeans/T-shirt/flannel shirt ensemble. A stray lock of dark brown hair had escaped from his ponytail to straggle down one side of his face. His lone earring gleamed in the light. He looked like a street punk, Molly had to admit. She took an unobtrusive step closer, inhaling to see if she could smell alcohol, or marijuana, on him. Nothing except crisp night air carrying a hint of leaf mold reached her nostrils. "Like we all do. First of all, you're almost an hour late. Where have you been?"

Mike shrugged. "Nowhere. The cops weren't really here because of me, were they?"

"They said you smoked pot, Mike!" Sam interjected excitedly before Molly could reply. "They said you drank beer too!"

"You are such a liar," Mike said, fixing his little brother with a disdainful look.

"He is not!" Susan took up the cudgel in her twin's defense. "Sam never lies!"

"That's what they said, Mike," Ashley confirmed. Mike's eyes widened, and he glanced at Molly. Lips compressed, she nodded.

"They said a group of teenagers was trespassing in a barn over at Sweet Meadow Stud. When they pulled up, the kids ran. They left behind evidence that they had been smoking pot and drinking beer in the barn. A witness identified you as one of the boys."

"What witness?" The very defensiveness of Mike's tone made Molly's heart sink.

"You *were* one of the kids in the barn, weren't you, Mike?" Oh, God, what was she going to do? Disciplining a teenage brother was a Herculean task, Molly was discovering. Taking away TV and phone privileges did not seem to be a strong enough response to this crisis. But what did that leave? Grounding him? Physical discipline? Her imagination boggled at the thought. Mike was bigger than she was.

Mike hesitated, his gaze unwillingly locking with Molly's.

"Maybe," he said.

"*Maybe?*" Molly's voice went up an octave.

Mike started to say something, then glanced at Will, who stood silently to Molly's left, his hands still thrust into his trouser pockets, his eyes on Mike's face.

"Does *he* have to be in on this?" Mike asked with a jerk of his head in Will's direction.

"He's on our side," Susan piped up. Ashley and Sam nodded agreement. Molly barely caught herself before she joined in.

"That was pretty rude," she told her brother. Mike shrugged.

"Anyway, he's going to get you a lawyer," Ashley said. "Before you talk to the police."

"I'm not talking to the police, and I don't need a lawyer. It wasn't me in that barn." Mike's face turned sullen, an expression Molly had lately become all too familiar with. He was lying. She knew it in her gut. All at once she got mad. How could he do this, to himself, to her, to all of them? Harsh words sprang to her lips. She had to grit her teeth to hold them back. Yelling at Mike was not the answer, she knew, although she couldn't seem to figure out what was.

"You don't believe me, do you?" Mike's question was angry. Looking at him, Molly suddenly saw before her the undersized eight-year-old he had been when he was restored to their family after years in a series of foster homes, and her own anger cooled. He had used belligerence to mask his fear then too.

"Whether I believe you or not, you're in trouble, bud," she said quietly. "This isn't going to go away. The deputies who were here want me to call them tomorrow to set up a time so they can talk to you. You can just bet they'll be talking to other kids, too, and I'd say there's a pretty good chance that somebody will spill the beans. And that's not even the worst of it. The worst of it is what you're doing to yourself. If you were drinking, or smoking pot, I need to know. You need to tell me the truth."

Mike glared at her. "Why? You never believe a word I say anyway."

Before Molly could reply, he turned his back and stomped away. Feeling helpless, she could only watch as he took the porch steps in a single bound and disappeared into the house.

"He's going through a phase," Ashley said, clearly wanting both to comfort Molly and to excuse Mike's conduct.

Molly took a deep breath. "I know."

She had told herself the same thing countless times, but it was cold comfort just at that moment. She glanced up at Will. "Do you really think he needs a lawyer?"

"Up to you," Will said, sounding indifferent. "You could just take him along to the police and let him 'fess up. If he really was smoking pot and drinking beer, a taste of the juvenile justice system might be what it takes to straighten him out."

"He's only fourteen," Molly said sharply.

"If he's smoking pot at fourteen, what will he be doing at twenty?" It was a reasonable question, one that Molly had already asked herself, and been unable to answer. Her shoulders slumped.

"If you could get us a lawyer, we'd appreciate it," she said to Will, knowing she might be making a mistake but unable to do anything else but come to her brother's defense. Will nodded.

"Mike won't have to go to jail, will he?" Susan asked, looking up at Molly. The child sounded scared, and Molly squeezed her shoulder.

"No, of course not," Molly answered stoutly, striving to reassure her little sister.

Her siblings, Ashley included, looked relieved, as though Molly's word were law. Will's expression was unreadable.

Susan yawned.

"You're tired, aren't you, Susie Q?" Molly asked. Susan shook her head in an instant, vigorous *no*, which Molly disregarded with the wisdom born of experience. Glancing from Sam to Ashley, she added: "We're all tired. Let's go inside."

"Him too?" Sam asked hopefully, looking up at

Will. Never having had a father, or a father figure, Sam was always eager to attach himself to an available adult male.

"No!" Molly said with more force than tact. Gaining a grip on her composure, she turned to Will, holding out her hand. "I'm sorry the evening ended this way. Thank you for offering to help us with the lawyer. Good night."

"Could I speak to you for a minute?" Will asked, ignoring her outstretched hand. To anyone else it might have sounded like a polite request, but Molly knew an order when she heard one.

Ashley, with a glance from her sister to Will, began to move away toward the house, shepherding Susan and Sam with her. "Come on, guys."

Ashley probably thought that, as her "date," Will wanted privacy to kiss her good night!

"What?" Molly asked abruptly when she and Will were alone.

"I expect you to get your job back tomorrow."

Molly, who was braced for a lecture on the merits of letting her brother take his lumps, had almost forgotten her Faustian bargain. "I'll try."

"Don't try. Do it," Will said, voice curt. He studied her for a moment, then reached into his inside coat pocket and drew out his wallet. "How much do you need to get your phone turned back on?"

"I don't want your money."

He opened the wallet and thumbed through the bills anyway.

"It's not my money, it's the government's money. You're working for Uncle Sam now, remember? And I need to be able to get in touch with you in a hurry if I have to. So you need to get your phone turned back on."

"You mean I don't get a shoe phone, like in *Get Smart*?" Molly tried to cover her humiliation with flippant humor.

"How much?" Will ignored her weak attempt to be funny. Grudgingly, Molly named a figure.

"I'll have a lawyer call you tomorrow," Will said, handing over a quintet of twenties. "If I were you, I wouldn't be too easy on your brother."

"That's too much"—Molly discerned the amount at a glance, and thrust the fanned bills back at him—"and how many teenagers have you raised lately?"

"Keep it. You might get another sudden urge for doughnuts, and I'd hate to find you out robbing a 7-Eleven." His mouth quirked at her. "As for raising teenagers, I have an eighteen-year-old son. A good kid. But I sure have seen a lot who've gone bad."

"Mike's not going bad!" The warning stung.

"Isn't he?" Will shrugged. "You know him better than I do. I'll be in touch. Good night."

With a brief inclination of his head, Will turned and walked to his car. Molly watched him go. Wind rustled through the treetops, dislodging a shower of leaves that swirled down around her. The car backed down the driveway and turned right, heading for town.

Alone in the dark, Molly was suddenly cold. Crossing her arms over her chest, she turned and headed for the house. Despite the chill in the air, she was in no hurry to get inside. Once there, she would have to deal with Mike.

And she simply did not know what to do.

About anything.

11

October 12, 1995

It was 3:00 a.m. The old woman sat straight up in her bed, awakened from a sound sleep. It was happening again. She was convinced of it.

The screams had invaded her dreams. Long-ago screams. Screams of an eviscerated pet mouse, a mutilated kitten. Screams of a parakeet, wings and tail aflame, streaking frantically through the house. Screams of a dog. A horse. A child.

Oh, God, the child. And she had never spoken out.

Breath catching on a sob, she fought to calm herself. It couldn't be happening again, it couldn't. That was twenty years in the past. Over. Done with. Forgotten, by almost everyone. Even for those who remembered, time had worked its magic to veil their memories and dull their pain.

The screams that had awakened her had been part of a nightmare, of course. Nothing more than that.

Though it was not a cold night, she was shivering. As she forced herself to lie back down again and pulled the covers up around her chin, she discovered why:

The thin silk nightgown she wore was drenched in sweat.

From the nightmare, of course.

She lay awake the rest of the night, afraid to close her eyes lest she sleep, and invite the nightmare back again.

12

October 12, 1995

Slicked with early morning dew, the lush bluegrass lawn shimmered in the light of the rising sun as Molly walked along a turf path to Barn 15. The crisp air was tinged with manure and sawdust. Neatly trimmed privet hedges underscored with masses of golden yellow chrysanthemums outlined the maze of walkways that led from the backstretch barns to the track and the stands and beyond.

Built of aged gray limestone, impeccably manicured Keeneland was one of the most beautiful racecourses in the world. Composed of more than nine hundred acres bordered by a three-foot-tall, ivy-covered stone wall, it was officially named Keeneland Race Course, in the European tradition, instead of race*track*, in the tawdry American fashion, when it was built in the 1930s. Billboards and signs were not allowed on the grounds, and it was the only major racetrack in the world without a public address system. This omission was deliberate, underlining the expectation that Keeneland's visitors would be knowledgeable enough to identify horses, riders, and silks without an announcer's assistance.

Just as it was meant to, Keeneland exuded an air of old money. Not nearly as well known as Churchill Downs, Saratoga, or Belmont, Keeneland had the exclusivity of a well-kept secret. Even this early in the day, men casually elegant in navy blazers breakfasted on the terrace overlooking the track, heads buried in copies of the racing form. The few women present were more colorfully dressed, but they, too, subscribed to the tasteful understatement that was the course's unofficial dress code. No outrageous fashions or enormous hats for this crowd.

An exercise rider, standing straight-legged in the irons, jogged a fidgety Thoroughbred down the path, heading toward the oval track. Molly stepped aside to let them pass. The colt lashed out at her with a back hoof as it went by, skittish rather than vicious, and was sharply called to order by its rider. Molly dodged, then continued on, unruffled. Like all true horsemen, she had been kicked, bitten, stepped on, and thrown too many times to count. The unpredictability of the animals was a given.

In the distance, the pounding of hooves told of other horses already on the track. It was just shy of 7:00 a.m., and morning work-outs were well under way.

"Mornin'." A uniformed security guard scrutinized with a glance the pass Molly had clipped to the front of her zip-up gray sweat shirt. Hired for the meet, he was no one she knew. With a nod she kept walking.

The white-painted barns were clustered beneath a sheltering grove of trees. Outside Barn 15, two eight-horse trailers and a lawn company truck were parked. Marta Bates, another Wyland Farm groom and a good friend, led Tabasco Sauce toward the paddock. Preoccupied with the colt, who was prone to acting up, she acknowledged Molly with an absent wave.

Molly felt as if she had never been away.

Except for the stamping of horses' hooves, it was quiet inside the barn. Kept as clean as a hospital, the vast interior gleamed with fresh white paint from the baseboards to the lofty rafters high overhead. Heavy double-wide doors mounted on rollers provided access from either end. At the moment only the side through which Molly had entered was open, allowing a waft of fresh air to drift through. Thirty-two stalls faced each other across a wide turf lane. Each stall bore a plaque inscribed with its resident's name on the bottom half of the Dutch door. Half-barrels of plum-colored chrysanthemums adorned the space between every third stall. The barn smelled of sawdust, disinfectant, and horse.

Molly took a deep breath, the action almost subconscious. The smell was as familiar to her as her name, and as welcome as the scent of her own home.

Wyland Farm's head groom, Rosario Arguello, whistled softly as he mucked out a stall just inside the entrance. Molly leaned over the half-open door.

"Hey, Rosey, where's Mr. Simpson?" she asked. Dark and compact, a native of Argentina who had once hoped to become a jockey, Rosey was an even closer friend than Marta. He glanced up, eyes widening as he saw who was asking.

"Molly!" he said in his heavily accented English, dropping his pitchfork and walking toward her. "Damn, Molly, what you doing, hmm? How could you go off and leave us? Just like that? What about a goodbye?"

Molly smiled at him as he caught her shoulders and gave her a rough hug. Fortyish, Rosey had a wife and four children, with another on the way. He had never once in the seven years she had known him treated her as anything other than a genderless fellow groom and friend, and she appreciated that.

"So, how's Mr. Simpson feeling today?" Molly asked, which was a roundabout way of inquiring whether the trainer was in one of his legendary foul moods. Rosey knew the code. He rolled his eyes.

"Bad, huh?" Molly grimaced. Just her luck.

"Lady Valor came up lame this morning."

"Oh, no!" Born at Wyland Farm, Lady Valor was—or had been—one of Molly's horses. Molly had cared for the two-year-old filly from birth, and had a special fondness for her.

"Mr. Simpson's with her now, I think," Rosey called after her, but Molly was already hurrying away. Most of the roomy stalls with their half-open doors were empty, she saw at a glance as she passed them. The horses were on the track. In the stall beside Tabasco Sauce's empty one, Ophelia lay with legs tucked beneath her. As Molly passed, the little burro clambered to her feet, furry rabbit ears pricking forward. She wanted the handful of sweet feed that Molly's presence usually presaged.

"Later, Ophelia," Molly promised, and strode on.

Lady Valor's stall was second from the far end, on the left-hand side that was Wyland Farm's row. Simpson, his burly form clad in khakis and a blue button-down shirt with sleeves rolled up, and veterinarian Herb Mott were in the stall with the filly. Simpson's thick gray hair, usually carefully groomed, was standing on end as if he'd been raking his hands through it.

Dr. Mott, seventyish and frail, was kneeling, running his hand over Lady Valor's leg, while Simpson, his back to Molly, leaned over the vet's shoulder. Angie Archer, a young hotwalker Molly assumed had been recruited as her own replacement, stood at the animal's head. Lady Valor had her ears back. Molly knew that look. For all her sweetness, Lady Valor was a biter.

"Can I help?" Not waiting for an answer, Molly entered the stall and went straight to Lady Valor's head. The filly greeted her with a soft nicker and a vigorous nod. After an identifying glance, Angie surrendered the shank with an expression of relief. Noting the quartet of small round bruises on the sturdily built brunette's bare forearm, Molly almost smiled. Lady Valor's displeased nips were as painful as a vicious pinch.

"She's injured her goddamned stifle!" Simpson threw Molly an anguished glance.

"Oh, no!" Molly said with genuine alarm. The stifle was the joint in the hind leg of a horse that was roughly equivalent to the human knee.

"Overnight, in her stall," Simpson continued almost on a groan.

"Is she still going to be able to run in the Spinster?" Molly asked, referring to the coming Sunday's big distaff stakes race. Lady Valor was an early favorite.

"Don't look like it."

The vet glanced up at that, shaking his head in confirmation of Simpson's opinion. Simpson swore.

"Sorry, Don," Dr. Mott said, gently putting Lady Valor's leg down and standing up. "This kind of injury just takes time to heal."

"I know." Simpson wiped the lower part of his face

with his hand, shook his head, and then recovered his composure enough to walk Dr. Mott to the stall door.

"She'll be fine in a month, six weeks."

"I know."

Dr. Mott left. Simpson latched the chest-high wooden door behind the vet, then turned back into the stall. His gaze met Molly's.

"Sometimes I feel like I oughta be one of them Hee-Haw characters: You know, if it weren't for bad luck I'd have no luck at all." He was talking more to himself than her, Molly knew, and she also knew that no reply was expected, or wanted. Suddenly Simpson's bushy gray eyebrows snapped together, and he frowned.

"What the hell are you doin' here?" he demanded, as if all the reasons she shouldn't be present had just registered on him. "I thought I fired you."

"You didn't fire me. I quit," Molly answered, frowning back at him. Being meek with Don Simpson was a mistake, she had learned soon after he had taken over the job a year ago. At sixty-two, he had once been a big-time trainer. A career-crushing string of losses over the last five years had sent him reeling to the relatively small potatoes of Wyland Farm, which, like himself, had once been a force to reckon with in the racing world. Wyland Farm, and Simpson, were considered has-beens by people in the know. But Simpson still thought of himself as a superstar. His ego had not shrunk along with his prestige. He was a bully with a vicious temper, happy to terrorize any poor soul who would let him. His one saving grace, in Molly's eyes, was that he had an almost intuitive understanding of horses, and a genuine love for them.

"Oh, yeah?" Simpson growled. "Then what the hell are you doin' here?"

"You owe me two weeks pay." Molly put up her chin belligerently.

"I'm keepin' it in lieu of two weeks notice."

"You can't do that! Anyway, how can somebody give notice if they're fired?"

"I thought you quit."

"If it's gonna cost me two weeks pay, I got fired." Molly said the last word through clenched teeth. Then, on the verge of forgetting her mission, she remembered, grabbed hold of her temper, unclenched her teeth, and forced out a smile. "Anyway, I—uh—thought you might need me to help out, at least until Keeneland's over."

Simpson stared at her hard. "We've been gettin' along just fine."

Molly glanced significantly at Lady Valor's stifle. "Looks like it."

Simpson's expression darkened. "You askin' for your job back?"

Molly swallowed her pride. "Yeah."

"You gonna call me an asshole again and tell me to go stick my head in the toilet?"

A spark of humor lit Molly's eyes, but she did not dare smile. "Not if I can help it."

"You better help it," he growled. "You get out of line with me again, and you're gone for good. Got that?"

Molly nodded.

"Then get your ass to work. You!" Simpson focused on Angie, who looked scared. "Get out of here. You're back to being a hotwalker. You make a lousy groom, anyway."

He glared at Angie, who flushed bright red and hurried past him, appearing on the verge of tears. Simpson watched with apparent satisfaction as she rushed away, head down.

Then he looked at Molly, as if daring her to say anything. Molly knew better. Lady Valor nudged her upper arm. Molly rubbed the filly's neck absently, knowing that if she didn't give the animal the attention she wanted, Lady Valor's next move would be to nip her arm.

"So get to work," Simpson barked at her, and left the stall.

Standing inside the lawn care truck parked by Barn 15, arms folded over his chest, Will watched the monitor with a frown. Seated in the computer chair in front of the desk, Murphy watched the monitor too.

"Whew! I thought for a minute there he was going to pitch her out on her ear," Murphy said.

Will grunted. With the surveillance system repaired—Murphy's job of the previous night—it had been an easy task to track Molly from the instant she entered the barn. He had been beginning to fear she wasn't going to show. The previous morning she'd arrived at the barn some three hours earlier. Why she was so late now he didn't know, and it didn't matter. What mattered was that she had accomplished the task he had set her to do: she had her job back. The vital inside link had been reestablished.

Fleetingly, Will thought of what had happened to his last inside link, then dismissed the little qualm that came with the memory. Lawrence's death had nothing to do with Molly. It was a suicide; Lawrence had been mentally unstable.

At that moment Molly was inside a stall, alone with a horse that looked big enough to crush her at will, murmuring to the animal as she wrapped bandages around its hind leg. The image of stall and horse and nubile young woman filled the screen.

"Not exactly Miss Tactful, is she?" Murphy observed.

Will grunted again.

"Sexy, though." Murphy grinned, and stood up to adjust the dial. The camera zoomed in on Molly, then panned her up and down. With her dark hair pulled back in a ponytail and her fine-boned face free of any makeup that he could discern, Will thought she looked about sixteen. He wondered why that made him cross.

"She sure does fill out a T-shirt and jeans," Murphy observed admiringly. Will felt his irritation increase. He had been trying not to notice how the worn jeans emphasized the shapely curve of her rear and the slender length of her legs, or how her plain white T-shirt clung to a pair of high, round breasts and, tucked in, revealed the suppleness of her waist. The gray sweat shirt that she had worn on arrival now hung over the stall door. Irrational as he knew it was, the fact that she had discarded it annoyed him.

Unwillingly, he focused on the one aspect of her anatomy that he couldn't seem to avoid. Her nipples were clearly visible, small nubs pressing against the soft white cotton, and her breasts seemed to move with unconfined freedom beneath. Was she even wearing a bra? he wondered.

"I bet she's hot in the sack," Murphy continued. At the image *that* conjured up, Will felt an unexpected gusher of heat explode through his veins. Gritting his teeth, he said nothing, just reached out to adjust the knob on the monitor so that it showed a panorama of the barn.

"Hey, we need to keep an eye on our informant," Murphy protested with a lewd chuckle, reaching for the knob in turn. It was all Will could do not to knock the other man's hand aside, but he stopped himself in time. As Molly once again filled the screen, he turned away.

13

It was a little after 6:00 p.m., the time of day when the air was growing cool and dusk was falling. Charcoal shadows stretched across the rolling landscape, enveloping grazing herds of horses so that they took on the unsubstantiality of ghosts, huddled together against the oncoming night. The scent of smoke from burning leaves hung in the air. The occasional backfiring pickup or barking dog were all that broke the silence. Clad in jeans, T-shirt, and a hooded gray sweat shirt that was zipped almost to her throat, Molly sat atop a black-painted board fence that ran along the crest of the small rise a little way behind her house. A gentle-eyed chestnut mare nudged her knee. Molly dug in the pocket of her sweat shirt, bringing forth the last handful of dog chow she had brought with her. The mare, Sheila, loved the stuff. Molly had little doubt that, given the opportunity, Sheila would gorge herself on dog food until she died.

Sheila's velvety muzzle greedily nuzzling her palm brought a slight smile to Molly's face. Sheila was sixteen, long retired from the racing world, left to finish out her days fat and happy in the Wyland Farm fields. Of them all, Sheila was Molly's secret favorite, and she treated the animal as a cross between a pet dog and her own horse.

It was peaceful in the gathering dark, alone except for Sheila, and Molly savored the moments of solitude. After a hard day's work, this was how she recharged. In just a few minutes she would have to go back inside to face fixing supper and helping with homework and a sullen, recalcitrant Mike. . . .

She had grounded him, forbidden him to see his friends outside of school for a month. Since he denied the beer and pot charge and she couldn't prove it, she rationalized the punishment on the grounds that he had been late for curfew. He hated her for it. So what else was new? As a solution to the real problem, Molly knew what she had devised wasn't really adequate. But it was the best she could come up with. At least while he was grounded he couldn't drink beer, or smoke dope.

No lawyer had been in touch, but then the phone was not yet reconnected, though she had stopped to pay the bill on her way home. But did she really expect the FBI man—Will—to come up with a lawyer for her brother? His promise of help had been just talk, she had little doubt. Though the idea was a good one. She would follow through on it, for Mike's sake. Tomorrow, during lunch or a break, she would look through the phone book and try to find a lawyer on her own. Today's lunch had been all of fifteen minutes long, and she had spent it on the phone making an appointment for Mike to speak to the deputies. After much haggling, she had gotten them to agree to let Mike come in on her next day off, Monday, at 3:30

p.m. No way was she letting Mike face them alone. Even with a lawyer present.

Afterward there would be the lawyer's fee to worry about. There was always something to worry about.

Ashley had been invited to the homecoming dance at school, she had confided when Molly arrived home. Ashley, a shy wallflower with boys, was so thrilled that happiness beamed from her like rays from the sun. Though her sister had not asked, nor probably even thought of it yet, Molly knew Ashley would need a dress. A special dress. An expensive dress.

Sam and Susan were going on a field trip the following Wednesday for which they were expected to pay ten dollars each.

And the mail had contained a postcard informing her that Pork Chop was past due for his rabies shot, as well as a shut-off notice from the electric company. If she did not pay what was owed within seven days, the power would be disconnected.

It was always something. But then, such was life.

"That's all, sweetheart," Molly said to Sheila, who was nudging her for more. "Sorry."

She patted the mare and swung down from the fence, turning toward home, then stopped short. A man was walking up the slope toward her. In one hand he carried a flat white box. Behind him, the lights inside the house had been turned on. A soft yellowish glow shone from the windows, turning the approaching man into little more than a dark silhouette. Molly got a glimpse of Ashley's head and shoulders, small at that distance, as she crossed in front of the rear kitchen window, then seconds later retraced her steps. A white car was parked behind her own blue Plymouth, the light from the windows making it clearly visible despite the yard's evening shroud of gray.

Even without the clue of the car, she would have recognized him anywhere. Maybe it was the suit, a gray one this time. The FBI man. Will.

Sheila nickered a soft greeting at the newcomer.

Leaning back against the fence, Molly waited, hands thrust deep into the pockets of her sweat shirt, one knee bent, her sneakered heel braced against the lowest board. When he was close enough so that she could discern his features, Will glanced up and saw that she was watching him. His mouth curved into a funny, lopsided kind of smile.

"Pizza?" he asked when he was just a few feet away, proffering the box. Then, "I tried to call."

"They won't turn the phone back on until tomorrow." The delicious smell wafting from the box made Molly salivate. Carry-out pizza was a treat in which the Ballards rarely indulged. They simply could not afford it. "The kids love pizza. If you don't mind, I'll give that to them. I'd just as soon have a sandwich."

"I dropped off two large pizzas with the works and a six-pack of Coke at the house. Your sister said you were up here—she even pointed the way."

"Ashley or Susan?" Molly inquired, making no move to reach for the pizza though her stomach rumbled longingly.

"The older one."

"Ashley." Molly took a deep breath, and looked up at him. "We're not starving, you know. There's plenty to eat in the house."

"I know." He studied her for a moment in silence, then shrugged and looked around. Spying a fallen log in a small copse of trees nearby, he moved over to it and sat down, balancing the pizza box on his lap. Pulling a half-pint carton of milk from his jacket pocket and balancing it on the log beside him, he flipped open the lid of the pizza box and extracted a large, cheese-and-pepperoni-laden slice.

As she watched him bite into it, Molly's stomach growled. She hadn't had anything to eat since a quick bowl of Cheerios that morning.

"Are you going to make me eat the whole thing by myself?" he asked her after a second mouthful. "I'll get fat."

The notion surprised a smile out of Molly. The idea of him as fat was absurd. If anything, he was too lean.

"Better you than me," she said, walking over to the log and looking down on both him and the pizza. The tantalizing aroma of pepperoni and pizza sauce teased her nose. His short sandy hair was, she noted from above, plenty thick. Nary a bald spot in sight.

"I never heard of anybody drinking milk with pizza," she observed.

"Hey, milk does a body good." He glanced up at her. "I brought you a Coke." Wiping his hands on a paper napkin, he reached into his other jacket pocket and pulled out a familiar red can, which he offered to her.

"Thanks." After no more than an instant's hesitation, Molly took the Coke, then moved around his legs and the open pizza box to sit on the log. She was hungry. He had brought pizza. It was silly to let pride keep her from enjoying the treat. "And thanks for the pizza. But you didn't have to."

"I know I didn't have to. But I did. So you might as well eat it."

Lifting a slice from the box to her lips, Molly was

relieved to discover that he was focusing on his own meal rather than on her. Thin, crisp crust, tangy sauce, flavorful cheese, spicy pepperoni: Molly enjoyed that first bite with an intensity that was almost sexual.

"It's good," she said after a couple of moments during which they both munched companionably.

"You didn't have lunch, did you?" He glanced at her over the pizza box, which rested between them. It was more a statement than a question, as if he already knew the answer. Was it that obvious that she was famished?

Molly shook her head. "I didn't have time. By the way, I got my job back."

"I knew you would." He didn't sound surprised. But then, Molly reasoned, he didn't know Don Simpson like she did.

"The deal's still on? Five thousand dollars for checking horses' mouth tattoos?"

"Yeah."

"You swear?"

Glancing up from extracting another piece of pizza from the box, he met her gaze. "You don't trust people much, do you?"

Molly shrugged, downed a mouthful of Coke, and reached for a second slice of pizza. "If you really want me to trust you, you could pay me in advance."

He grinned. "Then I'd be left wondering how much *I* could trust *you*. I like things better this way."

"I bet you do." The wry smile she sent him was a little mocking, but friendly.

"Is that your horse?" He indicated Sheila. Head over the fence, the mare watched the humans inquisitively. Probably wondering how pizza tasted, Molly thought.

Molly shook her head. "She belongs to Wyland Farm. She used to be a racehorse, but she's retired. She had over a million dollars in career winnings, though."

Will whistled. "Pretty impressive."

"Probably why she didn't end up in a glue factory."

"Is that what they do to them when they're done racing?"

"Sometimes. Or they get turned into dog food. Or fertilizer."

"You're joking, right?"

"You don't know much about this business, do you?"

"Not much."

"Where are you from, anyway? Up north someplace, I can tell by the way you talk."

"Chicago." He grinned suddenly. "Funny, and here I was thinking *you* had a regional accent."

Ignoring the jibe at her softly slurred southern syllables, Molly studied him. "So how did you end up down here in Kentucky investigating horse racing?"

Will shrugged. "Luck of the draw."

"You really *are* an FBI agent, aren't you?"

"There's that lack of trust I was talking about again."

"That's not an answer."

He sighed. "Yes, Virginia, I really am an FBI agent. Do you want that last piece of pizza?"

Molly shook her head. Will picked it up.

"So what did you do about your brother?" he asked between bites.

"Grounded him. For a month. No TV. No visits with friends. Although he swears he wasn't in that barn."

"Do you believe him?"

"No."

"I spoke to that lawyer I told you about last night. His name's Tom Kramer. He'll go with your brother to talk to the police." Finished with the pizza, Will wiped his fingers on a napkin and reached into an inside jacket pocket for a folded scrap of paper. "Here's his number. Just give him a call."

"Thanks." Molly took the piece of paper and stuck it in her sweat shirt pocket. She hesitated, but the point had to be clarified whether it embarrassed her or not. "Did he say how much he'd charge?"

"I told you, don't worry about it. It's taken care of."

"*You're* not paying for it, are you?"

"For somebody who not too long ago took five thousand dollars that didn't belong to her, you're awful picky about where things come from."

Molly flushed. "Can't you forget that?"

"Nope," he replied, opening his carton of milk with one hand.

"I don't generally steal, you know. In fact, I never steal. Just that once. It was just—an impulse. I looked in that bag, and saw the money—and I took it."

"Anybody would have done the same."

"Anybody in my shoes would!" He had not sounded sarcastic, but Molly was defensive anyway. She was hypersensitive about what she had done—and, if she was honest—about what he thought of her as a result.

"There aren't too many people in your shoes—a twenty-four-year-old raising four younger brothers and sisters on her own. How long ago did your mother die?"

Molly took another swallow of Coke. She didn't talk

about her parents—the wounds went too deep, the subject was too personal.

"Look, Mr. FBI man, if we're asking questions, I've got a few for you: Are your parents alive?"

"Will." The quiet emphasis in his voice reminded Molly of his warning of the night before.

"All right, then, *Will:* Are your parents alive?"

He looked at her for a moment, then nodded. "Yup. Both."

"Divorced?" Molly knew she sounded almost hopeful. There had to be some misery in his life somewhere.

He shook his head. "Married forty-five years next month."

"How long have you been married?"

"I'm not."

"You said you have an eighteen-year-old son."

"I do."

"So you're divorced."

"Nope."

"What are you, then, an unwed father?" Exasperation at his failure to give her a straight answer laced the question.

"My wife died fifteen years ago." No trace of pain or grief colored the words. He made a simple statement of fact.

"I—I'm sorry." Molly was sobered nevertheless.

"It's in the past." Seemingly unconcerned, Will guzzled his milk.

Molly said nothing more. She had not stopped to think that he might have his own wounds, and she had certainly not meant to touch on them.

The sound of a motor coming steadily closer across the fields was a welcome distraction. Sheila nickered sharply, wheeling and bolting away from the fence with her head high and tail streaming, showing the form that had once made her a champion racehorse. With a smiling glance at Will, Molly put down her soft drink, got to her feet, and headed toward the fence.

A black Jeep Cherokee rolled to a stop where Sheila had been. A big man wearing a tan Stetson, jeans, cowboy boots, and an open duster coat got out of the driver's side of the vehicle, a large handgun, barrel pointed toward the ground, in his hand. The other man was around thirty, handsome and dark-eyed, with pale skin and straight, jet-black hair. He rolled down the passenger-side window and stuck his head out. Both men focused on Molly.

14

"Yo, Molly," the big man said by way of greeting. He was in his late twenties, beefy rather than handsome, with a florid, coarse-featured face and shoulder-length dirty-blond hair.

" 'Beauty is power; a smile is its sword,' " the black-haired man quoted, casting his companion a sideways glance before bestowing an ironic smile on Molly.

"Yo, J.D. Hi, Tyler." Molly ignored that cryptic utterance, which she suspected was a jab at both herself and J.D.

"You okay?" J.D. glared menacingly at a point just beyond her. Glancing around, Molly realized that that look was directed at Will, who was coming up behind her, and grinned. J.D. made two of the FBI man, and it would be ridiculously easy to sic J.D. on him. Not that she would do anything like that, of course. Still, it was fun to think about.

"I'm fine, thanks, J.D. This is Will Lyman. Will, J.D. Hatfield, Tyler Wyland." Having joined her at the fence, Will replied to the introductions with a nod. J.D. replied with a grim jerk of his head, his expression just a hair short of a scowl. Tyler Wyland nodded too. Wry amusement curled his lip.

"I don't think Mr. Lyman's a threat, J.D., either to the horses or to Molly," Tyler chided gently.

"Something's been spookin' these here horses these last few nights," J.D. said, reddening but stubborn. "I was comin' by to ask you, Molly, if you seen or heard anything out of the ordinary."

"No, I haven't." Molly shook her head, and barely stopped herself from smiling. A local boy, J.D. had had an outsize crush on her for years. For all his size and intimidating appearance, he was gentle as a kitten, and Molly was loath to hurt him. She treated him as a friend, and ignored his hints that he might want anything more. J.D., to his credit, had never tried to force the issue.

"Well, I just thought you might've." J.D. shot another lowering look at Will. "Guess I better get back to work. You keep your eyes and ears open, Molly, and if you come across anything out of the way, you let me know."

"I will," Molly promised.

J.D. climbed back inside the Jeep with a flourish, slid the handgun into its accustomed place above the dashboard, and shifted the vehicle into reverse. With a bellowed "Hang in there, y'all!" and a wave, he wheeled the Jeep in a sharp semicircle and it jolted off across the field.

"What was that?" Will asked as the Jeep rattled away into the dark. Turning away from the fence, he looked, Molly thought, somehow both amused and a little grim at one and the same time.

"J.D.'s the night watchman. He patrols the perimeter of the farm, and keeps an eye on the horses and barns and that kind of thing."

"I wonder if he has a permit for that pistol?" Amusement seemed to gain the upper hand. "Probably not. Does he come by every night to ask if you've seen or heard anything unusual?"

"No," Molly replied with a look designed to squash any teasing in its infancy. "Probably he just wanted to impress Tyler with what a good job he's doing. They've been friends for years, but Tyler's sort of his boss, you know."

"I don't think it was Tyler he wanted to impress," Will said dryly. Molly fell into step beside him as he headed back toward their log. He glanced sideways at her. "Poor kid, I think I cramped his style."

Molly bristled. "Look, J.D.'s a nice guy, and a friend, but that's all."

"If you say so."

"I say so!"

"I'm not arguing," Will pointed out mildly. With the wind thus taken out of her sails, Molly was left with nothing to say. Sitting down on the log, she eyed him for a moment without speaking.

"Tyler Wyland—is he the poet?"

Surprised that he recognized the name, Molly nodded. Scuttlebutt on Tyler Wyland had it that his work was gaining an international reputation, but Molly was just a tad skeptical about that. It didn't seem likely that a homegrown Woodford Countian would turn out to be a writer of real caliber. Besides, she had read a couple of his poems out of curiosity, and they didn't seem all that great. But then, she wasn't a big fan of poetry, so she guessed she really couldn't judge.

"He's good," Will said thoughtfully.

"You've read his poems?" Molly couldn't keep the surprise out of her voice.

"All in the course of a day's work, so don't fall backward off that log," Will said. "When I'm conducting an investigation, I always make it a point to find out as much as I can about the people connected with it. Saves time and trouble in the long run."

"You checked out *Tyler Wyland*? You can't possibly suspect him of being involved in this. He doesn't even go to the races. I don't even think he's *interested* in horses. He told me once he drives around with J.D. at night to get inspiration for his *poems*."

"He's a member of the family who owns one of the stables under investigation. So I checked him out, just like I checked out everybody else with any type of link. Although I must have missed J.D." This last was said with a flickering smile.

"You checked *me* out," Molly said, unsmiling.

He looked at her. "Yeah."

There was no apology in his voice, or his gaze.

"Then why ask me questions?" she flared, her fists clenching against the log at the idea of him methodically uncovering her past. "If you already know everything about me there is to know, why ask me anything?"

"Background checks deal in facts. Date of birth, educational history, criminal records, things like that. Just the facts, ma'am. That's all. Not a thousand-page exposé of the intimate details of your life."

Blue eyes looked steadily into her own. Despite his reassurance, Molly felt exposed, vulnerable, hideously naked—the idea that he knew all about her was insupportable. Just the facts, ma'am—but what, exactly, did the facts reveal?

"Did you have a reason for dropping by, other than to bring pizza?" Molly asked coldly.

"I had a reason." He looked down at her for a moment. When he spoke again, his manner was businesslike.

"The first race tomorrow is an eight-thousand-dollar claimer. I want you to check out these horses before the race. If one of the numbers doesn't match, let me know." Will withdrew a business card from the breast pocket of his jacket and passed it to her. The front advertised Lawn-Pro Turf Professionals, John Murphy, proprietor, with a phone number. On the back were scribbled the names of three horses.

"What am I supposed to do, call you on my shoe phone?"

"I'll be around."

"Great."

"If one of those horses should win, you need to check his ID number immediately afterward."

"How can I do that? The winner is always surrounded—I'm not going to be able to just run into the winner's circle and yank down the horse's lower lip."

"That's for you to figure out. But do it. And don't let anybody catch you."

"Easy for you to say," Molly said under her breath, reading the names with some difficulty through the gathering gloom. All the horses were from different stables, of course. Had she really expected this to be simple? "Why these horses?"

"They all have odds of twenty to one or better."

"Do you really think one of them is going to win?" A germ of an idea entered her mind. As it took hold her annoyance abated. To be angry with an FBI agent for doing a background check on his informant made about as much sense as being angry with a bird for flying. It was the nature of the beast. She'd been foolish not to have expected it.

"Why?" Something about her tone must have alerted him. He looked at her suspiciously.

"Because I just might want to place a wager. With those odds, a twenty-dollar bet to win would pay—four hundred."

Will reached for the empty pizza box. "Any winner that was found to be fraudulent would be disqualified. So if I were you, I'd hang on to that twenty dollars."

He smiled at her as he picked up his empty milk carton and balanced it on top of the pizza box. "I've got to go. Come on, I'll walk you to the house."

"I don't need you to walk me to my house. I'm perfectly capable of getting there on my own."

"It's almost dark."

"What, do you think a bogeyman is out here in the dark somewhere, just waiting to catch me by myself? This is Versailles, Kentucky, not Chicago."

He shrugged. "So humor me. I need you around to check horses' mouth tattoos tomorrow. Anyway, your friend J.D. said that somebody's been spooking the horses."

Molly snorted. Will grinned, and Molly realized that she had just confirmed that she, too, doubted J.D.'s story. Like Will, she thought J.D. had made the whole thing up as an excuse to come see her. The glance she sent him was not friendly.

"I think I'll sit out here for a little longer, thanks."

"Suit yourself." He shrugged again, and sat down on the log beside her, pizza box in his lap. Seeming quite contented, he steepled his fingers in front of his nose, and gazed off into the distance.

"What are you doing?" Irritation edged her voice.

"Waiting."

"For what?"

"You to be ready to go in. I'm not leaving you out here alone in the dark."

"You'll be sitting there a long time, then," Molly said with an icy smile.

Will shrugged. Molly said nothing more. For several minutes the two of them sat on the log with about two feet of space between them, staring into the gathering night. As the dozens of chores that awaited her inside ran through her mind, Molly grew increasingly restless. Will, on the other hand, seemed prepared to sit there forever. In fact, he appeared lost in thought.

She was going to have to go in. It was ridiculous to sit on a log on an increasingly cold, damp night just to prove that she could.

She stood up. "I'm going in."

He glanced up at her as if he had, momentarily, forgotten who she was. Then he got to his feet. "I'll walk you to the house."

"Fine," Molly said through her teeth, and started off.

"Molly," he called after her softly. From his voice she could almost swear that he was laughing.

"What?" She whirled to face him, spoiling for a fight. But he appeared perfectly straight-faced as he nodded at the ground by the log.

"Don't forget your Coke can."

The bright red metal shone through the darkness. "To hell with my Coke can," Molly said with perfect civility. Turning, she headed down the hill, back stiff, head high.

After the briefest of delays, she heard him following.

Though she refused to so much as glance around, she would be willing to bet a month's rent that he had retrieved the can himself.

Of course he had. Mr. FBI man would never, ever litter. He was far too perfect for that.

"See you tomorrow," he called softly as she reached the front steps.

Her dander rose, but what could she say? If he wanted to, he would.

Molly walked with regal dignity into the house, and slammed the door.

15

October 13, 1995

The noonday sun was hot on Molly's back as she cinched the girth on Winnebago's saddle and let the irons down. Chattering crowds swirled around the edges of the unfenced paddock, watching as the horses scheduled to run in the first race were saddled. To Molly's left a flashbulb popped. Winnebago, a six-year-old gray past his racing prime, stood placidly amidst the commotion, apparently not minding it a bit, or objecting to having a stranger saddle him in place of his own groom. Molly rewarded his docility with a scratch behind the ears. He was the last horse on the list of three that Will had given her the previous night. Like Winnebago, the other two had checked out negative. No ringers here.

Winnebago belonged to Cloverlot Stables, which had been in disarray since the suicide of Howard Lawrence two days before. Molly's offer to "help out" by walking Winnebago to the paddock and saddling him had been gratefully accepted by Lawrence's harried replacement. Having memorized all three ID numbers, Molly needed only a quick glance inside Winnebago's lower lip to ascertain that this horse, too, was the genuine article. Winnebago was definitely Winnebago.

Checking out the other two horses had posed even less of a problem. She had simply walked into their barns and, under the pretext of rubbing one's neck and feeding the other a carrot, pulled down their lower lips. The fact that they were claimers made it easy. Security focused on the stars and up-and-comers, not the has-beens or never-weres.

Molly wondered if she would still get the promised five thousand dollars if Will never found his ringers. She wondered if maybe he had got hold of the wrong end of the stick entirely, and there were no ringers to be found. As long as she got paid, she hoped that proved to be the case. It would do the mighty FBI man good to be taken down a peg.

"All set?" Steve Emerson, the jockey, appeared, his diminutive body resplendent in the green and gold silks of Cloverlot Stables. Molly nodded, passing the shank over to the pony rider as the jockey climbed aboard. From the track, the bugler announced the post parade. It was just a few minutes before 1:00 p.m. The first race of the day would soon begin.

Like the other horses, at the sound of the bugle Winnebago was away, off toward the track and one more shot at glory. Molly watched him pick his way through the thinning crowd for a moment before turning to head back to Barn 15. The spectators had a race to watch. She had work to do.

Will, elegant as always in a navy sport coat and khaki slacks that stood out against a shifting backdrop of butterfly-bright ladies' dresses, stood watching her from the edge of the crowd. He waited near the path that led to the barns, a rolled racing form in one hand, in the lee of the chest-high boxwood hedge. It was the first time she had seen him that day, and his presence was totally unexpected.

Molly spotted him without warning. While sweeping the thinning ranks of onlookers with casual curiosity, her gaze simply caught his and held. To her surprise, her initial emotion upon discovering him was not dislike, or aggravation, but a warm burst of pleasure. Unlikely as it seemed, she realized with a sense of shock that she was actually glad to see him.

Will's arms were crossed over his chest, his eyes narrowed against the sun that turned his hair to gold and his skin to bronze. He looked distinguished, she thought. Even handsome. For an old man of forty-something, of course.

To her surprise, she found that she was smiling at him.

Will smiled back at her, slowly, his eyes crinkling at the corners. There was something about that smile—a kind of intimacy, a declaration that the two of them shared a special bond known to no one but themselves. His acknowledgment of their relationship took Molly aback. Then she remembered: Their association wasn't a secret. Only his identity was.

As she headed toward him, her smile widened, and warmed. For whatever ridiculous reason.

"Good golly, it's Miss Molly!" A pair of strong male arms snatched her off her feet from behind, whirled her around, and set her back down again. As soon as her feet touched the ground, Molly yanked free of those imprisoning arms and turned to confront her tormentor.

"You grooming for Cloverlot now?" Thornton Wyland grinned down at her, not one whit abashed by the anger sparkling in her eyes. "After you told Simpson where to go I figured you'd never work in the horse business again."

"Then you figured wrong. I'm still working for Wyland Farm." Thornton Wyland was about her own age, a handsome, black-haired stud who had had practically every girl for miles around panting after him for years. Since he'd dropped out of Cornell University (the fourth college he'd attended) the previous March and returned home to Wyland Farm, he had made the pursuit of happiness his full-time occupation. Molly tried her best to avoid him, but it wasn't easy. He thought he was God's gift to women, and couldn't understand why Molly wouldn't just give up and fall into bed with him like everyone else.

Molly smiled at him, but it wasn't a sweet smile. "And if you ever put your hands on me again, I'll chop them off at the wrists. I swear to God."

He laughed, his hazel eyes twinkling. "You're somethin', Miss Molly, you know that? How about going out with me on Friday? I'll take you somewhere fancy."

"No way in hell," Molly said pleasantly, and turned her back on him. Walking toward where Will still waited—his expression was impossible to decipher, but his smile was gone—Molly half expected to be the recipient of a slap to the posterior, which was one of Thornton's favorite methods of riling her. Apparently Thornton wasn't totally stupid, because today he refrained.

"You oughta be nicer to the boss." He fell into step beside her. "I could make things a lot easier for you."

"The day you're my boss is the day I quit," Molly

said, talking to the air in front of her instead of to him, and quickening her step.

"It'll happen. You know I'm gonna inherit one day."

"You'll be an old man by then, and I'll be long gone. Thank God."

"Since Grandpa died, Aunt Helen's been talkin' about turning the running of the farm over to me. Uncle Boyce wants to hire a manager, but Uncle Tyler wants to keep it in the family. And you know how Aunt Helen listens to Uncle Tyler."

Old John Wyland had died in December. His wife, Sarah, had divorced him a dozen years before and was currently living in Switzerland. Estranged from the family, she did not even return for her former husband's funeral. His death left their only daughter, Helen—who lived in the Big House with her husband, Walt Trapp, and daughter, Neilie—to manage the horse operation. Boyce, eight years younger than Helen, was a lawyer who shuttled between opulent houses in Lexington, Lake Placid, New York, and Palm Beach, while Tyler, the youngest sibling, occupied the farm's guest house. Tad Wyland, Thornton's father and the oldest boy, had died some ten years previously. Helen Trapp had raised Thornton after that, and he considered Wyland Farm his home.

He'd been chasing Molly since she was eighteen.

"Your uncle Boyce is right."

Thornton laughed again. "Sweet thang, you keep fightin' it, but I know that underneath that prickly exterior you really like me. I can tell. What're you doin' Saturday night?"

"Washing my hair."

"We could do it together."

"Not a chance, pal."

"We could have a lot of fun if you'd just relax and let it happen."

"I'm allergic to your brand of fun."

He caught her hand, imprisoning it as he playfully kissed her knuckles, then sucked on her fingertips. On the second try, Molly managed to yank her hand free.

"Buzz off, Thornton, why don't you?"

Quickening her pace, Molly reached Will's side and stopped, turning to face Thornton angrily.

"Bye," she said with a saccharine smile.

Thornton stopped, too, an expression of curiosity on his face as he glanced past her at Will, who was looking him up and down in a way that would have given Molly pause if such a glance had been directed at her. The men were about the same height, and both wore navy blazers, though Thornton's slacks were gray and his tie was decorated with red triangles instead of the stripes that adorned Will's. Leanly muscled and unsmiling, creases visibly etched into the tanned skin around his eyes and mouth, Will looked hard and cold next to Thornton's exuberant, youthful handsomeness.

But Will was the one Molly would have chosen to be with anytime. Will was the one who made her feel safe.

To Molly's surprise, she once again felt her hand caught and carried upward. Glancing sideways, she tried not to appear round-eyed as Will, gaze focused on Thornton, slowly and deliberately pressed the back of her hand against his mouth.

And held it there. His lips were dry and warm. Hot, almost. Molly could feel his breath against her skin. She didn't struggle, but let him do with her hand what he chose. He turned her hand over, kissing her palm.

To her amazement, lightning bolts of sensation exploded across the surface of her skin.

Will never once glanced her way. He was kissing her hand strictly for Thornton's benefit, Molly realized. To warn him off.

Meanwhile, Molly was having trouble catching her breath.

Thornton's eyebrows rose as he observed and registered Will's gesture of possession, as he was meant to do.

"New boyfriend, Moll?" he asked.

Will lowered her hand at last, but kept her fingers tightly enclosed in his. Molly was so unnerved she could barely think, let alone answer. Will answered for her.

"You got it," he said, very pleasant. As a back-off message, it came through loud and clear. Even Molly heard the unspoken warning.

"Hey, you can't blame a guy for trying," Thornton said with a shrug.

"Thorn! Thorn, come on! The race is about to start!"

Thornton glanced around, saw the pretty blonde hurrying toward him from the other side of the paddock, and grimaced.

"Gotta go. Allie's impatient, just like all my women. No hard feelings, I hope?" he asked Will. Beginning to feel like a bone between two dogs, Molly tried to summon indignation at being discussed as if she weren't even there. But her senses were still in too much turmoil from the touch of Will's mouth on her skin.

Thornton had kissed her hand, sucked on her fingers, even, and she felt only annoyance. Will pressed his lips to her palm and her bones threatened to melt.

It was scary.

"Not at this point." Will still held her hand, a point that was not lost on Molly—or Thornton.

"See ya around, Miss Molly." Turning to leave, Thornton tweaked the end of her ponytail.

"Not if I see you first," Molly mustered the will to mutter after his retreating back, but she doubted that he heard her.

"Thornton Wyland, I presume," Will said dryly, releasing her hand as casually as if he'd felt none of the fire that had so shaken Molly. Still trying to regroup, Molly kept her eyes on Thornton's diminishing figure as he was claimed by the blonde and hustled toward the grandstand.

"How do you know—oh, of course, I keep forgetting, you know everything, don't you? What, do you have files on everyone in the Bluegrass?"

Will's grin was quick and appreciative. "Just the people who interest me. And remember, just the facts. How long have you known young Mr. Wyland?"

"Off and on since I was eighteen."

"Ever dated him? Given him any encouragement?"

Molly snorted. "Thornton Wyland doesn't need encouragement."

"You don't like him?"

"He's a pain in the ass." Now that Will was no longer touching her, Molly was able to think normally again. But she was still shaken by what had happened. Surely she was not—could not be—sexually attracted to the FBI man.

"Is he?" Will seemed to lose interest. "I doubt if he bothers you again for a while. Did you check the numbers?"

"Yes." Copying his tone, Molly turned businesslike. "They all matched. None of them are ringers."

"Damn." Will frowned. "You sure they matched?"

"I'm sure." She was having trouble looking him in the eye. She forced herself to.

"Damn," he said again, staring beyond her with a pensive expression. After a moment he seemed to gather his thoughts, and glanced down at her. "We may be in this for the long haul. You have any trouble?"

"No."

"I didn't think you would."

"What happens if we don't find any ringers?" Molly asked.

"They're here. We'll find them."

"If we don't, do I still get paid?"

His glance at her was sharp with humor. "Always focused on the bottom line, aren't you? I'm surprised you keep turning Thornton Wyland down. His family's rich. He'd be a good catch for somebody like you."

"He doesn't want to buy me, just rent me for a while," Molly replied tartly. "I'm not stupid, you know. And what do you mean, somebody like me?"

"Broke," Will said, a smile flickering at the edges of his mouth. His gaze slid over her, returned to her face. "But beautiful."

Taken aback, Molly couldn't think of a reply. When she didn't answer, he gave a wry half smile and tapped her on the cheek with the rolled racing form.

"You better get back to work. If you get fired, you won't be worth a damn to me—and you can kiss that five thousand dollars good-bye." He turned away, heading toward the grandstand. "See ya."

Thoroughly rattled now, Molly stood stock-still and

watched as he disappeared into the crowd. Then, when she realized what she was doing, she gave herself a mental shake, and went back to work.

And refused to allow herself to think of Will Lyman for the rest of the day.

16

That night he brought Kentucky Fried Chicken.

Molly was at the stove, stirring cheese into macaroni noodles and at the same time drilling Sam, who stood nearby, on his spelling words. Susan sat at the kitchen table hunched over a sheet of math problems. Ashley sat beside her, attempting without much success to explain to Susan why the answer she'd so painstakingly arrived at was wrong. Mike was in the living room, working on a history research paper that was due the following week. He'd carried an encyclopedia in there with him, and a notebook. Molly could only hope that he was actually committing words to paper. Mike's modus operandi was to wait until the last minute, then stay up all night doing a project that was not half as good as it could have been if he'd put in the time and effort it called for. He was only working on the paper tonight because she had insisted—and anyway there was nothing else to do. Grounded, with no TV or phone privileges, he was a sullen prisoner in the house.

"Integration," Molly said to Sam.

"E-n-t . . ."

Molly's glance was enough.

"I mean *I*-n-t . . ."

Molly listened, stirring, then nodded approval as Sam got it right. Giving the boy another word, she set the spoon aside and turned down the heat on the burner. The hamburger patties were sizzling, and a glance told her they were ready to be turned. Canned brown gravy, mouthwateringly aromatic, bubbled at the back of the stove, along with a pot of green beans from Mrs. Atkinson's garden, cooked up with bacon. Refrigerated biscuits browned in the oven.

"There's an *i* in the middle of business, not a *y*," Molly said, taking a pancake turner to the burgers. Sam tried again, getting it right this time. Not a great student at best, Sam did worst at spelling, because he just could not be convinced that it was important. Math, on the other hand, was Susan's Waterloo. It was the only school subject at which she was not completely competent.

"Molly, do *you* know what the zero property of numbers is?" Ashley asked with exasperation, looking up from where she and Susan pored over an open text. "Susan doesn't, I can't remember exactly, and we can't find it in this stupid book."

"Got me," Molly said with an apologetic shrug.

"I hate math," Susan muttered. "It's so dumb."

"Math's easy," Mike chimed in scornfully from the other room. The house was small enough so that a conversation held in one room was completely audible throughout the entire upper or lower level, depending on where it occurred. "The zero property of numbers says that if you multiply any number times zero it equals zero."

"Thanks, Mike," Ashley called back. With a clear lack of enthusiasm, Susan wrote her sibling's words down.

"Barometer," Molly said to Sam just as there was a knock at the door.

Glad to be diverted, even momentarily, from homework, the four Ballards in the kitchen looked up. Pork Chop erupted barking from beneath the table. Mike, encyclopedia in hand, appeared in the living room doorway.

"I'll get it," Susan and Sam volunteered in the same breath. Susan, by virtue of already being closer to the door, beat Sam there by a fraction of a second, and yanked it open, nearly treading on Pork Chop's paw in the process. The dog scrambled sideways without missing a beat. The noise he made was deafening.

Will stood on the porch. Despite the darkness outside, and the veiling effect of the black mesh screen, Molly recognized him instantly. A curious warmth pulsed to life somewhere in the region of her breastbone. A welcoming smile sprang unbidden to her lips—until she realized it was there and banished it.

"Hi," Will said to Susan, who unhesitatingly opened the still-broken screen door to admit him. It dipped downward as she swung it outward, and he juggled something he held to catch the handle and take the door's weight himself. Stepping inside, he pulled the door shut behind him, nodded at Ashley and Mike, grinned at Sam, rewarded Pork Chop for ceasing to bark with a quiet "good dog," then looked across the kitchen at Molly.

"I brought supper," he said with an engagingly crooked smile, and held aloft a bucket of Kentucky Fried Chicken for her inspection. A half-gallon of milk was tucked beneath his other arm. The warmth inside Molly spread. She *was* glad to see him, there was no use denying it. Fried chicken and milk or not.

"What, does he think the way to your heart is through *our* stomachs?" Mike asked with a growl, turning to disappear into the living room.

Molly shot a warning look after her brother, which missed its mark because he was already gone.

"Thank you," she said to Will, staying back by the stove and purposely keeping her voice as distant as her person, "but as you can see I'm already fixing something. I *can* cook, you know."

Sam made a rude sound of dissent. Susan elbowed him hard in the ribs, and he howled and whacked her back.

"Homework!" Molly said sharply, pulling the plug on the brewing sibling battle before it could escalate into a full-scale war. "Susan, if you don't finish your math before supper, you won't be able to watch TV afterward. Sam, come on, let's get these spelling words out of the way."

"I bet *he's* good at math," said Susan with the hopeful air of one whose siblings were not. As she closed the heavy wooden door, her big brown eyes focused on Will. Clad in jeans and a ruffled-collar denim shirt, her blond hair pulled back in a curly ponytail and tied up with a length of blue yarn, Susan looked sweet as cotton candy. Clearly beguiled, Will smiled down at the child.

"I'm not bad," he answered with suitable modesty, advancing into the room and surrendering the bucket of chicken and container of milk to Molly, who at last came forward to take them.

"It was nice of you to bring this," she said grudgingly, referring to the food. Then, even more grudgingly, "We're having hamburger patties with brown gravy. You're welcome to stay."

"Hamburger patties with brown gravy are my very favorite." He met her gaze, smiled at her. For all her wariness of him, his motives, and the circumstances that threw them together, Molly was caught off guard by the sheer charm of that smile. Before she could catch herself, she smiled back. She doubted that he had ever eaten hamburger patties with brown gravy in his life. But he seemed right at home in her small, poor kitchen—stranger, northerner, FBI man or not.

"Can you multiply fractions?" asked Susan, tugging at the sleeve of his navy sport coat.

"I think so," Will responded with good humor. "If I still remember how."

"I always get it mixed up. Fractions are stupid anyway," Susan complained, leading him unresisting toward the table. Her assumption that Will was naturally prepared to assist her with her homework both amused and alarmed Molly. Susan was not an overly trusting child—and Will was only a temporary visitor to their lives. Molly didn't want Susan—any of them—to get too used to having him around. In just a couple of weeks he would be gone.

"You don't have to do this," she said to Will over the children's heads as Susan pulled the bench out farther so that he could sit down. Ashley relinquished her place at the table with a sympathetic smile for her replacement, crossed the kitchen to relieve Molly of the chicken and milk she still held, and put them down on the kitchen counter. Embarrassed that she had not had the presence of mind to set the food down herself, Molly quickly turned her attention to the stove.

"No problem," Will said to her back. "Actually, I *like* multiplying fractions."

This whopper earned him a sideways glance brimful of silent skepticism. Will grinned.

"It beats the heck out of a lot of things I've done. Here, Susan, let me get ready for action and I'll see what I can do to help you wrestle those fractions into submission."

Will slid out of his jacket while Susan giggled and Molly, ostensibly checking on the biscuits, watched out of the corner of her eye. Draping his coat across the bench, Will pulled his tie free of its knot and slid it from around his neck. It joined his coat over the bench. Loosening the top button of his collar and rolling up his sleeves with exaggerated motions, Will gave the impression that he was bent on getting down to some serious work, much to Susan's amusement.

As he settled down at the table beside her youngest sister, Molly noticed that his shoulders in the blue oxford cloth shirt were very broad, and his throat and forearms were as bronzed as his face.

A scattering of gold-tipped chest hair was clearly visible where the shirt opened at his throat.

"You're burning the biscuits," Ashley hissed in her ear.

Mortified to discover that she had been standing with the oven door cracked all that time while she watched Will out of the corner of her eye, Molly gathered her wits, grabbed a potholder, and reached for the biscuits. The ones at the back of the oven—it cooked unevenly—were browner than they should have been, but still edible. She pulled the pan out and set it on the counter, where Ashley waited to whisk the biscuits into a napkin-lined bowl.

It was only a yellow paper napkin, but still that was a pretty fancy embellishment for home cooking at the Ballards'.

"Can't we do this tomorrow? It's Friday night," Sam complained, tired of being ignored. He leaned against the cabinets near the stove, watching Susan and Will at the table a little jealously. Molly, reminded of her obligations, reached for a spoon and stirred the gravy as she glanced at the sheet of notebook paper with Sam's spelling words on it that lay on the counter nearby. Every Monday morning without fail his class had a spelling test, and it would take an entire weekend of daily practice for Sam to get a decent grade on it. Tempting as it was occasionally to let it slide till Sunday, Molly had learned from bitter experience that the rule to abide by with homework was, it gets done first. Even on the weekend.

"You know the answer to that," Molly said to Sam. "Ambition."

"A-m-" Sam began without enthusiasm.

"Let me do this." Ashley came up behind her to whisper while Molly determinedly smashed and flipped hamburgers. "You need to go brush your hair—and put your shoes on! And some lipstick!"

"-i-t-" Sam continued.

Molly, attending to each of her siblings with half an ear, glanced down at her feet. They were bare again, as they usually were when she was at home. Tonight she wore a pair of ancient, slightly too small gray sweat pants and another of Mike's oversized flannel shirts, this one a red-and-black buffalo plaid with sleeves rolled to her elbows. Her face was scrubbed clean, and her hair was pulled back into a ponytail at her nape. She could not be said to be looking her best by any stretch of the imagination.

She hadn't been looking much better earlier in the day, when Will had called her beautiful.

"-i-o-n."

Clearly Ashley wanted her to impress Will. Which meant Ashley liked and approved of Will, and would like to keep him around. Which was both foolish and impossible, though of course Ashley had no way of knowing that.

Under the circumstances, looking good for Will was the last thing Molly wanted to do. She had no intention of forgetting for so much as a moment who he really was and why he was showering so much attention on her and her family.

He wanted something. While he waited for her to provide it for him he was playing the part of her boyfriend, and making it look good. The man should be an actor, not an FBI agent.

But an FBI agent was what he was, and his presence in their lives was strictly temporary.

"You don't think I look sexy like this?" Molly whispered to Ashley with a teasing smile.

Ashley shook her head in an emphatic *no*.

"Molly, are you listening?" Sam demanded in outraged accents.

"Of course I am," Molly said to him, shrugging at Ashley to signify, Oh, well.

"You are not! I deliberately left out the *b* and you didn't even notice!"

"What makes you think I didn't notice? I was just about to tell you to spell it again."

"You're a liar!"

"Ambition," Molly said with bite, giving Sam a look that silenced his budding smart mouth.

"A-m-"

"I'll set the table." Ashley gave up the fight to make her sister more presentable, and turned away to get the plates out of the cabinet.

"-i-t-"

"What about that *b*?"

"Just checking to see if you were listening."

"I'm listening. Now spell it again. If you don't get it right this time, you're going to have to write it down five times."

"I hate spelling," Sam said with loathing. "A-m-*b*-i-"

"I don't get it! Why would you multiply both the top number and the bottom number by four?" Susan wailed from the table.

"-t-i-"

"It's called finding the lowest common denominator," Will responded with quiet patience, and began to explain the finer points of multiplying fractions one more time.

"Molly, you're not listening!" Sam said furiously.

"Yes, I am," Molly lied, lifting the burgers from the skillet and sliding them into the white glass casserole dish that Ashley had placed at her elbow. "You got it right. Good job. Successful."

"S-u-c-"

The telephone rang. Molly answered it, cradling the receiver between her shoulder and her ear and pouring gravy over the hamburger patties while she listened to both the caller and Sam's spelling. The call was for Mike, of course. Molly glanced toward the living room doorway, hesitated, hardened her heart, and told the caller her brother was unable to come to the phone.

She hung up, tossed the final word to Sam, exchanged speaking glances with Ashley, who shared her anxiety over what to do about Mike, and dumped the green beans into a bowl.

"Supper!" she announced just as Susan closed her math book with a snap and a beaming smile that pronounced her homework done, and carried the casserole dish and bowl of green beans to the table.

17

The phone rang three more times during supper, twice for Mike, who went into a major sulk when he wasn't allowed to speak to his friends, and once—surprise!—for Ashley.

"It's a *guy*," Sam announced as he held out the receiver to his sister.

Ashley pinkened, cast a self-conscious look around the table, and left her seat to take the call. Once his sister was safely behind him, Sam, on his way back to the table, rolled his eyes expressively and grinned. Molly frowned him down, and initiated some inane conversation to give Ashley the illusion that her end of the conversation was not being avidly listened to. Molly herself thought her ears might fall off from the strain of trying to hear what was being said. She was only able to catch an occasional word as her sister leaned against the wall with her back toward the table, talking much more softly than usual, her shoulders hunched protectively to afford the maximum privacy. A boy calling Ashley was so unusual as to be unprecedented. To a man, the Ballards were agog.

Ashley was still blushing when she returned to her seat, but she was also smiling and there were stars in her eyes.

"Got a boyfriend now, Ash?" Mike asked with an aggravating smile as his sister sat down. An enthusiastic eater, he was already working on second helpings of everything.

"What's his name?" Susan breathed, vitally interested. Only half finished, her supper was forgotten in her excitement. Susan frequently had to be reminded to eat. Food didn't have the importance for her that it did for Mike and Sam.

"Eat, Susie Q," Molly prompted in an aside as she always did.

"I hope you're not going to be as bad as Molly," Sam said to Ashley. "All the guys who hang around her, it's enough to make you sick. And most of 'em are real jerks too."

"Sam!" Ashley hissed, directing a speaking glance at Will, while a thump from under the table and a pained look from Sam indicated that his twin had rewarded him for his tact with a well-placed kick. Mike snickered behind his hand. Molly narrowed her eyes warningly, dividing the speaking glance between her two brothers.

"Uh, I didn't mean you, Will." The look Sam sent their guest was brimful of wide-eyed entreaty. "I *like* you."

"Thanks, Sam, I like you too." Will continued eating, apparently unperturbed. Despite Molly's misgivings, he had tucked into the meal with enthusiasm, and was almost finished.

"That was Trevor." Ashley glanced down at her plate, which she had barely touched, then across the table at Molly. Her cheeks were so rosy with embarrassment, her eyes so bright with joy, that Molly wanted to walk around the table and give her sister a hug. She refrained, but her answering smile was warm with understanding and an echoed pleasure.

"He wanted to know what color dress I'm going to wear to the dance. He's going to buy me flowers to match!" Ashley broke into a huge grin. "Oh, gosh, Moll, he wanted to know if I'd prefer a corsage to pin on my dress, or a wrist corsage!"

"Oh, wow!" Susan said enviously, laying her fork down again.

"Flowers, sick!" Sam put in with a groan.

"Women!" Mike muttered, and slumped lower in his seat. Fork in hand, he attacked the food remaining on his plate with an enthusiasm that appeared undiminished despite his distaste for the topic under discussion.

"What did you tell him?" Molly asked, doing her best to continue casually with her dinner. In truth, she was as excited as her sister. Though Ashley never talked about it, Molly knew Ashley's lack of a social life bothered her. A group of kids at school persistently teased her, calling her "egghead" and "brain." To the boys she was apparently invisible.

"I said I'd let him know. I said I didn't have my dress yet. Oh, Molly, what am I going to wear?" Ashley started to eat again, but it was clear her supper no longer held any interest for her. Molly doubted if she even knew what she was putting in her mouth.

"The dance is next Friday?" Molly asked, although she knew the answer. In a gentle aside, she prompted, "Eat, Susie Q."

Reminded, Susan picked up her fork again.

Ashley nodded in response to Molly's question. "We'll go shopping next week."

"I could just wear that yellow lace dress I got for Rosalee's wedding last year." Clearly the expense of buying a new dress for the occasion had just occurred to Ashley, and troubled her. The beginnings of worry shadowed her eyes and voice. Ever conscious of the family's financial needs and limits, Ashley would resist spending money on something as unnecessary as a new outfit for a dance.

Molly shook her head determinedly. "You need a long dress, honey. Anyway, it'll be fun to shop for something new."

She'd scrape the money together somehow, Molly vowed, if she had to hock the TV to do it. Unfortunately, her regular Friday paycheck wouldn't stretch to cover the cost of a new dress, and Simpson, the so-and-so, had not yet paid her for the two weeks he'd owed her when she quit. Then a happy thought occurred to her: Maybe they'd be able to find something suitable in the secondhand shops that had recently sprung up all over Lexington's downtown. That would keep the cost down.

"Get pink," Susan counseled. "You look really pretty in pink, Ash. With a big full skirt like Cinderella. And lots of ruffles."

"Cinderella, yuck." Sam put both hands to his throat and made noises as if he were gagging.

"Finish your supper, Sam," Molly told him. Then, remembering their guest who occupied the place of honor in a chair pulled up to the end of the table, she explained, "Ashley's been invited to her high school's homecoming dance next weekend."

"I gathered something of the sort was up." He grinned at Ashley. "Sounds fun."

"It should be." Ashley's answering smile was shy but happy. Her gaze swung around to Molly. "Only it just occurred to me—I don't even know how to dance."

Mike hooted. "All you gotta do is get out there and shake your booty, Ash. You know, like this." He mimed a jerky version of the Swim from his place at the table.

"Eat, Mike," Molly said.

"Shut up, Mike," Ashley echoed, then glanced at Molly. "I can't just get out there and flail around. I can't!"

"Do you think any of the other kids know how to dance?" Molly asked. "I mean, anything besides what Mike just showed us?"

Ashley nodded. "A lot of them went to cotillion. Trevor did. He was telling me about it right before he asked me to the dance. He said he hated it, but his mom made him go."

"What's cotillion?" Will asked, sounding genuinely interested.

"You never heard of cotillion?" Susan was scandalized.

"He's from Chicago," Molly excused with an amused glance at Will, who grimaced an apology for his ignorance.

"Strictly for preps," Mike said. "Total nerd city."

"*I'm* not going," Sam chimed in. "No way."

"You couldn't get in," Susan said scornfully. "None of us could. You have to be *invited*. By one of those women's clubs."

"You have to be rich," Mike said. "A rich snob."

"Trevor's not a snob," Ashley objected. "He's nice."

"Ashley's in *lo-o-o-ve.*" Mike made kissing sounds at his sister, who reddened with anger.

"Mike!" Molly reproved. She glanced at Will. "Cotillion is kind of a dance club that some of the kids go to from about fifth to ninth grade. They meet twice a month, and they learn ballroom dancing."

"And manners," Ashley put in.

"The girls get all dressed up, and the guys have to wear *suits and ties*," Sam added with revulsion.

"How do you know?" Mike stared at his brother. Such knowledge seemed totally foreign to everything his siblings knew about rough-and-tumble, sports-mad Sam.

Swallowing a forkful of macaroni, Sam shrugged. "Some of the kids in my class go. They talk about it sometimes."

"You've been to dances before, Molly. You can teach me, right?" Ashley looked hopefully at her older sister.

"Sure," Molly said, though she had some doubts. She had not had formal dance instruction either. "Actually, Ash, the truth is, you just follow the guy. He leads, and you just do what he does. Only kind of backward."

"Great," Ashley said gloomily. "I don't even know the steps, and I have to do them backward."

"She'll fall on her a—uh, butt," Sam said with glee, glancing quickly at Molly to see if she'd noticed his near profanity. Ashley's coltish lack of grace was something of a family joke.

"Sam!" Molly warned, having noticed.

"She will not!" Ever loyal, Susan stuck up for Ashley.

"I probably will," Ashley said, and stabbed her meat with her fork with rather more viciousness than was called for. "Trevor will think I'm a total dweeb."

"All you need is a little practice," Will spoke up from the end of the table, his gaze on Ashley's downcast face. "Which I'd be glad to provide, if you like."

"You know how to *dance*?" Ashley and Susan spoke in unison, while every eye at the table focused on Will.

"I'm no Arthur Murray," Will said dryly. "But then, I doubt Trevor is either. I can teach you the basics, that's all."

"How great!" Susan exclaimed, clapping her hands.

"Thanks, Will," Ashley said with fervor. "If you could, I would really, really appreciate it." Pushing her plate away, she started to get to her feet there and then.

"After supper," Will added, and Ashley sank back down with a self-conscious grin.

Sam's expression made it clear that he was shaken by Will's admission that he could dance. Mike's lip curled with derision, but he said nothing, concentrating on his meal. Susan and Ashley were both starry-eyed, while Molly wondered why she was even surprised. What would be astonishing was if a man of Will's age and background had never been to a dance.

"Eat, everyone," Molly ordered. For a few minutes only the clink of flatware against china broke the silence.

"I'm finished." Mike pushed his end of the bench out from the table.

" 'May I be excused,' " Molly corrected automatically.

"Whatever," Mike answered with a dismissive wave, and disappeared into the living room. Molly thought about calling him back, or at least sailing a reprimand after him for his rudeness, but then decided it wasn't worth the scene that would almost certainly result.

"I'm done, too," Sam piped up, scrambling away from the table. Molly opened her mouth to repeat the same admonition she had given Mike, sighed, and closed it again. Might as well count her blessings, she thought. At least he had swallowed that swear word.

"Are you going to teach Ashley to dance now?" Susan asked Will eagerly.

"I'm game if she is," Will said, looking at Ashley with a smile. Ashley's cheeks pinkened, but she smiled back. Shy as Ashley was, that smile and her willingness to allow Will to teach her to dance spoke volumes. She no longer saw Will as what he was—a near stranger—but as someone she trusted, and could turn to for help. A friend.

"I'm game—but I just remembered it's my turn to do the dishes," Ashley said.

"I'll do them," Molly offered abruptly. What harm could it do for Will to teach Ashley to dance, after all? It was such a simple thing. . . .

As long as she took care to impress on her sister, and her other siblings, that Will was not going to be a long-term addition to their lives. She didn't want them getting attached to him, only to have them wake up one morning to discover that he was gone for good.

"Can I watch?" Susan asked as everyone stepped away from the table.

"Fine with me," Will said with a smile, while Ashley nodded.

"It's fine with me, too," Molly put in, "as long as

you clear the dishes while you watch. It's your turn, remember?"

Susan groaned.

"Sam, your turn to sweep," Molly reminded him. Calling into the living room, she added, "Mike, to-night's your night to feed Pork Chop and take the garbage out."

"Yeah, yeah," came Mike's answer. By the time he appeared in the doorway, Susan already had a big pile of scraps scraped onto one plate. Mixed with a generic brand of dry dog food, the scraps constituted Pork Chop's dinner.

"Okay, step back on your left foot," Will said to Ashley.

Squeezing a frugal amount of dishwashing liquid into the water running into the sink, Molly watched the proceedings out of the corner of her eye. Slim in her white painter's pants and fluffy pale blue turtle-neck, Ashley was laughing as she tried to follow Will's instructions. Her glasses slid down her nose, and she pushed them back, then returned her hand to his shoulder. Her right hand was clasped in his. His other hand, long-fingered and tan, rested at her waist.

Will smiled into Ashley's eyes.

Molly was surprised to feel a tiny spurt of something that felt very much like jealousy. Of Ashley? she thought, amazed. The notion was absurd.

Then she realized that it wasn't so much Ashley she was jealous of, as Ashley's left hand, because it rested on Will's broad shoulder; Ashley's right hand, because Will's fingers curled around it; Ashley's waist, because Will held her there.

She wanted to be where Ashley was with an inten-sity that frightened her.

"Now slide left," Will instructed. Ashley went right instead, bobbled as Will slid left, and was dragged along willy-nilly.

"I'm sorry," Ashley said to Will, her brows drawn together in concentration. Her face was flushed, her body stiff, and even renegade strands of her curly fair hair seemed tense with effort.

"That's okay," Will said soothingly. "Now come forward left, and slide right. Then we do it all over again."

"Come on, Pork Chop," Mike said to the dog, who was frisking around his feet in his eagerness for dinner. Susan, her gaze hardly leaving Ashley and Will, brought the pile of scraped plates to the counter as Mike and Pork Chop went out the door.

"All right now, come forward left, then slide *right,*" Will said. He stepped backward, Ashley forward—but on the wrong foot. Her slim foot in its soft blue sock landed on the toe of Will's well-polished black shoe.

18

Susan winced in sympathy.

Leaning on the broom, watching with transparent derision, Sam hooted out loud.

"Sam!" Molly said. She was elbow-deep in sudsy water, trying with indifferent success to focus on the task at hand rather than her sister and Will. If she was attracted to him, it was a fluke, a case of chemistry run amok, Molly told herself. Ignore it, she was sure, and it would go away. Just as he would.

"I'm sorry," Ashley said again, lifting her foot.

"No harm done," Will answered. "Just remember: left, left, left, right."

"I'll never get it," Ashley moaned.

"She'll never get it," Sam echoed with conviction.

"Shut up, Sam!" Susan hissed.

"*Sweep*, Sam," Molly said, plunging glasses into hot water. Unable to resist, she cast the dancing pair a sideways glance. Will looked relaxed, patient—and too sexy for Molly's peace of mind. Not that Ashley seemed to think so. It was clear that Ashley, far from being smitten with Will, was hard at work. Ashley was chewing on her bottom lip, concentrating for all she was worth on where she would next put her feet.

While Molly, Mike, and Sam were natural athletes, at ease with their bodies and good at most sports, and Molly at least loved dancing, Susan and Ashley tended to be less physically coordinated. Ashley had fallen so many times when trying to learn to roller-skate that she had eventually given up the attempt; almost every time she sat on the back of a horse she managed to tumble off; she was a slow runner, a clumsy pitcher, and a lousy batter; one year at school she had fallen off the balance beam and broken her arm. She could not do the splits, a cartwheel, or even a somersault, and gym was the only class where Molly had ever feared she might earn less than an A.

It did not look like she was going to be a natural dancer, either.

Just as it did not look like Ashley had the slightest awareness of Will as a male. Or vice versa.

"Left, left, left, right," Ashley said, counting off the steps as she moved rigidly in Will's wake.

"You can do it, Ash," Susan encouraged.

"Man, this is *so* dumb," Mike muttered as he passed back through the kitchen. With a last scornful look at Ashley and Will, he disappeared into the living room.

"Garbage, Mike," Molly called after him.

"Left, left, left, right."

"You're doing great," Will said.

"You look like you've got a poker up your butt," Mike told Ashley as he came back through the kitchen, grabbed the garbage can, and headed for the door. "Loosen up."

"Shut up, Mike!" Molly and Susan said in almost

the same breath, then looked at each other and grinned.

"I hope this doesn't look as stupid as it feels." Ashley sounded discouraged as she and Will paused to untangle their feet for the dozenth time.

"It looks pretty stupid," Sam assured her. Having finished the sweeping, he perched on the edge of the kitchen table to watch with critical interest. Clad in jeans, sneakers, and a royal blue Kentucky Wildcats sweat shirt, a drift of shining blond hair hanging across his forehead almost into his eyes, he looked as sweet in his own way as Susan did in hers.

Too bad he isn't, Molly thought, exasperated.

"It does *not* look stupid," Molly said, casting Sam an evil glance, while Susan, in the act of restoring butter and milk to the refrigerator, chimed in with "What you need is music," and ran from the room.

"You're doing great," Will said to Ashley yet again. "It just takes practice."

"She can practice till the cows come home, and it's not gonna help," Mike observed, passing through again on his way back to the living room. "Face it, Ash, you can't dance."

"Mike!" Molly snapped, but he was out of the room.

"Maybe I should just tell Trevor I can't go." Ashley stopped moving, disengaged her hands from Will, and sent Molly a miserable glance.

Molly scowled at her sister. "Don't be silly, Ash. Of course you're going. You're going to look beautiful, and you're going to dance as well as anyone else there, and you're going to have a wonderful time."

"So there?" Ashley asked with a faint smile, her hands tucked under her elbows against her sides.

"So there!" Molly echoed.

"I wish someone would teach me to dance," Susan said enviously, returning with the small brass music box from Molly's top dresser drawer. "Who taught you, Will?"

He shrugged. "I just picked it up."

"Who taught you, Molly?" Susan was winding the key.

"I guess I just picked it up too. All you really have to do is listen to the music and follow your partner's steps." Molly rinsed the last of the plates, and started on the silverware.

Susan opened the lid of the music box. The clear, lilting melody of "Edelweiss" filled the kitchen.

". . . *small and white, clean and bright, every morning you meet me* . . ."

"Try it with music," Susan suggested.

Will held out his arms to Ashley, who sighed, rolled her eyes, and assumed the position.

". . . *small and white, clean and bright, you look happy to greet me* . . ."

Will and Ashley began moving in awkward squares across the kitchen floor, while Molly, listening to the tune she loved, felt tears mist her eyes.

"*Blossom of snow, may you bloom and grow* . . ."

The music box had been a gift from her mother. Every time she heard its tinkling notes, she was reminded of small happinesses and large sorrows and much that she would sooner forget. Which was why she hardly ever listened to it.

". . . *bloom and grow forever. Edelweiss, Edelweiss, bless my homeland forever.*"

She was surprised Susan even knew where the music box was kept.

"Will you show me, Molly?" Ashley asked.

The music stopped. Molly looked around in surprise. Ashley and Will had stepped apart. Both were looking at her.

"If you'd dance with Will for a minute, maybe I could see how it's done. I'm not getting the hang of it very well, I don't think."

Blinking away both moisture and memories, Molly met her sister's gaze. The soft brown eyes pleaded.

"Show her, Molly, please," Susan begged, her finger on the tiny button that, when depressed, stopped the music. "I want to see how *you* do it."

"You gotta be better than Ash," Sam muttered, shaking his head.

"Ashley's doing fine," Will said. "But it might help if she could watch someone else. Molly?"

He reached for her easily. Molly was reminded of how he had kissed her hand earlier in the day and appeared to experience absolutely no reaction, while she had received the shock of a lifetime. If, against all the laws of reason, she was attracted to him, he didn't seem to reciprocate.

"My hands are all wet," Molly protested. Susan, who was drying the silverware, wordlessly handed her a towel. Unable to think of another objection that would not leave her looking foolish—Will *was* supposed to be her boyfriend, after all, and it was only a dance—Molly dried her hands and went into his arms.

His shoulder felt hard beneath her hand. The material of his shirt was a fine, soft cotton. His fingers grasping hers were warm, strong. She could feel the firm possession of his other hand at her waist.

Her instinct was to drop her gaze, to shut herself off

from him by refusing to look at him. But what would he, and her watching family, read into that?

She raised her chin, looked him in the eye, and pinned a smile on her face.

Susan lifted her finger from the music box's button, and the evocative strains of "Edelweiss" spilled forth.

". . . *you look happy to greet me* . . ."

Molly tried not to listen, either.

So caught up was she in not revealing her reaction to either the man or the music, she danced without conscious volition. She simply followed Will's lead, her bare toes skimming over the floor. Thus she appeared extremely proficient at the waltz, which she had danced perhaps three times in her life.

". . . *blossom of snow* . . ."

There were a few silver hairs among the gold ones above his ears, Molly noticed, and grooves beside his mouth that were deeper than the crinkles at the corners of his eyes. His lips were thin but well shaped, stretched now in a slight smile as he looked down at her.

". . . *bloom and grow forever* . . ."

His eyes were bluer than Ashley's sweater.

"*Edelweiss* . . ."

The top of her head would fit perfectly beneath his nose.

". . . *edelweiss* . . ."

His throat was a brown, strong column, and despite its gold tips the hair on his chest was darker than that on his head. Molly caught herself wondering if his chest was very hairy. Probably not, she decided. Not with that blond hair.

". . . *bless my homeland forever.*"

His body radiated heat, or something did. Whatever

its source, she was absorbing heat in waves. She felt very, very warm.

The music stopped. Will swung her around in a theatrical twirl, and released her.

Molly felt dizzy. Susan, Sam, and Ashley applauded.

"You're a good dancer," Will said, smiling at her.

"Thank you," Molly replied, pleased to discover that she sounded a lot more normal than she felt. "So are you."

"Hey, the basic box step goes a long way."

"Ashley? Your turn." Molly walked away, leaned against the counter, and began to recover. Ashley and Will took up where they had left off, but Molly no longer felt remotely jealous. If Ashley was experiencing anything halfway near what Molly had felt in Will's arms, she wouldn't be able to hide it. If nothing else, her fair skin would give her away. It was clear, watching, that neither dancer was romantically interested in the other. They were friendly, and that was all.

Molly wondered how she had looked, dancing with Will. She doubted that *friendly* was quite the word to describe it.

Though her brothers and sisters would not have noticed anything amiss. Will was supposed to be her boyfriend, after all.

Susan screamed. The sound, loud and shrill as a siren, came out of nowhere to shatter the cozy serenity of the kitchen. The music box fell from Susan's hands to the floor with a crash. The music stopped.

White-faced and wide-eyed, Susan stared at the small window. The homemade curtains, which never quite met in the center anyway, were open. Beyond the glass was impenetrable darkness.

"What is it? What's wrong?" a jumble of voices, Molly's among them, demanded.

Susan pointed a shaking finger at the window.

"There was somebody looking in!"

"Susan! Are you sure?" Again the chorus.

"There was! There was!"

"Stay here!" Will commanded, and ran outside. Mike, who had appeared in the kitchen seconds after Susan screamed, grabbed the shotgun from the corner next to the refrigerator and followed him. The door banged shut behind him.

Outside, Pork Chop began to bark. Molly scooped up the music box from the floor. Her fingers found a slight dent in one smooth oval side, and as she set it on the counter she hoped that that was the only damage. But she would check the music box later; her first priority was her sister.

Mike was back within moments, slamming the door behind him. Molly, who was comforting a shaken Susan, looked an inquiry at him.

"He's an asshole," Mike said through his teeth, and kicked the baseboard furiously.

Molly's brows rose. She and Ashley exchanged questioning looks. Before they could say anything, Will entered.

"Nobody there," he said, closing the door. Molly realized that Will now held the shotgun, and glanced at her brother's resentful face with sudden comprehension: he must have taken it from Mike.

"There was somebody there. He—they—were looking in," Susan insisted. "I saw them!"

"Must have been a ghost, then. Pork Chop was eating his supper when we went outside. *He* didn't see anybody—but then he wouldn't, would he, if it was a ghost," Mike taunted her.

"He's barking," Ashley pointed out.

"Cat," Will said briefly. "He chased it to the fence, but he can't get over."

"Oh." Everybody knew how Pork Chop felt about cats.

Will crossed the kitchen and leaned the shotgun against the far wall.

"You shouldn't keep this thing at all, much less where kids can get at it," he said to Molly.

"It's not loaded. I told you." There was a furious, goading note to Mike's voice.

Will gave him a level look. "It's still dangerous. What if that had been a police officer out there? He might have shot you, thinking you were armed and dangerous."

"Well, it wasn't a cop. It wasn't anyone. Just a figment of little sister's imagination!" Mike sneered.

"Mike!" Molly rebuked him, with a quick glance at Susan.

"It was not my imagination! There was someone there, truly there was!" Susan cried.

"Maybe you saw Libby Coleman," Mike offered maliciously. "Maybe she heard the music, and she wanted to dance."

Susan gasped.

"Mike!" Molly glared at him, while Susan turned three shades paler.

"Who's Libby Coleman?" Will inquired, checking the kitchen window to make sure it was locked, and peering out into the backyard beyond. Not that he would be able to see anything, Molly thought. Not even FBI agents came equipped with X-ray vision.

"She's our local ghost," Molly explained, striving to keep her voice light. "Except no one knows for sure that she's dead."

"She's one of the faces you see on milk cartons," Ashley added. "She disappeared, oh, more than ten years ago, when she was about twelve years old. Just disappeared."

"Right after she'd been to cotillion," Mike put in, with a teasing glance at Susan. "Dancing, you see. I bet she still likes to dance."

"Shut up, Mike," Susan said with loathing.

"It was thirteen years ago. I remember, because she and I were about the same age, and that made it scary. It was all over TV, and the papers. For months afterward, none of us were allowed to so much as set foot outside alone," Molly recalled.

"Was that when you were living at the Home?" Ashley asked, frowning. Molly nodded. Glancing at Will, she hoped that he hadn't noticed the reference to the modern-day orphanage where she had spent a good part of her adolescence. Though his background check on her had probably revealed that tidbit of information. But maybe not. Just the facts, he'd said. Not for the first time, Molly wondered what "just the facts" entailed.

Apparently he hadn't noticed Ashley's question, or wasn't interested in following up. "Coleman," he said thoughtfully. "One of the Greenglow Stables' Colemans?"

Molly nodded, glad to pursue that instead of the more sensitive subject. "Their younger daughter. They had—have—an older girl, and a boy."

"And she disappeared, after a cotillion class, thirteen years ago?" Will rubbed his chin. "That's interesting, but I don't think it was her at your window."

"It was somebody," Susan insisted. "I saw them, I really did."

"If you did, they're gone now. Don't worry about it." Will glanced at Molly. "Still, just to be safe, I'd like to check the house. Do you mind?"

Molly shook her head. Will walked through the downstairs, tugging at window sashes, testing locks. Then he went upstairs. When he came back, he spoke to Molly.

"The lock on the window in the boys' room upstairs is broken. I shoved a piece of wood in there to hold it. I'll fix it next time I come over."

"Thank you," Molly said, and smiled at him.

Mike's expression darkened. "What is he, man of the house now?" he muttered, and took himself off upstairs. They could hear his angry footsteps echoing through the house.

For a moment everyone was silent.

"It's a phase," Ashley said apologetically to Will, who nodded.

"I've got to go," Will said to Molly. "Unless you're scared. I'll stay, if you want me to."

"We're fine," Molly answered, her arm still around Susan's shoulders. "But thanks for the offer. And the chicken. You saved me from having to cook supper tomorrow night."

"Sure?"

"Yes." Molly retrieved his coat and tie from the bench and held them out to him. He rolled down his sleeves, slipped into the coat, and draped the tie around his neck.

"We'll practice that box step a couple more times,

and by next Friday night you'll be a pro," Will promised Ashley.

"I hope so." Ashley hugged herself and smiled at him. "Thanks, Will."

"Bye, Will," Sam said glumly. Molly wondered when the children had started calling him Will. The intimacy sounded natural—but she wasn't sure she ought to allow it. Given the circumstances.

Not that there was much she could do about it. They would think she was nuts if she insisted they call him Mr. Lyman. All her other boyfriends they had called by their first names.

"Bye, Sam. Bye, Susan. Don't worry. What you saw was probably some kind of animal, a possum or an owl or something, out there on the windowsill for a second before your scream frightened it away."

"Yeah." Susan was clearly unconvinced.

"I'll walk you to your car," Molly offered, thinking he probably had instructions for her.

"No." His refusal was abrupt. Molly looked questioningly at him. He caught her hand, pulled her close, and leaned down to whisper in her ear. "I didn't see anything out there, but you never know. I want you—all of you—to stay inside tonight, and keep the door locked. Just in case. Understand?"

Molly nodded. Will still held her hand, and his breath was warm against her ear. Molly felt the heat of it clear down to her toes.

"You've got my number if you see or hear anything else. Call the police first, then call me, because they can get here quicker. Got it?"

Molly nodded again. He was scaring her, a little—but that was ridiculous. Woodford County was not exactly a hotbed of crime, and even a Peeping Tom was unlikely. The nearest neighbors were the Atkinsons, and they were half a mile away.

Besides, J.D. patrolled the farm all night long.

Will released her hand, waved a general good-bye to her watching family, and let himself out.

His parting words to Molly were a stern "Lock the door. And for God's sake, get rid of that gun."

19

October 14, 1995

When Molly pulled her car into the driveway, it was about 5:30 p.m. Already she was bone tired. Saturdays at Keeneland were hectic at best; it was the busiest day of the week. With Lady Valor out of the Spinster, there'd been heartbreak to deal with as well. The filly's arch-rival, Alberta's Hope from Nestor Stables out in California, had won with a time Molly was sure Lady Valor could have bested. Don Simpson thought so too. As a result, he was as grouchy as a bear with a sore paw. Plus none of the horses whose names Will had slipped her the previous night had been ringers. It had taken a great deal of effort to check every one (this time he'd given her six!), and it was aggravating not to find anything amiss.

All in all, it had been a heck of a day.

Ashley's best friend, Beth Osbourne, was leaving the house as Molly slid out of the car. Molly chatted with her for a few minutes before going inside. Beth inquired slyly about her new boyfriend. With a mental kick for Ashley, Molly smiled and made an offhand reply. Beth laughed. Molly wondered what Ashley had told her.

With Beth gone, Molly went in.

"Hi, gang, I'm home!" she called, dropping her purse on the kitchen table and heading toward the refrigerator. There had been no time for lunch today, either, and she was starving. Supper was going to have to be something that cooked fast, she thought, and then she remembered the chicken Will had brought: perfect.

"Hi, Moll." Ashley walked into the kitchen, her head wrapped turban-style in a green towel.

"Why'd you wash your hair at this time of day?" Molly asked, pausing in the act of filching a cold chicken leg from the bucket she had pulled from the refrigerator. With biscuits and a salad, supper would be a snap.

"We were trying out hairstyles. Beth curled it on these foam sticks she has, and I ended up looking like I stuck my finger in a socket. The more I tried to brush it out, the frizzier it got. So I washed it."

"Oh." Still standing by the open refrigerator, Molly took a bite out of the chicken leg. "Is Beth going to the dance too?"

"Yes." Ashley's sudden smile was bright. "With Andy Moorman. The four of us are going to go out to eat together first. Isn't that great?"

Outspoken Beth had always been more popular with boys than shy Ashley, though in Molly's opinion Ashley was the prettier of the two.

"Great," she agreed, and took another bite of chicken. "Where are Mike and the twins?" she asked around the mouthful.

"Mike's upstairs, lost in some tape one of his friends

loaned him. Sam's over at Ryan Lutz's, and Susan's at Mary Shelton's. Susan called to ask if she could spend the night, and I said it was okay. Sam will be home around eight."

"So there's just you, me, and Mike for supper," Molly concluded, polishing off the chicken leg and tossing the bone, with commendable accuracy, into the trash. She closed the refrigerator door, one arm around the bucket.

"That depends." Ashley gave her a severe look. "Jimmy Miller called. He said to tell you he'd pick you up at six forty-five."

"Oh, my gosh! I forgot!" Molly clapped a hand to her mouth.

"You seem to be forgetting dates a lot lately." Ashley crossed her arms over her chest and cocked her head to the side. "You're not going, are you?"

Actually, Molly was just wondering whether it would be better to call Jimmy at the garage or at home, to tell him something had come up and she couldn't go. But as she thought about it, she realized *why* she didn't want to go, and the reason scared her: Will.

He is not my boyfriend! she reminded herself grimly.

"Sure I am." Molly turned her shoulder on her sister, gave the bucket of chicken a fleeting look of regret, and restored it to the refrigerator shelf. "Why not?"

"You can't!"

"Why can't I?"

"What's Will going to think?" Ashley burst out.

Molly closed the refrigerator door before replying.

"Does it matter?" she asked lightly, and walked out of the kitchen. If she was going out to dinner and a movie with Jimmy Miller—he had asked her on Monday, two days before Will entered her life—she had to shower and change.

"Molly!" Ashley followed her.

Crossing her tiny bedroom and pulling aside the curtain that served as a closet door, Molly surveyed her meager wardrobe. Ashley stopped in the open doorway. Molly did her best to ignore her sister.

"You can't do this," Ashley said.

"What?" Molly pulled out a black skirt and examined it. The garment was clean and pressed. It was even still in style. With a sweater or a shirt and blazer, it would do. "Can I borrow your gray blazer?"

"No!" Ashley sounded outraged. "Not to go out with Jimmy Miller, you can't! What about Will?"

"What about him?" Molly rifled through the items remaining in her closet and located the black turtleneck she'd been seeking.

"Don't you have a date with him?"

"No." Strictly speaking, it was true. Will would probably stop by—all right, she was almost certain he would stop by—but they didn't have a *date*. Any information exchange could wait for tomorrow at the track.

"You mean he's not coming over tonight?"

Molly shrugged. "He might. If he does, tell him I had a previous engagement."

"What do you think he's going to think about you going out with Jimmy Miller?"

"Know what?" Molly dropped to her knees to rummage in the bottom of her closet for her good black pumps.

"What?"

"I don't particularly care."

"Did the two of you have a fight?" Ashley sounded anxious.

"No, we didn't have a fight." Molly stood up, shoes in hand, gathered up the turtleneck and skirt, and turned to lay the outfit carefully on the somewhat faded but still pretty yellow floral comforter that covered her bed.

"Then why—" Ashley began, only to be interrupted by her sister.

"Will Lyman doesn't own me," Molly said fiercely, and crossed to her dresser. Yanking open the top drawer, she tossed fresh underwear on the bed, then dug beneath the music box and her lingerie to hunt for panty hose. The square mirror threw her reflection back at her. Mouth set obstinately, eyes flashing, she looked hell-bent on something. Molly just wasn't sure what that something was.

"I really like Will, Moll."

"Then you date him."

"We all do. Except Mike, but you know how he is. He'll come around."

"Look, Ash." Molly found the pair of black panty hose that she sought, shut the drawer, and faced her sister. "Number one, Will is too old for me. Number two, he's not really my type. Number three, he's from Chicago and he'll be going back there when Keeneland's over. So don't be imagining we're having some deathless romance. We're not."

"I bet you could turn it into a deathless romance if you wanted to."

"Can I *please* borrow your gray blazer?" Molly tossed the panty hose on the bed and turned to root through her small jewelry box for her silver earrings and chain.

"You've gone out with him the last two nights. You never date on weeknights. You must like him a lot."

"It's nothing serious, Ash. Trust me, it's not." Molly

found one earring and the chain, but the other earring eluded her.

"You ought to see the way you look at him."

"It's your imagination." Molly found the other earring and shut the jewelry box with a snap.

Ashley shook her head. "I know you, Moll. Don't tell me you don't have the hots for him big time. I know better."

"Shut up, Ashley, will you, please?" Molly said through her teeth. Gathering up her plastic bag of toiletries, she headed toward the bathroom. Ashley stepped back out of her way, and Molly sailed past her.

"I bet you could make him fall in love with you," Ashley said from behind her.

"You've been reading too many romances," Molly snapped, and closed the bathroom door in her sister's face.

When she emerged thirty minutes later, showered, shampooed, blow-dried, and made up, Ashley was nowhere in sight. Carrying her toilet bag and dirty clothes in one hand and holding the towel that was all she wore closed with the other, she made a beeline for her room. If she was quick, she could have the door shut and locked before Ashley realized she was no longer in the shower.

Her sister, minus the green towel, was sitting on a corner of Molly's bed, fluffing her drying hair with one hand. Her gray blazer lay across her lap with a small vial of perfume on top.

Molly stopped in the doorway. Ashley glanced up. The sisters exchanged measuring looks.

"You can borrow my blazer," Ashley said. "And I got a free sample of Knowing last time I was at the mall. You can use that too."

"Thanks." Molly walked into the room and took the perfume, which Ashley held out to her. "Why the switch?"

"I decided it would probably help things along if you made Will jealous. You know how men are." This from Ashley, the worldly-wise.

Molly groaned. "Would you get out of here? It's six-thirty, and I'm not even dressed."

"Will's just right for you, Moll," Ashley said seriously, standing. "If you were with him, I wouldn't have to worry when I leave for college next fall. He'd take care of you. And Mike and Susan and Sam too."

"Get out of my room!" Molly pushed Ashley out the door, slammed it shut, and locked it. She stood for a minute with her forehead resting against the white-painted wood panel. Finally she straightened.

"Will's going back to Chicago in two weeks! Get that through your head!" she yelled to her sister through the door.

"Jimmy Miller just pulled up," Ashley called back by way of a reply. Cursing under her breath, Molly began to dress.

Jimmy Miller had tobacco-brown hair, a stocky build, and a sweet smile. If his square, snub-nosed face was not precisely handsome, it was attractive. He was considered a catch by the local girls. After all, he would be sole owner of Miller's Garage one day. Everyone knew the volume of business generated by Versailles's only auto repair shop. To top it off, Molly liked him.

The problem was, that was as far as her feelings for him went.

He bought her dinner at the Sizzler, and she smiled at him while he told her all about his plans for opening a second shop in the nearby state capital of Frankfort. He held her hand during the movie, and she let him. When it was over, he tried to talk her into letting him take her on to a nightclub in Lexington, but she said no, she had to get up and go to work in the morning.

He said that was something he really admired about her: her sense of responsibility.

Like the good sport he was, Jimmy drove her home. It was not quite 11:30 p.m.

Will's white Ford Taurus was parked in the driveway behind her own blue Plymouth, Molly saw as they pulled in. She sat up straighter as every muscle in her body tensed.

"New car?" Jimmy asked, turning off the ignition and sliding his arm along the back of the seat.

"It belongs to a family friend," Molly answered. Jimmy was going to kiss her good night—he had kissed her before—and she was going to let him, to give him more than he had bargained for, even.

Because Will was in her house. And because deep in her heart she realized that the man she really wanted to be kissing her was Will.

Sock-footed, clad in a blue button-down dress shirt and a pair of gray slacks, Will was sprawled out in the surprisingly comfortable old lounge chair in the Ballards' living room when he heard the faint crunch of tires on gravel. Outside, Pork Chop began to bark.

She was home. His fingers closed over the chair arms, tightening, as he considered. He could stay where he was and wait for Molly to come in. Or he could go out on the porch like an overprotective father and cast a damper over her and her boyfriend's good-night kiss.

It annoyed him that he didn't much like the idea of that good-night kiss. And it annoyed him even more that he didn't feel in the least bit fatherly toward Molly.

Sam was curled up on the couch, having fallen asleep during the closing credits of the rented movie Will had brought with him. Ashley sat at Sam's feet, her eyes heavy-lidded as she watched Jay Leno exchanging chit-chat with Elizabeth Taylor. Mike was upstairs. He had retired to his room immediately after the movie ended. But not even to avoid Will's presence had Mike been able to resist the lure of seeing Arnold Schwarzenegger in *True Lies*.

"Molly's home," Ashley said, sliding a glance across the darkened room at Will. Not for the first time that evening, Will wondered what Ashley was up to. When he had arrived around seven-thirty, bearing sacks of groceries and a movie, he was greeted by the surprising, infuriating news that Molly was out on a date. Ashley insisted he stay. To watch the movie with them, she said. And continue her dancing lessons, if he didn't mind. And—and to protect them, because without Molly there she and Mike were just the teensiest bit afraid.

Will noticed that Mike wasn't anywhere around when Ashley said that. And he didn't think Ashley was afraid. But, since Ashley's invitation exactly coincided with his own desires, he had acquiesced. He'd fixed the screen door and the upstairs bedroom window, practiced dancing with Ashley—dancing didn't seem to be her natural thing—and wrestled with Sam. And watched the movie.

He carefully kept a lid on his temper all the while.

"Is she?" Will continued to stare at the TV, as if

engrossed in Elizabeth Taylor's recounting of her latest illness. In fact, he could have been watching a blank screen for all the show registered on him.

It was taking Molly a long time to get out of that car and come in.

"I think I'll go to bed," Ashley said, and stood up. "Thanks for staying, Will."

"You're welcome."

He continued to stare at the TV as Ashley roused Sam and pushed him before her toward the stairs.

" 'Night," she called softly.

" 'Night," Will answered, and hoped he didn't sound as sour as he felt.

It didn't take a lot of imagination to guess what Molly was up to in that car.

A well-to-do local businessman, was how Ashley had described Molly's date. Crazy about Molly.

Hell, half the men in the Bluegrass seemed to be crazy about Molly.

He wasn't about to join their ranks.

He was too old, and too experienced, to let himself get involved with a woman who drew men like a porch light did moths. A woman fifteen years his junior, with a face like an angel's—and a body that made men salivate.

His mama hadn't raised no fool.

But what the hell was she doing in that car?

Stupid question.

Will couldn't stand it any longer. If she wanted to screw the guy, she should damn well have the decency to do it somewhere other than her own driveway.

He wasn't going to sit twiddling his thumbs for an hour while she topped off her evening in some yokel's backseat. He was going to drag her out of that car, tell her what he had to tell her, then go back to his hotel room and go to bed.

He was already on his feet when he heard a car door slam, followed almost instantaneously by another. Either the yokel didn't believe in opening a lady's door for her, or Molly hadn't waited.

Two sets of footsteps crossing the porch were followed by the sound of the screen door being dragged open, and Molly's key in the lock.

Silence.

Will took a couple of instinctive steps forward, stopped himself, leaned a shoulder against the doorjamb, and waited.

It took her long enough to open the door.

"One more, Molly. Just one more," the yokel begged as the heavy wood door swung inward.

"Good *night*, Jimmy," Molly said, laughing, and stepped inside. Pork Chop pushed in with her, spied Will in the opening between the living room and kitchen despite the darkness, and came over to greet him, tail wagging. Molly and her swain never even bothered to look around.

"Next Saturday?" God, the yokel sounded abject. Will remembered how his body had reacted that day at Keeneland when all he had done was kiss the girl's hand, and felt a sudden spurt of fellow feeling for the yokel. Hell, even dancing with her made him hard, and her brothers and sisters had been watching the entire time!

The girl was a menace, and that was the truth. He wasn't about to join the pack that panted after her. After that dance, he had made up his mind: His policy toward her was strictly hands off.

"Call me," Molly promised without promising anything at all. The yokel grabbed her hand, pulled her forward for a kiss. He had brown hair, a thickset body, jeans with a crease down the center of each leg—and he burrowed his hand deep into Molly's hair as he kissed her.

What he appeared to lack in technique he more than made up for in enthusiasm.

Will straightened away from the doorjamb. Realizing how aggressive his stance was, he made himself relax.

She wasn't his, he reminded himself. Not for real, only for show. And he wouldn't have it any other way.

"Good night, Jimmy." Molly pulled free, smiling, and reached for the handle of the screen door.

The yokel stepped back with obvious reluctance as she pulled it closed.

"I'll call you tomorrow," he promised thickly.

"Okay. Good night," Molly said through the screen. Then, with a smile and a wave, she at last shut the door. The lock clicked home. Molly turned away into the room.

Will reached over and switched on the kitchen light.

20

Molly's hair tumbled around her face and shoulders in a dark, wavy cloud. Her eyes, rimmed with kohl and enhanced with mascara, looked heavy-lidded and sensuous as they met Will's gaze. Faint traces of a deep red lipstick clung to the tender curves of her mouth.

Will didn't like to think about what had happened to the rest of that lipstick.

She wore a fingertip-length gray blazer, a skirt maybe two inches longer, and a tight black knit turtleneck that clung like a second skin.

Her legs in black heels and stockings were slim, shapely, and endless. Of course, the effect was heightened by the fact that her skirt ended at approximately mid-thigh.

"What are *you* doing here?" Her voice and the sudden bright gleam in her eyes were insolent.

"Waiting for you." Having gotten himself under control, Will leaned a shoulder against the doorjamb again.

"If I'd known, I'd have stayed out later." Molly walked toward the refrigerator, shedding her blazer as she went. She dropped it on the table. Will was left to stare at her back as she opened the refrigerator door and extracted a can of soda.

"Want a Coke?" she asked over her shoulder, as if she was just remembering her manners. With a grimace she added, before he could reply, "Oh, yes, I forgot: I mean, want a glass of milk?"

"No." Her outfit was too tight, too short, too—everything. She looked very slender, fragile even, except for the tantalizing curve of her butt and, when she closed the refrigerator door and turned to face him, the soft fullness of her breasts.

Will realized that he had never seen her with her hair curled and makeup on, or dressed in a skirt and stockings and heels.

She was naturally beautiful, with her hair pulled back and wearing sweat pants or jeans. Got up like she was tonight, she took his breath away.

She was the sexiest thing he had ever seen in his life.

"Did you want something? If not, I'm going to bed." Molly popped the top on her Coke and took a sip, her eyes challenging him over it.

Will tried in vain to banish the instant erotic image of Molly in bed. His eyes narrowed at her.

"Did you do what I told you?" he asked, keeping his voice low. The TV in the other room was loud enough to cover their conversation, and the kids were in bed, but still he wanted to take no chances of being overheard. When she had reported to him that afternoon at Keeneland the results of the daily mouth tattoo checks—negative, as he was learning to expect—Will had given her another assignment: to photograph the files in Don Simpson's office. He had provided her with a pen-camera for that purpose.

"Did I have a choice?" Molly took another sip of her Coke.

"No."

She sipped without replying.

"Well?" Will prompted, holding on to his patience with an effort.

She moved. Despite his best efforts, Will couldn't keep his eyes off her legs as she crossed to the cabinets, opened a drawer, extracted the camera, which looked exactly like an ordinary Parker pen, and threw it at him with rather more force than was necessary.

"Catch."

Will did, one-handed, and stowed it in his shirt pocket.

"Good job," he said.

"There wasn't anything in our deal about me sneaking into Mr. Simpson's office and taking pictures with a spy camera. I want extra pay."

"I'm paying you enough."

"I thought it was the government that was paying me."

"It is. But I authorize the disbursement of funds."

"So I guess you think that makes you the boss."

"You're right. I do."

Molly didn't like that, he could tell. She took another sip of Coke.

"Now that you got what you came for, would you please go? I'm tired."

"I bet you are." The words with their snide edge came out before Will could stop them.

Molly stiffened. "Why shouldn't I be? I got up at four a.m., worked all day, went out to dinner and a movie, and now it's almost midnight. And I have to get up at four tomorrow morning."

"Tomorrow's Sunday."

"So? Horses don't observe the Sabbath. They need care on Sundays just like they do on any other day of the week."

"I need you to go to Howard Lawrence's memorial service with me tomorrow." Will revealed the other reason—the *official* other reason—he had waited around to talk to her.

"I can't. I have to work."

"So call in sick."

Molly laughed.

Will reconsidered. "The memorial service isn't until ten. The first race starts at one. If you can't call in sick, you'll have to duck out for an hour."

"Oh, right, and go to a memorial service in jeans and a T-shirt? I don't think so."

"So bring some extra clothes, and change in the car."

"You'd like that, wouldn't you?" On a mouth less luscious than Molly's, that twist might have been described as a sneer.

"You think I'd watch through the mirror?"

"You might."

"You've got me confused with your drooling boyfriend."

"All men drool."

"You may be right, but not necessarily over you." The implication that he didn't find her drool-worthy was a lie, but a necessary one, Will thought, for his own self-preservation. If she ever got an inkling of just how intense his physical response to her was, Will had a feeling he would be in a lot of trouble.

Molly said nothing, her gaze dropping to the bright red can she held. After a moment she glanced up at him again. "Why do you need me to go?"

"To identify some people."

"You mean your computer can't do that?" She was mocking him.

Will shook his head, refusing to be drawn.

"All right." Molly capitulated suddenly, wearily. "I'll tell Mr. Simpson I'm going. He won't like it, but he won't fire me over it."

"I'll pick you up at nine-thirty in front of the barn."

Molly shook her head. "I'd rather meet you away from the track. I don't want Mr. Simpson to think I'm skipping work to meet a man. He's going to be mad enough as it is."

"Where do you want to meet?"

"Where's the memorial service?"

"St. Luke's Episcopal Church in Versailles."

"How about the 7-Eleven on Versailles Road? Do you know where that is?"

"I know," Will said dryly, remembering the gum on his shoe. "Nine-thirty?"

"Nine forty-five. I can't be gone too long."

"Nine forty-five it is, then."

"Is that all?" She put the Coke can on the counter and crossed her arms over her chest, clearly wanting him to be gone.

"You weren't so anxious to get rid of your boyfriend a few minutes ago." Despite his firm intention of leaving, Will couldn't resist the gibe.

"But you're not my boyfriend, are you?" Molly replied with a saccharine smile and a toss of her hair. "Not for real."

"You've got a hickey on your neck." The small

brown bruise marred the pale curve of her throat just beneath her jaw. Her hair had hidden it till now. The sight of it jarred Will.

Molly flushed, lifting a hand to her neck. "So?" she said defensively.

"Better cover it with makeup tomorrow. I don't want people to think I did it. Hickeys aren't my style." Will was surprised at how annoyed he felt, looking at that love bite on her smooth skin.

"I guess not." Molly smiled that too-sweet smile at him again, and dropped her hand from its defensive position at her neck. "You're way too old."

"I'm thirty-nine," he replied, stung.

"Old." Molly nodded sagely.

Will felt the familiar burning in his stomach. It was his body's usual response to stress, frustration, and/or anger—all of which he was starting to feel in spades.

"Thirty-nine only seems old when you're twenty-four."

"I'll be twenty-five next month—and thirty-nine still sounds old. Drinks milk, doesn't give hickeys—old."

Will turned and padded into the living room without a word.

"In case you missed it, the door's the other way." Molly stood in the aperture watching him.

"I'm getting my shoes. And my coat. And my tie. So I can leave." Will picked up the items as he spoke. Shoes in hand, coat and tie over his arm, he turned to face her. Jay Leno was cracking jokes on TV. Except for the glow of the set, and the light spilling in from the kitchen, the living room was dark.

All that hilarity on the screen was too much. Will

turned the TV off with a semi-savage jab as he passed. Immediately he felt better.

Molly didn't move from the doorway as he padded up to her. With her blocking his path, he had to stop. Will was surprised to find that, in her high heels and with him in his stocking feet, her eyes were nearly on a level with his.

So was her mouth.

Will looked at that soft mouth with its parted, red-stained lips, and instantly he grew rock hard.

He wanted to put his mouth on hers so badly that he was afraid she might be able to read it in his eyes. He lowered them, but that didn't help. Instead it brought into focus the bruise on her throat, the one that had been made by another man.

"I don't want you going out on any more dates until this is over," he said abruptly, hoping his voice didn't sound as thick as he feared. "We're supposed to have a romance going here, remember?"

"You can't stop me from dating." Her voice was a cool challenge—and she still hadn't moved out of his way.

Will's lids lifted. "Can't I?" he asked.

Defiant, Molly shook her head.

A drift of perfume wafted under Will's nose. Her eyes dared him. Her body did too.

Will reminded himself that the long-legged, big-eyed creature before him was the human version of a Venus's-flytrap, with men cast as flies. He reminded himself that she had just spent half an hour making out in a car with another man, and sported the love bite to prove it. He reminded himself that he never mixed his personal and professional lives. He reminded himself that he was older, she worked for him, and she was trouble with a capital *T*.

"Would you mind stepping out of the way?" he requested politely.

Her lips compressed, her eyes narrowed, but she moved. Will walked into the kitchen, sat down on the edge of a bench, and put on his shoes. He could feel her watching his every move.

He stood up and shrugged into his coat, stuffing the tie into his pocket.

"Lock the door after me," he said, moving toward it.

"With pleasure," she answered with bite.

He opened the door, then glanced over his shoulder at her. "Tomorrow, I'd appreciate it if you would wear something a little more—conservative."

"You don't like this outfit?" The insolence was back in her voice.

Will shook his head. "It's too damned short and too damned tight," he answered, and walked on out into the blessedly cold night.

21

October 15, 1995

Molly changed in the 7-Eleven's rest room. Just to be perverse—and because her wardrobe truly was limited, though she could have borrowed something of Ashley's—she wore the same short black skirt she had worn the previous night. With sheer black panty hose and her black high heels, her legs looked a yard long.

She had seen Will eyeing her legs.

A white nylon blouse primly buttoned up to the neck and a hip-length, double-breasted black sweater jacket made the outfit demure enough for church. The blouse sported a delicate ruffle down the front. Pearls were in her ears.

Her hair was down, brushed carefully under at the ends and forward to hide the mark on her neck. Layers of coverstick and powder rendered the bruise all but invisible.

Molly had almost left it alone in a fit of defiance at Will, but the thought of sitting in church with a clearly visible hickey dissuaded her.

Her skirt would be enough, she thought. She didn't have to suffer public embarrassment to provoke Will.

Just why she wanted to provoke him Molly refused to examine too closely. She only knew she did, and the urge was all but irresistible.

Looking in the mirror, she flicked mascara on her lashes, powdered her nose, and smoothed deep rose lipstick on her mouth.

Sweet and innocent, she decided, examining her reflection. Except, of course, for the length of her skirt.

Molly grinned wickedly at herself, snapped her purse closed, then turned away from the mirror. She only hoped Will was already outside, waiting for her.

She meant to put everything she had into her walk across the parking lot to his car.

Outside in the car, two men saw Molly emerge from the rest room and glance around. In the driver's seat, Will took one look at the teensy skirt, at the long-stemmed legs in black stockings and high heels, and felt his blood pressure start to rise.

She was wearing that skirt because he had told her not to. Will knew it as well as he knew his own name.

She spotted the car and began walking toward it. Though the way she moved bore absolutely no relation to the way his own two feet carried him over the ground. There had to be another name for what she was doing besides walking. Sex on the hoof, maybe.

In the backseat, Murphy, obviously also watching her approach, let out a low whistle.

"I don't believe it. I'm getting a boner just from watching her walk."

Will froze as the comment hit him, feeling his blood pressure soar and his stomach burn. He slewed around in his seat.

"Shut up," he said, fixing Murphy with a deadly stare. "Just shut up."

"Sorry," Murphy said, taken aback. To Will's fury, after a few seconds the other man's eyes began to twinkle. Then he grinned.

Molly had reached the car by that time. With one last glare at Murphy, Will got out. Murphy followed suit.

Will walked around the hood to open the door for Molly. He was furious, at her, at Murphy, at himself, but he was determined not to show it.

As he came up to her Molly smiled at him, a smile so sweetly innocent that Will recognized it as pure mockery. He swung open her door, waging a fierce inner battle to keep from scowling, snapping, or doing anything else that would give her the satisfaction of knowing that she had gotten under his skin.

"This is John Murphy. He'll be going with us" was what he said, indicating his partner, who ogled Molly more or less discreetly across the Taurus's roof. "Murphy, Molly Ballard."

"Hi," Molly offered with a smile.

"Pleased to meet you, ma'am," Murphy replied. When Molly ducked into the car, Murphy's gaze shifted to Will. A wide, knowing grin split his face.

The memorial was short and—even to Molly, who had barely been acquainted with the deceased—the service was moving. There was no casket. The body had been cremated. The church was packed.

Molly knelt between Will and Murphy in a back pew, providing at Will's urging a whispered biography of everyone who was anyone in the Bluegrass. Nearly all the big horse farms were represented: besides

Cloverlot Stables, whose personnel had turned out in force to pay last respects to one of their own, there were contingents from Sweet Meadow Stud, Greenglow Stables, Wyland Farms, Rock Creek Stables, Oak Hill, Mobridge Stud, and Hillside Farm.

"Those are the Wylands," Molly whispered in response to a nudge from Will as a pew emptied to approach the altar for Communion. "The woman in the hat is Helen Wyland Trapp. Her daughter Neilie is behind her, and that's Helen's husband Walt Trapp with Neilie. You already know who Tyler is, and Thornton. The blonde with Thornton is Allison Weintraub. She and her mother—that's her mother with them—have been chasing Thornton for years."

"Jealous?" Will mouthed with a sideways glance.

"No." Molly didn't even dignify that with indignation. Because the church was so crowded, she knelt very close to Will, her shoulder brushing the sleeve of his dark blue suit. She wondered if her nearness was having any effect on him. She hoped it was. His proximity was certainly having an effect on her.

On her other side, she was barely aware of Murphy's pants leg touching her calf. He could have been a mannequin for all the notice her body took of him.

Unlike her, Will seemed right at home amidst the quiet, luxurious trappings of moneyed worship, Molly thought. His suit and tie were as elegant as any man's there. She was beginning to feel her own miniskirt might have been a mistake—except, of course, for the irritation it caused Will. The other women were all dressed in knee-length or longer suits or dresses, very conservative. Every time Molly glanced around, she was reminded that her blouse was nylon, not silk, and she'd bought the sweater-jacket two years ago at T.J. Maxx for $29.99.

The church was all mahogany paneling and stained glass and candles. A robed choir sang softly from behind the altar. Incense scented the air. Will's head was bowed, his face in profile both austere and ruggedly handsome. His skin looked very bronze against the pristine whiteness of his shirt; his close-cropped hair shone gold even in the subdued light. Molly caught herself tracing the outline of his features with her eyes, and dropped her gaze to her clasped hands.

Another nudge drew her attention to the next group to leave their pew.

"Those are the Colemans from Greenglow Stables. Remember we were talking about Libby Coleman, the little girl who disappeared?"

Will nodded.

"The white-haired woman in front is her mother Clarice. That's Clarice's daughter Donna Coleman Pierce behind her, with her husband, Ted Pierce. And Clarice's son Lincoln Coleman, with his wife, Diane. Behind them is Tim Harden, Greenglow's trainer, with his wife. And behind them is Jason Breen, Sweet Meadow Stud's trainer. Mr. and Mrs. Armitage, who own Sweet Meadow, are behind them."

Molly continued to identify anyone Will indicated, until it was time for their pew to join in. Will stood back to allow her to precede him up the aisle. With him and Murphy behind her she approached the altar, knelt, and was given Communion.

Will knelt beside her, with Murphy on his other side. Molly watched out of the corner of her eye as he took the wafer in his mouth. Kneeling beside Will in church felt so—so right, somehow, that it was unsettling. He was a good man, she thought, a decent man, kind and strong. The kind of man who took care of his own.

What she had to remember was that she was not his.

When they returned to their pew, she was careful to keep enough distance between them so that their bodies no longer touched.

The congregation prayed, the choir sang, and then the service was over.

Will drove her back to the 7-Eleven to change and pick up her car. Molly barely spoke. What she didn't notice was that Will barely spoke either.

"I can't get it out of my head that Lawrence's death was too convenient," Will said to Murphy after they had dropped Molly off.

"The coroner's report said suicide." In the passenger seat now, Murphy chewed on a thumbnail.

"I know what the coroner's report said."

"The body's been cremated. The coroner's report is all we have to go by."

Will said nothing, just stared out through the windshield thoughtfully. The day was gray and overcast, with the threat of rain in low-hanging clouds.

"Molly hasn't found a mismatch yet. Lawrence said their practice is to put ringers in claiming races a couple of times a week. If we're not finding any, then it's possible that somebody's tipped them off. Maybe somebody knows we're here, and they've decided to cease and desist until we give up."

"Do you really think they're on to us?" Murphy was frowning.

Will shook his head. "I don't know. It's possible. Maybe they found out Lawrence was talking to us, and they killed him to shut him up. The next logical step would be to keep the races clean while we're sniffing around. It's possible that we're not finding any ringers because there are no ringers to be found."

"It's also possible that Lawrence committed suicide, and we just haven't gotten lucky yet," Murphy pointed out reasonably.

"Yeah, that's possible too."

Both of them were quiet for a minute, thinking. Murphy glanced at Will.

"You ever considered that Molly might be playing a double game?"

"What?" Will threw him a startled glance.

"Maybe she's tipped them off to what we're doing. After all, not many people know we're here. Just the guys in Chicago, you, me, and her."

"Molly didn't tip them off," Will said, cold and sure.

"Look, I know it's hard to see past the fact that she's a beautiful girl, and I know there's some kind of personal thing going on between you two, but you shouldn't dismiss the possibility out of hand."

"I don't have any kind of 'personal thing' going on with Molly." Will's voice was sharp.

Murphy shrugged. "None of my business if you do. Not that I blame you. Believe me, if I were single and in your shoes, I'd be balling her brains out."

"Listen, Murphy," Will said through his teeth. "I am not sleeping with Molly. She's not much more than a kid—twenty-four years old. She's our informant. I feel sorry for her, okay? She's had a tough row to hoe in life. But I am not, I repeat, *not*, balling her brains out."

"Strictly your business," Murphy said with a shrug.

Left with nothing to say for fear of protesting too

much, Will contemplated wrapping his hands around Murphy's neck and squeezing until the idiot's face turned purple. His brain unwillingly grappled with the scenario Murphy suggested: Could Molly be double-crossing him?

"Wait. Lawrence kicked off the first time I talked to Molly, *while I was with her*," Will said triumphantly, remembering. "That lets her out. She didn't have time to tip off anybody."

"That's right," Murphy said, chewing on his thumbnail again. "So what do you think we should do next?"

Molly wasn't sure, but she thought it was around midnight, or maybe a little later. She lay awake in her bed, flopped on her back in frustration, arms flung above her head. Rain blew against her window. With a low cloud cover obscuring the moon and stars, the night outside was very dark. It was dark in her room too.

For one of the few times in her life, sleep eluded her. It was maddening, because she was dead tired, but her body just couldn't seem to relax.

At least tomorrow was Monday, and she didn't have to work. She could sleep late, if she liked.

Tomorrow was the day Mike talked to the deputies.

That was probably why she couldn't sleep. She was worried about Mike.

Her body was restless. Flopping over on her stomach, Molly punched the pillow into submission and closed her eyes, hoping by sheer force of mind over matter to make herself sleep.

Will's face materialized on the screen of her closed

lids. Molly imagined him stretching out in bed beside her, his hands running over her body . . .

Her eyes popped open again, and she gritted her teeth. She refused, absolutely refused, to have sexual fantasies about Will.

He hadn't come by tonight, though she'd seen him briefly at Keeneland just after the second race. With a shake of her head she had told him what he had seemed to already know—none of the horses she'd checked had a problem with its tattoo—and he had vanished into the crowd. She hadn't seen him since.

Maybe he was mad at her about the skirt.

Or the hickey.

This is ridiculous, Molly thought, and sat up. Swinging her legs over the side of the bed, she switched on the bedside lamp. Dressed in one of the oversized T-shirts she favored for sleeping, her hair a tangled mess around her face, she headed for the bathroom. The floor was cold beneath her bare feet. The ancient furnace groaned fitfully as it struggled to put out heat.

She was just coming out of the bathroom when she heard it: the shrill, whinnying scream of a horse in mortal fear, or pain.

22

October 16, 1995

Outside in the cold, drizzly night, a hand holding a knife rose and fell, the action frenzied, frantic with hatred and need. The razor-sharp blade sliced through hair and hide and sinew, unleashing rivers of blood so warm, they gave off little puffs of steam in the air. The mare stirred, moaning. The hand sheathed the knife and snatched up a broom handle. Plunging it, deep and hard, into the animal brought ecstasy, and release.

Down the hill, lights came on in the house.

The mare screamed once, twice, fighting to get to her feet. The owner of the hand watched the animal's struggles with exquisite pleasure. The creature was his, all his. It was under his control. He could cause it pain, or have pity. He could let it live—or die. To the mare, in that moment, he was God.

Someone stepped out onto the porch of the house, looking up toward the field, straining to see through the darkness.

The hand shook, and was still.

Still the mare screamed.

The figure on the porch came down the steps, running toward the field. For a moment the knife wielder watched almost hungrily. Was it time . . . ?

No, not yet, he decided. Turning away, he melted into the cold darkness of the night.

23

Will thought he had never driven so fast in his life. As his car skidded to a stop behind a convoy of police vehicles in Molly's driveway, he could see lights and activity on the hill behind the house. Flinging himself out of the car, not even feeling the icy drizzle that stung his face, he bounded up the slope, stopping only when he reached the black board fence. Pork Chop was there, ears pricked forward as he stared through the space between the boards. The dog greeted Will with a brief wag of his tail. Will followed his gaze. Flashlights and the headlights of a black Jeep Cherokee illuminated the scene in the field.

A horse lay on the ground, its legs thrashing feebly, its head in Molly's lap. She bent over the animal, cradling it, stroking its mane, protecting it as well as she could from the weather. Even from where Will stood he grasped the tragedy in her posture, the sense of horror in the air.

"What the hell?" he breathed, and vaulted the fence the way he might have done when he'd run track and field at age nineteen.

A bevy of people stood in a semicircle around the horse—Tyler and Thornton Wyland and Helen Trapp, and a half-dozen or so cops, two of them state boys. J.D. Hatfield was hunkered down beside Molly, directing the beam of a powerful flashlight along the Thoroughbred's massive body. The Ballards, coats thrown over their nightclothes, huddled behind Molly. Ashley held a battered umbrella over her sister's bent head, while Mike, of course, cradled the shotgun and the twins clung together. A thin old man in a pricey overcoat crouched by the horse's side, getting ready to plunge a filled syringe into the sleek, dark neck. Will noticed that the animal's hindquarters rested in an oily-looking puddle. Then as he almost stepped in it he realized the puddle was blood.

"Will." Ashley spotted him first. There was utter relief in the way she said his name. Ashley had called him, reaching him on his cellular phone as he'd been conducting a clandestine search of Howard Lawrence's office. Though she had been too upset to make much sense, what Will had gleaned from the conversation had brought him running: There'd been an accident, and Molly was in desperate need of him.

He wouldn't be surprised to learn he'd broken land speed records getting over here. It was a relief to discover that the casualty was not Molly, or one of the kids, but a horse.

Disregarding the sudden battery of eyes on him, Will crouched beside Molly. She was kneeling in the wet grass with her legs tucked beneath her, seemingly oblivious to everything but the trembling creature she was comforting. Even Will, who had absolutely no knowledge of horses, could recognize the flashing panic in the animal's rolling eyes. Red-flecked white foam covered its muzzle. There was a pungent smell in the air; he realized that it was a combination of blood and the terrified horse's sweat.

"Molly."

Her skin was freezing to the touch, and wet. Will saw that she was wearing some kind of loose short-sleeved T-shirt and that was all. Her legs from the knees down and even her feet were bare. The T-shirt was wet, too, Will discovered as he touched it. So was her hair.

Ashley must have been late with the umbrella.

"Molly."

She didn't move, didn't respond in any way. Will cursed under his breath, and stood up to shed the trench coat he was wearing over his suit. He wrapped the coat around Molly's shoulders, and once again said her name, with no result.

J.D., the closest person to him, glared at him over Molly's bent head. Molly didn't even look up.

"That'll take care of the pain," the vet said as he withdrew the syringe and got laboriously to his feet. "Where in the heck is that ambulance?"

"May God damn that pervert to hell!" Helen Trapp's voice shook. She was in her mid-forties, perhaps, with short, frosted hair and a weatherbeaten face. Dressed in Wellingtons and a hooded raincoat buttoned up over what appeared to be a nightgown, she huddled between her brother and nephew. Both Tyler and Thornton Wyland were fully if haphazardly dressed. J.D., who was clearly put out by Will's presence, was wearing the Stetson, boots, and duster coat he'd had on when Will had first made his acquaintance. Whether his jeans and shirt were the same, Will had no way of knowing.

The horse's legs moved convulsively. Molly talked to it, patted it. Listening to her broken murmurs wrung Will's heart.

"Can't somebody else do this?" he said to the Wylands, to Helen Trapp, to the vet, to the cops. "She doesn't need to do this. She's upset."

The only assent—a wordless grunt—came from J.D.

"The mare knows her," the vet replied. "We need to keep her calm until the sedative takes effect. It won't be long now."

The vet, like Helen Trapp and the Wylands, was clearly more concerned about the horse than about Molly. Will gritted his teeth and looked across Molly at J.D. Unlikely or not, he and the cowboy wanna-be seemed to be allies.

"She'll be all right," J.D. said. Will knew he was referring to Molly, not the horse.

"What happened?" Will's voice was grim. His every instinct shouted for him to stand up, flash his ID, and take charge, but the exigencies of the investigation he was already conducting stopped him. Secrecy was all-important to his success. Without it, he might as well head on back to Chicago.

"It's the horse slasher." J.D. shook his head. "Stabbed the mare's hindquarters a bunch of times. The maniac shoved a broom handle up her—up her—*you know*—too."

"Horse slasher?" It sounded ridiculous to Will.

"Could I get your name, sir?" A Kentucky State Police officer stood looking down at him, a pad and pencil in his hand.

"It's all right, he's Molly's boyfriend," J.D. said morosely with a glance up at the trooper.

"Molly?" The trooper nodded at Molly with raised eyebrows as Will stood up.

"Molly Ballard. I'm Will Lyman," Will said, and obligingly spelled it as the trooper wrote down names. "What's this about a horse slasher?"

"This is the sixth Thoroughbred attack in this area in four months. All mares, all assaulted in the hindquarters."

"Here comes the ambulance." J.D. got up as a white van about the size of a small U-Haul bumped across the field toward them, its headlights cutting twin swathes through the night.

Ignoring the rain that was wetting his hair and face and starting to seep through his suit coat, Will looked down at the girl huddled at his feet. Molly was still folded over the horse, stroking it, talking to it, but the horse was unmoving.

"Does it look to you like the sedative has taken effect?" he asked the vet. He strove to keep his voice at least minimally polite.

The vet glanced down at the horse. "Looks like it."

"Then we're out of here." Will crouched beside Molly again, wrapped an arm around her shoulders and spoke almost in her ear. "The ambulance is here. There are plenty of people to take care of the horse now. It's time to go inside."

When she didn't respond, Will began to feel the first faint stirring of alarm. He reached over and smoothed the wet, curling dark hair back away from her face. The curve of her cheek was paper white.

"Molly," he said, and touched her cheek. She felt as cold as a corpse. "Molly."

She looked at him then, and he saw that she was

crying. Her eyes were huge and wild; her mouth shook; her cheeks glistened with tears and rain.

"Will?" Her voice was high-pitched, tiny. "You've got to find out who did this. You *can*, can't you? After all, you're . . ."

She was in such emotional distress that she didn't know what she was saying, Will realized. To stop her before she blurted out anything she shouldn't, he leaned over and pressed his mouth to hers. It was more on the order of clapping a hand over her mouth than a kiss, but in an instant that changed. Her lips trembled and parted beneath his, and her arms wrapped around his neck as if she never meant to let him go.

Her mouth was warm and soft, and incredibly sweet. Her tears tasted salty on his tongue.

His body responded instantly. His mind reeled. His heart raced.

Shit, Will thought, but it was too late to turn back. With that kiss the Venus's-flytrap claimed another victim. The proverbial line he had drawn in the sand of their relationship was crossed. Everything changed. He felt protective, possessive, wildly territorial. Simply, the girl was now his for real.

He scooped her into his arms, trench coat and all, and stood up with her. Freeing his mouth, he kissed her cheek, whispered "hush" in her ear, and pressed her face into his shoulder.

Looking behind him, Will located the remaining Ballards, all of whom were watching him with their sister, wide-eyed.

"Back to the house," he said with a jerk of his head toward it. There was no doubt that it was an order. They didn't question him, not even Mike, but obediently began to move. Will walked toward the fence with Molly in his arms. The kids were already swarming over it.

Molly was crying. Will could feel the hot dampness of her tears as her face burrowed against his neck. Deep sobs racked her body. She drew in air in great broken gasps.

"Just a minute, sir. I need her statement." The trooper who had taken their names trailed Will to the fence.

Will stopped and turned to the man. "You'll have to get it tomorrow. She's in no shape to give a statement tonight," he said grimly. After a single glance at Molly the trooper nodded.

Will remembered the fence. "Hold her a minute, would you?" he asked the trooper, and passed Molly over without waiting for an answer.

Even as the trooper took her weight Molly murmured a protest, clung tighter to Will's neck.

"Just for a minute. Just till I get over the fence," he said in her ear.

She let go. The trooper held her awkwardly, ill at ease with a trembling, sobbing, tear-drenched woman, and looked relieved when Will reached across the fence to reclaim his burden.

"Thanks," he said to the trooper as Molly wrapped her arms around his neck, and he started down the hill.

Inside the house, Ashley had taken charge of her siblings, supervising their change into dry garments and handing out towels for their hair. She looked up in concern as Will walked in with Molly in his arms, kicking the door shut behind him because he didn't have a free hand to close it. Darting inside just ahead of the closing door, Pork Chop shook himself, sending drops of moisture flying everywhere. The kids all dodged; Mike cursed.

"Do you have coffee?" Will asked, heading for the living room. When Ashley nodded he said, "Fix some. Strong, with lots of sugar. And bring me some towels and a blanket, would you please, and something dry she can wear."

By juggling Molly from one arm to the other, Will managed both to shed his wet suit coat and switch on the lamp by the couch without putting his weeping burden down. Then he sank into the Naugahyde armchair with her on his lap, and turned his attention to stopping her tears. She kept her face pressed to his shoulder so he couldn't see her face; her arms hugged his neck. He kissed her averted cheek, then her ear, murmured to her, brushed her wet hair away from her face with his fingers. Still she sobbed and shook. Her feet were left bare by the wrapped folds of his coat, he saw, and reached for them, trying to warm her toes with his hand. They were long, delicately made feet, cold as blocks of ice.

Susan and Sam peeked through the living room doorway. Hair tousled from being towel-dried, wearing dry pajamas (in Sam's case) and a gown (in Susan's), they took one look at their usually all-powerful sister crying like a child in Will's arms and seemed to shrink. Spying them, Will lifted his head. His hands stilled in Molly's hair.

"Is Molly all right?" Susan asked in a small voice, coming over to the side of the chair.

Will was beginning to wonder that himself. He wasn't surprised that the thing with the horse had upset her, but her reaction seemed extreme. Molly must have realized Susan was there, that she was frightening the girl by weeping so, because suddenly her sobs were no longer as shattering. Instead her shaking increased, until she was shuddering in his arms. Her face pressed hard against his shoulder as if she was trying to stifle her anguish the only way she could.

"She's a little upset, but she'll be fine," Will said with false heartiness just as Ashley entered carrying towels, a quilt, and a pink cotton T-shirt with a bunny and some writing on it. Ashley's hair stood out around her face in a frizzy cloud. Her glasses were sliding down her nose, and she wore a blue chenille robe over what looked like the T-shirt's twin.

"Molly, I brought you a dry sleepshirt," Ashley said louder than was normal, looking down in dismay at her sister.

Molly burrowed closer. Will realized that she was ashamed for her siblings to see her cry, and that nothing short of brute force was going to get her out of his arms at the moment. He shook his head at Ashley.

"Leave it on the table. She'll get to it in a minute. Dry her feet, and tuck the quilt around them. And give me the other towel for her hair."

Ashley did as she was told. Will rubbed as much moisture from the dark curls as he could. Ashley took the damp towel from him, then patted her sister's shoulder through the stiff twill of Will's trench coat. Molly's sobs had quieted down even more, but Will could feel the violent tremors that racked her body and knew that she was making a supreme effort not to frighten her siblings any more than she already had.

Looking down at her sister, Ashley's eyes filled with tears.

"Good God," Will said, exasperated. "Don't you start."

Ashley sniffed, but shook her head.

Sam and Mike, who was wearing only a pair of jeans and the ubiquitous earring, ventured into the room. Will assumed that Mike slept in his underwear, and the jeans would be shed once the kid was upstairs.

He felt uncomfortable cuddling Molly on his lap before such a young and observant audience. His hands dropped to link loosely at her back. She lay curled against his chest, trembling so much that he kept expecting to hear her teeth chatter. Despite the fact that her sobs had dwindled to occasional hiccuping gasps, she was crying still. He could feel the wet spill of her tears against his neck.

"It was the blood," Mike said, eyes solemn as he looked from Molly to Will. "Molly can't stand the sight of blood."

"Hush, Mike," Ashley said sharply.

"If she's going to cry all over him, you ought to tell him why. He'll think she's some kind of nut case."

"She won't want us to tell."

"Tell me what?" Will looked from Mike to Ashley.

"Susan and Sam, go to bed," Ashley ordered.

"Do we have to?" Sam whined.

"Yes," Will said, in a tone that brooked no argument. That seemed to clinch it. The twins left the room with only a below-the-breath mutter or two.

"So tell me," Will said.

Ashley and Mike exchanged glances. Ashley shook her head.

"Our mom committed suicide four years ago. She got in the bathtub at her boyfriend's apartment in Lexington and slit her wrists. Molly found her. Since then, the sight of blood flips Molly out. And tonight there was a lot of blood up there," Mike said.

Ashley scowled at him.

"Jesus." Will winced at the horror of it. Molly shuddered. Will could feel her mouth shaking against his neck. But she didn't make a sound. Will suddenly, fiercely admired her for that.

She needed comforting, but he needed to be alone with her to do it. No way could he so much as whisper in her ear under the interested eyes of a fourteen-year-old boy and a seventeen-year-old girl.

24

"Mike, I appreciate you telling me. Now go to bed," Will said. Mike looked at him, affronted. For a moment Will thought the kid's natural rebelliousness was going to assert itself and he would refuse. But Mike surprised him by merely pursing his lips in a thoughtful way before leaving the room.

"Did you make coffee?" Will said to Ashley.

"I'll get it," Ashley said, and hurried out, taking the damp towels with her. Will shifted Molly into a more comfortable position on his lap and pressed his mouth to her thick mass of damp hair, and then Ashley was back. She carried an earthenware mug filled almost to the brim with steaming coffee.

"I put three spoonfuls of sugar in," she said, setting the cup down on the table within reach of his hand.

"Good."

"Now you want me to go to bed," she guessed.

"Yeah."

"Okay. Good night."

"Good night."

"Will?"

"Hmm?"

"Take care of Molly."

"Good night, Ashley." His voice was dry.

" 'Night. 'Night, Molly."

Ashley left. Seconds later the kitchen light went out. Will could hear Ashley climbing the stairs.

Will slid his hand beneath the thick fall of Molly's hair to the back of her neck, stroking the velvety nape. They were alone in a pool of soft light. He looked thoughtfully at the tangled mass of coffee-brown waves that were snuggled against him, at the slender shoulders almost buried by the bulk of his coat. She wasn't heavy. Will realized that she felt as if she belonged on his lap, and realized, too, that he was in serious trouble.

At the moment he didn't much care.

"Molly."

No response. He couldn't see her face. Will brushed the hair away from her ear—the only part of her his lips could reach—and kissed it.

"Hey," he said. "You're scaring me."

She drew in her breath in a kind of hiccuping gasp, then turned her head so that her cheek was pillowed on his shoulder. Her hold on him loosened. Instead of strangling him, her arms slid down to drape tiredly over his chest. She didn't open her eyes, but at least now he could see her face. She was weeping still, her tears silent and seemingly endless. Her body trembled in his hold.

"Molly." He pushed the hair back from her face, brushed gently at the flowing tears with a forefinger. "I want you to sit up and drink some coffee. Can you do that for me, please?"

When she didn't respond, he slid his lips over her

wet cheek, touched them to the corner of her mouth. Her lips quivered, then turned, seeking his. Will kissed her mouth, careful to be tender, surprised that he succeeded so well. For quite a while now he hadn't been able to so much as think about her without an accompanying surge of hard, hungry desire. Tonight he found that taking care of her took precedence.

He freed his mouth before the kiss could heat up to the point where it was out of control, then took a deep breath to clear his head.

Her eyes were still closed, her head still rested on his shoulder, but one of her hands had crept up to curl around his neck.

Also, her face had a little more color to it, he decided. He fought the urge to kiss her again.

"If you don't do what I tell you, I'm going to put you in the car and drive you to the hospital," he threatened. "They'll treat you for shock. Do you want me to do that?"

He interpreted the small movement of her head as a negative answer.

"Then sit up and take a drink of coffee." He employed the same stern, brook-no-disobedience voice he had used on her siblings.

Molly shivered, and her eyes opened. Then she pushed away from his chest and sat up, pulling his coat more closely about her. She didn't look at him, but kept her eyes downcast. Will wondered if she was embarrassed, or just shy.

At the thought of Molly being shy he almost smiled. Brazen, maybe; feisty, definitely. Shy, no.

"Here." Will handed her the cup of coffee, and watched while she drank. Her hands were unsteady, but, though he was ready to help her, she managed without spilling any.

Her hair must have a natural tendency to curl, he decided, because, damp, it formed a tumultuous halo of near-black waves around her face and shoulders. Her lashes were dense and long and darker than her hair, and still wet with tears. Her brows were thick, with only the faintest suggestion of an arch. Her nose was fine and straight, her lips soft and eminently kissable. Her chin and cheekbones were perfectly sculpted and delicately carved. The creamy smoothness of her skin was marred only by the silvery tracks of tears. Lost in the folds of his coat, she looked like a fragile, slightly bedraggled version of a Pre-Raphaelite angel. The quilt had fallen away from her legs and feet. With her legs draped over his, her feet did not quite touch the floor.

"I'm cold," she said in a small voice, still without looking at him, and shivered.

Will remembered the wet nightshirt and took the half-empty coffee cup out of her hands.

"We'll fix that," he said, striving for a light tone.

Gathering her up in his arms again, he got to his feet, picking up the nightshirt Ashley had left on the table as well.

"You don't have to carry me. I can walk." Despite her low-voiced protest, Molly curled in his arms as if there were nowhere else on earth she would rather be.

Will looked down into her tear-washed brown eyes as he headed for the kitchen. "Just shut up and let somebody take care of you for a change, okay?"

He thought Molly fought against it for another instant, but then she surrendered with a tired sigh and rested her head against his chest. Her eyes closed and her breathing slowed. Intermittent tremors shook her as Will carried her through the kitchen into the bathroom, turning on lights as he went.

He hoped her shivers were from the cold.

Once in the bathroom, he assessed the facilities with a glance. The tub was ancient, one of the original claw-foot variety with the rubber stopper in the bottom to keep the water in. The shower attachment had obviously been rigged up more recently. It consisted of a thin brass pipe extending halfway up the green-tiled wall with a showerhead tilting down over the tub. An oval-shaped metal rod suspended from the ceiling supported a plain white shower curtain.

Hanging on to Molly as best he could, Will leaned over and managed to fit the plug into the drain. He turned on the taps. Water spurted into the tub. Will tested the temperature, waited a minute, then pulled his trench coat away from Molly's body, dropped it and the dry nightshirt on the closed toilet lid, and lowered her into the tub.

He thought, briefly, about stripping the soaked white T-shirt with its incongruously cheerful picture of Mickey Mouse over her head, but the garment was already so wet, it couldn't get any wetter. And at the moment, under the circumstances, stripping her didn't seem quite the thing to do.

Her eyes opened as she turned loose of his neck. Huge and dark and lost-looking, they rested on his face. The pain in them hurt him as well. Crouched by the tub, Will caught her hand, pressed the icy fingers to his cheek, kissed her palm.

"It was Sheila," Molly said, closing her eyes. Her head rested tiredly back against the lip of the tub. Her hair spilled behind it, almost reaching the floor. "It was Sheila."

The words made no sense to Will. He kissed her palm again.

"It's all right," he said. "Everything's all right."

Tears spilled from beneath her lashes. She shook her head. Then she pulled her hand from his hold and opened her eyes again.

"I can manage now," she said steadily. "Thanks."

Will realized he was being dismissed. He looked at her, hesitated, and stood up.

"You sure?"

"Yes."

"Call me if you need anything," he said, and left the bathroom, pulling the door shut behind him.

25

When Molly finally got up the nerve to emerge from the bathroom, Will was leaning against the kitchen counter drinking a glass of milk. He was wearing black sweat pants and a white short-sleeved T-shirt that said NIKE on the front. White sweat socks were on his feet. He met her gaze over the rim of his glass, his eyes moving swiftly from her scrubbed-clean face to her bare feet and back. She had brushed her hair and teeth and splashed cold water on her face until her skin felt tight, but still her eyes were red around the rims and swollen. Not that there was anything she could do about that, or about her nightshirt, which sported a sleepy-eyed bunny in curlers with the motto *I don't do mornings!*

"Milk again?" she questioned, wrinkling her nose at him. Embarrassment had kept her in the bathroom long after she had both finished bathing and recovered her composure. What was she supposed to say to a man she had just kissed and cried all over and who had just learned one of the most painful secrets of her life?

Especially a man to whom she was wildly, crazily

attracted. A man who, before tonight, had seemed determined to keep her at arm's length.

A man there was no future in loving, even if she were stupid enough to fall hard.

"Milk again?" was the best she could do.

"I have an ulcer," he said easily. "The doctor who diagnosed it said I don't handle stress well."

He took another swallow of milk, watching her over the rim of the glass. Molly realized that he had made her a present of the information as sort of a trade-off for what he now knew about her.

"Where'd you get the clothes?" She walked into the kitchen carrying his raincoat, which she placed over the back of a chair. Then she headed for the coffeepot, careful not to get too near Will. Things had gone too far between them already for one night. She felt as if she were standing on the edge of a precipice where he was concerned. One more misstep and she would fall over.

"I keep a gym bag in the trunk of the car. In case I should get a chance to get some exercise."

He must get that chance fairly often, Molly thought with a sideways glance at him. He looked even better in sweats than he did in his expensive suits. His was the strong, toned body of an athlete. His shoulders were broad, his arms solid with muscle, his waist and hips narrow, his stomach washboard flat. His legs were long and powerful-looking. Even his neck looked strong.

"Do you lift weights?" she asked, turning to face him. She used the filled coffee cup she held as a kind of barrier between them, raising it to her lips. A jolt of caffeine was what she needed, she thought, sipping. Maybe it would shock her back to reality.

"Sure. Where do you think I found the strength to cart you around all night?" He grinned at her, a boyish grin, and Molly realized he was teasing.

"I don't weigh all that much." A smile trembled on her lips. It felt good, and Molly was grateful that he had provoked it. It helped push the hideous events of the night farther away, toward the black canyon where all her painful memories were buried.

"You don't, do you?" He finished his milk and moved to the sink. Molly watched as he rinsed his glass before setting it down.

He must have caught the surprise in her look as he turned around.

"Hey, I can wash dishes with the best of them. You'll have to try me out."

She would love to, Molly thought. But he would be going back to Chicago soon, so she wasn't likely to get the chance.

"You don't believe me?"

He seemed able to read her expressions without any trouble at all.

"I'll take your word for it."

"So where'd the smile go?"

"I guess I'm tired," she said, setting her coffee cup on the counter behind her. She would rinse the cup out later, when he was not standing in front of the sink. Her emotions were too close to the surface tonight. Putting them out in the open where they could get trampled did not seem like a smart idea.

"You ought to go to bed." He was watching her steadily. Molly hoped her cheeks didn't turn pink. Going to bed sounded wonderful, but only if he joined her—which she did not want him to do, not really. At least that's what she told herself.

Sleeping with him when he was only a temporary visitor to her life would rank right up there as one of the stupidest things she had ever done.

"Are you leaving?" she asked, hoping she merely sounded polite.

He shook his head. "Under the circumstances, I'm going to sack out on your couch for what's left of the night. I'll have someone out here first thing tomorrow to install a security system for you. Until then you're stuck with me."

"A security system? Do you really think we need one?"

Will looked at her without replying for a moment, his expression unreadable. "No, not really. But the other night Susan thought she saw someone at the window. J.D. said someone was spooking the horses. And tonight—well, tonight. I can't be here all the time, and I can't do my job if I'm worried about you and your brothers and sisters. So you're getting a security system."

"Security systems are expensive. We can't afford it."

"The government protects its informants."

"The government must have pretty deep pockets."

"It does."

"What if I told you I don't want you sleeping on my couch?"

Will's eyebrows rose. "Are you by any chance making me a more interesting offer?" A smile tugged at one corner of his mouth. He was teasing again—wasn't he?

"No." Molly couldn't help it. She couldn't seem to locate her own sense of humor. Her eyes slid away from his.

"Too bad." He *was* teasing.

"I'll fix the couch." Glad of something to do, Molly hurriedly left the kitchen. The spare bedding was kept in a cubbyhole of a closet under the stairs. When she returned with it in her arms, the kitchen light was off and he was sitting in the chair in the living room, thumbing through one of Mike's car magazines.

He glanced up and saw her in the doorway.

"Just dump the stuff on the couch and I'll spread it out when I'm ready," he said.

Molly shook her head. "I'll do it."

She crossed the room, put the little pile of bedclothes on the table beside him, and started to shake out a sheet.

Will stood up without warning. The action so startled Molly that she whirled, dropping the sheet. He was close. Too close. She took a step backward instinctively.

"Go to bed, Molly," he said. There was a wry expression on his face as he looked at her. He was handsome and sexy and strong, Molly thought, and exactly what she would ask for for her upcoming birthday if there was a God in heaven who saw to such things.

"I will when I'm done with the couch," she said, retrieving the sheet. Falling for Will was the last thing she ought to do, she told herself. It was a mistake and she knew it. She could turn back from the edge, now, and at least try to save herself a bushelful of grief. Instead she took a deep breath, and stepped out into space. "By the way, thank you for—taking care of things earlier. For taking care of *me.*"

"You're welcome." He was still on his feet, watching her. Though she didn't look at him, Molly could feel the weight of his gaze.

"Do you usually kiss your informants?" she asked, shaking out the sheet.

"What?"

"You heard me."

"No, I don't usually kiss my informants. But then, I've never had one who looked like you before—or one who wrapped her arms around my neck and cried her eyes out on my shoulder, either."

"I see." Molly smoothed the sheet over the cushions and tucked it in at the corners. Then she reached for the top sheet, still without looking directly at him.

"You kissed me back," Will said.

"I know I did." She unfolded the sheet.

"Care to tell me why?"

Molly shrugged, shaking the sheet out. "Hey, you said yourself you're the boss. Maybe I thought kissing you was part of the deal."

"Molly." There was a note somewhere between amusement and irritation in his voice as he took the sheet out of her hands. "Forget the damned couch."

Will turned her around to face him, his hands on her arms just above her elbows. Molly looked up at him to find that he was frowning as he studied her expression. His eyes were intent and very blue as they met her gaze.

"I want to make this clear: You don't have to do this if you don't want to," he said. "It's not part of the deal."

"Do what?" He was making her nervous, wonderfully, deliciously nervous, in a way she couldn't ever remember being made nervous by a man. Usually men were the supplicants, and she was the grantor, or not, of her favors as she chose. Always she had the upper hand. But with Will—Molly was very much afraid that in this case, *he* might have the upper hand. The scariest part of it all was, she kind of liked the idea.

"Sleep with me," Will said.

To hear him put it so baldly made Molly's senses reel.

Mere inches separated them now. Suddenly she savored the freedom from pretense his words offered, savored the freedom to touch him if she wished. Her hands found his chest, flattened against the hard muscles beneath the cotton T-shirt, taking pleasure in the feel of him. Molly discovered that, with him in his stocking feet and her barefoot, he was quite a bit taller than she was after all.

"Sleeping with you isn't part of the deal?" she questioned carefully. Her hands moved up his chest. His eyes flared in response, and his grip on her elbows tightened. The solid warmth of him beneath her palms was intoxicating. His head, which had been dipping toward her, lifted at her question. His eyes narrowed and he shook his head.

"Too bad," Molly said with regret and a Mona Lisa smile, her hands sliding up over his broad shoulders to link behind his neck. "And to think I had my sexual harassment suit all planned."

Will laughed, and while he was laughing she rose up on tiptoe and kissed his mouth.

It was a practiced kiss, soft, provocative. She slanted her lips over his and slid her tongue inside his mouth and did her level best to knock his socks off. His body was hard as a board, Molly discovered as she plastered herself against it, and the arms that came around her were strong enough to break her in half with ease. She loved his hardness, and his strength.

For that first moment she was the aggressor. Then

he was kissing *her*, short-circuiting her effort to assume control, his mouth experienced, sure. He shifted her so that her head was cushioned against his shoulder; one hand came up to mold her jaw, stroke her throat. Molly felt a spurt of surprise as the balance of power shifted, followed by an electric thrill. Her single conscious thought as his tongue explored her mouth was that the man certainly knew his way around women. She realized with a delightful little shiver that it was she who was in danger of getting her socks knocked off.

If she'd been wearing any socks, that is.

It was a while before Will lifted his head. Then he looked down at her, cupping her face in his hands.

"You're beautiful," he said, his voice husky.

"You're not bad yourself," she whispered, and reached up to press a string of kisses to the hard line of his jaw. Blond men did get five o'clock shadow, she discovered, and ran her tongue along the sandpapery ledge. Beneath her fingers she could feel his shoulders tighten. One hand slid down her back, smoothed the curve of her spine, and splayed over her bottom, pulling her tight against the hard bulge in his pants.

Then he kissed her again.

Molly wrapped her arms around his neck and pressed her body against his, reveling in the strength of his muscles, in his masculinity, in the evidence of his desire. He squeezed her bottom, kneaded it, caressed the soft curves through her nightshirt. Bunching the pink cotton in his hand, he pulled the garment inexorably upward. Molly tingled with anticipation, and caught fire waiting for the touch of his hand on her bare skin.

She wanted his hands on her flesh with an intensity that made her knees quiver.

His hand slid under her nightshirt at last, flattening over her bottom and lifting her upward so that her pelvis was crushed against him. His hand was hard, and warm, and masterful, and Molly's bones felt as if they were melting in response. She was left in no doubt whatsoever about who was in charge of their lovemaking: Will.

His other palm covered her breast. His thumb found her nipple through her sleepshirt, teasing the nub that was already pebble-hard. Fireworks went off against the screen of her closed lids.

Molly fought against succumbing to a spiraling passion that was nearly overwhelming. He was on the verge of reducing her to a supplicant in his arms, and that she couldn't stand. What she needed for her own self-respect was to turn the tables, to work her wiles on him.

Molly's hands slid down, found the edge of his T-shirt and wormed inside, then moved up, over the smooth, warm skin of his back.

"Molly, I—oh." Susan appeared in the doorway, blinking sleep from her eyes. Will and Molly jumped about a foot apart. Will yanked down his shirt. Molly's nightshirt dropped into place on its own.

"Oh, hi, Will. Are you still here?" Susan asked, yawning.

"He's spending the night—on the couch. To make sure we're safe," Molly said, flustered, and to her horror felt herself start to blush. Will, too, she saw, looked less than his usual cool, controlled self. A tinge of red stained his cheekbones. He ran a hand through his hair.

"Kind of like a bodyguard?" Susan asked, looking from one to the other of them.

"Like that," Molly agreed, and Will nodded.

"Then I don't have to be afraid anymore." Susan sounded relieved. "That's good, 'cause I'm really sleepy. Are you all right now, Molly?"

"I'm fine, Susie Q."

"I knew Will would make you feel better," Susan said with satisfaction, then turned and padded toward the bathroom. The kitchen light came on. After a moment during which Molly didn't dare glance at Will, the kitchen light was switched off again and Susan was back.

"I'm going back to bed," she announced in passing, heading for the stairs. "G'night."

"'Night, Susie Q."

"Good night, Susan."

Molly listened to her footsteps ascending. Then she crossed her arms over her chest and glanced at Will. He stood about three feet away, his hair ruffled, his expression rueful.

"Sorry about that," she said.

"Not your fault." He reached out, hooked her elbow, pulled her close.

More footsteps on the stairs. By the time a quilt-wrapped Mike trekked past the doorway on his way to the bathroom, Will and Molly were no longer touching. Mike did his business and headed upstairs again, all with no more than a cursory glance at the pair in the living room.

Molly looked at Will.

"This isn't the time or place, you know," she said softly.

Will rubbed his hands over his face. "I'm beginning to realize that."

"I don't think it's a good idea to—do anything—with the kids around."

"I agree."

"I think I really will go to bed now."

"Good idea."

"The couch . . ."

"Would you please quit worrying about the damned couch? I can make it up myself if I want to."

"All right." Molly started walking. Will stood between her and the door. He looked uncharacteristically grumpy, and that made Molly smile. She stopped in front of him, ran a hand up his muscled arm, tiptoed to plant a quick kiss on his lips.

"Good night," she whispered against his mouth.

"Good night, hell." He wrapped his arms around her. His kiss was hard and hot. Molly melted against him, her head tilted back by the pressure of his mouth, her arms sliding around his neck. His body was urgent against hers. She moved her hips in sinuous response.

"Kissing, yuck!" This disgusted comment sent them leaping apart. Molly, breathing hard, looked around to discover Sam in the aperture staring at them.

"What are you doing up?" she managed, not daring to look at Will.

"I need a drink of water."

"The kitchen's that way," Molly said, pointing.

"I know." Sam turned to head for the kitchen. "I just wanted to see if you were awake. I didn't know Will was still here. I don't know how he can do that kind of stuff."

This last muttered comment was accompanied by a disgusted shake of Sam's head.

Molly sent a sidelong glance toward Will. He looked so disgruntled she had to grin.

"Forget it," he growled. "Go to bed."

Molly couldn't help it. She chuckled. "It's called family life," she said, semi-apologetically.

"Go to bed." It was an order.

"I'm going." Still chuckling, she headed for the door. Sam was in the kitchen. She could hear him running water in the sink.

"Molly?" Will's voice was husky.

"Hmm?" She glanced back over her shoulder. Will stood by the half-made couch, holding in both hands the white-cased pillow she had brought him. He looked tired and cross, and so sexy it was all she could do not to retrace her steps.

"What are you doing for dinner tomorrow night?"

A slow smile lit her face. "Anything you want."

"Is that a promise?"

Molly nodded, and his eyes darkened. Sam came out of the kitchen with a big glass of water and a speculative look on his face.

"Do you think I could watch TV for a while? I can't sleep."

"No!" said Molly and Will in unison. Sam glanced from one to the other.

"I was just asking! Sheesh!"

Sam headed for bed. Molly did likewise. She was just snuggling under the covers when she heard the sound of the refrigerator door opening.

Will, she assumed, getting himself another glass of milk. She fell asleep smiling over the most recent cause of his stress.

26

Morning came early, as morning always did. Groggy with sleep, Molly opened her eyes when a quick, hard kiss landed on her lips.

"See you tonight, beautiful," Will said, straightening away from the bed. Then he was gone.

Blinking, Molly glanced at the bedside clock: 6:45 a.m. The rattle of dishes in the kitchen told her that the kids were up and getting ready for school. She groaned, then, resigned, rolled out of bed. She should have felt refreshed; this constituted sleeping late for her.

As she pulled on jeans and a sweat shirt and headed for the kitchen, the memory of what had happened to Sheila washed over her like a dark wave. Always, on the mornings when she didn't have to work, she went up to the field to feed Sheila a couple of handfuls of dog chow. Not today; maybe not ever again.

But Molly had learned long ago not to think about painful things she could not cure. She banished the terrible images of Sheila, and replaced them instead with thoughts of Will. At least, this time, something magical had been born of tragedy. It was time to face the truth: Last night she had fallen head over heels for Will.

Molly was smiling when she walked into the kitchen. Her brothers and sisters immediately suspended all conversation. With guilty looks, they hung their heads and applied themselves to their cereal bowls. It didn't take a genius to guess the topic of their conversation: it had been about her and Will.

They didn't keep their mouths shut for long.

"Hey, Molly, aren't you kind of old to be sitting around on Will's lap like you did last night?" Sam asked critically after a few seconds.

"She was *crying*. You can sit on somebody's lap if you're crying even if you are grown up." Susan came to Molly's defense.

"A girl can sit on a guy's lap anytime," Mike said, dripping scorn. "Guys like it. Don't you know that?"

"Are guys supposed to like kissing and stuff too?" Sam asked his big brother, sounding anxious.

"Molly and Will were kissing," Susan put in. "Does that mean you're going to marry Will, Molly?"

"Of course it doesn't. People don't have to get married just because they kiss," Mike told her, then looked suspiciously at Molly. "If you *are* going to marry Will, I'm out of here. He's too bossy."

"I like him!" Susan said. "I think Molly *should* marry him!"

"Me too!" Sam seconded.

"Me too!" Ashley agreed.

"You guys are so dumb!" Mike gave his siblings a withering look.

"For everyone's information, I am not going to marry Will," Molly said, "and if you don't hurry, you're going to miss your bus. It's almost seven-fifteen."

There was the usual mad scramble for the bathroom and out the door. The twins' bus came first; the one Mike and Ashley rode, fifteen minutes later. A white van with *DTM Security Services* emblazoned on its side pulled up just as Mike and Ashley were leaving the house.

"We're getting a security system put in?" Ashley asked Molly in a disbelieving tone as Molly joined her, Mike, Pork Chop, and the van's driver on the porch. The morning was crisp but cloudless, the night's cold drizzle no more than a memory.

"Yes," Molly said as she signed the purchase order, hoping to get by with no more explanation than that. She should have known better.

"You've got to be *kidding*." Both Mike and Ashley stared at her as the driver went inside to, he said, check out the number of windows and doors.

"Molly, did you see how much it cost?" Ashley whispered, not wanting the driver to hear. "It was on the bottom of the bill: fifteen hundred dollars!"

"Will's paying for it," Molly admitted, defeated, knowing there was no other way to explain away something that expensive.

"*Will's* paying for it!" her siblings chorused in astonishment.

"Yes," Molly said, then, looking down the road, spied deliverance. "Here comes the bus."

"You aren't going to marry him, are you?" Mike asked, his cool facade slipping enough to allow him to sound a little anxious.

"No, of course not," Molly said. "He just is worried about us, is all."

"You better not," Mike said, heading for the bus.

"Don't forget I'm picking you up after school. We have an appointment with the Sheriff's Department at three-thirty," Molly called after him.

"Yeah, yeah." Mike didn't *sound* nervous. If he truly wasn't, Molly thought, he had to have rocks in his head. She certainly was.

"Molly, I just thought you'd like to know: Will was *whistling* when he left this morning," Ashley confided in a conspiratorial tone.

"Would you get on the bus?" Molly almost yelled. Ashley grinned, waved, and sprinted down the driveway toward the bus. Frowning direly, Molly watched the slim, blue-jeaned figure retreat. Ashley bounded on board, the bus pulled off down the road—and Molly pictured Will whistling. The image was irresistible. Molly never even noticed when her frown changed to a smile.

The security system was not completely installed and functional until early afternoon. While the installer was working, Molly cleaned house, sorted clothes for a trip to the Laundromat, and, finally, with great reluctance, called Dr. Mott to inquire about Sheila. While waiting for the vet to get on the line she almost hung up, so certain was she that the news would be bad. But Sheila was holding her own, the vet said. She was badly injured and under heavy sedation, but she had a chance. Putting down the phone, Molly said a little prayer for Sheila: Please, God, don't let her die.

A state police car pulled into the driveway just as the security system van was leaving. By the time Molly had answered the officers' questions and they left, she was on the verge of tears. She drank two cups of coffee and took a long shower, and finally managed to push the whole nightmare out of her mind again.

For the meeting with the deputies, Molly raided Ashley's closet. She chose a cream-colored turtleneck dress of knit, ribbed cotton, set off with a tan leather belt. Its below-the-knee length was Ashley, not her, but the effect was attractive, especially when paired with gold hoop earrings, flesh-toned panty hose, and Ashley's tan heels. She curled her hair with hot rollers, applied cinnamon-colored lipstick and a flick of mascara, and on the whole, she thought, looked very nice.

She was willing to bet dollars to doughnuts that Will would approve of her outfit. It was just the kind of demure getup that a man like him would want his girlfriend to wear.

Now that she was his girlfriend for real, she might even—occasionally!—oblige. Although she meant to trot the black mini out every once in a while too.

The meeting with the deputies did not go well. Tom Kramer, the lawyer, met them at the sheriff's office, a one-story brick building in the middle of downtown Versailles. He was portly, with a bald spot at the crown of his head and a cheerful face. He was also, Molly discovered, well known to the deputies, who treated him with vast respect. Molly was thankful for his presence. With him at Mike's side, the deputies were scrupulously polite. If she and Mike had faced them on their own, Molly feared to think what might have happened.

With his ponytail and earring, his faded flannel shirt and grungy jeans, Mike, Molly admitted to herself, looked like bad news. It didn't help that he was in his cool mode, his responses monosyllabic, his attitude verging on the sullen.

While one deputy questioned Mike under Kramer's watchful supervision, the other drew Molly aside. His name was D. Hoffman, according to the narrow plastic tag attached to his shirt pocket.

"How much do you know about satanism, Miss Ballard?" Hoffman asked without preamble.

Molly remembered him from the night at her house: He was the deputy with the beer gut. The tall, lanky officer talked to Mike. His name tag read *C. Miles*.

"About what?" Molly was distracted trying to hear what C. Miles was asking Mike, and thought she must have misunderstood the question.

"About satanism, Miss Ballard. You know, devil worship."

"I don't know anything about it at all." She was impatient; what had devil worship to do with anything?

"We know you are aware that a Thoroughbred mare was attacked in a field at Wyland Farm last night. In fact, we understand that you—and your brother—were first on the scene."

"That's right."

"How did that happen? That you and your brother were first on the scene, I mean?"

"Look, I already gave a statement to the state police, and I really don't want to talk about it anymore, all right?" Molly couldn't bear to relive the details again.

"All right." With a glance at Kramer, the deputy backed off. He looked down at a clipboard in his hand. "Another Wyland Farm animal was attacked several months ago, is that right? A burro?"

"Ophelia. Yes."

"Ophelia. I'm assuming that's the burro's name?"

Molly nodded. He wrote it down.

"You obviously are familiar with the burro. Were you familiar with the horse who was attacked? Did the animal know you?"

"Yes." Molly's voice was tight.

"What about your brother?"

"What about my brother?"

"Was either animal familiar with your brother?"

Molly stared at him. "Could you please tell me what this has to do with what we're here for? I thought you were trying to find the kids who were drinking beer and smoking pot over at Sweet Meadow Stud."

"We are." Hoffman hesitated, and glanced toward Kramer again. The lawyer, his back to Molly, was talking to the other deputy. Mike was staring at the opposite wall, looking, Molly thought with vexation, as if he were mentally out to lunch.

"We're also investigating the horse slashings," Hoffman continued. "The burro—Ophelia—was apparently the first. Since that time, six Thoroughbreds have been attacked. Four have died. Were you aware of that?"

"No, I wasn't. What is the point of this conversation, if you don't mind telling me?"

"We think the horses are being slashed in some sort of ritual. A ritual involving devil worship. We've found signs that lead us to believe a satanic cult has formed in this area."

"A satanic cult?" Molly was disbelieving.

Hoffman nodded. "It's more common than people think. Usually it's a group of teenagers, kids who don't fit in, who are kind of rebellious. Like your brother."

It took a couple of seconds for the portent of that to sink in.

"You think that *Mike* . . . ?" Molly gasped, then shook her head. "No *way*. Beer or pot, maybe, but not devil worship! And he would never, ever harm an animal! Mike loves animals!"

"Are you sure of that, Miss Ballard?"

"Absolutely sure. I would stake my life on it!"

"You may be." Hoffman was unsmiling. "Or somebody else's. Sometimes these cults move from attacking animals—to attacking people. This past spring, we had reports of rabbits and squirrels and birds being mutilated. Over the summer, domestic animals—cats and dogs—were attacked. Now horses. What would you say is next, Miss Ballard?"

"You've got to be crazy!" Molly said, and looked around for Kramer. He had to hear these accusations—and deal with them.

It turned out that he already had. Deputy Miles was asking Mike almost exactly the same questions. On advice of counsel—Tom Kramer—Mike refused to answer. As there was no proof even of the existence of a satanic cult, much less of Mike's involvement in it, there was nothing the deputies could do but terminate the interview when Kramer declared that the meeting was over.

If they had additional questions, they could call him at his office, the lawyer said. He was putting them on notice that they were not to question his client without his being present.

"Are they serious?" Molly asked as she, Mike, and Kramer walked out into the bright October afternoon together. Indian summer was back, but the beautiful weather was no panacea for Molly. She was so worried, she was nauseous; even Mike, she was relieved to see, looked subdued for once.

"I never did that," Mike said earnestly, looking from Molly to the lawyer.

"I know you didn't." Molly was glad to be able to state her belief in him with absolute conviction.

"Oh, they're serious," Kramer said, unsmiling. "But they don't have any evidence. Look at it this way—it took their minds off the other charges."

"Great." Mike's response was gloomy.

"If and when they get some evidence that this group exists and Mike is a part of it, they'll be in touch with me. Until then, I wouldn't worry about it. Just stay out of trouble, young man."

They reached the end of the walk leading from the sheriff's office to the street where both their cars were parked at the curb, one behind the other. The blue Plymouth with its rusted-out spots, fading paint, and bald tires looked even more like the junker it was compared to the lawyer's opulent gray Mercedes. Molly noted the difference between the vehicles with a wry inner grimace, and tried not to think about how much the lawyer's services were costing the government—or Will. Instead, she stopped and extended her hand. Mike, of course, slid into the car without a word of either thanks or good-bye.

"I don't know what we would have done without your help," Molly said, casting a reproving glance at Mike, who didn't see it. He was already rifling through the tapes in the glove compartment.

Kramer took her hand and smiled at her. "Glad to be of service," he said. "If I hear any more from the deputies, I may want to come out to your place and look around, see where the horse was attacked, that kind of thing. Is that all right?"

"You're welcome anytime," Molly assured him.

"Don't worry too much," he advised, releasing her hand. "I doubt anything will come of this. From what I gathered, they were grasping at straws. And they seem to have forgotten about the other charges."

"I hope you're right." Molly's reply was heartfelt. With a smile and a wave, she walked around the car and got in.

The Plymouth would not start. Mike muttered and sank low in the seat with embarrassment as first Molly and then Tom Kramer tried everything they knew to make the engine turn over. Finally Molly was forced to admit defeat, and called Jimmy Miller's garage. Jimmy was not in. A mechanic promised to come out and look at the car as soon as he could, but said that since he was the only one in the shop it might be a couple of hours before he could get to it.

Tom—Molly was on a first-name basis with him by this time—offered to drive them home. He said he'd kill two birds with one stone and check out the scene of the attack while he was there.

By the time they reached the house it was almost five-thirty. Late afternoon sunlight slanted across the fields, lending the trees and the grass and even the farmhouse a golden glow. Susan and Sam, in jeans and sweat shirts, were tossing a football back and forth in the yard. Pork Chop sat beneath the large oak, looking up into the red-gold foliage with an eager expression at what Molly hoped was a squirrel. A black Jeep Cherokee was already parked in the drive, Molly saw. Stetson in hand and minus his long duster, J.D. stood at the front door talking to Ashley, who was holding open the screen. J.D. turned, brightening, at the sound of the car pulling up, only to scowl as he realized that

Molly was arriving in a Mercedes with an unknown male escort.

"Bet you a dollar I know who *he's* here to see," Mike muttered to Molly as they got out of the car.

Molly ignored him, waving at the twins, who continued with their game, and patting Pork Chop, who quit barking when he realized who the new arrivals were. Tom walked up to the house with them.

Rolling his eyes at J.D.'s too-hearty greeting, Mike went on inside as Molly introduced Ashley, who had stepped out on the porch, and J.D. to Tom, and they all stood chatting for a moment. In the yard, Susan yelled as she missed catching Sam's throw and Pork Chop absconded with the ball. Both twins took up the chase as Pork Chop ran with ball in mouth and tail wagging, appearing to find this new game tremendous fun. The temperature, even so late in the afternoon, was seventyish. No one wore a jacket except for Tom, and his was part of a suit.

"I just came by to see how you were doing," J.D. said in a low voice to Molly under cover of Tom's exchange of pleasantries with Ashley.

"I'm fine," Molly answered. Before she could say anything more, the crunch of gravel heralded the arrival of another visitor. With a grimace, Molly recognized the red Corvette: Thornton Wyland.

Tyler was with him, she saw as the pair got out of the car. Pork Chop dropped the ball to bark at the newcomers, and the twins scooped it up and resumed their game. Thornton grinned and waved at Molly on the porch, while Tyler gave a sardonic smile.

Ashley took one look at Thornton, blushed, and retreated into the house. Molly had noticed before that Ashley was especially shy around Thornton, and guessed her sister found his good looks intimidating. J.D., obviously put out by the arrival of the two other men, remembered he worked for the Wylands and tried not to scowl at them. Tom Kramer shook hands all around as Molly performed the introductions. Then, not knowing quite what else to do, she invited them all to sit.

"Tyler and I just came by to check on you," Thornton said with a devilish grin. "We all saw how upset you were last night. I don't mind telling you that I, for one, was shocked to discover that our own tough little Miss Molly could actually cry."

"The soul of tact, as always, Thorn," Tyler murmured, then smiled at Molly. "We're lucky you live so close. We would have lost that mare."

"Have you heard anything? Is she going to be okay?" Molly sank down on the glider, grateful to Tyler for allowing her to ignore Thornton's teasing. Thornton immediately availed himself of the opportunity to perch on the metal arm next to her. Molly ignored him too.

"Dr. Mott says it's touch and go." J.D. obviously considered claiming the vacant space beside Molly, remembered who his rivals were, and remained standing with a disgruntled expression. Tom sat down in his stead, listening to the conversation with obvious interest.

"We're offering a reward," Thornton said. "Two thousand dollars for information leading to the apprehension of the person or persons responsible."

"You think it might be more than one?" Tom asked. After hearing what the deputies had had to say, Molly wondered at the note of innocent inquiry in his question. If the Sheriff's Department was investigating the possible involvement of a satanic cult, then the Wylands would know all about it. They probably even knew Mike was a suspect. That was just the way things worked in Woodford County.

Molly's spine stiffened at the idea. If the Wylands were meaning to catch Mike with that reward, they had another thing coming, she thought fiercely. In this case, her brother was as innocent as she was herself. Molly was as sure of that as she had ever been of anything in her life.

J.D. shrugged. "The police seem to think so. They said they don't hardly see how one man could subdue a twelve-hundred-pound mare for long enough to do that to her."

At that moment a beige Chrysler pulled into the driveway, followed by Molly's blue Plymouth. Pork Chop barked. The conversation paused as they all watched Jimmy Miller get out of the Chrysler. He wore a tan sport coat and brown slacks, a mode of dress that was unusual for him. A young male garage employee in a blue mechanic's uniform slid out of the Plymouth. Both men headed toward the porch.

"You got my car fixed already?" Molly greeted Jimmy with delight as he came up the steps.

"It just needed a jump," Jimmy said, smiling at Molly and nodding at the other men. "The battery was low. You must have left your lights on, or something."

"Thanks." Molly smiled back at him. "And thanks for driving it out. You didn't need to do that."

"My pleasure." Jimmy gave her a look that remembered the kisses they had shared in his front seat just the night before last. Reminded of the hickey that, though fainter, lived on beneath the turtleneck and a layer of Coverstick, Molly felt both embarrassed and guilty. Embarrassed because, under ordinary circumstances, she never would have let him kiss her like that; and guilty because Jimmy clearly imagined that those kisses meant more than they really did.

"Let me get you all some coffee, or a Coke," Molly said, standing up.

"A Coke would be fine by me." Jimmy sat down on the steps. His employee stood irresolute for a moment, then sank down beside him. "For Buddy here too. Oh, Molly, this is Buddy James."

"We've met," Buddy said, smiling rather shyly over his shoulder at Molly. He had a black buzz cut and a teenager's round face and blemishes. Molly nodded acknowledgment of his comment, though if they had ever met she couldn't recall where or when.

Molly performed the requisite introductions all around, then asked, "Gentlemen—coffee or Coke?"

She was just making a mental note of their answers when another car turned in the gravel driveway.

It was a white Ford Taurus.

27

Shades of Scarlett O'Hara! That was the thought that popped into Will's head when he stepped out of the car with an absentminded pat for Pork Chop and got a load of the scene on Molly's front porch. Five—no, six—men, two on the steps, two on the glider, two standing, all gazing raptly at a bodacious babe with a come-hither walk and a flirtatious smile.

His bodacious babe.

As Will headed toward the porch, Molly turned that smile on him. Will's answering smile was wry.

If you're going to fall for the prettiest girl around, he told himself, you can't be surprised if there's competition. It goes with the territory.

"Will! Will!" The twins spotted him, and Will found himself plucking a football out of the air. "Wanna play?"

"Later," he promised, throwing the football back. Sam leaped into the air and caught it, and the twins resumed their game.

Molly had her back to him by that time, heading inside the house. Will watched the enticing sway of her hips with appreciation. When the screen door swung shut behind her, cutting off his view, he glanced around in time to notice that every other male present had been appreciating the same thing.

Will reached the porch and stopped because two men occupied the steps. One was a pimply kid. Will dismissed him at once as a potential rival. The other was thirtyish, solid and prosperous-looking. Something about him seemed vaguely familiar. Will frowned, trying to place him, as his gaze skimmed to the others on the porch. He nodded without enthusiasm at J.D. and Thornton and Tyler Wyland. The other man was Tom Kramer, the lawyer. Will recognized him from his visit to the man's office last week. As Molly's boyfriend who was footing the bill for legal help for Mike, Will had paid the man's retainer. What was he doing at Molly's house? Surely he had not followed her home after one meeting! He didn't look the type to form part of Molly's court.

Will supposed he didn't either.

"Oh, sorry," said the solid-looking man on the steps, standing up to let Will pass. The kid stood up too. "I'm Jimmy Miller. This here's Buddy James."

"Will Lyman," Will said, shaking the hand that was held out to him. Jimmy Miller—the name rang a bell. Oh, yes, the yokel. Immediately on the heels of recognition came a less pleasant companion thought: the hickey. Will had to exercise control not to put more force into the handshake than civility called for.

The kid shook hands too.

"You're a friend of the family, aren't you?" Miller said with a good-humored smile. At what must have been Will's look of surprise, he added, "I recognize the car. From the other night."

"You might say that," Will replied, just as Molly pushed open the screen door with her hip and stepped outside bearing a glass-laden tray. Will went up the steps to help her, only to be forestalled by J.D., who tried to take the tray from Molly. She shook her head at him, managed a deft balancing act with one hand and her hip, and passed J.D. a glass of fizzy dark liquid Will assumed was Coke. A single ice cube floated in each glass. Molly was clearly not prepared for mass hospitality, Will thought with some amusement. Not that any of her admirers seemed to mind. She handed glasses of Coke all around to the accompaniment of murmurs of appreciation.

"This is yours," she said finally to Will.

The glass Will accepted was scratched plastic decorated with a pink flamingo—and it held milk.

"Thanks," he said, smiling at her. She smiled back at him, a wide, beguiling smile that matched the impish twinkle in her eyes. Will felt himself being dazzled, and reminded himself once again that standing before him was a Venus's-flytrap. Every man on the porch was watching her, enthralled, drinking warm, fizzy Coke from scratched, mismatched plastic glasses with expressions that equated the beverage with crystal goblets of French champagne. And he was no exception. Grimacing at his own folly, Will took a sip of milk and switched his attention to the twins' ongoing football game.

"Does everybody know everybody else?" Molly asked brightly, turning that megawatt smile on the assembled company.

"We haven't met officially," Thornton Wyland said to Will with a lazy smile. He stood up, offered his hand. "I'm Thornton Wyland."

"Will Lyman." Will shook hands.

"Uh, Molly, are you doing anything for supper tonight?" Jimmy Miller asked in a low voice. Though Will was turned away, he heard. His back stiffened reflexively. It took conscious effort on his part to get his muscles to relax.

"Oh, Jimmy, I'm sorry, but I have plans," Molly said as quietly, sounding more regretful than Will thought the situation called for. Turning away from Thornton Wyland with a nod, he watched as Molly dealt with yet another swain.

"We could grab a pizza," Miller continued with dogged determination. He was an earnest-looking guy with freckles, and almost certainly didn't deserve the wave of dislike Will felt for him. Miller was on his feet now, on the top step, which meant his head did not quite reach as high as Molly's nose because she was standing on the porch, and his heart was in his eyes as he looked at her. Will thought he had never seen a man so openly lovesick, and felt a spurt of acute annoyance.

The girl was his.

"I can't . . ." Molly began.

Will took a sip of milk and came up behind her.

"She's having dinner with me," he said to the younger man. Miller looked at him, blinked in surprise, then focused on Molly with wide-eyed disbelief that darkened to reproach. His mouth opened as if he would protest, but he didn't. From his position behind her, Will couldn't see Molly's face, but he imagined what emotion Miller had found there to shut his mouth: compassion.

He hoped like hell Molly never looked that way at him.

"Some other time, then," Miller managed with creditable composure, then glanced at his watch. "Well, I have to be taking off. Come on, Buddy, I'll drive you back to the shop."

With their going, the rest of the fan club took the hint and departed too. Will was left helping Molly gather up dirty glasses as the cars pulled out of the driveway. She was silent, her expression pensive. Will looked at her as she crouched to retrieve a glass from beside the glider. The cream knit dress she wore covered her from her ears to her knees, but it fit like a glove and clung in all the right—or wrong, depending upon your point of view—places. Her legs in their sheer stockings and high heels were every bit as luscious as they had been sheathed in black the day before. Her hair was a loose fall of luxuriant coffee-brown waves that reached past her shoulder blades. She was slender, curvaceous, staggeringly sexy, and—when she straightened with a graceful turn and smiled at him—charming as well.

That smile was an arrow aimed straight at his heart.

"We still on for dinner?" he asked.

"You bet." Her smile was warm and gay and it bewitched him. Will realized that he had it bad. Maybe worse than the yokel, though he hoped it didn't show.

The Venus's-flytrap was getting ready to swallow him whole, and he was too far gone to even want to put up a fight.

28

"So have you always had a problem attracting men?" Will asked dryly halfway through dinner. They were at the Merrick Inn, a small, wood-paneled Lexington eatery that Molly had not even known existed. With oil paintings on the walls, white tablecloths and green votive candles on the tables, the restaurant was the epitome of quiet good taste. Will told her that he had stumbled across it during the course of his investigation. The horse crowd ate there often, and the food was fine old southern cuisine. The prices were out of this world, but Molly tried not to think about that.

Molly swallowed as scrumptious a bite of country ham as she had ever tasted, and looked at him consideringly. The navy suit he wore tonight had subtle pinstripes. His shirt was white and his tie was red. His hair gleamed gold in the candlelight. By contrast, his face was bronzed and hard-planed. And there was something about his eyes as he looked at her that gave her the shivers. Nice shivers. Had she ever not thought him handsome? Molly wondered. She must have been blind.

"Always," she answered with a saucy smile, and took another bite.

"I bet you had to beat them off with a stick as far back as elementary school."

"I never carried a stick." The ham was delicious, but salty. Molly washed it down with a sip of iced tea. Will, of course, was drinking milk, and had ordered a steak. Molly had a feeling she should be thankful they were not eating Italian.

"You just let them swarm all over you, hmm? Like today. I don't think I've ever arrived to pick up a date before and found six other men there ahead of me."

Molly swallowed a sinfully good bite of green beans flavored with ham and almonds and looked at him with wide-eyed delight.

"You're jealous," she said.

Will stopped cutting his steak and met her gaze. For a moment he just stared at her, surprised. Then he gave her a wry little smile.

"You're right."

"I like it."

"I don't."

"For your information, the only one of those men I've ever been out with is Jimmy Miller."

"The yokel who gives hickeys." There was such a caustic note to this that Molly laughed.

"You can blame yourself for that."

"For what?"

"The hickey," she whispered, mindful of the other diners who, though intent on their own dinners in the dark, quiet room, might overhear.

"I can blame myself because you let some yokel give you a hickey?" Will didn't lower his voice. Molly shot a quick glance around, but no one seemed to be paying any attention.

"Shh!" She nodded.

"How do you figure that?"

"I pretended he was you."

"What?"

"You heard me."

"Jesus." Will took a deep breath. "Are you about finished?"

"Not really." Molly glanced down at her plate with surprise. She still had half her meal to go—and it was good.

"I'll feed you again later." Will stood up, signaling for the waitress. Molly took a hasty bite of ham and then a swallow of tea while he waited for the waitress to bring the check. As he glanced at the check and handed the waitress cash, Molly pulled on her sweater—then succumbed to the lure of the ham again.

"Was there something wrong with the food, sir?" the waitress asked, concerned, glancing at their half-eaten meals.

"It was fine. Something just came up, and we have to go," Will said, reaching for Molly's hand. With a last, lingering look of regret at the ham, she grabbed her purse and allowed herself to be pulled from the table and hustled toward the door.

"What just came up?" Molly asked when they were outside walking toward the car. It was dark now, and colder than it had been during the day. The brown wraparound sweater she wore over Ashley's turtleneck dress was welcome. Overhead, stars twinkled like fireflies on a midsummer's night. The half-moon rode low on the horizon.

Will laughed. "Me. Get in the car, Molly."

Will opened the door for her. Molly got in, both bemused and unsettled by his admission, and he slammed the door shut behind her. She was reaching for her seat belt when he slid into his seat. Molly heard his door shut just as she was dragging the belt across her body. His hand closed over hers and she looked up at him in surprise. He was very close, leaning over her, in fact, his broad shoulders blocking out her view of the night through the windshield, his eyes intent. Molly stared up at him for an instant, at the hard, handsome face she had never thought would be able to make her heart beat so fast.

Without a word Will kissed her. Molly let go of the seat belt, wrapped her arms around his neck, and kissed him back.

After a few minutes he lifted his head and said thickly, "I am too damned old to be making out in cars."

Molly took a deep, shaken breath and whispered, "I'm not."

Will gave a ghost of a laugh. "I know."

"So?"

Will kissed her again, quick and hard, and rested his forehead against hers.

"We've got an audience," he said.

Molly looked, and saw that two well-dressed older couples, having obviously just finished dining inside, were staring at them with disapproval as they walked past the car. Molly's face heated with embarrassment. The car was parked right by the sidewalk leading to the restaurant, leaving them in full view of anyone who passed.

Will lifted her arms from around his neck and

reached for her seat belt. He pulled it around her, fastened it, then kissed her mouth again.

"I have a hotel room," he said.

Clearly it was decision time, but Molly knew as soon as the thought entered her head that there was no decision to be made. Whatever came of it, this was what she wanted. *He* was what she wanted.

She nodded.

Will put on his own seat belt, started the car, and pulled out of the lot.

His hotel was close. Molly read the illuminated sign EMBASSY SUITES as he slowed the car and pulled into the parking lot. By the time he had the car parked and was coming around the hood to open her door, Molly's pulse was racing. She was scared, she was excited, she was out of her head—over Will.

He reached in and took her hand. Molly allowed him to pull her from the car. He kept her hand in his, warm and strong, as he walked her across the parking lot and through the double doors into the brightly lit lobby. It took a moment for her eyes to adjust. By the time they did, he had already steered her halfway across the thick gray carpet toward the bank of polished stainless steel elevators in one corner. The two men and one woman at the reception desk, she was relieved to see, paid no attention to their passing. A large TV set played quietly in a sunken sitting area of overstuffed couches and glass tables beside the elevators. The lone occupant of the area never even spared them a glance.

The elevator opened. Molly stepped into the mirror-lined space with Will beside her.

He still held her hand. He raised it to his mouth as the doors closed, and kissed its back. Watching him, and watching their reflections in the mirror as his blond head bent close to her dark one, Molly experienced a feeling of unreality. Was she really going upstairs in a hotel to sleep with the FBI man?

It seemed impossible.

"You look scared to death," Will said, glancing at her from beneath lowered lids.

"I'm not." Her answer was about half bravado, because she was scared. But she wasn't going to admit it—or turn back.

"I can take you home." He turned her hand over to kiss her palm. Molly felt the heat of his mouth clear down to her toes. She shivered.

"No."

"Sure?"

Molly nodded just as the elevator pinged to announce its arrival on the third floor. The doors slid open. Will let go of her hand, and Molly stepped out into the gray-carpeted corridor on her own. Will followed. Glancing around, Molly saw that he held a key card in his hand.

The hall was deserted. Will walked ahead of her to a door with the number 318 on a brass plaque set into the wall beside it, and inserted his key into the lock. The tiny light on the door flashed green. Will turned the handle, pushed the door open, and stood back for her to precede him.

Molly held on to the strap of her shoulder bag so tightly that she felt her nails dig into her palm, and walked past him into his hotel room.

The door closed. Pitch blackness descended. Her skin prickled as she sensed him moving through the dark. Molly was so nervous, she felt queasy. Her hands were freezing cold. Her body was freezing cold. It was all she could do to keep her teeth from chattering, though the room was comfortably warm.

Any second now she expected Will's arms to come around her. She expected him to turn her around and kiss her and . . .

A soft light illuminated the room. Molly saw that Will was withdrawing his hand from beneath the tasteful beige shade of a floor lamp, which he had turned on. He stood in front of a wall of draperies in an abstract pattern in which gray and beige predominated. On either side of the lamp was one of a pair of gray velour armchairs. To the left was a kitchenette with dark wood cabinets and shiny appliances. In the carpeted area beside the kitchenette, beneath a beige-shaded lamp dangling from a gold chain, were a round table and four chairs. To Molly's right was the bathroom. Farther into the room, on the same side as the bathroom, were two double beds. They were neatly made up, the bedspreads custom made to match the drapes, the headboards half circles of brass-trimmed dark wood set flush against gray-painted walls.

Will was watching her, Molly discovered as her gaze fled from the beds to him. Legs braced slightly apart, he stood with his hands buried deep in the pockets of his perfectly tailored trousers, his coattails pushed back behind his hips. The expensive navy suit, the pristine white shirt, the elegantly knotted red tie, were so different from the style of her usual run of boyfriends, it seemed impossible that she was there with him. Her uncertainty must have been apparent, because as he looked at her he was unsmiling, almost grim.

"I'll take you home," he said.

He would, she knew. All she had to do was nod her

head. Suddenly Molly recognized the one essential quality in him that attracted her so strongly: Of all the men she had ever known, he was the one who made her feel safe.

Molly looked at him, at the close-cropped blond hair and bronzed lined face and athlete's body in the expensive suit, and knew that if she turned tail and ran now, she would kick herself for it for the rest of her life. Whatever happened later, however much she eventually got hurt, right now he was what she wanted, and she wanted him as she had never before wanted anything in her life.

"I don't want to go home," she said, and crossed the room toward him.

29

Will's hands came out of his pockets as Molly approached. He reached for her, caught her elbows through the nubby-textured wool sweater, drew her close. Her bag's strap slipped sideways. Will removed it from her shoulder and dropped the purse on the chair behind him. When he turned back to her, Molly slipped her arms around his neck, loosely linking her hands at his nape.

"I don't want to go home," she repeated.

"You sure?" he asked.

"I'm sure."

Molly smiled at him. He didn't smile back, but instead examined her face with a thoughtfulness that worried her a little.

"Why do I feel like I'm cradle-robbing here?" Will's hands shaped her face. The feel of his warm hands against her cool skin sent a shiver down her spine. His mouth curved in a crooked half smile, but his eyes were dark blue and intent as she met his gaze.

"I'll be twenty-five in two weeks, Will. I'm all grown up, believe me."

"You don't look it." His gaze flickered down her body. "Well, maybe you do."

"Thanks. I think."

Will brushed back the hair that tumbled over her right shoulder, tucking it carefully behind her ear. His hand slid beneath the thick fall of hair, cradling the back of her head, tilting it slightly. His other arm slid around her back, and he pulled her close, so that she was tight up against his chest. She could feel the heat of his body, the steely strength of his muscles, all along her body. His head bent. His mouth found the soft skin below her ear, as he nudged down the high cotton neck of her dress. It fastened, hard and possessive, against her throat just below her jaw. The sensation was so unbelievably erotic that it was a minute or two before Molly realized what he was doing: replacing Jimmy Miller's love bite with his own.

"I thought giving hickeys wasn't your style," she managed when Will lifted his head at last.

His lips were parted, his eyes hot. "The damned thing's been driving me nuts," he said, and pressed his mouth to her throat again. A weakness seemed to afflict her muscles. It was all she could do not to sag against him.

"Has it?" Molly could barely breathe, let alone talk. His chest was hard against her breasts, making them tingle and swell. The arm around her waist was solid, possessive. One hand cradled her head, stroked her cheek, smoothed the hair back from her face.

"Insane." He slid his mouth along her jawline. Molly shivered, and closed her eyes.

"Really?" she got out, relieved to discover that her voice was relatively normal.

"You don't have to sound so happy about it." He

kissed the corner of her mouth, and Molly's lips parted in instinctive response. "At least now when I see it I'll know it's mine."

"Jealous," she whispered, just before his mouth slid over hers.

"Damn right," he said into her mouth, and then he was kissing her and she was kissing him and neither of them was talking at all.

She loved the way he kissed, Molly thought as his arms tightened around her and her head fell back against his shoulder. She counted herself something of an expert on kisses. As she had already learned, he was no slouch in that department himself. Actually, she decided as he traced the outline of her lips with his tongue, he was a worthy foe. His mouth was hard and hot, his tongue seductive as it coaxed rather than demanded her response. She kissed him for all she was worth, pressing herself against him, clinging to his neck, wanting to provoke an even greater response in him than he was evoking in her.

It was a duel of masters, she concluded dizzily as he pulled her so tight against him that she rose on tiptoe, her arms curling close around his neck, letting his strong body support most of her weight. He kissed her until she had to free her mouth to catch her breath, and then he kissed her again.

His hand was between them, moving up her rib cage, finding and flattening over her breast. His palm pressed against her through layers of sweater and dress and bra, caressing her softness with an urgency that caused her already pebble-hard nipples to throb and burn.

"These have been driving me nuts too." Will's hand

shifted to her other breast and reworked its rough magic.

"Have they?" Molly could hear the unsteadiness of her own voice, but she couldn't help it. Her head was whirling, her body was on fire, and she was finding it difficult to think, much less speak, coherently.

"Insane."

His lips found hers again. Molly arched her back, gasping into his mouth, pressing her breast closer into that knowing hand.

Will lifted his head. Molly's lids fluttered up, and she drew in a shuddering gulp of air. She was relieved to see that he was breathing hard too. A dark flush stained his cheekbones. His eyes reflected the golden lamplight, making them look as if there were flames in the blue depths.

Will glanced down, and Molly followed his gaze. His fingers were long and tan against the brown bouclé knit of her sweater. The sight of his hand on her breast was intimate, erotic, fanning to life flames of desire that raced through her blood.

His hand left her breast, moved to the self-tie belt that was all that held her sweater closed in front. Molly watched as he tugged the bow loose. The sweater fell open, revealing the cream knit dress that had seemed so demure when she had donned it earlier. Now, with her nipples pressing visibly through the cloth, the dress seemed anything but modest.

It seemed to beg for his touch.

With the barrier of her sweater removed, Will's hands found her breasts again. Watching as he covered both full, round globes with his palms, Molly felt a quiver run through her body. His hands tightened, and the quiver turned into a full-fledged quake.

He was deliberately going slowly, she realized, giving her plenty of time to call a halt if she wished. That was Will: ever the gentleman. It was both maddening and reassuring at the same time.

As well as being sexy as hell.

Molly looked up to find that his gaze was on her face. Her tongue came out to wet her lower lip, because her mouth was suddenly dry. His eyes darkened. He lowered his head and drew her tongue into his mouth, sucking on it. His mouth was warm, wet, devastating.

Molly shivered and fought back, stroking the warm skin above his shirt collar at the nape of his neck, running her fingers through the short, crisp hair that covered the back of his skull. But her battle plan backfired, because she loved the textures, loved the feel of him. She loved the fact that he was not rushing her, not insisting, though part of her wished he would just do it, just hurry up and take what he wanted and be done with it.

Part of her wished she didn't have time to think. Part of her wished she could just tell herself *He made me do it*, and thus be absolved of all responsibility.

His hands caught her elbows, tugging her arms down. He eased the sweater off her shoulders and dropped it on the chair with her purse, all the while kissing her as if he never meant to stop.

Molly wound her arms around his waist beneath his jacket, pressing herself ever closer as his arms slid up her back. She felt her hair being lifted, and then his fingers were at her nape. She felt a tug, heard the faint sound of a zipper being lowered, felt a drift of air on the bare skin of her back, and realized that she was being undressed.

The flames in her blood raged hotter. Molly fought against giving in to it, fought for control. She dragged her mouth away from his, drew in a deep breath to try to steady her reeling senses, and reached for his tie. It was cool, heavy silk, elegantly knotted, expensive in look and feel. She tugged at the knot, and then his hands were there helping her, sliding the narrow end free. He left it loose around his neck, dangling vivid red stripes against his white shirtfront. Shrugging out of his jacket, he dropped it on the chair and pulled her back into his embrace.

When Will kissed her, Molly had the uncanny sensation that the room was tilting. Her arms went around his waist and her hands clutched his back through the fine cotton of his shirt as she tried to regain her equilibrium and at the same time kiss him back.

Finally he lifted his head. Molly opened her eyes, struggled both to breathe and to command her senses, and looked past the lean, sandpapery jaw that was so temptingly close to the hollow of his neck, where his shirt was still buttoned up tight.

If there was undressing to be done, she meant to do her fair share.

Sliding her hands up his shirtfront, trying not to be mesmerized by the feel of the hard muscles beneath the smooth cloth, Molly began to unbutton his shirt. He kissed her cheek, her ear, then pulled aside the loosened neck of her dress and started to kiss her throat.

All her life Molly had heard tales of long-ago southern maidens who swooned at a gentleman's kiss. Now she knew just how they must have felt.

Only about a third of his shirt was unbuttoned when she forgot what she was doing and her hands stilled.

His mouth was painting a line of fire across her bare skin from her right collarbone down over the swelling slope of her breast. He used his teeth, his lips, his tongue. The effect was devastating.

Her dress sagged halfway down her arms. Will unfastened her belt and tugged at her dress. The dress slid free of her arms and down her body until it dropped in a pool around her feet. Molly barely retained the presence of mind to step out of the garment, nudging it aside.

She was left wearing a lacy white bra and matching bikini panties, sheer-to-the-waist panty hose, and high heels.

Will was very still suddenly, and Molly looked up to find his gaze on her body.

His face was flushed and his eyes were bright as they rose at last to her face. Molly thought she detected a fine tremor in the hands that settled on either side of her waist.

"Nice. I like white," he said in a voice that sounded as if he had to work to keep it steady.

"I thought you might." She had to work, too, to produce that cool-sounding response.

"Did you wear these for me?" Despite the heat in his eyes, a faint smile lifted a corner of his mouth.

"Who else?" There was a flippancy to her response because she didn't want to admit the truth—that she had indeed chosen the lacy white scanties because she had guessed they would turn him on. And she wanted, badly, to turn him on. To turn him on like no woman in his life ever had.

"Nobody else," he said, his voice almost a growl. "Not if you know what's good for you."

Before she could reply to that, his hands slid up her

rib cage to gently tug aside one cup of her bra. He looked down at the breast he'd bared, while her gaze rose to his face. His jaw was set, his mouth tight. A dark flush stained his cheekbones. His breathing suspended.

He cupped her bare breast in his hand.

That was when Molly realized that the duel was over, and she, master duelist that she was, had just been bested. For the first time in her life, she was conquered. She, who usually reduced men to putty with no more than a glance, was herself putty in the hands of this man.

She never lost her head over kisses. Never lost her head over lovemaking. Never lost her head over men. But now her senses were swimming, and she was spinning out of control.

She was losing her head over Will.

At the realization her heart shook along with her knees.

30

Hot and wet, his mouth closed over her nipple. Molly clutched his shoulders, gasping his name as exquisite tremors of pleasure raced along her skin. Will pulled her close with one arm around her waist while his mouth drove her crazy and his hand eased her other breast free.

Molly found herself thrust against the hard bulge in his pants. She pressed closer, rubbing herself against him, as undulating waves of heat radiated down her thighs. Her movements set off mind-boggling explosions of desire in her own body. What it did to him she couldn't have said, because suddenly everything had changed. For once in her life she could think of no one but herself and her needs.

She needed him to make love to her. There. Then.

His hand was in the middle of her back. Without any fumbling at all, he found and released the clasp of her bra. The straps slid toward her elbows. Will caught the lacy garment, tugged, and the bra was tossed aside, to land on the floor.

It was her best, most expensive bra, and she didn't even care.

Across the room, Molly caught a glimpse of movement in the full-length mirror she had not until that moment noticed was affixed to a closet door, which stood slightly ajar. She was standing at an angle to the mirror, and to see her reflection properly she had to turn her head. She did, and stared, pulse pounding, at the most carnal image she had ever seen in her life: herself, naked to the waist, dark hair cascading over her shoulders, lips swollen from Will's kisses, eyes huge and drugged-looking, cheeks flushed with desire. Her sheer panty hose might as well have been nonexistent. They provided no coverage for the tiny white panties that kept her from being completely nude. Her tan high heels blended with the color of her skin, making her legs look impossibly long and slender. Her stomach was flat, her bottom rounded, her waist supple. Her breasts were the size of oranges, and just as firm and ripe-looking. The pale globes were topped with pink nipples still shiny wet from Will's mouth. One of his tan, long-fingered hands rested on her back. It was dark against her creamy skin, its position intimate, possessive.

Will was still fully clothed, Molly realized, looking beyond herself at him. His shirt was buttoned at the wrists and two-thirds of the way up his chest, a narrow black belt circled the waist of his still-fastened trousers, and he even wore his socks and shoes.

While she was naked, or nearly so, in his arms.

Her gaze met his in the mirror, and held.

"You're beautiful," he said.

As they both watched, his hand came up to cup and caress a breast. His thumb ran over her already distended nipple. His touch shot through her body like a lightning bolt. Molly caught her breath. Her knees threatened to buckle, and she had to cling to his shoulders for support.

"I want you." His voice was suddenly thick. Without warning one arm encircled her back and the other slid beneath her knees. Then the room really did tilt because she was being swung off her feet and carried over to the bed. He put her down, then came down beside her, his weight on the mattress making her roll toward him. Molly went into his arms willingly, her arms locking around his neck, her mouth seeking his. He kissed her with a torrid hunger that turned her brain to oatmeal and her body to fire.

His hands were scaldingly hot as they slid beneath the waistband of her panty hose, pushing them down over her hips. He delved inside her silky panties, his palm flat against her stomach, his fingers gentle as they found and caressed the triangle of sable curls between her thighs. Then he was pushing her panties down, too, and sliding his fingers between her legs.

"Oh, yes," Molly gasped into his mouth as he found the tiny bud that awaited. He touched her there, pressing and stroking until she thought she would die of need. She writhed desperately beneath that knowing hand, then moaned a protest as it was removed. His body followed. Molly was left trembling as he sat up to pull her remaining clothes down her legs. Her shoes were gone, she discovered as he finished stripping her with quick efficiency, though how she had lost them she didn't quite know.

Will was taking off his own clothes, his movements jerky. Molly watched for a moment as he yanked at his belt buckle, then sat up to help him with his shirt buttons. But she was soon distracted by the sheer masculine beauty of the chest she uncovered. Wide and muscular, its center covered with a wedge of gold-tipped brown curls, it cried out for her touch. She complied, running her palms over the hard contours with sensuous delight. A pulse throbbed at the base of his brown throat. She moved to kiss it just as he freed his belt at last and stood up to shuck his pants. Arms around his neck, Molly refused to let him go, and thus she wound up kneeling naked at the edge of the bed, pressing a string of kisses from the hollow of his throat down the center of his chest.

Will shed his shoes and underwear along with his pants. Straightening, he ran a caressing hand over her bottom and up her spine, then turned his attention to the buttons securing his left cuff. Except for his white shirt, which was still buttoned at the wrists, and his black socks, he was as naked as she.

While he tugged at the uncooperative button with uncharacteristic impatience, Molly's downward glance found his member: it was swollen, huge, and standing stiffly upright. Molly let go of his neck and slid down, taking the burning hot thing in her mouth.

For a moment Will went very still. He caught his breath sharply. Then his hands were on either side of her head and he was pulling her off him and tumbling her backward and falling on top of her. No sooner had her back hit the mattress than he plunged violently inside her. Molly cried out at the fierce pleasure of it. His lips came down on hers, stopping her mouth.

His arms crushed her to him. His mouth and tongue were wet and scaldingly hot as he kissed her with a ferocious need. Molly kissed him back with a burning passion of her own. Her hands burrowed beneath the shirt he still wore, her nails digging into his neck, his back, her hips arching off the bed to meet his frenzied thrusts. He was so hot she felt branded, so big he filled her to bursting. He drove into her with an urgency that made her writhe and buck and strain against him in shattered response. He kissed her mouth, her neck, her breasts. His hand slid down between their bodies to touch her where they joined. Molly buried her face in the hollow between his neck and shoulder and wrapped her legs around his hips and clung, moaning, trembling, while electric arcs of ecstasy danced from her body to his.

She, who was used to being in control, was instead being controlled. He was dominating her, taking what he wanted from her, and it was the most erotic, soul-shattering experience of her life.

He was making her his, and she reveled in it.

"Will, oh, Will! Oh, *Will*!" Her release, when it came, was mind-blowing. It detonated with the force of an explosion inside her, smashing through her body with wave after wave of licking flames.

She was whirled away on the firestorm, barely aware of his answering groan as he thrust deep into her trembling body and was still, holding himself throbbing inside her.

Her arms still clutched his back as he shuddered and collapsed atop her.

Little things—like the fact that her feet were cold and the bedspread was bunched into an uncomfortable knot in the small of her back and she had to sneeze—roused her. It couldn't have been more than twenty minutes since she had walked into the room with him,

Molly calculated, but in that brief period of time her whole world had shifted on its axis.

The thing she had most feared had happened: She had fallen in love with Will.

31

The knowledge terrified Molly. She lay very still and stared up at the textured white ceiling and tried to reject it.

There was a cobweb in one corner.

Will was lying sprawled on top of her, and he weighed a ton.

The smoke alarm near the ceiling had a light like a tiny blinking red eye.

Her hands rested on Will's strong back beneath the shirt he still wore. His skin was warm and damp with sweat.

A crack bisected the ceiling across one corner.

Will's head turned, and his sandpapery jaw brushed her cheek. One hand tightened on her waist. He pressed his mouth against the soft skin just below her ear.

Molly went rigid, and pushed at his shoulder.

He raised his head and smiled at her. It was a sweet smile, heart-stoppingly tender, just like the look in his eyes.

Molly withdrew her hands from beneath his shirt,

trying not to feel the satiny texture of his skin, the hard resilience of his muscles. She wanted to know no more of him than she already knew.

Which was already far too much.

"Let me up, please."

"Now?" He frowned a little, appeared to consider that she might have an urgent reason for her request, and rolled off her. Molly slid off the bed and stood up, looking around for her clothes, trying not to notice that he now lay on his back with his hands folded beneath his head, watching her. Except for the open shirt that covered no more than his arms and the sides of his rib cage, and his socks, he was naked. And clearly unconcerned about it.

She was naked too. Her first instinct was to reach for something, anything, with which to cover herself. His gaze on her body was attentive, appreciative, and it embarrassed her. But to cover herself would reveal that embarrassment, and to reveal embarrassment was to make herself vulnerable. She dared not appear weak at all where Will was concerned.

So Molly stood naked near the foot of the bed and pretended not to care. She held her head up proudly and shook her hair back away from her face and let him look where he would, and told herself that being on display didn't bother her at all, though it did.

She was a past master at presenting an invulnerable face to the world, and it had served her well. The core of her, the soft underbelly of her personality, she kept carefully concealed beneath a harder outer surface, like a crab in its shell.

It was, she had found, the only way to survive.

Will's pants lay next to the bed. They were nearly inside out. His wallet and some loose change and a gold foil condom packet had spilled out of his pockets across the carpet. Molly assumed that he'd been carrying the condom in her honor. He had never used it. The end when it had come was too hot, too fast, too shattering, to allow for such practicalities.

When she spotted, first, her panties and hose and then her shoes, Molly moved with carefully sinuous grace to scoop them up.

To scuttle, which was more in tune with the way she felt, would have been demeaning.

"What are you doing?" It was a lazy inquiry.

"Getting dressed." Molly's reply was short. As she gathered up her bra and dress, she heard rather than saw him sit up.

"What's the matter?" Will was frowning, Molly saw as she dared a glance at him. Sitting in the middle of the bed with his hair ruffled and his knees bent, dressed only in an open shirt and black socks, he was the sexiest thing she had ever seen in her life.

"I hate making love to men in socks," she said nastily, grabbing her purse and heading for the bathroom. He swung his legs over the side of the bed, but he was too late. She reached the sanctuary and closed the door behind her, locking it.

Then she rested her forehead against the cool, gray-painted wood.

The knob rattled.

"Molly. Let me in."

She stepped back from the door. "I'm busy," she said, and flushed the toilet to prove it.

"Molly."

"Go away," she said, depositing her belongings on the counter. Her reflection caught her eye. For a moment she stared at it. Her hair was a tangled mess, her mouth was swollen from kisses, and her eyes had an odd, almost shell-shocked expression. Lower than that, she refused to allow herself to look.

If her body bore the marks of Will's lovemaking, she didn't want to see.

"Molly!"

"I'm taking a shower!" she called, turning away from the mirror, and suited her actions to her words.

By the time she emerged from beneath the warm spray, she was cool, composed, and in control again. She dried, dressed, brushed out her hair, and touched up her makeup. When she was done, no one would ever have guessed that she had just gotten up from having earth-shattering sex with the man she loved.

The man she loved. The very notion sent tendrils of panic curling through her. She refused even to consider it.

To love someone was to get your heart broken. She'd learned that from many hard lessons over many hard years.

She'd been a fool to let things go so far with Will. What on earth had she been thinking of? How could she not have foreseen that her atavistic yearning for a strong, kind man to take care of her would mix with potent sexual chemistry and a good measure of genuine liking to form something highly combustible? Add a dose of mind-blowing sex to the concoction, and of course she had fallen in love with him. It was a no-fail recipe.

But what had she supposed the outcome was going to be? That he would carry her off into the sunset for a happily-ever-after? He would be going back to Chicago in just a couple of weeks. Did she think he was going to take her with him? Kids, dog, and all?

Yeah, right. One thing she had learned was, there are no happy endings in life.

Beyond the bathroom door there was silence. Molly listened, but could hear nothing. She knew he hadn't left her, however. He was out there, waiting, and had to be faced.

Molly squared her shoulders, lifted her chin, and picked up her purse. Then she opened the bathroom door, and stepped out into the hotel room.

Will was sitting in one of the gray velour armchairs. He was wearing his shirt, which was buttoned about halfway up his chest, a pair of narrow light blue boxer shorts, and his black socks. One bare leg was crossed over the other, its foot idly swinging. He was drinking a glass of milk, which he set down on the table as she emerged.

"Ulcer acting up?" Molly asked with a mocking smile. She meant to push him away any way she could, to try to salvage what was left of her heart before he lodged himself in there any deeper. Using her knowledge of his ulcer was dirty pool, she knew, when he had presented it to her as a quid pro quo for what he knew about her mother. But she would fight dirty if she had to, to save herself from pain.

"You might say that."

If being twitted about his ulcer bothered him, Will didn't reveal it. Instead he took another sip of milk. His eyes ran over her thoughtfully before returning to her face.

"Could you take me home, please? It's getting late."

"It's barely nine o'clock."

"I'm tired."

"Kind of a short date, isn't it?"

Molly shrugged.

Will stood up, and padded across the carpet toward her. It was all Molly could do not to retreat. She stood her ground, chin up. She was wearing heels, he was sock-footed, and the top of her head almost reached his eyebrows. Still, he was far larger, his frame broad-shouldered and muscular, and she knew from recent experience that he probably outweighed her by about seventy pounds.

By rights he ought to intimidate her. And he did, but not because of his size. She found him intimidating because of the way he made her feel.

Will stopped in front of her, reaching out to curl his hands around her upper arms. Molly jerked free of his touch.

Will looked at her for a second, his gaze speculative, then folded his arms over his chest.

"What's the matter, Molly?" This time the question was almost tender.

Molly's lips tightened. "Nothing's the matter."

Will sighed. "That's what women always say when something's the matter. It doesn't take a genius to figure out that you're mad at me all of a sudden. The question is, why?"

"I'm not mad at you. I just want to go home. If you won't take me, I'll walk."

"Twenty-plus miles in the middle of the night? I don't think so."

"I'll hitchhike, then. Or call Ashley to come and pick me up."

He looked at her. Something in her face must have convinced him that she was serious, because his tone changed. "You really want to go home?"

"Yes."

"Then I'll take you. Let me get dressed."

Molly tried not to watch as he walked over to the closet and extracted a sweat suit, which he threw on the bed. His undershorts were snug-fitting and reached only about a third of the way down his thighs. She couldn't help but notice that he had nice legs, tanned and well muscled and roughened with hair. He unbuttoned his shirt and took it off with as little self-consciousness as if he'd been alone, while she shifted from foot to foot and tried to look at anything but him.

"There's Coke in the refrigerator, if you want it. I got it especially for you."

She glanced at him then, and it was a mistake. He was wearing only his light blue boxers. His body, which she hadn't really gotten a good look at earlier, was now revealed in all its glory. It was gorgeous. His shoulders were bronzed and thickly muscled and broad; his arms, too, were well muscled. His chest was wide and tapered and covered with just the right amount of curling gold-tipped hair. His abdomen was ridged with muscle above the waistband of his shorts. His hips were narrow, his legs long and powerful-looking.

Molly stared, and then averted her eyes. What had happened between them would not happen again. She would not allow herself to feel so much as a flutter of desire for him. Or any other emotion.

"I don't want a Coke," she said.

"There's food, too, in the refrigerator. Cold chicken." Will stepped into the sweat pants and pulled them up his legs, his movements as leisurely as if he had all night.

"I'm not hungry."

"You were earlier." There was a double meaning to that that Molly couldn't miss.

"I got over it," she said shortly.

"So all this because I didn't take off my socks, hmm?" Will tied the drawstring around his waist. Molly glanced away again.

"Could you hurry, please? I really need to get home."

"Why? The last time you were out on a date, you didn't get in till nearly midnight." Will pulled the sweat shirt over his head and thrust his arms through the sleeves. Like the sweat pants, the sweat shirt was gray, with some sort of athletic logo.

The date he referred to had been with Jimmy Miller, of course, and Will had been wildly jealous of the result. The knowledge of that jealousy now shimmered in the air between them, though his tone was mild. Molly thought of the hickey, felt her neck burn in silent reminder that she sported a new one, courtesy of Will, and mentally fled from the memory.

"Look, are you one of those guys who has to hash things to death afterward? So we had sex, all right? You wanted it and I wanted it and we did it and now it's out of our systems. Life goes on from there."

For a second or two Will merely looked at her.

"Are you trying to tell me that as far as you're concerned I'm just a one-night stand?" Will sounded almost amused. Molly crossed her arms over her breasts and watched as he thrust his feet into black sneakers and tied the laces. She was on edge, as jumpy as a frog in a frying pan, and his deliberate movements were all she needed to drive her around the bend.

"I wouldn't have put it that way, but yes, more or less," she snapped.

"Don't call me, I'll call you?" he asked, standing up.

"Yes."

Will walked toward her, fully clothed now, looking impossibly sexy in the collarless gray sweats. He was unsmiling. Molly expected—what? That he would try to take her in his arms and kiss her? That he would tell her she was behaving foolishly, and ask her to reconsider? That he would be angry, or hurt, or pleading?

"If that's the way you want it," Will said with a shrug, and handed her her brown sweater, which he had retrieved from the chair.

32

When they arrived at the house, Will insisted on walking her to the door. Molly marched ahead of him, brushing past Pork Chop, who greeted them with the inevitable barks of delight. The house lights were on. The windows glowed warm incandescent yellow. The porch was shadowy, but not so dark that she couldn't see. When she reached the door, Molly turned to face Will, who had of course followed her up onto the porch.

"So nothing grabbed me, okay? You can leave now."

"Not till you're inside," Will said calmly. He was being so good-humored about being dumped that it was driving Molly crazy. Every other boyfriend she had ever had, whether she had slept with them or not—and to tell the truth she had slept with remarkably few—would have been begging her for explanations by this time. In fact, being dumped seemed to act on men like the most powerful of aphrodisiacs. The more you told them they weren't wanted, the more abjectly in love they fell.

Except for this man.

"All right," she snapped, whirling to pull open the screen and fit her key in the lock. The light was on in the kitchen, she saw as she pushed the door open, but the room was deserted. The TV blared from the living room, and she assumed her siblings were in there.

"Molly, is that you?" Ashley called, confirming her guess.

"Yes, it's me," Molly answered, then turned to Will, blocking his access to the house.

"I take it you're not asking me in." He sounded almost amused again. He had hold of the edge of the screen, so she could not pull the door closed in his face.

"No, I'm not."

"You're not going to kiss me good night?"

Molly did not even dignify that with an answer.

"What will your brothers and sisters think?"

Hard as it was to believe, the man was actually teasing her! Molly gritted her teeth.

"To tell you the truth, I don't particularly care. I just want you out of here and out of my life."

There was a brief pause, and then Will smiled at her. "You're forgetting something, I think."

"What?" Molly asked suspiciously.

"However you may feel about me personally, professionally nothing's changed. You still work for me, you still do what I tell you, and to all intents and purposes I'm still your boyfriend. Got that?"

Molly stared at him. She *had* forgotten that. She was not going to be able just to cut him out of her life. She was going to have to deal with him, every day, until he returned to Chicago.

On his terms.

"Get some sleep, honey," Will said on a caressing

note. Behind her, Molly glimpsed Ashley entering the kitchen, and assumed the loving tone was for her sister's benefit. Then Will curled a hand around her nape and bent his head to drop a quick, hard kiss on her mouth.

"Don't do that again," Molly growled so that only he could hear when he released her. To her fury, he chucked her under the chin with avuncular indulgence, called a cheerful good night to Ashley, and then, and only then, left the porch.

She couldn't even give herself the pleasure of slamming the door behind him. With Ashley as a witness she had to close it quietly, and could only give vent to her spleen by the secret savagery with which she locked it.

"You're home early," Ashley said in all innocence. "Didn't Will want to come in?"

Molly forced a smile as she faced her sister, and proceeded to spin one more in what was beginning to seem like a positive web of lies.

Then she retired to her room, went to bed, and lay awake the rest of the night.

It was around midnight when Will found himself driving past Molly's house again. After taking her home, he had made use of his unexpected free time to resume his interrupted search of Howard Lawrence's office. This time he found something of more than passing interest: a blackmail note. Or at least what appeared to be one.

Composed of different-size letters cut from magazines and pasted onto plain white typing paper, the note said simply, *I kNow WhAt yOU did.* There was no specific threat, no demand for payment. That led Will to suspect it was one in a series of notes, but he came up empty searching for others. Still, his instinct, which was rarely wrong, told him that this was it: the smoking gun. He'd never bought the story of Lawrence's suicide. His reading of the man had been that he wasn't the type. Here was the first concrete evidence that he was right. Someone, somehow, had apparently known that Lawrence was talking to him, and had found the knowledge fertile ground for blackmail. Was Lawrence killed as a result? It seemed likely.

There was no envelope—a return address was really too much to hope for—and the paper was not creased as it would have been had it been folded for mailing, so Will deduced it had been hand-carried to the recipient. He would have it tested for fingerprints first thing in the morning. He would also check Lawrence's bank records for any unusual payouts. Not that he was likely to find that the trainer had written his blackmailer a check, but an unusual transaction would at least serve to confirm his theory.

It was the first crack in the case since Lawrence's death. Despite the debacle with Molly earlier in the evening, Will felt almost mellow as he headed back toward Lexington.

Although it was not precisely on the way, Will turned down the road that led past Molly's house. Horse folk, by and large, were early-to-bed, early-to-rise types, and nearly every house he passed was dark. Molly's was no exception. It was quiet beneath the starry sky. The only movement came from the swaying branches of the gnarled oak in the front yard, and the shifting shadows caused by clouds playing tag with a ghostly moon.

Molly—and the rest of them—would be asleep.

He was fifty kinds of an idiot to be driving past her house in the middle of the night, he knew. Will thought of the lovesick yokel and almost snorted. Surely he was not that bad. Or at least if he was, he'd be damned if he'd let it show.

He still hadn't figured out precisely what had gone wrong between him and Molly earlier that evening, but he knew this: A universal truth of life is, the harder you chase something, the faster it runs away. He was too old a hand at the games women play to go whining after Molly when she was walking away.

The correct strategy in that situation was to walk away himself.

Though in this case it was hard. The sex they'd had had been fantastic, and there'd been just enough of it to whet his appetite. He wanted more. A whole lot more.

It looked like he was going to have to work to get it.

Fool, he called himself for the dozenth time. He'd known from the beginning that he was falling for a mantrap. A sexy little she-devil of a mantrap who chewed men up and spit them out like bubble gum.

So what had he expected? Certainly not forever. Anyway, he wasn't into forever himself. He didn't *want* forever.

He wanted to take Molly to bed and keep her there for about a month and after that . . .

After that he'd probably have her out of his system. He'd kiss her good-bye and go back to Chicago and get on with his life.

But he'd be the one to make the break, damn it. Not her. And not yet.

Will was almost past the house when he saw it: a dark figure skulking across the yard. Unable for a moment to believe what he was seeing, Will blinked, stared—and almost drove into a tree.

After righting the car just barely in the nick of time, his first impulse was to slam on the brake, jump out, and give chase there and then. But he controlled himself, drove on around the bend, doused his lights, and turned the car around.

Coming back, he pulled off onto a bumpy dirt track that led through a stand of tall sycamores not far from the house, unscrewed the interior light bulb so that he could open the door without being seen, and got out of the car. The pistol he kept in the glove compartment was in his hand.

The moon was high overhead, providing plenty of illumination. Will skirted the perimeter of the yard, keeping to the shadows, his eyes moving carefully over the bushes near the house. They were some kind of evergreen, overgrown and badly in need of trimming. For a Peeping Tom, or a burglar, or whatever, they would provide perfect cover.

For a moment Will thought that he was too late; whoever had been prowling about the house was gone.

Then he rounded a corner, and saw a dark shape creeping around the rear of the house. Creeping toward Molly's bedroom window, in fact.

Will was suddenly, furiously angry.

Low to the ground, gun drawn, Will raced toward the figure.

The interloper glanced around, saw him, and ran.

"Freeze!"

Will aimed his pistol at the fleeing figure, which kept right on fleeing. Cursing, Will stuck the pistol in his waistband at the small of his back, and gave chase. This was the creep Susan had seen in the window that night he had danced with Molly, Will had little doubt. It might even be the sicko who had hurt the horse. Whoever he was, he had no business outside Molly's bedroom window.

His days as a track-and-field star had left Will nearly matchless in any ordinary footrace between creep and cop. He was on the guy's heels in a matter of minutes, then brought him down with a flying tackle not far from the road.

It was not until Will had his knee on the culprit's spine and one of his arms jerked up tight behind his back that he realized he'd captured a kid.

Mike, to be precise. The dark ponytail and glinting earring made him unmistakable.

"You stupid little shit," Will said, easing his grip slightly but not releasing the kid, thankful that he never had been one to shoot first and ask questions later. "Don't you know enough to freeze when somebody tells you to? I could have shot you."

"Get the hell off me, asshole," Mike panted over his shoulder.

"What are you doing outside at this time of night? It's after midnight."

"It's none of your business what I'm doing out here. Just because you're fucking my sister doesn't give you any rights over me."

"Hey," Will said, tightening his grip again.

"Let go!"

"You don't talk that way about your sister."

"She's *my* sister and I'll talk about her any way I want to. Now, get off."

"Or what, tough guy?" Will shifted position and gave Mike a quick, one-handed pat-down. The kid's pockets were full.

"You can't do that! I'll kill you! I swear to God I will!" Mike struggled futilely as Will began to pull an assortment of items from his pockets. The last treasure revealed was a Baggie with a small amount of what looked like cigarette tobacco in the bottom. Will grimaced, and dangled the Baggie in front of Mike's face. "What's this, hero?"

Mike gave a particularly ferocious heave, and when that didn't work to dislodge Will he let loose with a string of curse words that would have shocked Madonna. Will was unmoved.

"None of your business, is what it is," Mike finally ground out.

"Okay." Will kept his knee on the kid's back. His grip secure on the arm he held, he was quiet for a moment. Then he said, "The way I see it is, you have three options: I can call the police right now, and pass this interesting substance on to them; we can go wake up Molly, tell her the whole story, and let her decide what to do; or you can come with me and try to persuade me why I shouldn't do either of the above."

Mike seemed to think that over. At any rate, he quit struggling. "Come with you where?" he asked suspiciously. Will almost smiled. Like Molly, the kid wasn't big on trust.

"To my car. It's parked by the road."

"What are you, some kind of pervert? If you think I'm going to give you a blow job or something in return for keeping quiet, you can just think again."

Will tightened his grip on Mike's arm, and Mike yelped.

"Another remark like that and you no longer have a choice to make," Will said grimly.

"All right, I'll go to your car!" Mike gasped.

"I don't hear an apology."

"Sorry!"

"That's better."

Will released his prisoner and got to his feet. Mike scrambled upright as well, scooping his belongings back into his pockets. Will kept the Baggie, tucking it into his own pocket.

"Asshole," Mike muttered.

33

"Run, and I call the cops," Will said, knowing the kid was thinking of doing exactly that. Mike's sulky expression confirmed it.

"Come on." Will headed for his car. A quick glance around told him that Mike was following. Will slid behind the wheel, restoring the pistol to the glove compartment just as Mike got in the passenger side.

"Were you headed out, or in?" Will asked when Mike shut the door. It was dark inside the car, but despite the shadows Will could see Mike's expression. The kid shot him a glance of intense dislike.

"In."

"Where you been?"

"Is that any of your business?"

Will gave him a level look. "Yeah, it is."

Mike's expression turned sullen. "I was meeting friends."

"Over at the barn at Sweet Meadow Stud?"

"We're not *stupid.*"

"Found a new meeting place, hmm?"

"Yeah."

"So what's with the pot?" Will asked.

"I smoke it sometimes. So what?"

"So it's illegal, and if you get caught with it you could end up in a juvenile facility. To say nothing of how much it'll hurt your family, and how much it'll cost to get you out of trouble, if it can even be done."

Mike shrugged.

"It's also really *stupid*, because the cops have their eye on you already. They know you were one of the kids in that barn, but they can't prove it. That kind of thing makes cops mad. They catch you with pot on you, and you're gone. They'd also like to hang something else on you—like the horse mutilations. So you get in trouble, and you're just helping them out."

"That's such shit. I never touched that horse."

"That's what Molly said, and I take her word for it. But the cops don't know that. They think you and maybe some of your friends did it, and if they catch you with pot it's just going to help them make their case."

"Even if they do catch me, what are they gonna do to me? I'm fourteen."

"If the crime's serious enough, they can charge you as an adult anyway. That means a juvenile facility until you're eighteen, and then adult prison after that. You ever been in a juvenile facility, Mike?"

"No," Mike said. Then, "Molly has. She says it wasn't so bad."

Will paused, processing the information. "Molly likes to pretend she's tough. A juvenile facility *is* bad, Mike. I wouldn't want to see you end up there."

"What do you care? You don't even like me."

"I like your sister. If it comes to that, I like your whole family. How far off the gene pool can you be?"

Something that was almost a smile emerged from Mike.

A thought occurred to Will. "How'd you get out of the house without waking everybody up, anyway? Isn't the alarm system on?"

"The one you bought?" The hostility was back in Mike's voice. "It was. I turned it off."

"There wasn't a key in your pocket. How are you going to get back in? Tell me you didn't come out and leave the door unlocked with the alarm system off." With everything that had been going on, the idea of anybody being able to walk into a house where Molly lay sleeping made the hair rise on the back of Will's neck.

"You had no business going through my pockets—and anyway I went out the window. The one you fixed. The lock works great, by the way."

"Thanks." Will's voice was dry. "You know, somebody could go in that window as well as come out it. You ever think of that?"

"Who's going to go in the window?" Mike asked scornfully.

"Whoever Susan saw peeping in, maybe."

"That was just Susan's imagination. She always has been a 'fraidycat."

"Maybe. Maybe not. The point is, you're putting your sisters and brother at risk every time you sneak out that window and leave it unlocked." Will decided to quit there. From his dealings with his own son, he had learned that belaboring a subject to death was a good way to get a teenager to tune you out. Any points that were scored were usually scored with subtlety, not haranguing.

"You're a sophomore in high school, right?"

"A freshman." Mike sounded wary, as if he didn't much trust this change of subject.

"You like school?"

"It's okay."

"You play sports?"

"No."

"Why not?"

"Sports are for boneheads."

"You don't like basketball?" Will sounded shocked.

Mike shrugged.

"You ever *played* basketball?"

"Sure I've played basketball. In gym." Mike's voice was defensive.

"Your school got a team?"

"Of course it's got a team. What high school doesn't have a team?"

"You're not on it."

"No."

"Did you try out?"

"Why would I try out? I've got about as much chance of making the team as I do of getting run over by a herd of buffaloes in the front yard."

"Is that so? I'm surprised. You're tall. You're fast on your feet. You seem plenty coordinated. What's the problem?"

Mike shrugged.

"When I was in school, the girls went for the jocks. Basketball, football, wrestling, track and field—man, we had the girls lined up."

"You were on a team? Which one?" There was a note of unwilling interest in Mike's voice.

"Track and field. And basketball. I liked girls."

"Yeah." Mike sounded so gloomy that Will realized he'd hit a nerve.

"Things have probably changed, though. Girls nowadays are too smart to like a guy just because he's a jock."

"Not really."

"Oh, yeah?" Will cast him a sideways glance. "I know where there's a basketball court. You interested in shooting some hoops, sometime?"

"I can't hit the broad side of a barn."

"We could work on that. It's all in the technique, you know. I taught my kid how to play, and he's a pretty fair shot. In fact, he's going to college on a basketball scholarship."

"You got a kid?"

"A son. Kevin. He's eighteen. He's a freshman at Western Illinois this year."

"Really?" A thought apparently occurred to Mike, and he frowned. "You telling me you got a wife too? And you're going out with Molly?"

Will laughed, glad the kid had enough feeling for his sister to object. "No, I don't have a wife. She died a long time ago."

"Jeez," Mike said. "You're old, aren't you?"

Will laughed again, but with less amusement. "I'm not that old. I can run circles around you, kid, and stuff a basketball in your eye anytime I feel like it too."

"Trash talk," Mike said, but he grinned.

"You think so?" Will looked at Mike. "I'll make a deal with you. You promise to stay in the house at night and lay off the pot, and I'll teach you how to play basketball. How about it?"

"Really?" Mike's response was wary. Will was once again reminded of Molly.

"Really. We can start tomorrow. I'll be over—oh, probably around six."

"You usually take Molly out."

Will shrugged. "Molly's mad at me, for the moment. Anyway, I'd enjoy teaching you the finer points of basketball. I've got a feeling you could be good."

"Really?" This time Mike sounded both wary and pleased.

"Really." Will said firmly. Then, "Uh—Mike."

"Yeah?"

"You could do me a favor."

"What?" The wariness was back in spades. Will wondered what the kid was expecting, remembered the pervert accusation, and grinned.

"Nothing horrible," he said. "Just tell me something about what Molly was like, growing up. About how things were for all of you, your family."

"Ah," Mike said, slanting him a sideways glance. "You want to know about things like our mom's suicide?"

"Yeah," Will said. "I'd like to know what makes your sister tick, but Molly doesn't like to talk about stuff. Your parents, for example."

"Molly always says that looking back is a mistake. All we can do is look forward." Again that sideways glance. "Actually, she just doesn't like to remember. Molly hasn't had what you'd call a really great life."

"I gathered that much. You told me your mom killed herself. What happened to your dad?"

"My dad's in prison. For armed robbery." Mike sounded almost proud. "Molly doesn't know where her dad is. He took off when she was a baby, and she hasn't heard from him since."

"You had different dads?"

"We all did. Except for the twins, of course."

"So your mom was married a bunch of times."

Mike shook his head. "She was married to Molly's dad, and I think to Ashley's. After that I don't think she bothered with getting married to the others."

"Was she a good mom?" Will tried hard to keep his voice neutral.

"Sometimes. Sometimes she was just the best mother in the world." Mike's voice faltered, and he took a deep breath. Will realized that, like Molly, Mike still suffered from their mother's death. After a second Mike continued softly, "And sometimes she wasn't. Sometimes she'd just take up with a man and go off and leave us. Or she'd try to kill herself, and they'd come and take her to a hospital. Social workers were always coming to get us and putting us in foster homes. I was in about seven."

"What about Molly?"

"She was, too, only she kept running away. Finally they put her in a home for girls. She liked that better, she said, but then she got caught shoplifting and that's when they put her in reform school."

"How long was she there?" Will's voice was quiet. Here in this pitiful little tale was the answer to the mystery of Molly, he realized. Her pride, her outward toughness, her inability to let anyone get too close. Her defenses had been forged in a hard school, one that he wasn't sure he could have survived himself.

"About two years, I think. They let her out when she turned eighteen. Then she went to live with our mother. See, they taught her how to be a groom in reform school, and when she got out she had this job with Wyland Farm. So Mom was glad to have her." This cynical view was expressed without bitterness.

"Were you living with your mom then? Any of you?"

Mike shook his head. "When Molly found out she

could rent our house as part of her pay, Mom came and got us all out of the foster homes we were in. Mom and Molly took care of us, and Molly worked, and even when Mom went off or had a spell it was okay, because Molly was here. We were all pretty happy, I thought, and then Mom went and killed herself. Molly said she was just sick, sick like somebody with cancer, only in her head. She didn't really mean to do it, she just couldn't help it." This last was said softly.

Will had to battle the impulse to put a sympathetic hand on the boy's shoulder. He had a feeling that Mike wouldn't receive the gesture kindly. The kid was too much like Molly.

"So you didn't have to go back to foster homes when your mom died?" Will asked after a moment.

Mike shook his head. "I don't think Molly ever notified any of the authorities that Mom died. She just kept on taking care of us, and Ashley was big enough to help by then, and we just all kind of stayed together."

Will was silent for a moment, mulling this over. Then, deliberately reaching for a lighter tone, he asked, "Has Molly always had a lot of boyfriends?"

Mike gave him a look. "You're pretty gone on her, aren't you?"

Will shrugged and smiled. "Yeah, I guess I am. But don't tell her, okay?"

"Okay." Mike was pleased by that bit of masculine bonding, Will could tell.

"So?" Will asked.

"Oh, the boyfriends." Mike thought a minute. "Yeah, she's always had guys after her ever since I can remember. She's really pretty, you know."

"I know," Will said dryly.

"Will," Mike said, shifting in his seat so that he was facing him. Will realized that it was the first time Mike had ever called him by name. He realized, too, from the kid's earnest tone that Mike was getting ready to say something that he considered important.

"Yeah?" Will prompted, according Mike his full attention.

"Molly's a really good person. A lot of guys hang around her, but she's not—she's not . . ."

Will knew what Mike was trying to say. "Easy? I know."

"I just wanted you to know."

"I appreciate that. I appreciate your telling me all this too." Will glanced at the clock on the dashboard. "You know, it's after one o'clock. Don't you have school tomorrow?"

"Yeah," said Mike, with a notable lack of enthusiasm.

"Then you'd better get to bed. Come on, I'll walk you back to the house. You climb back through the window and lock it and stay in there, you hear me?"

"I hear," Mike said.

34

October 17, 1995

The next night Will showed up at suppertime just as if nothing had happened between them. It had been another beautiful Indian summer day, all sunshine and gentle breezes, and it was still warm even at dusk. The oak in the front yard had disgorged almost all its leaves. They rustled whenever anybody or anything moved. Busy fixing the evening meal, Molly glanced out the open door as Pork Chop started to bark. Through the screen she could see Will's car parked in the driveway, and Will himself walking through the carpet of crimson and gold leaves toward the house. He was dressed in his gray sweats and carrying a large, gaily wrapped package under one arm.

Molly's reaction was a jumble of contradictions: The mere sight of him made her heart ache like a sore tooth; reflecting on the gall it took to continue to visit just as if he thought he were welcome made her angry; and despite her determination to have nothing further to do with him on a personal basis, she felt a spurt of very human satisfaction at the sight of the gift. She had every intention of cutting the man firmly out of her heart and life, but it was nice to see that he intended to grovel while she did it.

Bringing her a present wasn't going to change a thing, but it was a typical male peace offering.

Men were just the same, every one of them: They all panted after whatever it was they couldn't have.

Molly had had a busy day. Since she hadn't had to work, because it was a Tuesday and Keeneland wasn't running, she had done a million other things instead, determined not to give herself time to think about Will or anything else. She cleaned house, went to the Laundromat, and drove to Lexington to visit the resale shops to see if she could find something for Ashley to wear to the homecoming dance, which was only a few days away. Meaning to take her sister back with her if she found anything worth trying on, she had fallen in love with an ankle-length ivory silk slip dress with tiny spaghetti straps and a slight flare at the hem. She'd bought it for a ridiculously low price, with the understanding that it could be returned if Ashley didn't like it. Ashley had already tried it on and pronounced herself delighted with it, though Molly had a few misgivings. It was, she thought, too old for her sister. But unless they could find something better before Friday, it would have to do.

Molly would just have to see if she couldn't persuade Ashley to cover up some of that slinkiness with a sweater.

Ashley was in the kitchen now, humming happily as she mashed the potatoes. Using a fork, Molly turned coated pieces of chicken in a frying pan of sizzling hot grease, and kept an eye on the green beans simmering on the back of the stove. Sam and Susan were at the table finishing up a homework project that called for them to make an entire Comanche settlement out of homemade modeling clay. Mike was in the living room, supposedly working on his research paper.

"It's Will!" Susan said excitedly when Will tapped at the screen. Scrambling to let him in, she saw the present and stared at it big-eyed.

"Is that for Molly?" Susan asked with hushed respect as Will walked past her into the kitchen. Molly, turning her back on the newcomer, prepared to treat the gift—and the giver—with disdain.

"Nope," Will said cheerfully, ignoring Molly's icy silence and casting no more than a cursory glance over her flannel shirt, sweat pants and bare feet. "It's for Ashley."

"For me?" Ashley looked at him with amazement as he held out the beautifully wrapped box to her.

Will grinned and nodded. Ashley dropped the potato masher into the pan with a clatter and took the present. She looked down at it for a moment, then up at Will.

"Open it," he said.

"Open it, open it!" the twins echoed. Sam abandoned the Indian village to join Susan in crowding around Ashley. Mike, apparently drawn by the noise, came to lounge in the kitchen doorway and watch.

Trying not to feel affronted, Molly shifted the chicken from the skillet onto a serving platter, and observed the proceedings out of the corner of her eye.

Ashley removed the wrappings slowly, much to the twins' loudly expressed disgust, folding the paper with care and setting the ribbon aside for later reuse. The box was shiny white cardboard with the name of an exclusive retailer swirled across the lid in gold. When

Ashley somewhat hesitantly removed the lid, layers of white tissue paper billowed out.

"What on earth . . . ?" Ashley breathed, setting the box on the table and delving beneath the tissue paper, suddenly more eager than shy. "Oh, my!"

Gasping, Ashley lifted a dress from the box. A prom dress, to be precise, in a delicate shade of rose pink, with a demure off-the-shoulder neckline adorned in the middle by a silk rose. The dress was made with a fitted bodice and a filmy skirt that fell to the floor in layers of ruffles.

"Oh, my!" Ashley said again, staring at the dress as she held it at arm's length in front of her.

"Ashley, it's beautiful!" Susan breathed.

"It's a dress," Sam said to Mike with obvious disappointment. Mike grimaced in sympathetic response.

"Molly, look!" Ashley turned to hold the dress out for her older sister's inspection.

"It's gorgeous, Ash," Molly said, loath to rain on Ashley's parade just because she was determined to have nothing more to do with Will. The dress would suit Ashley like a dream, and it had clearly cost the earth. Far more than they could have afforded to spend. "Absolutely gorgeous."

"But I already have that white dress." Ever conscientious, Ashley remembered the dress Molly had bought for her and looked troubled.

Molly shook her head. "This one is perfect. I can take the other back."

"I love it." A smile trembled on Ashley's lips. Her eyes shone as she looked down at the pink dress again. At her sister's transparent delight, Molly felt a glow of gratitude toward Will, which she immediately suppressed. Yes, he was kind—and strong and handsome and sexy, too, if she were honest—but he was leaving. By the time he left, she was determined to feel nothing for him at all.

"Thank you, Will," Ashley said softly, her gaze swinging around to where he stood grinning at her. Then she crossed the room, put a hand on his shoulder, and stood on tiptoe to kiss his cheek.

"You're welcome," Will said as she stepped back to smile at him. "I figured it was the least I could do after stepping on your toes so many times."

"Stepping on *my* toes . . . !" Ashley laughed, a merry sound of pure joy, and shook her head. For an instant Molly got a glimpse of the lovely woman Ashley would be when she finally grew into herself.

"Try it on," Susan urged. Ashley, more than willing, picked up the dress and headed toward the bathroom.

"I suppose you're going to want to stay for supper," Molly said in a sour aside to Will as she rescued the potatoes Ashley had abandoned, and began to wield the potato masher on them with more force than was necessary.

"Not tonight." He glanced over to where Mike still lounged in the living room doorway, and raised his voice. "Mike and I are going to go shoot some hoops. I thought we'd grab a bite somewhere afterward."

"You are?" Astounded, Molly looked from Will to her brother to find that Mike had straightened away from the door frame, his expression more eager than she had seen it in months.

"Yeah," Mike said, carefully casual. Then, to Will, "Ready to go?"

"As soon as we admire your sister's dress," Will said as Ashley emerged from the bathroom with a shy "What do you think?"

She looked beautiful, was what Molly thought as Ashley pirouetted rather awkwardly before them. The soft rose of the dress made her skin seem creamy rather than pale, and the off-the-shoulder neckline was both flattering and modest. It was the perfect gown for a young girl to wear to her first dance. Molly was suddenly fiercely glad that Ashley possessed it, even if it was Will who had bought it for her.

"You look fantastic," Molly said, and everyone else—even Mike and Sam—echoed the compliment. Flushing at the praise, Ashley nevertheless looked supremely happy as she went to take the dress off.

"Ready?" Will said to Mike when Ashley had retired to the bathroom again.

Mike nodded and headed toward the door.

"I won't keep him out late," Will called back over his shoulder as he followed Mike out the door. "See ya."

Molly was left staring after them with the potato masher suspended over the pan.

"Do you believe that?" she said to Ashley, who had emerged from the bathroom in her jeans and was reverently folding her new dress back into its bed of tissues.

"What?" Ashley asked with dreamy inattention. It was clear from her sister's face that she was now so in charity with Will over the dress that she didn't see anything the least bit odd about Mike's going off with him so readily, so Molly forebore saying anything more. But she was frowning as she dished up supper, and cross for the rest of the night.

35

October 18, 1995

Before dawn the next morning, Will sat in front of the monitor in the van and moodily watched Molly muck out a stall. Her back was to the camera, as it had been pretty much the entire time he had been sitting there. He had been up all night going over the contents of Don Simpson's files. His eyes felt grainy as they followed Molly's movements. By this time he had every barn at Keeneland wired, copies of the office files of the four men under investigation, bank records, employment records, criminal records and racing records for just about every horse at Keeneland. It all added up to exactly nothing. He was getting desperate to find even one ringer. The puzzling thing about it was, the suspect trainers were still winning with long-shot horses—but *legitimate* long-shot horses, at least as far as he could tell. That left two possibilities: Either there were no ringers, which meant he had completely screwed up from the beginning and Lawrence had lied to him, or he was missing something. Much as he hated to face it, Will had a feeling that the second possibility was the correct one: He was missing something. But what?

It was galling to think that crooked horse races were being run right under his nose and he could not uncover how it was being done, but he was afraid that was the case.

Lawrence's "suicide" was another sticking point. For Will's money, it was just too convenient.

The blackmail note on which he had pinned such high hopes had not provided any enlightenment either; the only fingerprints on it belonged to Lawrence himself. If it even was a blackmail note. At this point, who knew?

His usual instinct for a case seemed to have deserted him on this one. Will had a pretty good inkling as to the reason why: He could not focus on it with his normal degree of concentration. The answer to the "why" to that was even now filling his monitor's screen: Molly. In the schmaltzy words of the old song, she had him bewitched, bothered, and bewildered.

Horny, too, though the song hadn't said anything about that.

His relationship with Molly was interfering with his work.

The van door opened. Will glanced up as Murphy, clad in his faux lawn service uniform and a good half-hour early, stepped inside. Murphy looked surprised to see him. They had agreed that Will, in his guise as Molly's boyfriend, would stay away from the van unless absolutely necessary.

One glance at the monitor appeared to answer Murphy's unspoken question concerning Will's presence, however. Will flushed, and had to fight an urge to flip the dial.

"Nothing happening in Barn 15," Will said as he turned casually away from the monitor.

Murphy was not deceived. He eased himself down on the couch and pulled a chocolate-covered doughnut out of the brown paper bag he held.

"So how's the belle of Woodford County today?" he asked, cocking an eyebrow at Molly's image on the monitor as he offered the paper bag to Will.

The belle of Woodford County. It was a good name for her. Will shrugged, and waved the bag away.

"Fine, as far as I know."

Murphy took a bite out of his doughnut, and glanced at the monitor again. "Don't look like she's fine to me."

"What do you mean?" Will swiveled around to look at the monitor himself.

"She's crying."

Molly was on her knees spreading fresh straw on the floor of the stall. She was facing the camera now. Will could clearly see the tears running down her cheeks.

For a moment he watched, paralyzed.

"Shit," Will said, and got to his feet. Murphy, the dog, was grinning widely as Will exited the van.

Though it was growing brighter by the minute outside, the lights in the barn were on. Will nodded at a security guard who was strolling out as he entered. The man nodded back without much interest. In a stall near the door, a swarthy little groom was holding on to a halter and crooning in Spanish to an obviously agitated horse. The groom glanced around as Will went by, but said nothing. The horse nickered and stomped its feet. There were some empty stalls, then the fuzzy donkey—burro—with the name Will couldn't remember twitched its ears at him. Farther along, another horse put its head out of its stall and watched him pass with almost human curiosity.

Molly was in a stall at the far end. Will reached it and rested his arms on top of the partly closed Dutch door, watching her. She was still on her knees, turned away from him, spreading straw for all she was worth. The overhead light lent a glossy sheen to her wavy dark hair, which spilled over her shoulders and down her back. When he thought about it, Will realized that he had never seen her wear her hair loose to work before. Then he figured out that she must be trying to hide the mark on her neck. He hadn't given a girl a hickey since high school. Remembering the particulars surrounding the giving of this one, he felt a stab of desire that aimed straight for his ulcer. As he eyed her back, Will's mouth twisted in wry amusement at his own reaction. Clad in old jeans and sneakers and an open flannel shirt over a turtleneck, Molly was still lovely enough to give him a stomachache.

As he watched, she lifted a hand to her eyes, brushing at them angrily. He heard an audible sniff.

"What's the matter, Molly?" His voice was tender. She jumped as if she had been shot, stumbled to her feet and whirled to glare at him, scrubbing at her cheeks with both hands.

"What are you doing here?" She was actively hostile—but then she spoiled it with a loud sniff.

"I just happened to be in the neighborhood . . ." he said with irony as he opened the stall door and walked inside. "You want to tell me what's wrong, or do I get to guess?" His voice sharpened. "Is it Mike?"

He stopped in front of her. She looked up at him, and he saw that despite her efforts her big brown eyes still brimmed with tears. He wondered if she had been crying long. From the look of her, she had.

"Go away," she said as a tear coursed down her cheek. She brushed it away with a muttered curse, and glared at him.

"Did something happen to one of the kids?" Will was surprised at the degree of anxiety he felt. Like their older sister, the younger Ballard siblings had in some inexplicable fashion managed to worm their way into his heart to a surprising degree.

"No." Molly's voice was curt. She turned her back on him and picked up a pitchfork, using it to spread out the straw. "Go away. I don't want to see you, and anyway you're going to get me in trouble if Mr. Simpson catches you in here. We're not supposed to have visitors while we're working."

"I'm not leaving until you tell me what's the matter. Somehow I don't think you're the type to cry just because you're having a virulent attack of PMS."

Will had dealt with enough women to know that any male reference to PMS was the equivalent of waving a red flag before a bull, and it worked that way with Molly too. She swung around to face him, eyes glittering, teeth gritted, and a pitchfork in her hands.

"Get," she said, sounding as if she meant it.

"Not till you tell me why you're crying." Will stood his ground, but eyed the pitchfork warily.

"If you have to know, it's Sheila," she said after a moment.

Will had heard the name before, but he couldn't quite place it. Reaching out, he caught the shank of the pitchfork, pulled it out of her hands, and leaned it up against the side of the stall.

"Sheila?" he questioned, turning back to her.

"The mare." Molly spat the words at him.

"The mare?" Will repeated stupidly, still not quite making the connection.

"The mare in the field. The mare the horse slasher attacked. Remember her?" Molly threw the words out as if she hated him. Her fists were clenched and her eyes sparkled with anger. Will might have been fooled into thinking that she was furious rather than hurting—but then another fat tear coursed down her cheek.

Will looked at her, said a swear word under his breath, caught her wrist, and pulled her into his arms. Molly resisted, her body rigid, her hands pushing against his chest.

"What about Sheila?" Will asked, his voice as soft as his eyes as she glared up at him. His arms were locked around her waist. He had no intention of letting her go.

Molly's lower lip quivered. All the fight went out of her suddenly. Her gaze dropped and she leaned into him, resting her forehead against his chest.

"They put her down this morning," she said in a muffled voice to his expensive silk tie.

Her shoulders shook. Will realized that she was crying, and realized, too, that what she had told him meant the horse was dead. He tightened his arms around her slender form, bent his head and pressed his lips to her hair. Murmuring almost meaningless words of comfort, he rocked her back and forth, kissing the tip of her ear, her temple, whatever he could reach. She snuggled closer, burrowing against him like a small child seeking warmth, and wrapped her arms around his waist beneath his jacket.

It was only when she looked up and he bent his

head to kiss her mouth that Will remembered they were on *Candid Camera.* Moving one hand behind his back, he gave Murphy the bird. Then his lips found Molly's, and he forgot all about Murphy again.

Approaching voices broke them apart. Molly pushed against his shoulders, Will glanced up, and then she was out of his arms, frantically tidying her hair and clothes and wiping at her face with the tail of her shirt. Will straightened his tie and buttoned his coat, watching her quizzically. She didn't so much as look at him as she hurried to the stall door and stepped out into the wide barn corridor, closing the door behind her.

"Yo, Miss Molly!" The exuberant greeting left Will in no doubt as to the identity of at least one of the newcomers: Thornton Wyland. He started to follow Molly, to make his presence known. Then he hesitated. She'd said his presence would get her into trouble. Will realized if he emerged from the same empty stall that she had just exited, that might very well be true. So he stuck his hands in his pockets and stayed where he was, feeling like a fool as he skulked out of sight.

"Hello—Molly?" The voice, with its slight hesitation, as if the speaker couldn't quite remember Molly's name, was a woman's. Peering through a crack in the wooden wall and feeling about ten years old, Will recognized Helen Trapp.

"We're looking for Don," Helen Trapp continued. Will realized she was referring to the trainer. "Do you know where he is?"

"Probably trackside," Molly answered. "He wanted to clock Tabasco Sauce's workout. Mr. Simpson's got high hopes for him in the Bluegrass Stakes this Saturday."

"So do we all," said Helen Trapp, smiling, then turned as though about to leave the barn.

"Speaking of the Bluegrass Stakes," Thornton said to Molly. "We're having a party at our house afterward. A humdinger. Fancy dinner, dancing, black tie. I could pick you up at seven."

Helen Trapp looked surprised and a little disapproving of her nephew's sudden invitation. Will disapproved himself, though he supposed it was futile to hope that Wyland—and every other man too—would simply give up and leave Molly alone. He waited for Molly to tell the slimeball, in some more or less polite way, to get lost.

"That sounds like fun," Molly said, smiling at Thornton in a witchy way that did bad things to Will's blood pressure. "I'd love to come."

Will's jaw dropped. He could scarcely believe his ears. Molly considered Thornton Wyland an opportunistic creep, he knew. Almost as soon as he had the thought he knew, too, why she accepted, when she had turned Wyland down so many times before: because she knew he could hear.

Molly was accepting Wyland's invitation for no other reason than to torment him.

Will's fists clenched. His muscles tightened. His stomach roiled.

He realized that there was absolutely nothing he could do.

Except pretend he didn't care.

"You mean you're saying *yes*?" Wyland sounded as surprised as Will felt. When Molly nodded, he grinned at her like a man who had just won the lottery—which in a way Will supposed he had. "We'll have a great time. I promise."

"I'll look forward to it." Molly, who had fallen into step with Wyland and his aunt as they walked away, sounded as if she didn't have a care in the world. If Will had not known it for a fact, he never would have guessed that just minutes before she had been crying in his arms, and kissing him as if it meant something.

Watching the three of them walk out of the barn together, Will didn't know whether to curse or kick the wall.

So he did both. Not that it helped.

All it did, Will realized with disgust, was provide further amusement for Murphy via the monitor.

36

October 21, 1995

Molly realized she had made a bad mistake before the evening was barely under way. To begin with, there was Thornton. His hands were all over her every chance he got. Driving to the Big House in his bright red Corvette, he'd rested his hand on her knee; at the dinner table, he'd put his arm around her shoulders so many times, she'd felt like asking him if he'd ever considered a career as a mink stole; now they were dancing, and he was nuzzling her neck while his hands slid perilously closer to her rump with every step.

He seemed to feel that by accepting his invitation, she had also agreed to fall into his bed. The hideous thing was, Molly had known he would feel that way, had known how he would expect the evening to end. And she had accepted his invitation anyway. Because Will had kissed her and she loved him and no matter how she tried to deny the feeling it didn't seem to be going away.

She had tried to tell herself that one man was as good as another, and that Thornton, who was handsomer, younger, and richer than Will, would be a good bet to help her get Will out of her mind.

The problem was, Thornton wasn't kinder than Will, or a gentleman like Will. He wasn't solid, steady, and dependable. He didn't make her feel safe.

And for all his looks and money, he didn't turn her on.

With Thornton, there were no sparks. When he held her in his arms, all she wanted to do was kick his shins.

One or the other of Thornton's friends had been watching them all night. Allison Weintraub was the worst. Molly knew the slender blonde with the jealous blue eyes by sight, though they'd never been introduced before tonight. From something the other girl said, Molly realized that she had been with Thornton at Keeneland the day Will had kissed her hand; Molly hadn't recognized her at the time. Gossip had it that she meant to be Mrs. Thornton Wyland. In any case, Allie, as Thornton called her, clearly considered Thornton hers. She just as clearly resented Molly to the point of hatred. If Allison had had a knife, Molly knew she would have felt it in her back.

Thornton's male friends, few of whom Molly knew because they ran in such different circles, watched Molly too, but not with dislike. They were avid to make her acquaintance.

They upbraided Thornton for keeping her a secret from them, and tried to cut in. Thornton rebuffed them with good-humored firmness. Molly, he said to her annoyance, was private stock.

"I really like the way your dress feels. What is it, satin?" Breathed in her ear, this gambit presumably was designed to explain away Thornton's stroking hands.

"Silk," Molly said pleasantly, knowing that she looked good in the ivory slip dress that she had bought for Ashley, and knowing, too, that her dress could not hold a candle, style- or costwise, to any of the other women's gowns. "And if you don't keep your hands where they belong, I'm going to knee you where it counts right here in the middle of the dance floor."

Thornton laughed, pulling her tighter against him and twirling her around. In a classic black tuxedo, he looked so handsome that by rights Molly knew she should have been dazzled. But she wasn't, and when he kissed the side of her neck it was all she could do not to carry out her threat.

The only thing that held her back was the potential embarrassment of making such a scene in front of all these people—there must have been at least two hundred crowded into the Big House's ballroom, and more circulating through the twin double parlors off which the ballroom opened. Molly felt outclassed by the company, no matter how fiercely she told herself otherwise.

Across the room, Helen Trapp, resplendent in a glittering gold gown that must have cost the earth, watched them with a worried expression as she stood on the sidelines talking to Tyler. Whatever Tyler said must have reassured her, because after a moment her frown cleared, and she turned to chat with a woman friend.

Molly presumed Tyler had assured his sister that nothing permanent was likely to come of Thornton's infatuation with one of the grooms.

From the time she'd entered the Big House, with its twelve-foot ceilings and glittering chandeliers, its gorgeous oriental carpets and stately antiques, Molly had felt out of place. Helen Trapp and her daughter, Neilie, a statuesque brunette, were not responsible for that, but they had made their own small contribution to Molly's sense of unease. In line to greet the arriving guests, they had in the most subtle way possible looked down their noses at Thornton's date, smiling and chatting politely all the while.

Molly guessed they feared she might somehow manage to snare Thornton permanently.

But she had news for them, she thought as Thornton's hands slid too low again, she didn't *want* Thornton permanently. She didn't want him at all.

"Excuse me, I have to go to the rest room," Molly said as the music ended and Thornton showed every inclination to keep his arms around her until it started up again. The band in the corner had so far played nothing but slow dances. Molly wondered who she had to thank for that.

She wouldn't have been surprised to learn that Thornton had something to do with it, but because he had not left her side since she had walked through the door several hours before, she could only speculate. It was possible that slow dances were all they played at these fancy parties. Never having been to one before, she had no way of knowing.

"If you're running away to powder your nose, baby, don't bother. You already look good enough to eat." Thornton grinned at her and took a playful bite out of one white shoulder.

"I'm not," Molly said, pulling herself out of his arms. "I have to pee."

She said that last deliberately, enjoying its shock value, determined not to let herself be intimidated by the upper-crust crowd or rich surroundings. Thornton chuckled. Molly could feel his gaze on her back as she walked away.

The powder room—they actually called it that—was off the front hall. It was larger than Molly's bedroom. The floor and vanity top were of gray marble, the wallpaper featured what appeared to be hand-painted birds, and the white china sink had been custom made to match. A huge gilt mirror over the sink reflected the light of two elaborate crystal sconces that had been set right into the glass. Making use of the facilities, Molly discovered that the toilet made no noise at all when it was flushed, and the exquisite pink soaps that looked exactly like tiny rosebuds actually *smelled* of roses too. A filagree-over-crystal dispenser by the sink held hand lotion, Molly discovered when she touched the handle. Rubbing some into her hands, she fell in love with the soft floral scent.

Vaseline Intensive Care it wasn't.

Molly brushed her hair, powdered her nose, and freshened her lipstick, then stood back to regard herself critically in the glass.

It was easy to see why she had fallen in love with the dress in the resale shop, she thought, because it might have been made for her, not Ashley. The thin spaghetti straps and lingerie neckline bared her shoulders and the soft uppermost curves of her breasts. The lustrous silk clung to her every curve and shimmered when she moved. That particular shade of ivory enhanced her dark hair and eyes, and made her skin look as creamy as her favorite Baskin-Robbins flavor, French vanilla.

So the dress was secondhand, and had only cost thirty-seven dollars. So what? No one here was aware of that, and it looked fabulous on her. Molly knew it did.

Why then did she feel so out of place?

You can take the girl out of the reform school, but you can't take the reform school out of the girl. The thought made Molly squirm.

But she wasn't going to let it defeat her. She was good enough, she told herself stoutly, for the Wylands or any of them. As her mother used to say, it's not where you come from but where you're going that counts.

Right now, Molly decided, she was going home.

She'd been stupid to come, and she was only going to compound her stupidity if she hung around till the end of the evening. Thornton's plans for her were very clear.

She could fight him off, of course, but it *would* be a fight and she was not up to it. The smart thing to do would be to ditch him now and walk home across the fields.

Two other women were waiting outside the powder room when she emerged. Molly smiled at them as she passed, and they smiled back. Molly felt a sudden renewal of confidence. Those two strangers with their elegant hairdos and beautiful designer gowns had seen nothing wrong with her. She had to keep telling herself that her background did not show, like a badge of shame.

As she walked toward the kitchen she was smiling.

In the ballroom, the band performed a drumroll. Cymbals crashed and some sort of announcement was made. Molly couldn't quite understand the words.

"Champagne, Miss Molly?" To her consternation, Thornton came out of the kitchen just as she reached it. He was carrying a champagne glass full of golden bubbly in each hand. "We have to drink a toast to Tabasco Sauce's victory, you know."

Tabasco Sauce had won the Bluegrass Stakes hours earlier. *That* was what the announcement had been about, she had no doubt. Seeing no help for it and in any case not loath to celebrate something that touched her as nearly as anyone there, she accepted the glass. The win made it a great day for Wyland Farm.

"To Tabasco Sauce," Thornton said, clicking his glass with hers. He gulped at his champagne, while Molly took a sip of hers. For all its vaunted reputation, champagne wasn't much to her taste.

"And to our first date." Thornton drained his glass and set it down on the tray of a passing waiter. "It's been a long time coming, but I mean to see that it's worth the wait."

With that he reached for Molly. She jumped back to avoid being caught in his bear hug, and sloshed champagne all over her dress. Looking down in dismay at the stain spreading across her skirt, Molly didn't demur when Thornton took the goblet from her with a teasing "Tssk!"

"There's a bathroom right through here," he said, pulling her into a nearby wood-paneled den. The den did indeed have its own bathroom, masculine in decor but no less elegant than the powder room. Setting her glass down on the vanity and picking up a towel, Thornton dabbed at her skirt.

"It doesn't matter." Being alone with Thornton in a bathroom was not a situation in which she cared to stay. Tugging her skirt from his grasp, Molly edged toward the door.

"Oh, no, you don't." Grinning, he did his bear hug

thing again. This time he caught her, and wrapped both arms around her waist, pulling her against him. "I've got you alone at last, and I'm not letting you go."

His breath hit her full in the face. Molly realized that Thornton had had too much to drink.

"Give me a kiss, beautiful," he growled, his mouth swooping down on hers. He tasted of champagne and garlic, a combination Molly found repulsive. Thrusting his tongue into her mouth with bold confidence, Thornton kissed her. Molly let him, and was disappointed to find his sloppy technique less than thrilling. Thornton was so very handsome, with a hard male body every bit as masculine as Will's and a moneyed background to boot, that by rights he should have been able to knock the memory of Will's kisses clean out of her head. No such luck, though, as she should have known. The chemistry simply wasn't there. Molly waited the kiss out, hoping he would be satisfied with that and let her go.

She should have known better.

His mouth crept down her throat at the same time as one hand slid up her rib cage to cover her breast.

"Stop it, Thornton!" she said, pushing at his shoulders in an unmistakable demand to be released. He ignored her, fumbling about in a less than deft attempt to thrust his hand down the front of her dress. She struggled, and one of her straps broke, sending the left side of her neckline south. Grabbing at her dress with one hand, sputtering with rage, Molly doubled up her fist and socked Thornton smack in the nose.

"Ow!" He released her, stumbling back, his hand flying to his face. Blood gushed from his nostrils. Molly could not help but feel smug as he tilted his head back, pinching his nostrils shut with one hand. There was something to be said for an upbringing like hers, after all: She had learned to take care of herself.

"Serves you right," she said to Thornton, who was groping along the counter, presumably for a towel. She handed him one, then walked out the door.

Minutes later she was running along the pea-gravel path that bisected the Big House's back garden, and letting herself out the wrought-iron gate that separated the lawn from the fields.

Home was not more than two miles distant. Molly had walked it many times. The problem was, she had walked it wearing sneakers or boots and jeans. Tonight she was wearing heels and a very bare evening dress with a long, tight skirt.

Fortunately it was a warm night, with a beautiful starry sky and a three-quarter moon to light the way.

She even had company, in the form of tight little groups of grazing Thoroughbreds dotted about the fields. Since the attack on Sheila—as soon as the mare entered her mind Molly pushed her out again, refusing to allow herself to remember—another security guard had been hired to assist J.D. with his nightly rounds. But neither J.D. nor his colleague was in evidence now.

Molly lifted her skirt high as she trudged over the spongy ground, stepping carefully to avoid the occasional horse pile. Tall hemlocks and spruces ringed the fields, creating dark, shadowy borders where the moonlight did not reach. The sounds of the night—a hooting owl, the squeal of a rodent that might have been its prey, rustling leaves, the soft swish of her own passage through the ankle-high grass—were familiar. She was no stranger to the rolling pasturelands at night.

But something about this night was different. Eerie.

Hard as she tried to repress it, the memory of Sheila rose in her mind.

Something evil walked these fields by night.

The thought made Molly shiver, and stop in her tracks to cast quick glances all around.

She was no coward, but she was not stupid either. Belatedly, it occurred to her that choosing to walk home across the fields at night might not have been the smartest thing she had ever done.

But it was too late now. There was no way she was going back. Anyhow, she was almost a third of the way home.

Molly shivered again, and told herself it was because the wind was picking up. She resumed walking, deliberately conjuring up pleasant thoughts.

Ashley in her pink dress had been absolutely beautiful.

Molly's face softened as she remembered how her sister had blushed and smiled at the boy who had come to pick her up the night before. Like Ashley, Trevor was seventeen, tall and thin with glasses, blemishes, and a dirty-blond bowl cut. Ashley had looked at him as if he were the handsomest thing in the world.

There was no accounting for taste, Molly thought, shaking her head. Take herself, for example: Thornton Wyland, with his good looks, money, and fine old name, turned her off.

What turned her on was Will.

Without warning Molly set her foot down in a hole, and fell sideways, landing on her hip. For a moment she sat there, more surprised than hurt. Getting to her feet, she discovered that she was standing on the cover of what seemed to be an old well. The lid was a stone circle not more than three feet in diameter. It was very old, Molly guessed, because grass grew thickly around and over it. She never would have seen it if her foot had not found the one place that had broken away, and plunged downward.

Starting off again, Molly stumbled and realized that her encounter with the well had broken the heel off one shoe. They were Ashley's, actually, sparkly silver slippers that she had bought to go with her prom dress. Molly grimaced. Ashley was not going to be happy when she saw her shoe. Molly wondered if she could repair the heel with superglue.

Hobbling, she made it a few more yards before stopping once more. Cursing under her breath, she pulled off the intact shoe and did her level best to break its heel. Of course it was impossible; that was how life worked. Slipping the shoe back on, Molly stayed where she was, darting quick glances everywhere to reassure herself she was alone. She could not limp all the way home. The idea of walking barefoot did not appeal either. Anything, from horse piles to snakes, might lurk in the grass.

The intelligent thing would have been to call home and ask Ashley to come to the Big House to pick her up.

Hindsight was always twenty-twenty.

Glancing around again, Molly realized that all might not yet be lost. The farm's veterinary hospital–equine swimming pool complex was perpendicular to the route she'd been taking. But it was only about a tenth of a mile distant, just off the road. Molly could see its cupola against the star-studded sky. It was empty, at present, since Wyland Farm found it more economical to take its animals to a nearby equine vet practice than to keep its own vet, but it had a phone in it, and as far as Molly knew the phone still worked. Don Simpson used the premises for storage.

Even if the hospital's phone didn't work, she could at least walk home along the road. She would feel much, much safer on the road.

It was ridiculous to be afraid, she knew, but—where, oh where, was J.D. when she needed him?

Probably parked outside her house, Molly thought with a snort, staring moonstruck at the windows.

When she reached the hospital, after about a five-minute hobble, Molly found to her dismay that a padlock secured the double doors. Stymied, she stared at the lock for a minute, contemplated the long walk to her house, and limped around the building, trying the doors and windows. All were locked.

Her legs were aching, she was growing increasingly nervous, and she was not much closer to home than she had been when she had left the Big House.

To heck with it, Molly thought. Picking up a rock, she smashed a window. Once the tinkle of glass died away, the night was as quiet as before. She was standing deep in the shadow of the barn. The Plexiglas dome covering the empty swimming pool glowed silver in the moonlight. The effect was downright weird.

Molly realized that she was letting herself be spooked.

Putting her hand inside the hole she had made, she unfastened the lock. Then she opened the window and climbed inside.

37

Inside the hospital, it was so dark that Molly could barely see her hand in front of her face. She stood motionless for a moment, getting her bearings. Cool, musty-smelling air caressed her cheek. For a moment Molly stiffened, unnerved by the sensation. Then she realized that a breeze was blowing through the open window, stirring up dead air inside. The building had only one story of usable space; divided into a small office, a lab, two stalls, a large operating room, and a smaller recovery room, it encompassed about fifteen hundred square feet.

She thought she must be in the office. As her eyes adjusted, Molly saw a line of metal file cabinets pushed against one wall. A desk hugged another wall. A phone was on the desk.

Molly was reaching for the phone when she heard a muffled thump from somewhere inside the building.

She froze, listening. Her every instinct warned her that she was not alone.

The thump came again, followed by a huffing

sound. Molly frowned. The sound was familiar—a horse blowing on its feed?

There shouldn't be a horse in the hospital. It hadn't been used for anything but storage since the year she'd been hired.

Another thump, a rustle, and the huffing sound drew Molly toward the corridor.

At the door she paused, thinking hard. If a person, friendly or otherwise, was in the building, he or she would already be aware of her presence thanks to the noise she'd made breaking in. Sneaking around in the dark was therefore a waste of time. Moreover, if someone *was* there, already aware of her and with evil intent, she would far rather face them in a blaze of light than in complete darkness. Sliding her hand over the wall, Molly felt for the switch.

The light was hardly a blaze. More like a dim glow, from what couldn't have been more than a forty-watt bulb under a frosted-glass globe on the ceiling. A quick glance around confirmed Molly's impression of office, file cabinets, and phone.

She walked out the door. Light from the office illuminated the corridor. The lab was next to the office. Its door was open, too, and a quick glance revealed nothing but more file cabinets. Across the hall, the operating room was empty except for a dusty-looking sling hanging forgotten from a hydraulic lift on the ceiling. The recovery room was piled with discarded tack.

A series of thumps and a soft whinny led Molly to the second of the two stalls. A chestnut filly stood there, calmly munching oats while she looked at Molly out of soft, liquid dark eyes.

The filly was a Thoroughbred of racing age, around

three, maybe four years old. Thoroughbreds of the same general size and color and age are difficult to tell apart unless one knows them well. Molly couldn't be sure, but she didn't think she'd ever seen this particular animal before.

She didn't think the filly belonged to Wyland Farms. Even if she did, what was she doing in the hospital?

A quick glance around confirmed Molly's impression that no horse piles steamed on the floor. Molly surmised that she had been put in the stall not long before.

"Whoa, girl." Molly entered the stall, moving carefully so as not to frighten the filly. She touched her flank, then ran her hand along the animal's neck while the filly stomped and shook her head.

Molly had spent so much time lately checking horses' mouth tattoos that by now doing so was almost second nature to her. She ran a quieting hand down the filly's muzzle, murmuring to her, and pulled down her lower lip.

The filly had no tattoo. The lip was bare.

All Thoroughbreds were given lip tattoos as yearlings for identification purposes. If this filly didn't have one, something was wrong.

Molly absorbed the import of that, and left the stall. When she got to the office, the first thing she did was dig in her purse for the scrap of paper on which Will had jotted the number of his cellular phone. The second was to flip off the light.

Then she called Will.

38

Will arrived not more than fifteen minutes later. Molly was waiting for him by the side of the road. She moved out of the shadows, flagging him down. The car pulled in beside her. Will got out.

He listened to what she had to say, his gaze following her pointing finger to the hospital.

"Come on," she said, impatient to show him what she had discovered.

"I'll go. Alone. You're going to wait here in the car." Will's voice brooked no disobedience. A glance at his face showed no trace of the charming, tender man with whom she had fallen in love. His eyes were grim, his jaw set hard.

"But . . ." Molly began, only to be silenced when Will caught her arm, propelled her around the hood of the car, opened the door, and deposited her in the passenger seat. He reached into the glove compartment and withdrew a pistol.

Molly's eyes widened. Her FBI man carried a gun after all.

Will dropped the keys on her lap.

"As soon as I leave, you lock the doors. Stay inside the car. If you see something that makes you nervous, drive away. If I'm not back in fifteen minutes, drive away. Don't go home. Go to the Sheriff's Department in Versailles. Whatever you do, don't get out of the car, and don't let anybody in. Got it?"

Molly nodded. With the gun in his hand, Will was suddenly a formidable stranger. Molly was reminded that he was a federal agent, and that this was serious business.

Maybe killing business.

"Be careful," she said. He nodded. Then he shut the door.

Molly watched him moving up the overgrown driveway to the deserted hospital, where he disappeared around the side.

Exactly twelve and a half minutes later—Molly timed him on the dashboard clock—Will walked back into sight, coming down through the grass and talking on his cellular phone at the same time.

When he reached the car, he stood outside for a minute, presumably to finish his conversation. Minutes later he got in.

"Well?" Molly asked as he leaned across her to return the pistol to the glove compartment, then placed the phone on the console between the seats.

"I think you found it," he said, unsmiling. "I'll bet every dime I've ever earned that horse is a ringer."

"Yes!" Molly beamed in triumph, shooting her clenched fist in the air. To her surprise, Will didn't seem to share her jubilation. He was quiet, his jaw still grim. Molly was reminded that they were no longer on good terms. Since he had kissed her in the barn and she had walked out and accepted Thornton's invitation, they had said no more to each other than was strictly necessary. He had given her the names of horses to check, and twice asked her to photograph files with his trusty pen-camera. At night when he came by to take Mike to play basketball, he treated her like Mike's older sister. No more, no less.

In her excitement over finding the ringer, she had forgotten all that. His stern demeanor reminded her.

"Are we waiting for something?" When he made no move to start the car, Molly grew puzzled.

"Murphy's on his way," Will said. "I don't want this horse to get out of our sight until I see what they're planning to do with it. When Murphy gets here, I'll take you home. Then I've got to come back."

His gaze slid sideways to her face. Something about his expression puzzled Molly. He was not reacting as she would have expected to having his case all but solved for him.

"While we're waiting," he said, "maybe you can tell me exactly how you came to be in that building in the middle of the night."

A car came down the road, its headlights cutting bright swathes through the darkness. Their beam must have illuminated the Taurus, because it pulled in behind them.

"Murphy," Will said, getting out of the car. "Stay put."

He was back minutes later, sliding into the driver's seat. Murphy's car drove away as Will started the engine. Molly looked an inquiry.

"He's going to find somewhere less obvious to park."

Will pulled out, made a U-turn that Molly was surprised didn't land them in the ditch opposite, and headed in the direction of her house.

"Now," he said. "Suppose you tell me everything that happened, right from the beginning. I thought you were supposed to have a date with Thornton Wyland tonight."

"I did," Molly said. "We were at a party at the Big House. I—decided to walk home. The quickest way is across the fields, so that's the way I came. Only I broke the heel of my shoe—Ashley's, actually—and it was colder than I thought, and when I saw the hospital I remembered that there was a phone in there. I thought I would call Ashley to come and pick me up."

Will made an indecipherable sound. Molly glanced at him.

"So you broke a window to get in," Will said. Molly had already told him that part when she had phoned him. She presumed he had climbed through the same window himself.

Molly nodded. "When I was in the office I heard something, so I turned on the light and went to investigate. It was the horse."

Glancing out the window, she was surprised to see that they were passing the farmhouse.

"Hey, you're driving by my house," she said.

"I'll take you home in a minute. First I want to finish this conversation without hordes of kids interrupting at every juncture," Will said, pulling off onto the dirt road near the house. He stopped the car, doused the lights, and turned in his seat to face her.

The moon was high overhead now, but its light did not penetrate the sheltering stand of trees. Will was nothing more than a large, dark shape beside her in the car. She could not see his features.

"Let me get this straight," he said. "You decided to walk home by yourself across deserted fields in the middle of the night. Didn't you consider a small detail like the fact that one or more lunatics who get their kicks from mutilating horses are on the loose?"

"I forgot about that until I was already out there," Molly said with a trace of guilt. "Then I got a little nervous, I admit. That's another one of the reasons I broke in to use the phone. I didn't want to walk the rest of the way home."

Will said nothing for a moment. Then, "So you broke in to use the phone. You heard a sound in a supposedly deserted building. *And you turned on the light and went to investigate?*"

"It was a horse," Molly said. "I could tell it was a horse."

"And could you tell that there were no humans there with the horse? Humans who might have been really bad news for a stupid little girl who stumbled across them?"

"Don't call me a stupid little girl," Molly said, eyes narrowing.

Will took an audible breath. "I'm sorry," he said politely. "I meant stupid big girl. Or woman. However you like to think of yourself. The important word is *stupid.*"

"I found your ringer for you!"

"Yes, you did." The overhead light came on. Will dropped his hand away from the switch, his gaze moving over her. "So what happened to your dress?"

Molly glanced down at herself. She had forgotten about her broken strap, forgotten that her neckline drooped perilously low on one side. She was decent, but just barely.

"I broke a strap," she said.

"Is that blood?" Will touched a smattering of brown spots that dotted her abdomen. Molly supposed that Thornton's nose had erupted with more force than she'd thought.

"Probably."

"Are you hurt?" His voice was sharp.

"It's not mine."

"Whose is it, then?"

"Thornton's," Molly admitted unwillingly. A glance at Will's face goaded her. "All right, you want the whole story? Here it is: Thornton drank too much and he tried to kiss me and he stuck his hand down the front of my dress and broke my strap. I gave him a bloody nose. Then I ran out of the house and started across the fields and got scared and saw the hospital and decided to call Ashley to come and pick me up. Only I found the horse and called you instead. Big mistake."

"Big mistake," Will agreed. His mouth was tight and his eyes were so dark, they didn't look blue at all. Molly realized that he was angry. "I almost feel sorry for Wyland. When you agreed to go out with him, you must have known what to expect. I doubt the poor bastard expected to get punched in the nose for something you knew was coming as well as he did."

"Go to hell," Molly said, opening her door. "I don't have to listen to this. You don't own me, Mr. FBI man."

She got out of the car, slamming the door, meaning to walk the short distance home. The interior light went out. Will was out of the car, too, moving fast and meeting her in front of the car's hood.

He caught her arm. He was close, looming over her. Despite the shadows, Molly could see his eyes. They were dark, intense—and angry.

"Let me go!" she said, trying to pull free. Her leg brushed the car bumper through her dress.

"Do you have some kind of death wish?" Will asked with deceptive calm. His hold on her arm was unbreakable. "You go out with a slimeball who can't keep his hands off you, and you don't expect him to try anything. You walk home, at night, alone, across deserted fields with a maniac on the loose and don't think twice about it until it's too late. You know we're investigating a criminal conspiracy, I've told you it could be dangerous, yet you break into a deserted building, hear a noise, and decide to check it out. Is that not the most self-destructive behavior you've ever heard of?"

"So what's it to you?" She was standing so close to him that she had to tilt her head back to see his face. In her stocking feet—she had kicked her damaged shoes off in the car—he was much bigger than she, taller and broader and almost menacing.

Only she wasn't one whit afraid of Will Lyman, menacing or not.

"What's it to me? What's it to me? *This*," he said through his teeth, and kissed her.

At the touch of his mouth, Molly's anger melted, while his seemed to detonate. Will was always so cool, so calm, so much the man in charge. Ever since she had first met him she'd been itching to make him lose control.

Now she had what she'd wanted. He was out of control, furiously angry, shaking with it, and she was going to bear the brunt of the explosion she had sought.

His mouth was hard and fierce, his hands on her arms almost punishing. His tongue was wet and scalding hot as it thrust into her mouth. He wasn't operating on technique now, but on raw emotion. Molly shivered, closed her eyes, and was lost. She clung to him, kissing him as devouringly as he kissed her, catching fire as his hands slid over her slinky dress, caressing her everywhere, pulling her against him. When a large warm hand closed on each separate cheek of her bottom, she moaned, and pressed closer. She was barely aware that he was lifting her until she found herself sitting on the hood of the car, her feet resting on the bumper.

She opened her eyes. He pressed her backward, yanking her skirt up with rough hands. Molly lay back against the hard, cold metal and spread her knees for him. He was wearing a dark suit and tie. His shirtfront was white in the darkness. Above it, his face was lost in shadows. His thighs were hard against hers through the smooth wool of his pants. The feel of them opening her legs wide, the sensation of his pants brushing against her own panty hose–clad thighs, was unbearably exciting. His mouth slid away from her lips, down her throat, across her chest. Molly clutched the back of his head, guiding his mouth to her breast. He pulled at the delicate silk of her dress. Molly felt it slither down as the other strap gave.

His mouth closed over her nipple.

Molly's eyes closed. She moaned, and pressed his head closer. His mouth was hot and wet as he suckled her like a babe. Molly arched her back, offering him her breasts with abandon, clutching his head with both hands as he kissed and sucked and nibbled and she squirmed like a wild thing beneath him.

His hand was between them, yanking at the crotch of her panty hose, ripping them, ripping her panties. He touched her, finding the tiny bud that quivered desperately beneath his caress, then slid lower and inside.

Molly clung to his shoulders, gasping her need into his mouth as he abandoned her breasts to kiss her. He was leaning over her, supporting his weight with one hand while the other took ruthless possession of her body. She lifted her hips in wordless suppliction, welcoming his touch in a way that was as old as woman.

"Will!" She gasped his name against his neck as he lifted his mouth from hers. He bent his head. His teeth closed on her nipple with a force that would have hurt if she had not been so far gone with passion. His hand withdrew from her body. Molly whimpered and strained, begging wordlessly for its return.

"Love me, Will," she whispered, her eyes opening. For a moment he was above her, looking down at her, his face hard and fierce, his eyes black.

Then he slid inside her, enormous and hot, filling her to capacity and then some. He thrust, caressed, took, gave, and made her feel more and more and more until she was sobbing her ecstasy into his mouth. Molly was mindless with pleasure, her nails digging into his back through the layers of his jacket and shirt.

"Will, Will, Will, Will, *Will*!" she cried as her world exploded into a million brightly colored starbursts of delight. Groaning in response, he found his own release, grinding himself deep into her shaking body.

Afterward, Molly lay beneath him, eyes closed, body

limp except for the tremors that still racked it. She had lost the war, totally and finally. Heart, mind, and body, she had been conquered. All belonged to Will.

The problem was, Will did not belong to her.

39

Will lifted himself away from her and stepped back. Molly saw that his trousers and shorts were around his knees. He pulled them up, tucking in his shirt and fastening his belt, all without a word.

Molly sat up, tugging the top of her dress over her bare breasts. There was nothing she could do about her shredded hose or panties other than to drop her skirt so that they were hidden. The undergarments were ruined beyond repair.

It was hard to believe that she had just made passionate love to a man on the hood of a car. Never in her wildest dreams would she have fantasized about that—or imagined how good it would feel.

Or how bad she would feel when it was over. What happened now? She loved him. He would be leaving soon. Her heart would break.

Molly slid off the hood. Her knees were unsteady, but she locked them into place and they did not let her down. She had to hold her gown up or it would have slithered around her waist.

"You're the next thing to naked." Will's voice was a

growl. He still sounded angry. Molly's chin came up in response.

"It's called an evening gown," she said, surprisingly cool. "Or at least it was."

"You're not even wearing a bra."

"So? I didn't have one that worked with the dress. Besides, I don't need one." Still holding her gown up, she turned sideways and mockingly thrust her silk-covered chest out for his inspection. "See? No sags."

Will said nothing for a moment, but Molly had the impression that he was gritting his teeth.

"You can't go home like that. I've got some clothes in the trunk you can wear." He moved around to the back of the car. Molly followed, watching as the trunk light came on and he fished through a blue gym bag.

"Since we found the ringer, your investigation's basically over, right?" To her credit, the question sounded indifferent.

Will pulled some items from the gym bag, zipped it up, and shut the trunk. "If everything pans out, yes. Here."

Molly caught the clothes he tossed at her: sweat pants and a T-shirt, she saw. His answer was like a blow to her heart.

"So when do I get paid?" Not for anything in the world was she going to let him know how she dreaded to hear the answer. She was no longer even interested in the money. Because when she got paid, he would go.

He laughed, but it wasn't a pleasant sound. "Before I leave."

"And when will that be?"

"I'll let you know. Soon, probably."

"You shouldn't have been so nice to the kids. Doing homework with the twins, buying Ashley a dress, teaching Mike to play basketball. They don't have a clue that you're getting ready to vanish from their lives."

"They'll get over it."

"Yes, I guess they will," Molly said bitterly, knowing that his words applied to her too. Only she wouldn't get over it. Not for a long, long time.

"I'll give you my number in Chicago. If you need anything—any of you—you can call me."

"Oh, right, the charity hotline. I don't think so. We were fine before we ever laid eyes on you, and we'll be fine long after you're gone."

"Just another notch on your bedpost, hmm?"

Molly stiffened angrily. "You got it."

"Are you going to change? I have to get back."

"Sure. I wouldn't want to keep a dedicated public servant from his work." So saying, Molly released her grip on the top of her gown. The shimmery silk fell with a soft sound to her waist, baring her breasts. His gaze was on her as she slid the dress down her legs, and her ruined underthings with it. For a moment she stood naked in the moonlight, knowing that her boldness angered him and glad of it.

Just another notch on your bedpost. The words hurt more than she ever would have imagined words could. He thought she was easy, promiscuous. Well, she told herself, having him think that was better than having him guess the truth: that she was only easy with him because she was so in love with him, she was sick with it.

He was going to leave.

"Maidenly modesty is not your strong suit, is it?" he asked.

"Nope." Her tone was insolent, because she knew insolence would infuriate him.

But he said nothing. His gaze ran down her body one more time, and then he turned away, getting into the car. Stepping into his sweat pants, she pulled them up and tied the drawstring around her waist. They were miles too big, and they reminded her of him, and the reminder made her ache. Pulling the equally oversized T-shirt over her head, Molly gathered her ruined clothes from the ground and joined him inside the car.

"You know, I'm going to miss you," he said as he backed the car toward the road.

"You are?" Molly looked at him, suddenly hopeful. Maybe, just maybe . . .

"Yeah, I am. I have to hand it to you, you're the best lay I've ever had."

Molly sat frozen for a moment, while the cruel words reverberated inside her head, pounding themselves mercilessly into her consciousness. Then fury, blessed, healing fury, erupted to save her.

"Oh, yeah?" Her voice was polite, even cordial, a perfect mask for the pain-filled rage that seethed inside. She smiled at him, too sweetly. "I wish I could say the same, but I can't. Close, but no cigar."

That was how they left it. Will took her home, made sure she got safely in the door, then turned and walked out of her life. Molly didn't see him again, not even to say good-bye. Three days later, she got a package from Federal Express: a certified check for five thousand dollars, and a lawn service company business card with three phone numbers scribbled on the back.

The charity hotline, she had no doubt. Looking

from it to the check, Molly hurt so bad, she thought she was going to die.

Because she knew they meant that Will was really, truly gone from her life.

40

November 15, 1995

More than three weeks had passed. Keeneland was over, and Molly was back carrying out her regular duties at Wyland Farm. Rumors of grand juries being convened and indictments being prepared against several area trainers were the scuttlebutt among the local horse people, but no one seemed to know anything for sure and nothing happened. A few of Wyland Farm's horses had been shipped to tracks in different states to compete in various races, but none in Molly's charge had been fit enough, and so she stayed home. Don Simpson was away with Tabasco Sauce, which meant that work was less stressful than it might have been. That was just as well, because Molly was not functioning at peak capacity. It was all she could do to drag herself out of bed each morning and make it through the day.

She felt Will's absence like a physical pain that would not go away, though she tried not to dwell on it. But for the first time in her life, she wasn't able to push something unpleasant down the black hole she had created in her mind. This ache wouldn't be denied, and it wouldn't go away.

Her siblings all missed Will, but to Molly's surprise Mike took his defection worst. The teenager moped at first, then got angry, and finally turned sullen with a vengeance. Molly suspected that he was running around with the wrong crowd again, and feared to think what might come of it. Talking to him was a waste of time. He turned a deaf ear and a smart mouth to everything she said.

Trevor dropped Ashley and started dating Beth Osbourne, leaving Molly to cope with her sister's broken heart as well as her own. Ashley handled heartbreak far better than she did, Molly had to admit.

Another Thoroughbred was attacked, this time in a field at Cloverlot. The deputies notified Tom Kramer that they wanted to talk to Mike again. The state police came by. Fortunately, Mike had an airtight alibi for the attack: He had been home in bed. All four of his siblings could vouch for that.

Jimmy Miller and Thornton Wyland both kept badgering her for dates. Several of Thornton's friends from the party called too. Molly turned them all down. The way she felt at the moment, she would never date another man as long as she lived.

If she didn't feel anything for them, what was the point? And if she did, it hurt too much.

During the seond and third weeks in November, the Lexington Hunt Club was out in full force, ballyhooing through the fields on their jumpers in pursuit of a nonexistent fox. The annual appearance of the society types in their full scarlet-coated regalia always presaged cold weather. Sure enough, the temperature dropped to the forties, and stayed there. The leaves vanished from the trees, and the lush bluegrass turned brown. The landscape took on a seasonal bleakness that exactly matched Molly's mood.

It seemed as though the sun would never shine again.

The one bright spot was that Susan was thrilled to get a part in her school's production of *The Wizard of Oz*. She played the Wicked Witch of the West, and spent her after-school time rehearsing. The biggest difficulty, Susan said, was with the bucket of water. The girl who played Dorothy kept missing her. It was hard to die convincingly when she wasn't even wet.

It was a Wednesday night. Molly was in the kitchen scrambling eggs for supper, listening to Susan rehearse her part with half an ear. Sam sat at the table doing homework. Ashley and Mike were in different parts of the house, studying. Ashley had a big chemistry test on Friday on which she needed to make an A. Mike had a test, too, in social studies. Molly would be happy if he brought home a C.

"I'll get you, my pretty . . ." Susan intoned with a wicked cackle as Molly scooped the eggs out onto plates. Molly had heard Susan's part so many times, she thought she could play it herself. Susan's version of the witch's laugh was starting to give her a headache. Molly realized that she was feeling irritable, which was nothing new for her lately. Since Will had left, her moods seemed to teeter between anger, grouchiness, and depression.

It wasn't fair to the kids, she knew, but she couldn't seem to help it.

"Put these on the table, would you?" Molly interrupted Susan's monologue ruthlessly, indicating the plates. She picked up platters of bacon and toast, and headed for the table. Behind her, Susan did as she was asked, grimacing. With a yell, Molly summoned the others in to eat.

"Did you start on my costume yet?" Susan asked as they ate.

Participants in the play had to provide their own costumes. Though Molly would never say so to Susan, privately she wondered if getting a part was a privilege or a penance.

"No, but I will."

"I need it by next Wednesday."

"I know." A visit to Goodwill would, Molly hoped, yield a suitably ancient black dress. If not, she would start combing the resale shops. Thanks to the five thousand dollars she had earned working for Will, money was not so tight that she could not afford to scrape together an acceptable costume for Susan.

So some good had come out of her association with Will after all.

"I hope you don't expect me to come watch the stupid play, because I'm not going to," Mike said.

"I don't care if *you* don't come," Susan said. "Your pimply face would probably scare everybody else away anyway."

"Shut up, you little brat! At least I don't have rabbit teeth!"

"No, you just have a rabbit brain," Sam chimed in in his twin's defense. "You're so stupid you're probably going to flunk out of school."

"Stop it, all of you! That's enough!" Molly glared around the table. "What's the rule?"

"If you can't say something nice, don't say anything at all," Susan and Sam parroted in a high-pitched singsong.

Mike scowled at them, and at Molly too.

"That's such bullshit!" he said. Standing up, he grabbed his plate and glass and left the table, stomping into the living room. Seconds later Molly heard the TV come on. She knew she ought to call him back, or at least reprimand him for swearing, but she didn't have the heart. Her sour mood seemed to have affected all of them lately. Molly couldn't remember the last time they had bickered so much. Or so unpleasantly.

After supper, Ashley helped her with the dishes. Susan and Sam were released to practice and finish homework, respectively. Mike was so much trouble of late that Molly had just about quit even asking him to do his chores. If he forgot and she reminded him, they just ended up screaming at each other. It was easier to do them herself.

"Have you heard anything from Will?" Ashley asked as Molly washed and she dried. At first, after he had left, her siblings had asked her that several times a day apiece. Now it had been two whole days since anyone had even mentioned him, so Molly supposed she should feel grateful for the respite.

"No," Molly said shortly.

"Love's tough, isn't it?" The sympathy in Ashley's voice grated on Molly like fingernails on a blackboard. She knew Ashley only meant to be kind, and perhaps to share some of her own hurt, but Will's absence was like an open wound Molly couldn't bear to have touched. Even talking about it was painful.

"Life's tough," she said, handing Ashley the last of the pans. Turning away from her sister, she picked up the plate of scraps she had put together for Pork Chop and headed outside. The dog, who'd been waiting patiently in front of the door, almost knocked her down the porch steps in his eagerness for the food. Molly yelled at him and immediately felt bad. Setting the plate on the ground, she gave him an apologetic pat as he put his nose in the food and began to wolf down his dinner.

For a moment Molly stood, arms wrapped around her, taking in great gulps of cold night air. The moon, huge and yellow, was just rising over the horizon. Tiny stars sparkled across the sky. The wind was up, rustling through the branches of the denuded oak. Ordinarily Molly would have heard a whinny, or the stamping of feet, or something to announce the presence of horses in the surrounding fields. But the Thoroughbreds were being kept in stalls now, partly because there was no longer any grass for them to eat and partly to protect them from the attacker who stalked them. J.D. and company watched the barns all night, which was good for the horses. But the animals' absence, and the knowledge that J.D. was not out on his nightly rounds, made Molly feel lonely.

Gazing up at the moon, she imagined what Chicago must be like: tall buildings, the constant hustle and bustle of people, traffic on the streets at all hours of the day and night. Right now, Will would probably be in a little Italian restaurant somewhere, having lasagna for supper. With him would be his newest girlfriend, or maybe an old girlfriend who'd been waiting back in Chicago for him. She had never asked if there was somebody like that.

Like sailors, Molly supposed, FBI agents had a girl in every port.

The thought was so painful that Molly closed her eyes, fighting back tears. She would not cry over him.

She absolutely refused. It was stupid, and useless, and did no good at all.

Taking another deep breath, she turned and went back inside.

41

It was after midnight. A shadowy figure crept across the yard toward the house. He moved quietly, knowing that a careless noise would disturb the dog, ruining his plans. The animal slept downstairs in the kitchen. Earlier excursions, test runs if you would, had revealed that it was a sound sleeper.

Just like the children upstairs.

He was excited. No, elated was a better word. The thrill of the hunt was a more intense high than any drug could provide. Thanks to the horses, he had been experiencing it in increasingly larger doses over the last few months. Tonight would be the ultimate rush. For a long time he had dreamed of, and planned for, tonight.

Everything was ready. He patted his pocket to make sure he had the chloroform, the rag. Of course he did. He was careful, always careful. This time he didn't mean to get caught.

In a way, it was just like before, which was as it should be. Because it was the anniversary of the first time he had embarked on such a hunt. Thirteen years ago, to the day.

He had planned it that way.

Overhead, the golden ball that was the moon watched blindly, as it had before. It loomed large in the night sky, larger than at any other time of the year.

They called it a Hunter's Moon.

Which was fitting, because he was the hunter.

42

November 16, 1995

Howard Lawrence's death still bothered Will. It was a loose end, and he didn't like loose ends. Loose ends meant he had missed something.

Though everybody else seemed perfectly willing to write it off as a suicide.

His gut told him they were wrong.

Not that it mattered. Not really. Suicide or murder, Lawrence was just as dead. Homicide investigations were the province of the local cops. Not the feds.

He tapped a key. His computer screen glowed green at him, then data started scrolling across it. All the information he had compiled from Operation ChaseRace—that was the tag the Bureau had given his investigation—had just been transferred via modem to the Lexington field office. They would handle the arrests, the prosecutions. His job was done.

"You want to go get a drink, Will?"

Dave Hallum popped his head in the door of Will's small office. Lean and balding, Hallum reminded Will of a greyhound. Today even his suit was gray.

"Not tonight, thanks."

Hallum's question reminded Will that it was five-thirty. Time to go home. Home to what, though? Now that Kevin was gone, home was an empty house. He could order in a pizza, eat in front of the TV.

Will decided to opt for the gym. Later, he could always call up Lisa, though since he had returned from the sticks Lisa seemed to have lost her appeal.

For a long time now she'd been pressuring him to get married, but Will had always resisted, using Kevin as an excuse. Now that his son was no longer home to act as a shield, Lisa was growing more insistent.

She was thirty-seven, divorced, and heard her biological clock ticking, Will knew.

The thought of giving Lisa babies made his stomach act up. He didn't like her all that much, Will realized. He certainly wasn't in love with her.

Hallum walked into the room. "What're you working on?"

"Finishing up that Kentucky thing. I just lobbed the last of the paperwork to—what's the guy's name?"

"The agent in charge of the Lexington office? Matthews."

"Right. Matthews. Now the ball's in Matthews' court."

"You did a good job on that."

"Thanks."

"They were shipping horses in from Argentina, right? And substituting them for American horses? I'll be talking to George Rees tomorrow, and I want to make sure I've got it straight."

"The report's on your desk," Will reminded him.

"I haven't had time to read it," Hallum admitted, crossing the room to perch on the edge of Will's desk. "Fill me in."

"A group of horse trainers entered into a conspiracy to fix certain races so that they could bet small and win big. To do that, they substituted fast horses for slow horses. Since all horses racing in this country are identified by mouth tattoos, they flew in horses from a country that has no such requirement—Argentina. Then they had the fast horse's mouth tattooed with the slow horse's ID number, ran the fast horse against other slow horses at long odds, and pocketed the winnings. End of story."

"Sounds simple enough. I'm surprised it took you two weeks to figure it out." Hallum grinned at him.

Will knew when he was being teased. "It wouldn't have, except the first informant I recruited lied to me. Once I figured out how the scheme really worked, it was a piece of cake."

"The first informant being the guy you think may have been murdered?"

"Yeah."

"Murphy doesn't think so. Anyway, that's for the local cops to decide."

"That's what I figured."

"So case closed?"

"Yeah," Will said. "Case closed."

There was a tapping at Will's open door. He glanced over to see Murphy and two other agents—Warren Roach and Ben Markey—at his door. He motioned them inside. If it had not been for Hallum's presence, he knew they wouldn't have bothered to knock.

"You ready to go?" Murphy asked him.

"Go where?" Will frowned.

"Don't tell me you forgot," Roach said. He was tall and thin, with carefully combed brown hair and nice taste in suits. Divorced, he fancied himself a lady-killer. Will had the sudden hopeful thought that maybe he could fix him up with Lisa.

"Hey, man, it's my bachelor party!" Markey grinned at him. In his late twenties, short with black hair, Markey was never still. He jiggled the change in his pocket now, looking at Will.

"That's right, I remember. In fact, I wouldn't miss it for the world. At DiGiorno's, isn't it? You guys go on, and I'll be there a little later. I've got a few things to do here first."

"You still working on Operation ChaseRace?" The absurd name made Murphy grin.

Will shook his head. "Just finished it up."

"What was Kentucky like, Will?" Roach was teasing him. Murphy had spent the last three weeks regaling everybody in the office with his and Will's experiences in the Bluegrass. Will had found himself the butt of much humor, none of which he particularly appreciated. Not that he was stupid enough to let his lack of appreciation show.

"Like being trapped in an endless *Green Acres* rerun," Will said dryly.

The group chortled. "You even had your own Elly May, didn't you?" Markey asked.

"That's not *Green Acres*, idiot. That's *The Beverly Hillbillies*," Roach corrected him.

"I don't care. I just want to hear about Elly May." Markey was grinning.

"Get out of my office." Will said it with far more good humor than he felt. Hearing Molly referred to as Elly May was starting to get on his nerves.

There was another tap on the door. His secretary—no, the new PC terminology was administrative assistant—stood there.

"Will, you have a call on line two," she said. "A Miss Ballard."

The trio of fools in front of his desk looked at each other in delight.

"Elly May!" they crowed, even as Will reached for the phone.

"Will Lyman," Will said crisply into the mouthpiece. Watched by a grinning audience, he'd be damned before he'd let any emotion show.

"Will?" Molly's voice hit him with the force of a baseball bat to the stomach. It was soft, and low, and southern, and it made his mouth go dry. Will suddenly couldn't imagine how he had lived without hearing it for three weeks.

"Molly." He ordered the Three Stooges—and Hallum too—from his office with a gesture. They ignored him.

"Oh, Will." Molly's voice broke. Will was suddenly alert. For Molly to sound like that, something must be very wrong.

"Susan's gone," she said, sounding as if she was having trouble talking.

"What do you mean, she's gone?" His voice was sharp.

"She's missing. She went up to bed last night, and this morning she was just gone. Her bed was empty. She wasn't anywhere in the house. We searched everywhere, inside, outside, and then I called the police. They act like they think she's run away. Will, she didn't run away. You know she didn't. I think somebody must have gotten into the house and stolen her out of her bed."

"Jesus God."

"Will you come? Please? Now?"

"I'll be there as soon as I can catch a plane," Will said into the phone as his blood slowly froze. "Just stay calm, and hang on."

"Hurry. Please hurry." Molly's voice broke again. There was a click in his ear as she hung up.

Will replaced the receiver and got to his feet. The four men in the room were no longer grinning. Hallum rose from the edge of Will's desk.

"There's been a kidnapping," Will said. "A little girl. I've got to go."

43

Susan awoke in the dark. Her head hurt, and she was sick to her stomach. She didn't know where she was, but she did know she wasn't in her own bed. She'd gone to sleep in her bed last night just as she always did, but somehow she'd woken up—here.

Where? That was the question. Susan scrambled up, crouching on what felt like a dirt floor. Wherever she was was cold and dark and moldy-smelling. And quiet. Echoingly quiet. Like a cave.

Could she be having a nightmare? Susan pinched herself to make sure. The pinch hurt. Did pinches hurt in nightmares?

Susan knew she was awake.

A whimper formed at the back of her throat. Susan held it back. She was afraid to make a sound, afraid to move, in case the beast that inhabited this place should hear her and pounce.

She didn't know why she pictured a beast, but she did. A huge, shaggy creature with horns and claws and fangs that captured children and ate them for breakfast. She could almost hear it now, sneaking through the dark toward her.

Something ran over her fingers. Susan snatched her hand off the floor and screamed. Even as the sound died away she was scuttling backward like a crab until her head crashed into a stone wall.

She saw stars, and subsided in a shuddering heap. Drawing her knees up close to her chest and wrapping her arms around her legs, Susan made herself as small as possible. Stone walls, dirt floor, the smell of rot. Tiny beady eyes glowing at her from a distance: mini beasts?

Was she in a cellar—or a grave? The thought that she might be buried alive terrified her. Around her, the darkness seemed suddenly alive, listening, breathing, waiting to pounce on her.

"Mommy," she whimpered. Then, "Molly."

44

By the time Will arrived some four hours after Molly had phoned him, the house was filled with people: neighbors, friends, and cops. It served as a command post for a bewildering mix of federal agents and local police. Will had set the wheels of that in motion before ever leaving Chicago. There was a tap on the house phone in case a ransom call should come in, and an agent monitoring the tap. Molly had provided pictures of Susan, along with a list of her friends, identifying information, and a description of what she had been wearing when last seen—an ankle-length white flannel nightgown sprigged with pink flowers. Molly, Sam, Ashley, and Mike had been questioned so extensively about their movements of the night before that Molly felt she could retell her story in her sleep. The house had been dusted for fingerprints. Susan's room had been photographed from every angle. A BOLO—Be On the Lookout For—had been issued with Susan's description, and a search had been made of the house, yard, and nearby fields. A more extensive search was being organized for the coming of daylight, if Susan had not turned up by then.

Molly prayed that Susan would turn up by then.

Will phoned from the plane to tell them what time he would be landing. The FBI agent in charge of the phone tap passed on the message to Molly—Special Agent Eaton, he said his name was. Molly, Ashley, Sam, and Mike sat around the kitchen table with untouched plates of meatloaf and mashed potatoes before them, courtesy of their neighbor Flora Atkinson. Molly had dated the Atkinsons' son Tom, and had been good friends with their daughter Linda before Linda had married and moved away. Mrs. Atkinson was a plump, motherly woman of sixty. She bustled about the kitchen, preparing food and talking in hushed tones to other neighbors as they came in and out.

Susan's disappearance was a nightmare, they all agreed, the kind of thing that happens on TV, or to other people. Not to them. Not to Susan. Not to a child they knew.

Pork Chop's excited barks as a car crunched into the driveway at about 10:00 p.m. sounded so normal, it was bizarre. They all, Special Agent Eaton included, went out onto the porch, hoping. Hoping it was Susan being brought home. Hoping for news. Hoping for . . .

Will. He strode toward the house, his blond hair bright in the moonlight. He was wearing a trench coat unbuttoned over a dark suit. Molly was so glad to see him that her throat constricted.

"Will!" Ashley and Sam swarmed down the steps toward him. When they reached him they threw themselves upon him, hugging him as if he were a long-lost family member. He hugged them back, then looked over their heads at Molly standing on the porch with Mike beside her.

For a moment their gazes met and held.

"You didn't tell us you were an FBI agent!" Sam's voice was accusing. Molly had told them that afternoon, just before she called Will. His real identity was the only ray of hope she had to offer them—and herself.

Will looked down, ruffling the boy's hair.

"It was a secret," he said.

"Susan—" Ashley broke off, obviously too overcome with emotion to continue.

"Don't worry, everything's going to be all right," Will said, then with an arm around each of them came on toward the porch.

From the moment Ashley and Sam flung themselves at him, Will knew he had been wrong. Wrong to think that his fondness for the Ballards was something that would pass, wrong to leave without a word the way he had. At the time, it had seemed like the best way to handle things. He had been afraid that they—and he—were getting too attached, and to what purpose? His life was in Chicago, their lives were here. When the job was done, he would walk out of their world as abruptly as he had walked in. As Molly had said on that last, never-to-be-forgotten night, under the circumstances he should never have gotten involved with her brothers and sisters in the first place. It wasn't anything he'd planned; he'd felt sorry for them, at first. They'd been so obviously needy, not just financially but for adult male attention. It was easy to help Susan with her homework, to toss a football with Sam, to teach Ashley to dance. Mike seemed at first to need stern discipline rather than attention, but he was just as vulnerable as his siblings, Will had discovered. Showing the kid the rudiments of basketball had been fun. Straightening him out in other ways wouldn't have been so enjoyable, though Will was confident it could be done. But teaching Mike and the rest of them to depend on him would have been cruel. Will had no forevers to offer them.

But they'd wormed their way into his heart, all of them. The truth was, he had missed them.

He was as sick with fear over Susan as he would have been if she were his own child. He understood the ramifications of the horror that had befallen her far better than did any of her siblings, and it terrified him.

What he most feared was a pedophile. When he remembered the night Susan had seen someone at the window, his blood ran cold. Perhaps whoever had taken her had been stalking her for some time.

Another possibility was a kidnapping that stemmed from Molly's help with the investigation. Someone could have taken the child for revenge.

There were lots of possibilities, but not much time to explore them. He knew that the longer a child was missing, the less likely it was that the child would be found at all, much less alive.

But he didn't mean to tell the Ballards that, not until he had to. They were already scared to death; a glance at them had been enough to tell him so.

Standing there on the porch as he walked up the driveway toward her, Molly said nothing, did not even so much as lift a hand in greeting. She was very pale. Since he had seen her last, she had lost weight that she didn't need to lose. Dressed in faded jeans and a nondescript gray sweater, she still managed to look both sexy and beautiful. And fragile, so fragile the moonlight almost seemed to pass right through her. Her arms were crossed over her breasts. She kept her lips pressed tightly together, as if she were afraid they would tremble if she didn't. Her eyes were huge and ringed with shadows. Will met their gaze and felt his world tilt on its axis.

For three weeks he'd been telling himself that what he and Molly had had been great, but it was over: a classic case of a hot, brief love affair.

Only it wasn't over. As soon as he set eyes on her again Will knew that. What he felt for her was too strong; what was between them was no brief affair.

Will wanted to walk up on that porch and take her in his arms and kiss the breath out of her.

But she had called him not because she wanted him, but because she needed him. He was here in his capacity as an FBI agent, not as Molly's lover.

Until Susan was found, he had to remember that.

"Hello, Molly" was what he said as he came up the steps with Ashley and Sam clinging to either arm.

"Thank you for coming," Molly answered in a low voicc.

On the other side of the steps, Mike made a restless movement. Will looked at him.

"Hey, Mike."

"Hey, Will." The boy didn't sound openly hostile, as Will had expected. Will supposed he had the trauma of Susan's disappearance to thank for that. They were all on the same side until Susan was safely home.

Please God it worked out that way.

"I'm Special Agent Ron Eaton." The man in the suit standing behind Molly held out his hand. Will would have known at a glance that he was with the

Bureau. There was something about feds, he supposed, that allowed them to recognize each other.

"Will Lyman." Ashley and Sam released him, and Will shook hands.

"And I'm Flora Atkinson." A gray-haired woman too heavy for the navy polyester slacks and long-sleeved white blouse she wore nodded at him. Besides Eaton and Mrs. Atkinson, there appeared to be about a dozen strangers crowded onto the porch staring at him. With a glance Will separated them into the teenage crowd—friends of Mike's and Ashley's, he supposed—and the adults, who with the exception of Jimmy Miller appeared to be neighbors.

Miller nodded at him without enthusiasm.

"Will." Molly's voice was scarcely louder than a whisper. He was standing beside her. As he glanced down at her she put a beseeching hand on his sleeve. Her eyes were huge and dark. "Find Susan. Please."

"We will," he said reassuringly, hoping he was telling the truth. Then, purely for the purpose of comforting her, he put an arm around her and ushered her back into the house.

The whole crowd of them followed. One glance at Molly's exhausted face in the light told Will that she was nearing the end of her rope. He beckoned Eaton over, said a word in his ear. Eaton handled the situation like a pro. Within minutes the group was leaving.

Mrs. Atkinson kept saying, "I can stay if you need me," up till the very moment when she got into her car. Miller pressed a kiss on Molly's white cheek and murmured something in her ear before walking out the door. The rest of them departed with various farewells. Finally the Ballards, Will, and Eaton were left alone.

"You're on the phone, I take it?" Will asked Eaton,

who nodded. "In a few minutes I'll want you to brief me about the status of the search. Right now I want to talk to the family."

Eaton nodded, and vanished into the living room. Will looked at Molly, Ashley, Mike, and Sam sitting limply at their kitchen table, and felt a pang for the Ballard who wasn't there. Then he took off his coat and suit jacket and loosened his tie, and sat down on the bench beside Molly.

"Tell me what happened," he said.

They did, singly and together, their voices sometimes dropping to a shaky whisper and sometimes faltering altogether as they described waking up that morning to find Susan gone.

That was all they knew, really. She'd gone to bed the night before just like always, and when they woke up the next morning she was gone. Even Ashley, with whom she shared a room, had heard nothing. Her initial assumption, when she awakened to find the other twin bed empty, was that Susan had simply gotten up early to go downstairs.

"Was there any sign of a break-in?" Will asked.

They all shook their heads.

"The doors were all locked, and the alarm was on," Molly said. "That's what I don't understand: How could Susan simply disappear from a locked house?"

"It seems impossible," Ashley said. "But that's what happened."

Will had a moment of blinding revelation. He looked at Mike, to find the teen was eyeing him nervously.

"You go out last night, Mike?" Will asked.

Molly shook her head. "We all stayed in. Ashley and Mike were studying, Sam did homework and watched

TV, and Susan was practicing for her p-play." Her voice broke on the last word.

"Mike?" Will asked again.

Mike nodded.

"Same way?"

Mike nodded again. His siblings stared at him.

"What time did you get in?"

"Around one-thirty."

"You were out last night?" Molly asked. There was a high-pitched quaver to the words that worried Will. Molly was an emotional wreck over this, Will knew. He was surprised she'd managed to hold herself together as well as she had.

"Hush," he said in her ear. This was not the moment to scold Mike for anything he might or might not have done. They had to get at the truth if they wanted to help Susan.

He said to Mike, "You locked the window and turned the alarm on when you got in, right?"

Mike nodded.

"Did you notice anything out of the ordinary? Was Susan in her bed?"

"I never even looked in on Susan. Why should I? I locked the window and turned on the alarm and went to bed." Mike's chin quivered. Will realized that the tough teenager with the ponytail and the earring was on the verge of tears. "It's my fault, isn't it? Whoever took Susan came in the window, didn't they?"

"It's not your fault. You didn't know it was going to happen," Will said. "And in a way it's a help. At least we can pinpoint the time she was abducted with a good degree of accuracy. What time did you leave the house?"

"Around eleven-thirty," Mike said.

"So we have a two-hour window of opportunity where someone could have entered the house and taken Susan. In order to have hit that, somebody had to know you snuck out at night through the window. One of the friends you meet, maybe, or someone they told. I'll want a list of your friends. Or it could be that somebody has been watching the house pretty closely. Did you pick last night at random? Or do you usually go out on Wednesdays?"

"I've been going out most Tuesdays and Wednesdays for a couple of months, except when you and I had our deal."

"Yeah." Will could tell from Mike's expression how much their deal had meant to him. Will felt bad about leaving the kid high and dry, and thus his response was gruff. But now wasn't the time for apologies or explanations.

"What deal?" Molly asked, looking from Mike to Will. Then, to Will, "Did you know he was sneaking out nights?"

"I caught him at it, and we agreed that if I coached him in basketball he wouldn't do it anymore," Will said briefly. "But then I left."

"Yeah," Mike said, the single word bitter.

Will put aside his guilt to concentrate on the more important issue. "You didn't tell the police about going out the window? Or whoever took your statement?"

Mike shook his head. "I told them I was in bed."

Will frowned. Mike looked scared.

"I didn't want Molly to find out," Mike said. He seemed very young suddenly, more like a little boy than a teenager. His chin quivered again, and he glanced at Molly. "I know I'm a lot of trouble, and I worry you a lot, and now it's my fault that S-Susan's been kidnapped."

Tears welled into his eyes. He covered his face with his hands and began to sob.

"Mike," Molly said, getting up to go to him. She leaned over him, hugging his shoulders. "It's not your fault. You didn't know it was going to happen. None of us did."

Looking at the two nearly identical dark heads so close together, Will felt another shackle binding him to them tighten around his heart. He cared for them, both of them. All of them.

Maybe he'd better start believing in forevers after all.

"Is Mike going to get in trouble for lying to the police?" Ashley asked in a small voice. Both Molly and Mike glanced up to hear the answer.

"I'll take care of it," Will said.

He stood up, found a glass in a cabinet, and poured himself some milk. When he glanced back at the table, Mike had himself under control again. Molly was still on her feet with a hand on Mike's shoulder.

Under the pitiless glare of the overhead light, her skin was so pale it was almost translucent. Her eyes were huge, dark, and weary. She was so tired she was swaying on her feet.

"Bed," Will said firmly. "For all of you."

45

An hour later, Molly was in bed. She lay on her side with Ashley, who had flatly refused to stay in the room she shared with Susan, snuggled against her back. Her sister's breathing told her that she had finally fallen asleep.

Molly felt she would never sleep again.

She turned over onto her back, murmuring another of the endless prayers she had said since she had figured out that Susan was really, truly gone. The words were a chant now, running ceaselessly through her head: *Please, God, bring her back. Please, God, let her not be hurt, or scared. Please, God, she's only eleven years old.*

Moonlight filtered through a gap in the curtains. Molly got out of bed and went to the window, parting the curtains so that she could look out. Overhead, the moon glowed, round and full and yellow. Under the circumstances, it was almost obscenely bright and beautiful.

The night was alive with shadows. Wind blew through the trees. The stand of hawthornes and sycamores where she had last made love with Will formed the horizon to the south. Their peaked tops swayed against the cloud-dappled darkness of the sky. To the east was the fence, with the rolling fields beyond. To the west was the road, a glinting black ribbon curling away into the night.

Somewhere out there was Susan. Was she close, or had she been bundled into a car and driven far away?

It was cold now, dropping into the thirties tonight for the first time all year. Molly put her hand against the windowpane; it felt like ice.

Molly thought of Susan out there somewhere, pictured her little sister cold and frightened, and choked back a sob. Susan, she thought. Oh, Susan. Then she said her prayer again.

She couldn't stay in bed. The thought of sleeping was absurd. She had to do something—but what? Searchers had already combed the yard and nearby fields. Will said they would be back tomorrow with dogs. Will said everything that could be done was being done. Will said she should sleep, because she would need every bit of strength she could muster for whatever lay ahead.

Will said. Will said.

Thank God for Will.

Molly turned away from the window and padded barefoot across the hardwood floor. Opening her bedroom door, she started down the hall. Then she remembered there was a strange man in the house: Eaton. She was wearing a white Winnie-the-Pooh sleepshirt with a picture of the fat bear on the front above the motto *Honey forever!* She turned and went back into her room, rummaging through her closet by touch until she located the pink toweling-cloth robe she rarely wore. Pulling it on, tying the belt around her waist, she headed back down the hall.

The kitchen light was on, drawing her like a moth. Will and Eaton sat at the table, deep in earnest conversation. Will had the inevitable glass of milk in front of him, while Eaton had coffee. The girls' room was theirs for the night, though it was obvious at a glance that neither of them had yet been to bed. Will had removed his tie and unbuttoned the top few buttons at his neck, but he wore the same trousers and shirt he had arrived in. Eaton still wore his suit.

What was it with these FBI men and their suits?

"Miss Ballard. Did you want something?" Eaton saw her first and got clumsily to his feet. Assigned to the Lexington office, he was young, maybe thirty, maybe a little more, with dark hair nearly as short as Will's and a lean, intelligent face. Molly knew he admired her, had seen it in his eyes from the time he had first arrived on the scene a half hour or so after she called Will. The knowledge barely registered. She was accustomed to men admiring her.

"Some coffee maybe. I couldn't sleep." Both men watched as Molly padded toward the counter, finding a cup and pouring herself some coffee from the pot one of them—Eaton, probably, since Will never drank it—had already made. When her cup was full she turned around to face them, leaning back against the counter as she sipped the steaming brew.

"Have you heard anything?" Molly knew the answer even before Will shook his head. Of course if he had heard anything he would have told her.

"We're pursuing every avenue available to us, Miss Ballard. We've filed your sister's vital statistics with NCIC—that's the National Crime Information Center—and it's been wired to every police department in the country. We have the guys at VICAP—the Violent Criminal Apprehension Program—running a check to see if they can turn up any leads. They've got a national computer database capable of comparing missing persons cases from across the country to see if there's any connection. By tomorrow we should know if there's a match."

"Oh, dear God," Molly said, her gaze flying to Will as the enormity of the task before them suddenly sank in. People went missing all over the country all the time; the government had a database full of names and statistics from all fifty states. Susan was only one of—how many? Thousands? More? "It's just like what happened to Libby Coleman. Susan's not coming back, is she?"

Her voice cracked. Her hands shook so badly that coffee sloshed over the side, burning her fingers. She set the cup down on the counter.

"Susan's not going to be like Libby Coleman," Will said, getting to his feet and moving toward her. He stopped abruptly, standing in front of her. His hands flexed by his sides; Molly got the impression that he was making an effort not to touch her. She looked up at him. He was close, so close she could see the bristle of five o'clock shadow on his cheeks and chin. His eyes were very blue, very intense, and his jaw was hard and set. "We're going to find her. We're putting everything we have into the search, and we're going to find her."

"Oh, God," Molly said, closing her eyes and leaning her forehead against his chest. She thought he hesitated a moment, but then his arms came around her, warm and strong and comforting, to pull her close.

She had missed being in Will's arms.

"Libby Coleman?" Eaton questioned from behind them.

"I've got somebody on it," Will said over his shoulder. "It's another missing persons case in the area. Thirteen years old. We're checking for similarities."

So Will had already remembered Libby Coleman. Molly felt herself relax a little. Will wouldn't overlook something like that. Will was thorough, he knew his job, and he was smart. If anyone on earth could be trusted to find Susan, it was Will.

The scrape of the picnic table bench moving over the linoleum floor told Molly that Eaton was getting to his feet.

"I think I'll go to bed," he said. Molly realized from his tone that Eaton was being discreet. She should move out of Will's arms, she supposed, both to alleviate Eaton's discomfort and to save Will from further embarrassment before his fellow agent. But she badly needed him to hold her, and she couldn't bring herself to pull away.

If Will was embarrassed, he gave no sign of it. "I'll be up later," he said. Retreating footsteps told Molly that Eaton was gone.

Except for Pork Chop, snoozing outside the front door, she and Will were alone.

Her arms slid under his jacket and around his waist. She felt something brush her hair, and wondered if it was his lips.

"I missed you," she said into his shirtfront.

Will's arms tightened around her. "I missed you too."

"If it weren't for Susan, you wouldn't be here."

Molly had to keep reminding herself of that. She wanted him so badly, not just for now, but for keeps.

Will didn't say anything to that. The tacit acknowledgment hurt. Molly rested against him for a moment longer, then pulled out of his arms to lean back against the counter.

"It's almost two a.m.," he said, studying her. "You need to get some sleep."

Molly shook her head. Sleep was impossible. "I can't. Every time I close my eyes I think of Susan. I wonder if she's hurt, or cold—I know she's scared . . ."

"Torturing yourself doesn't do Susan any good," Will said firmly. "Do you have any sleeping tablets in the house?"

Molly shook her head.

"Do you feel like talking?"

Molly thought about it, and nodded.

"Okay, you got it. You lie down on the couch and rest, and we'll talk. I never have told you much about my son, have I?"

"Or your wife," she said. Just saying the word caused Molly a pang. She didn't like to think of Will with a wife, even one who had been dead for fifteen years.

"Come on." He headed for the living room, pausing to turn out the kitchen light and collect a quilt from the closet under the stairs. By the time Molly had been settled to his satisfaction, she was stretched full-length on the couch. The quilt was wrapped around her cocoon-fashion, and she had a pillow under her head.

Will sat on the floor near her head, his back leaning against the couch, his knees bent and his arms resting on his knees. When Molly turned on her side, her nose almost touched his shoulder. His face was very close.

"So tell me about your son and your wife," she said. Will had not turned on a lamp. They were alone in the dark with just enough moonlight filtering in through the curtains to turn the blackness to gray. As her eyes adjusted, Molly could see the curve of Will's ear, the jut of his chin, the straight line of his nose. He turned his head to look at her. She could see his mouth, unsmiling now, and his eyes.

"Kevin—my son—is at college at Western Illinois. He's eighteen, a freshman. He's a great kid, good at athletics, makes good grades, nice-looking, nice manners. Until August he lived with me, and stayed with Debbie's parents or my parents when I had to go out of town. Since he's been gone, I've been kind of at loose ends. Surprising how much life one fairly quiet kid can add to a house."

"Is that why you were so nice to the kids? Because you were missing your son?" Molly asked.

Will moved his shoulders in what Molly took for a shrug. "I liked them. I *like* them. They're good kids. Even Mike."

"Underneath it all," Molly said, smiling a little. She curled closer to him, so that her chest rested against his back and her chin touched his shoulder. "Debbie—was that your wife's name?"

He nodded. "Yeah."

"Tell me about her."

Will was quiet for a moment. Then he said, "We met in college. We dated, started going steady. She got pregnant, we got married. Kevin was born. Two days after his third birthday she was killed in a car accident.

He was in the car with her, but he wasn't hurt. Thank God he was in the back, in a car safety seat."

"Just the facts, ma'am?" Molly said softly. "What was she like? Did she have dark hair or blond? Did you love her?"

"She had brown hair and blue eyes—Kevin looks like her—and she laughed a lot. She was a jock, good at all sports, a killer at tennis. She was her parents' only child, a little spoiled but she knew it and could joke about it. When Kevin was born, she adored him. And yeah, I loved her."

At something in his voice, Molly cuddled closer, resting her cheek against his shoulder in silent sympathy. He glanced at her, then made a sound that was not quite a laugh.

"When she died I never thought I would love a woman that way again. But you know what? Time changes a lot of things. I remember what she looked like—hair color and so forth—but I can't really picture her in my mind anymore. She's just a shadow, a laughing shadow. Sometimes I think the boy who was married to Debbie died with her. The man that boy grew into is someone entirely different."

"I know what you mean," Molly said, because she did. "When I think about my mother now, all I remember is things like she loved chocolate ice cream and yellow dresses. I can't really picture her face. It's almost like she never existed at all. I feel guilty sometimes, but that's the way it is."

"Mike told me about her, a little."

"Did he?" Molly's mouth twisted wryly. "I had no idea Mike was such a blabbermouth. I know he told you about—how she died. I heard that one. What else did he tell you? That she was manic-depressive? That sometimes she was the greatest mom in the world, and sometimes she just seemed to forget about us? That she had terrible taste in men, and when she was in love—she fell in love a lot—she'd take off and leave us at the drop of a hat?"

"He told me that you supported the family—your mother too—from the time you turned eighteen. He told me that when your mother died you kept taking care of them just like they were your kids, not hers."

"Did he?" Something rough and warm in his tone sent a shiver down Molly's spine. Will turned sideways so that he was facing her. One hand came up to brush the hair away from her face.

"You know what I think?" he said.

"What?" Molly asked, turning onto her back so that she could look up at him. He was very close, his face just inches above hers. The hand that had been stroking her hair moved down to rest against her cheek. It was hard, and warm, and it felt like it belonged on her skin.

"I think that makes you pretty special. Pretty wonderful, in fact."

"Do you?"

"Yeah. I do."

"I think you're pretty wonderful too." She turned her head a little, and pressed her mouth to his palm. Will went very still as her lips touched the warm saltiness of his skin.

"I really have missed you," she whispered.

"I missed you too," he said.

Then he bent his head and kissed her with an intensity that shook her soul.

46

"Molly, I—" Will began, lifting his head.

A shriek interrupted. It was a hideous sound, shrill and echoing. It sliced down Molly's spine like the cold blade of a knife.

"Sam!" she gasped, scrambling up, knowing it was Sam instinctively. Will was on his feet, too, following her as she dashed for the stairs, the quilt left forgotten behind. As they reached the head of the stairs Eaton emerged from the girls' room with a pistol in his hand and a sheet wrapped hastily around his waist below his bare chest. The light came on in the boys' room moments before Molly reached the door. Mike was kneeling beside Sam's bed with his arms around his little brother, she saw as she ran into the room. Sam, who was in the stage where macho was all and who scorned anything that smacked of femininity, like tears, clung weeping to Mike.

"He had a nightmare," Mike said over his shoulder to Molly as she dropped to her knees beside the bed. As she took Sam in her arms she was vaguely conscious of Will and Eaton, with Ashley trailing them, crowding into the small room.

"Susan's in the dark," Sam sobbed into Molly's shoulder. "She's in the dark and she's scared. I saw her in my dream. The place she's in—it's like a big hole, or a cave. She wants to come home."

"Oh, God." Molly shut her eyes and held Sam close while she fought to keep control of her own emotions. For Sam's sake, for Mike's and Ashley's and Susan's, too, she had to stay strong. "It was just a bad dream, Sam. That's all. Just a bad dream."

"But I saw her—she was crying. Oh, Molly, are they gonna find her? She wants to come home."

"Shh, shh," Molly said, stroking his hair. "Shh."

It was a long time before they got settled down again. This time Sam was in Molly's bed sandwiched between his sisters, and Mike slept on a mattress dragged downstairs to lie beside them.

47

"Susan."

The coaxing voice made Susan shiver in horror. A man was in the hole with her, searching for her with a flashlight. She could see its yellow beam bouncing off the wall.

"Susan."

She pressed back farther into the fissure she had found in the stone. Instinct had sent her scrambling into it when she had first heard him coming. It was long and narrow, perhaps ten inches wide at the opening and tapering gradually inward until it came to a point some five feet inside the wall. Slender as she was, she had managed to wedge herself almost to the end.

Maybe the man wouldn't find her.

"Aren't you hungry? I've brought you something to eat. A pizza, Susan."

She could smell it. The spicy aroma wafted tantalizingly beneath her nostrils. Her stomach growled. Susan stiffened, terrified that the slight sound would give her away.

She was hungry. It had been a long time since she had eaten. Her last meal had been scrambled eggs. Susan remembered sitting at the kitchen table with Molly and Sam and Ashley and Mike, and almost whimpered before she caught herself. She couldn't make a sound. She knew the man who was looking for her was bad. She knew if he got hold of her he would hurt her. She didn't know how she knew, but she did.

She wanted to go home. She was hungry and thirsty and cold and dirty and scared to death.

"You're not afraid of me, are you, Susan? I'm not going to hurt you."

His voice was gentle, coaxing—and false. It chilled her to the bone. He was closer now. The flashlight played over the walls opposite where she hid. Susan turned her face to the wall and closed her eyes. Tears slid down her face.

"Oh, there you are," he said. Against her closed lids Susan felt the bright beam of the flashlight.

She dared a peek sideways to find that his arm was in the opening and he was reaching for her. With a shriek she pushed farther into the narrow crevice—just out of the range of that grasping hand. His fingers brushed the stone no more than three inches away.

He withdrew his hand and pressed his face to the crack, shining the flashlight on her while he looked at her consideringly. Meeting that dark, merciless gaze, Susan choked back a frightened cry. She was electrified, mesmerized, by the evil she saw there.

"Come here, Susan," he said, and reached for her again.

48

November 17, 1995

At just before seven the next morning, Will stood before a desk in the Lexington office of the FBI. A file was in front of him, lying open on the desk, turned the wrong way around so that he could read it. Libby Coleman's file. In 1982, when she had disappeared, computers had not been put to work on every crime as a matter of course. Her name was in the NCIC data bank, along with the standard identifying information. That was all. The rest of the story—the whole case, in fact—was contained in this thick sheaf of papers that no one had yet gotten around to entering into a computer. Grim-faced, Will sifted through the stack of papers, scanning ones that caught his eye.

"Want me to brief you?" asked the young woman entering the office behind him. A glance told him that she was perhaps thirty, attractive, with chin-length blond hair and a businesslike manner underlined by her navy suit. She carried a styrofoam cup of steaming coffee in one hand. "Special Agent Cindy Rayburn."

She set the coffee on her desk and held out her hand.

"Will Lyman." Will shook hands. From Hal Matthews, the veteran agent who was in charge of the Lexington office, Will knew that Special Agent Rayburn had spent most of the night locating the Coleman file and sifting through the information. According to Matthews, Rayburn was one of his best. The whole office had been working flat-out on finding Susan since approximately 6:00 p.m. the previous night, when Dave Hallum had phoned Matthews from Chicago to apprise him of the situation personally.

"Brief me," Will said.

"There is a difference in the MO," Rayburn said. "As far as we know, Libby Coleman was abducted from her front porch at approximately 7:30 p.m. Susan was abducted from her bed at some time between 11:30 p.m. and 1:30 a.m."

"What about the victimology?" Will asked, glancing down at a photograph of Libby Coleman dated approximately one week before she disappeared. The child had round, rosy cheeks and curly brown hair that did not quite reach her shoulders. In the picture she wore jeans and a sweater that did nothing to disguise the fact that she had not yet outgrown her baby fat. A brown-and-white-spotted horse stood beside her; it was saddled and she was holding its reins. She was laughing, her eyes sparkling, as if whoever held the camera had just said or done something hilarious. Happiness and exuberant good health radiated from her. If she felt the slightest premonition of what was to come, it did not show in the picture.

"Very similar: Libby Coleman, white Caucasian female, aged twelve years at the time of her disappearance; Susan Ballard, white Caucasian female, aged eleven years at the time of her disappearance."

"Other similarities?"

"Both disappearances occurred within five miles of each other. Both occurred on exactly the same date, thirteen years apart."

"*Exactly* the same date?" Will asked, glancing at Rayburn, suddenly alert.

"See for yourself." She extracted the NCIC form from the pile without any difficulty and tapped the date with a pink-polished fingernail. "November 15, 1982. November 15, 1995."

"That's it, then." The date was the clincher, as far as Will was concerned. He had learned long ago not to believe in coincidence. Susan and Libby Coleman were victims of the same perp.

"I think so too."

The phone rang. Rayburn spoke into it briefly, then hung up.

"They want me down in the lab," she said. "They're comparing fibers taken from Susan's bedroom to fibers saved as evidence in the Coleman case. Want to come?"

Will shook his head. "I'm going to look through this."

"You're welcome to use my desk," Rayburn said, picking up her coffee and leaving the room.

Will took advantage of her offer, sitting down in her chair and skimming the file for any information that might point to a particular individual as the perp. The investigators then had drawn a blank; working with the information they left behind, Will drew one too.

Like Susan, Libby Coleman seemed to have vanished into thin air. There was no doubt that someone had abducted her. But who? The disappearance of Libby Coleman had never been solved; she was still listed as a missing person. She was out there somewhere, dead or alive. And the same lunatic who had taken her had Susan.

Will was as sure of that as he was that the sun would come up in the morning.

He shut the folder, stood up, and left the office, taking the file with him. His next stop was the Woodford County Sheriff's Department.

As it always did when he was under stress, his stomach started acting up again. Will pulled into the nearest fast-food place to get some milk to soothe it. Frowning as he waited for change, he glanced through the open pickup window at the security monitor above the clerk's head without really seeing it; another car was behind him, distracting the clerk's attention. Will's milk was on the counter beside her; his change was in her hand. He watched impatiently on the black-and-white TV screen as the other driver placed his order into the microphone. The teenage clerk repeated it twice before she got it right. Finally she quoted a price, and the other driver pulled away from the order box and out of camera range, driving around the side of the building to stop behind Will.

"Have a nice day," said the clerk as she passed Will's milk and change through the window. Will dropped the change in the console, flipped the lid off the milk with his thumb, and drove. It was only as he was pulling out into the street and happened to glance at the restaurant's sign that he realized where he was: at the Dairy Queen where Howard Lawrence had died.

Will took a swallow of milk and headed out Versailles Road. Lawrence's death still bothered him. It was a loose end, another coincidence that he did not believe in. But it was not, he reminded himself, his problem. He had a far more urgent matter to worry about at the moment.

Susan had been missing for more than twenty-four hours. Everything he had ever learned about missing persons told him that time was running out.

"You're wasting your time, in my opinion," Deputy Dennis Hoffman said to Will half an hour later. Clad in his brown uniform, fingers thrust inside the front of his waistband, he watched as Will thumbed through the black metal cabinet that held all the department files from 1982. The file cabinet was one of many in the dimly lit basement of the sheriff's office. Will was looking for crimes, perps, anything out of the ordinary that was the same thirteen years ago as it was today. In his car he already had an *R. L. Polk Directory* listing area residents from the year 1982. It contained about thirty thousand names. Of course, once the names of those who'd moved out of the area since were crossed off, there would only be about twenty-five thousand left.

That was just Versailles and the counties immediately surrounding it. If he expanded the search to include Lexington and Frankfort—both easy commutes—and other nearby communities, he would be dealing with a cast of nearly a million.

And none of the information was on computer.

"You want to know what I think?" Hoffman continued after a pause during which Will, ignoring him, scanned the records of burglaries. Fortunately, Will thought, Versailles was a law-abiding community. There weren't that many.

"What?" Will asked over his shoulder, moving on to homicides, of which there were three.

"I think you ought to look at the brother."

"What brother?"

"The older one. Mike."

"Why do you say that?" Hoffman had Will's attention now.

"You think about it. The boy doesn't have an alibi for the time period in question; he was not asleep in the house as he first claimed; he was in fact outside in the middle of the night by his own admission; he runs with a bad crowd; I'm as certain as I can be without actually catching him with his hand in the cookie jar that he smokes marijuana, and he may be into other drugs too. We've been looking into a satanic cult in the area—devil worshipers, you know. My guess is he's a part of it, along with some of his friends. Just say, for a minute, that they took that little girl for some sort of ritual."

"Susan is Mike's sister. He loves her," Will said. At Will's insistence Mike had changed his statement to the police the first thing that morning. It hadn't endeared him to the locals, to whom Molly had originally reported Susan missing. They'd been the ones to dismiss her disappearance as a case of just another runaway. To have their judgment overruled, as it were, by the feds clearly stuck in this man's craw.

Hoffman snorted. "Fact remains, the boy lied to us, he lied to the state police, he even lied to you folks at the FBI. Why'd he lie, you have to ask yourself? What's he got to hide?"

"He was scared of getting in trouble with his sister for sneaking out at night," Will said. "He's just a kid."

"A *bad* kid."

"He is not." Will was surprised at the vehemence of his response. "Mike's just an ordinary mixed-up teenager like any other ordinary mixed-up teenager. What's surprising is when they don't get into trouble."

Hoffman looked him over for a minute in disapproving silence. "That's right—you been seeing the sister, haven't you? She's a looker, and I don't know anything to her discredit, but I'm telling you the older boy is one to keep your eye on."

Will didn't know why he was surprised to find that a deputy at the local sheriff's office knew about his involvement with Molly. He had already figured out that in little towns everybody knew everybody else's business.

God save him from little towns!

"Mike didn't have anything to do with Susan's disappearance," Will said evenly, and turned back to the files. Hoffman, who'd been on the force for only a decade and thus could tell him nothing about the Coleman case, was more annoyance than help. Will wished he would go away.

He was just opening his mouth to send the other man on a fictitious errand when a file caught his eye: *Animal Mutilations.*

Will pulled it out and skimmed its contents. Then he passed it, open, to Hoffman.

"Look at this," he said, pointing to a particular passage.

Hoffman read. When he glanced at Will, he was frowning. "It's the same darn thing that's going on right now. Somebody was cutting up race horses."

"Yeah," Will said grimly. "Know what that means? It means Mike couldn't possibly be involved in either the horse slashings or Susan's disappearance. Because the same things were happening in 1982, when he was only a year old. Horses were being mutilated in the months before Libby Coleman disappeared, just like they were in the months before Susan was kidnapped. Know what that makes me think? Susan and Libby were taken by the same perp who attacked the horses. He uses the animals to whip himself up to a frenzy before moving on to little girls."

"Could be a coincidence," Hoffman said.

"I don't believe in coincidence."

Hoffman stared at him. Will could see the wheels slowly turning in the other man's mind.

"If you're right," Hoffman said at last, "and I'm only saying *if*, mind you, where's he been for thirteen years?"

"I don't know," Will said. "We want to look for any area residents who were away for that time period. Say they moved, and came back. Or went to prison."

"I'll get on it," Hoffman said, shaking his head. "But I can tell you right now it's gonna be a hell of a job."

49

Will was gone even before the bloodhounds got there, and they arrived at 7:00 a.m. Daylight was just breaking when Molly came out of the house with a sweater of Susan's in her hand. The handlers, Bert and Mary Lundy, had asked for something that Susan had worn recently for the dogs to sniff. Mary Lundy took the sweater from Molly. She and her husband let the large brown dogs out of their crates in the back of the van, restraining them with firm hands on their harnesses. The sweater was held under each dog's nose; they snuffled eagerly, then put their noses to the ground. While Mary Lundy held one harness and Bert Lundy held the other, the dogs moved around the house, muscles rippling under their loose coats. The Ballards waited tensely, huddled together on the porch, as the dogs quartered the property.

All of a sudden one of the glossy-coated animals began to bay.

"They've picked up the scent!" Bert Lundy called out. Clinging to the dogs' harnesses, he and his wife led a contingent of police through the wooded area that ran parallel to the fields. In a few minutes the group was out of sight.

A crew from WTVQ arrived just after 10:00 a.m., followed shortly thereafter by reporters from the other local TV stations and the newspaper. Susan's disappearance was suddenly big news; Lydia Shelly, a local reporter, asked Molly if she would like to make an appeal to the kidnapper on the air. After a brief conference with Ron Eaton, Molly agreed.

Watching herself plead for Susan's safe return on *The News at Noon*, Molly felt suddenly light-headed. She'd seen other broadcasts like it before: distraught family members begging for the lives of beloved children. In every case Molly had ever heard of, there'd been no happy ending; the children had been found dead.

Please, God. Please.

The dogs and their handlers were still out as the afternoon progressed; more volunteers arrived to comb the fields. J.D. and Thornton and Tyler Wyland were among this group, along with Tom Atkinson, whose mother had come with him. Instead of heading off with the search party, Flora bustled into the kitchen. She had brought over a chicken dinner complete with all the trimmings, and was determined to feed anyone who needed feeding. Molly was grateful for her help. Though she herself could not eat, Ashley and Mike and Sam needed food, and Flora was the best cook in the county.

Watching Sam bite into a drumstick, Molly smiled at Flora and went out onto the porch. She could still see the search party in the distance. Restless, Molly decided to join them. She could not, for the life of her, just stay in the house and wait.

Trapped by the fence, Pork Chop whined with disappointment as Molly climbed it. His whines turned to barks and his barks to howls as she started to walk away.

"Hush, Pork Chop!" Molly told him as he leaped vainly at the fence. He was still howling as she crested the rise and disappeared from sight.

The day was cold and bright. Wrapped in a down coat of Ashley's, Molly kept her eye on the ground as she walked, looking for something—anything—that might indicate Susan had passed that way. A tiny white fuzzball in the brown grass, perhaps; the nightgown had a tendency to pill and shed. Or a blond hair. Or—or what, she didn't know. Because she loved Susan, Molly felt she might notice what the others had overlooked. She almost felt that her love could lead her to Susan like a divining rod to water.

Please, God. Please.

Molly had prayed more in the last thirty-six hours than in the entire rest of her life.

"*Su-san!*" Periodically the searchers called Susan's name as they progressed. Other search parties, farther away, did the same. Susan's name echoed forlornly over the countryside. The sound had a mournful, keening quality that clutched at Molly's heart.

Something was coming up behind her, moving fast and low over the grass. Molly heard its approach, saw it coming out of the corner of her eye, and turned her head.

"Pork Chop!" she said as the dog slowed his headlong gallop to come trotting up to her. He was panting. His tongue hung out and his paws and muzzle were covered with dirt, but he looked very pleased with himself.

"Did you dig under the fence?" she asked in a

scolding tone, because Pork Chop had done it before. The dog was not supposed to be on Wyland Farm property for fear he would spook the horses. But the horses were in barns now, so what harm could he do? Molly thought about ordering Pork Chop to go home—not that he was likely to obey—just from general principles, but then realized that she would be glad of the company. Pork Chop would keep her from feeling so alone.

"Come on, then," she said to the dog. He wagged his tail at her, snuffling small hillocks of grass as he trotted alongside.

J.D., the Wylands, and the others were by now almost an entire field ahead of her, Molly discovered. She glanced up in time to see them scaling another fence. They were headed toward the woods beyond the stallion barn, Molly knew. The consensus was that Susan could not be out in the open. The grass was too flat at this time of year to provide much concealment. If she was in the fields, she would have been found by now.

Nobody had said the words *her body*, but Molly knew that was what they meant. If Susan's body was in the fields, they would have found it; if she was alive, she wouldn't be in the fields.

Please, God. Please.

Sam would be devastated if Susan did not come back. He and his twin had never been separated, even when they were moved from one foster home to another. If for no other reason, Susan had to be found alive for Sam.

Molly remembered Sam's dream of the night before. Susan wanted to come home, he'd said. She was in a big hole, in the dark, and she wanted to come home.

Tears rushed to Molly's eyes; she blinked them back. Susan wanted to come home. Of course Susan wanted to come home.

She was in a big hole.

Out of nowhere Molly remembered the well. The one she had fallen over, breaking Ashley's shoe, the night she had found the ringer. Had anyone looked in the well?

She glanced up, suddenly excited, meaning to call the search party back and send them in a new direction. They were mere specks in the distance, already almost to the woods. She would have to scream her head off for them to hear her.

Molly decided to go herself. Turning in the opposite direction, she whistled for Pork Chop, who had been ranging farther and farther afield and was at this point nowhere in sight. When he didn't respond, Molly shrugged. The dog could find his own way home, she had no doubt. Walking very fast now, she headed for the veterinary hospital. She would have to use it as a reference point. Without it, she wasn't sure she could find the well again, as it blended completely into the ground.

A ten-minute walk brought the hospital into sight. Molly stood in the open field and looked at it, trying to remember at precisely what angle she had approached it. The Big House was about a half mile to the north. Glancing over her shoulder, she determined that she had crossed the field perhaps a hundred feet farther to her left.

"Susan!" Calling her sister's name, Molly walked toward the barn, scanning the ground carefully on both sides as she went. Even so, she would not have seen the well cover had it not been for the tiny strip of silvery leather from Ashley's shoe.

It still clung to the edge of the hole that had tripped her.

Molly hurried to the well. It did not look as though it had been disturbed in decades, but still . . .

"Susan!"

She put a hand in the hole, which was perhaps six inches in diameter, trying to shift the stone cover. It weighed a ton; she couldn't budge it.

"Susan!" she yelled down the hole.

"Molly!" It was a man's voice, and it came from behind her instead of from underground.

Molly glanced around to see Tyler Wyland striding toward her across the field. He must have seen her heading in the opposite direction from the search party and decided to join her. Molly was glad to see him. At that point, she would have even welcomed Thornton.

"What are you doing?" he asked as he drew closer.

"I just remembered this well," Molly said, standing up. "But I can't lift the cover. Can you help me?"

He was beside her, looking down at the stone circle that was barely visible beneath the spongy carpet of brown grass.

"How did you find it?" he asked.

"I tripped over it the other night when I was walking home from your party. I got my foot caught in the hole, and broke off the heel of my shoe."

"That's too bad," Tyler said.

Molly glanced at him impatiently. "See if you can lift it. If you put your fingers in the hole, you can get a grip on it. It's too heavy for me to move."

Molly dropped to one knee beside the well, inserting her fingers into the hole to demonstrate. The stone was rough and cold beneath her hand. The afternoon chill had her shivering despite the protection of Ashley's goose-down coat.

"The cover weighs about two hundred pounds," Tyler agreed. "But it's not a well down there. It's a hidey-hole. Local abolitionists used to hide runaway slaves in it in the days of the Underground Railroad."

Before Molly could ask him how he knew, something smashed with crushing force into the back of her head.

Molly felt a blinding pain, and then the world went dark.

50

Despite his preoccupation with Susan, Will could not keep Howard Lawrence's death out of his mind. Something about it bothered him. It kept niggling at the edges of his consciousness; he had the feeling that he was missing something, something important.

He could not waste time on Lawrence today. The man was dead; with every hour that passed, the chances increased that Susan might be too. She had to be found, soon.

Uncovering the link with Libby Coleman was a break. It narrowed down the list of possible suspects considerably. Right now a dozen assorted cops and feds were combing every available record to find anyone who had left the area just after Libby Coleman's death and returned before the latest round of animal mutilations began. Among the names they compiled should be that of the perp.

The records were not computerized. Time was running out. *Hurry, hurry, hurry* was the refrain that ran through Will's head.

Still, he could not get Lawrence's death out of his mind.

Finally Will stopped what he was doing and leaned back in his borrowed chair in disgust. Massaging his temples with his fingers and closing his eyes, he let his mind off the tight leash on which he'd been keeping it.

Free to wander, it went straight to Howard Lawrence.

There is no such thing as coincidence.

Given that assumption, then Lawrence's death was murder. The most likely scenario was that someone had found out that he had turned informant—witness the blackmail note—and killed him as a result.

Shot him in the head at the very Dairy Queen where Will had stopped earlier in the day, as a matter of fact.

Why, all of a sudden, did the case refuse to let him go?

Was there any way it could be connected to Susan's disappearance?

Will didn't see how, but he had learned to trust his instincts long ago. Suppose he was looking at the Lawrence case all wrong, he posited. Suppose he turned everything upside down. Suppose Lawrence's murder was not the result of his work as an informant; suppose the blackmail note had nothing to do with that.

Suppose Lawrence was killed for something to do with—not Susan because Susan had not yet disappeared—something to do with the Coleman case. Suppose Lawrence had known what happened to Libby Coleman. Suppose that the uncreased blackmail note with no fingerprints on it besides Lawrence's had not been sent *to* Lawrence, but was soon to be sent *by* Lawrence.

Suppose Lawrence had been blackmailing Libby Coleman's kidnapper. Suppose the kidnapper had retaliated by killing Lawrence.

At the Lexington Dairy Queen.

Will remembered the black-and-white security monitor that recorded customers placing orders, and his eyes popped open.

Lawrence would be on one of those tapes. Perhaps whoever killed him would be too.

Will was on the phone before the thought was fully formed. The time it took for the Dairy Queen's owner to be tracked down and the whereabouts of the October 11 tape ascertained had Will in a cold sweat. His greatest fear was that the tape might already have been destroyed, or erased.

Luck was with him. In the absence of a crime, the owner said, security tapes were erased and recycled monthly. But the Dairy Queen had been robbed in October. All tapes for that month had been sent to the police so they could check to see if the robbers had cased the restaurant before committing the crime.

Forty-five minutes later Will was seated before a TV screen in an office at the Lexington Police Department, reviewing the Dairy Queen security tape for October 11.

There was Howard Lawrence ordering a cheeseburger, onion rings, and a vanilla shake. The next driver was a woman with two children in the car. Then came Tyler Wyland in a gray Volvo that Will had seen around the farm, ordering an ice-cream cone with sprinkles.

Tyler Wyland.

As far as Will knew, Wyland had never left the area, and he would have been young—sixteen, seventeen—

when Libby Coleman disappeared. But he was on that security tape.

There is no such thing as coincidence.

Buying ice cream at a Dairy Queen was not a crime, even if the man two cars ahead died minutes later under suspicious circumstances.

Will had not a shred of hard evidence to charge Tyler Wyland with anything.

What he had was a gut feeling. He picked up the phone, and ordered Tyler Wyland brought in for questioning.

51

Molly opened her eyes. Not that it made any difference. It was so dark, she could see nothing. Dark and musty-smelling and cold, but not as cold as it had been outside.

Where was she? What had happened?

Her head hurt so badly that it was making her nauseous. Cautiously she moved, gritting her teeth against the pain. She was lying on her back on what felt like a dirt floor, she discovered. She could not see, but she had the impression of a vast, echoing space.

Susan. The well. Memory came flooding back. Molly realized that she was not in a well at all. Tyler Wyland had described it as a hidey-hole left over from the days of the Underground Railroad.

Tyler Wyland had knocked her unconscious and brought her down here. Why?

"Susan?" Molly called tremulously into the darkness, using her hands to push herself into a sitting position. Her head swam. She shook it, hoping it would clear.

Shaking her head was a mistake. The resulting pain

was crippling. Molly collapsed onto the floor again, wondering if she had a concussion.

"M-Molly?"

When she first heard it, Molly thought the voice was a hallucination. Still, she struggled up again, hoping against hope.

"Susan?"

"Molly?"

"Oh, Susan!" Ignoring the pain in her head, Molly scooted along the floor toward the voice. "Susan, Susan!"

"Molly?"

Suddenly Susan was there with her, in her arms, hugging her as if she would never let her go. Molly wrapped her arms around her little sister and thanked God.

"Oh, Molly, did he get you too?" Susan was shaking, crying, her head burrowing into Molly's shoulder. Molly held her sister close. Her initial euphoria evaporated.

Susan had not been found. Instead, they were both missing.

52

Waiting for Tyler Wyland to be picked up, Will drove back to the farmhouse to apprise Molly of the break in the case. There were so many vehicles crammed into the driveway and in the yard in front of the house that he had to park on the grassy verge across the street. Eaton was in the house, along with Mike, Ashley, and Sam, and assorted neighbors. Molly was not; she had gone out an hour or so previously.

Probably to join a search party.

Mrs. Atkinson pressed chicken and dressing on him, which Will politely declined. He comforted the children as best he could, giving them hope without promising anything he couldn't deliver. Then he went out on the porch, roaming restlessly through the yard. Where was Molly? Why was it taking so long to pick up Wyland?

The cellular phone in his pocket rang. Will answered it, talked to Captain Bill Sperry of the Lexington police, and hung up.

There were cops at Wyland's house and at his sister's house, but Wyland himself was not there. The word was that he had been with a search party that included his nephew Thornton, but the search party had been located and Tyler Wyland was no longer with them. According to members of the search party, Tyler Wyland had separated from them at around four o'clock, striking out over the fields on his own.

No one had seen him since.

It was 5:45 p.m. Night was falling, and the temperature was dropping. The search parties were trailing in. Will went into the house, talked to the kids, talked to Eaton, and came outside to pace again. It was full dark, though it was not yet six o'clock.

Where was Molly? She should have been back by now. A quick phone check confirmed that all the search parties were in. Molly had not been seen. Was she out in the fields looking on her own? In the dark?

Where was Tyler Wyland?

Wyland would have no reason to attack Molly. *If* he was the perp. Will had to remind himself that there was no proof yet that Wyland had done anything.

Just his gut feeling, after seeing that tape.

His gut feelings were usually pretty accurate. At the moment his gut was screaming at him that Molly should have been back by now.

Where was she? Will walked up the slope to the fence, staring restlessly across the fields. In the dark he couldn't see much. Just shadows dancing over the grass, and in the distance the gray shapes of hills and trees against the night sky.

The moon was rising on the horizon, yellow and swollen and round as a ball.

She would have been home by now, unless something had prevented her. Will knew it with a conviction that bordered on certainty. Remembering how she had gone to investigate the sounds she had heard that night in the veterinary hospital when anyone with a lick of sense would have hightailed it back out the window, Will grew increasingly alarmed.

What if Molly had found something that led her to Susan? What if Tyler Wyland had found Molly where she had no business to be?

It was after dark, all the search parties were in, and both Molly and Tyler Wyland were still missing.

There is no such thing as coincidence.

Will's blood ran cold. Snatching the phone out of his pocket, he dialed the Lexington office. He wanted those bloodhounds back out here, pronto.

They had drawn a blank with Susan, following an old trail to a playmate's house. Susan, of course, had on the night of her abduction presumably been carried from the house. But the dogs had at least proved they could follow a trail. Will wanted them put on Molly's trail. Now.

Matthews called back minutes later. The bloodhounds were on their way to an exhibition in West Virginia. They could not possibly get back before morning. He would see if he could scare up another pair of tracking dogs in the surrounding counties.

Will said a few choice words into the phone, and hung up.

At the idea that Molly might have joined the ranks of people who disappear never to be seen again, cold terror ran through Will's veins. He didn't think he could bear to lose another woman he loved.

That was when he faced the truth he'd been avoiding for the last twenty-four hours: He loved her. So much, it scared him. So much that the idea of someone hurting her made him homicidal. So much that he was going to go nuts if she didn't turn up at all, or turned up dead. Will acknowledged the strength of the emotion, clenching his fingers around the top rail of the fence and closing his eyes.

He wanted to offer her forever, more than he had ever wanted anything in his life.

A bark made him look down. Will saw Pork Chop loping toward him out of the dark.

"What are you doing over there?" Will asked as the dog reached the fence, reared up on his hind legs and pawed the top rail, barking. He'd never before seen Pork Chop in the Wyland Farm fields. As far as he had been aware, Pork Chop couldn't get over the fence.

"Where have you been, hmm?" Will asked the dog. Pork Chop dropped to all fours, barking. Will stared at him as the dog continued to bark, backing away from the fence.

Had Pork Chop been with Molly? Did he know where she was?

Responding to his gut again, Will went over the fence and followed Pork Chop into the dark.

53

A muffled grating noise made Susan stiffen in Molly's arms.

"He's coming," Susan whispered, trembling. "Oh, Molly, I can fit in the crack but you . . ."

The beam of a flashlight sliced through the darkness about a dozen feet to Molly's left. Coming from the surface, it shone downward, illuminating a stone-lined shaft about four feet in circumference. Iron bars formed a jail door–like barrier between the large chamber they were in and the shaft, which Molly presumed led to the stone cover.

The grating noise came again, followed by the sound of footsteps descending. Molly watched as black boots came into view, followed by lean legs in jeans. Iron rungs were set into the side of the shaft to serve as a ladder, she saw. He was climbing down them.

In her arms, Susan was shaking with fright.

"If you have a place to hide, go hide," Molly whispered, pushing her sister away. Susan hesitated only a second, then slithered away into the dark. Molly lay down, feigning unconsciousness.

Fear dampened her palms and dried her throat as she listened to the clink of metal against metal. Peeking from beneath one nearly closed lid, Molly watched as he inserted a key into the lock on the barred door. The door swung inward with scarcely a sound; the hinges must have been well oiled, and recently.

Probably in preparation for Susan's abduction.

Molly realized that to everyone on the surface she had now vanished as thoroughly as her little sister. They would be looking for her—Will would be looking for her.

But they hadn't found Susan. And they hadn't found Libby Coleman.

They might look for another thirteen years and never find this place.

She had to fight the terror that threatened to engulf her. Giving way to panic was the worst thing she could do. She had to lie very still, lips parted, breathing in and out, in and out . . .

The flashlight shone full in her face. It was all Molly could do not to flinch.

"You haven't come out to help your sister, Susan?" Tyler Wyland asked reproachfully, aiming the flashlight along the wall behind Molly. "Her head's bleeding; she needs you."

Susan said nothing. Wherever she was—the crack, she had said—Molly assumed that she was beyond Tyler Wyland's reach. That might be why she was still alive; but still, she couldn't stay in there forever. She would die just as surely in there as she would out here, just in a different way.

And no one would ever know.

"Now that Molly's here, I thought we might talk," Tyler said, still pointing the beam of the flashlight at the wall. "I really don't want to hurt either of you, you know."

Oh, right, thought Molly, and prayed Susan had enough sense not to fall for that. Tyler could hardly let them go; kidnapping was the least of the charges he would face.

Suddenly the flashlight was on her face again. The light filtering in through her closed lids made the throbbing pain in her head worse. Molly concentrated on her breathing as Tyler knelt beside her, touching her face with warm fingers.

Her stomach knotted with fright.

He picked up her left wrist. The action was sudden, and she had to concentrate hard on keeping her arm limp. Molly felt the cold slide of metal around her wrist, heard the click, and realized that she was being handcuffed.

Sheer black panic almost overwhelmed her.

Once she was handcuffed, she would be helpless, unable to aid herself or Susan.

He reached for her right wrist. It was now or never. Molly exploded off the floor with a shriek that would have been deafening even in the open air. Down in the hidey-hole, it bounced off the walls, amplified a thousandfold. As Tyler jumped back in surprise, Molly let loose with a roundhouse right to his nose. She felt the bridge smash under her fist.

Susan screamed in terror as Tyler staggered backward, a hand clapped to his nose, howling. The flashlight fell to the floor with a clatter. Molly dove for it, captured it, turned it off.

They were plunged into pitch darkness that was alive with the echoes of screams.

"I'm going to kill you, you bitch." The guttural

voice no longer sounded like Tyler Wyland's at all. Icy terror twisted around her heart as she realized that he was coming after her, feeling for her with broad sweeps of his arms that disturbed the still air. His harsh breathing told Molly where he was as she crawled along the cold dirt floor, flashlight in hand, taking care to make as little noise as she could. The handcuff that he had secured to her left wrist hit the stone wall with a clank. A shiver of panic shot down her spine. Molly quickly tucked the offending metal circle inside the sleeve of her coat, and rolled, moving at a ninety-degree angle from the direction in which she had been headed.

With a sound like a growl he lunged for the place she had been, cursing when he came up empty.

Molly hit the far wall and was still for a moment, fighting to control her breathing. He would be able to find her if he heard her breathe.

Not that she could hope to escape him for long. It was a large room, perhaps twenty by twenty-four feet, but the only escape was through the iron door and up the ladder. Even if she could make it before he caught her, there was still the two-hundred-pound stone slab that stood between her and freedom.

She would not be able to budge it.

It was impossible to steady her erratic pulse.

He was trying to be very quiet now, moving softly through the dark. Molly stayed still and listened, following his movements as she tried to formulate a plan.

What plan? she thought with despair. She could not hope to physically overpower Tyler Wyland. He wasn't a huge man, but he was taller than she and muscular despite his leanness. The blow she had landed on his nose had been so effective because of the element of surprise. Without that, she was lost.

"Do you remember the mare, Molly?" The voice coming at her through the darkness made her scalp prickle. He was moving closer, following the perimeter of the room. Molly crawled toward the middle, trying to keep a grip on her fragile control. To shriek her terror into the darkness would only hasten her own end. "Sheila? Do you remember what I did to Sheila?"

Hideous realization burst upon Molly: Tyler Wyland was the horse slasher. She gasped, caught herself, and immediately rolled left.

He lunged right past her, coming up with nothing but an armful of air. Suddenly he laughed, the sound high-pitched and horrifying. It was as if he was getting into the spirit of the thing, enjoying the chase.

"Remember what I did to her? That's what I'm going to do to you. And Susan too. Though I'm going to let Susan live awhile. Little girls are fun to hurt. Did you know that? But you—you're going to die tonight. It's just a matter of time until I catch you and then . . ."

The acts he described were so vile that Molly tuned them out. He was lunging around the room now, from corner to corner and across the middle without warning. Rolling, crawling, slithering across the floor, Molly just managed to elude him. Her heart was pounding; her head hurt so badly, she could hardly think. Susan was weeping; Molly could hear her gasping sobs.

But wherever she was, weeping or not, for the moment at least Susan was safe.

He passed so close to where she huddled against the wall that Molly actually felt his shoe brush her arm. He kept walking. Molly let out the breath she had been holding and slithered backward, her stomach pressed against the floor. Suddenly with a cackle and a whoosh of air he was upon her, his knee thudding into her back, his arm whipping around her neck.

Molly cried out in terror.

"Got you, got you, got you," he crowed, tightening his arm as Molly gagged and choked. She struggled, but he grabbed a handful of hair and slammed her forehead into the hard-packed dirt. For the second time that day, Molly saw stars.

Seconds later, he had her handcuffed and was shining the flashlight in her face.

"Molly!" Susan screamed from her hiding place.

"Don't come out, Susan!" Molly called urgently back. He was binding her legs now, with a rope he had apparently brought with him. Molly knew that the real horror was only just beginning.

"No, Susan, don't come out," Tyler agreed, hauling Molly into a sitting position with her back against the wall. "You can watch what I'm going to do to your sister from right there."

He pointed the flashlight at the opposite wall. Molly caught a glimpse of white, and then saw Susan, wedged deeply into a narrow fissure in the stone. Her sister's frightened eyes gleamed as the beam hit them. Molly could see a small fist curled in front of her face.

"Don't look, Susan," Molly ordered. A rag was stuffed in her mouth, silencing her.

"So you don't hurt my ears when you scream," Tyler explained with a ghastly smile. Blood streaked the bottom half of his face from the blow she had landed. Even without the distorting effects of the flashlight and the blood, he looked different, Molly thought. His eyes were wide and gleaming, black now instead of their usual brown. His forehead was wrinkled, and his eyebrows were drawn together so that they almost met over his nose. His cheeks were lined in a way she had never noticed before, and he was panting with anticipation. Molly realized that she was looking into the face of insanity, and began to shake.

She was sitting against the wall with her hands cuffed behind her back and her legs bound at knee and ankle. He squatted beside her, propping the flashlight so that it focused on her like a spotlight. Molly realized that he truly did want Susan to see everything he did to her; she supposed he wanted to heighten the little girl's terror.

Molly was terrified herself. Helpless now, she could only watch as he reached beneath his jacket and drew out a long, silver-bladed knife.

"This is going to hurt," he promised softly, lifting the blade toward her throat.

Susan began to scream.

Molly closed her eyes, praying. The blade slid into her coat, sawed downward. Molly realized that he was cutting off her clothes.

"Freeze!" The shout sliced through Susan's screams and caused Molly's head to whip around. There, framed in the opening between the shaft and the room itself, was Will. He stood, feet apart, arms raised, a pistol pointed at Tyler's head.

Tyler dived behind Molly, hooking her with an arm around her throat, dragging her in front of him like a shield. Molly felt the sharp blade of the knife dig into the soft skin just below her ear as she was pulled upright.

"I'll cut off her head," Tyler said. Susan had stopped screaming, and the threat echoed through the chamber. Will's face was hard and set; the pistol never wavered in his grip.

"Susan," he called. "Come here."

Susan wriggled out of her hiding place. Sobbing, casting a tearful glance at Molly, she ran to Will.

"It's okay," he said, motioning her on past him, his gaze never leaving Tyler. "Get out of here."

He pushed her behind him toward the ladder. With a last glance at Molly, Susan climbed.

Voices from above as Susan reached the surface told Molly—and apparently Tyler too—that Will had not come alone.

"Put down the knife," Will said to Tyler in an even tone. "You won't be hurt, I promise."

Molly could smell Tyler's fear. Held tight against him, she could smell the suddenly rank odor as sweat began to pour from his body. He was breathing fast, his arm hard around her throat, the hand holding the point of the knife to her jugular vein trembling.

"You can't escape," Will said, the pistol unwavering as it pointed at Tyler's head. "Put down the knife."

"If I can't escape, then I don't have anything to lose," Tyler said in a perfectly normal voice. A quick jerk of his hand, and the knife sliced into Molly's neck.

Boom! There was an explosion. Molly fell to her knees, pitched forward on her face. Then Will was beside her, turning her over, his hands trembling with fear.

"Molly, oh, God, Molly," he said, pulling the rag from her mouth and holding it to her throat to stanch what she assumed was the flow of blood. She didn't feel any pain, or even any fear. She felt cold, freezing cold; she was shaking in Will's arms.

"Get a medic down here!" he bellowed, his voice hoarse with fear. Men filled the room, hovered over her, pulled her away from Will.

The last thing Molly was aware of was a stranger kneeling beside her, and a needle plunging into her arm.

54

November 18, 1995

When they found Susan, and Molly, they also found Libby Coleman. Her skeletonized remains, still lying amidst the tatters of her white party dress, were buried under a shallow layer of dirt in the hidey-hole. Later, they were given an answer to the question that still plagued Will: Why, since Tyler Wyland had never left the area, had there been no victims in the intervening thirteen years?

A phone call came into the Lexington FBI office while Will was at the hospital with Molly, and the Bureau had it transferred to his cellular phone. The woman placing the call identified herself as Sarah Wyland, Tyler's mother. She was calling from Switzerland. At the outset of the call she had been informed by whoever had answered at the Lexington end that her son was dead. It made no difference. She said she had seen the story of the little girl's disappearance on CNN, and felt it was time to set the record straight.

"Any help you can give us in understanding what happened will be greatly appreciated, Mrs. Wyland," Will said into the phone. It was about 4:00 a.m. Lexington time God knew what time it was in Gstaad, where Mrs. Wyland said she was calling from—and he had been half dozing in a chair by Molly's bed. He stood up and moved to a corner of the room as he spoke. Not that his voice was likely to disturb Molly. She was under heavy sedation, sleeping like an angel.

Will's gaze slid to the bandage on her throat, and he felt his stomach burn. She could so easily have been an angel for real that he still got scared thinking about it.

Thank God he'd gotten there in time. Thank God Pork Chop had led him to the hole, and he had had his cellular phone with him to call for backup. Thank God Susan's screaming had masked the sound of his moving aside the stone cover and dropping into the hole. Thank God he had fired when he did, and his hand had been steady.

Thank God, period.

Mrs. Wyland began to talk. She said that as a child Tyler had tortured and killed his pets. When he got older, he mutilated farm animals. Finally he moved on to horses. She had been alarmed at what she called his "tendencies," and begged her husband to get help for the boy. John Wyland refused. He said he wasn't going to see the Wyland name dragged through the mud, and whipped Tyler instead. Of course, that did no good.

When the little girl disappeared—the first little girl, Libby Coleman, the daughter of a neighbor and good friend—Sarah Wyland did not at first suspect her son. It was not until one of the farmhands, Howard Lawrence—yes, the one who was now trainer for Cloverlot, and no, she hadn't realized he was dead—found a little girl's white satin hair bow in the field and brought it to her that she started to suspect. She recognized the hair bow from the extensive publicity about Libby Coleman's disappearance. When she confronted Tyler with her suspicions, he confessed. Sarah Wyland went to her husband preparatory to calling the police. He wouldn't let her, and insisted on covering the whole thing up.

Sarah Wyland did not agree, but she could not stand against her husband. Howard Lawrence was paid a large sum yearly to keep quiet about the hair bow. Tyler was put on medication: monthly injections of a drug that chemically castrated him. Her husband obtained the drug ostensibly to aid in controlling his stallions, and administered the injections himself. Without his sex drive, Tyler was no longer dangerous.

Unable to live with the strain, Sarah Wyland divorced her husband the following year. She left the country, and had never returned.

When she was informed that her ex-husband had died, she feared that it would all start up again. Tyler could always administer the injections to himself, but she was afraid he would not. Only her husband's threats to turn him in if he did not had made Tyler agree to submit to them in the first place. Seeing the clip of the second child's disappearance on CNN, she had realized her fears were correct.

She had called the FBI immediately. Thank God, in this case, the child had been saved, even if her own intervention might have come too late.

For Howard Lawrence too. If Lawrence had been blackmailing Tyler, it must have been a recent development. Tyler would have told his father, and John wouldn't have stood for that. Most likely the hush payments, like Tyler's injections, had stopped with her ex-husband's death. A yearly stipend of that nature was not the kind of thing one could write into a will, after all.

When Will hung up, he stood for a few moments just looking down at the phone and shaking his head. All these years, while the Colemans had been left to worry and grieve over their daughter, their friends and neighbors had been hiding a secret like this.

After suffering through first Susan's and then Molly's disappearances, Will's sympathies were all with the Colemans. He had had just enough of a taste of it to realize how devastating such grief could be.

He returned the phone to his pocket and went to stand beside the bed. Molly was hooked to an IV line. Her arms, bare beneath the short sleeves of the green hospital gown, lay limply across the neatly tucked beige blanket. Her coffee-brown hair formed a tangled halo around her face and her skin was nearly as pale as the white sheets. Her lips were parted as she breathed in and out, their usually rosy color blanched to a soft pink. Her lashes lay in dark crescents against her cheeks. Her breasts rose and fell in gentle rhythm beneath the bedclothes.

Will curled his fingers around her limp hand. To his surprise, her eyes opened and she looked at him.

"Will," she said, and smiled. Will realized in that instant that he loved her as he had never loved anyone else in his life. Then her eyes closed, and she was asleep again.

Will stood holding her hand for a long time.

55

By eleven o'clock that night everyone had left the farmhouse except the five Ballards and Will. Susan and Molly had been released from the hospital at about 2:00 p.m. Susan had been kept over the previous night for observation, although, as one doctor said, there seemed to be nothing wrong with her that a good meal and a night's sleep wouldn't cure. Molly was treated for shock, got a topical antibiotic on her scalp and a Band-Aid on her forehead, and received five stitches below her ear. The doctor who stitched her up told her that if the knife had gone a quarter of an inch deeper, she would have died.

Tyler Wyland had died. In that last instant, when he had started to cut Molly's throat, Will had blown off the top of his head.

But Molly refused to think about that. She lay on the couch in her *I don't do mornings!* nightshirt, cozily wrapped in a quilt, her head on a pillow, watching the end of *Speed.* Will sat on the floor in front of her, leaning back against the couch, his knees bent, his arms resting on his knees. Susan was curled up at Molly's feet, while Sam and Mike sprawled on the floor and Ashley claimed the recliner. Pork Chop, as was his habit, snoozed in front of the kitchen door.

It was a cozy family scene, with all the Ballards in nightclothes and Will in sweats. Molly glanced from one engrossed face to the other and felt her heart swell with happiness and relief. *Thank you, God,* she prayed as she had a million times since waking up in the hospital. The only fly in the ointment was that Will was not family; he would be flying back to Chicago on Monday.

But just for tonight, Molly wasn't going to think about that.

The closing credits of the movie rolled across the screen. Will stood up and turned off the TV.

"Bed," he said.

"It's Saturday," Mike protested, rolling onto his back and sitting up.

"Yeah, it's not late!" Sam seconded.

Ashley yawned, and got to her feet.

"I'm tired," she said, narrowing her eyes at Sam.

"Me too," Susan said, uncurling herself from the couch and giving Sam a monitory look. "Come on, Sam."

"There's no way . . ." Mike began heatedly, then met Will's gaze. As Will's back was to her, Molly couldn't see his expression, but Mike broke off in mid-gripe and rolled to his feet. "Okay."

Molly watched in astonishment as her siblings, with hardly another grumble among them, trooped from the room.

"How did you do that?" she asked Will, impressed.

"They obviously know the voice of authority when

they hear it," he said, coming to stand over her. "How do you feel?"

"Great, considering," Molly said, smiling up at him. He looked very serious suddenly, and she wondered what he was thinking. She reached out and caught his hand, giving it a little tug to encourage him to sit on the edge of the couch.

"You scared the life out of me, you know," he said, resisting. "When I realized you were nowhere to be found, I nearly had a heart attack."

"I didn't know you cared," Molly teased, batting her eyelashes at him flirtatiously.

"I do," Will answered, unsmiling. "Too damn much."

His voice was grim, and Molly's eyes widened on his face.

"Is something wrong?" she asked, releasing his hand and sitting up. Will looked down at her, opened his mouth, closed it again, and took a quick turn about the room.

"What is it?" Molly asked, thoroughly alarmed.

Will came back to stand in front of her. Molly saw that twin flags of red had risen to stain his cheekbones.

"Molly," he said, then paused. "I'm no good at this."

"Are you trying to tell me you're leaving tomorrow?" A sinking feeling hit Molly's stomach at the thought. He had promised to stay through the weekend, but something must have come up. His son, perhaps, or work. She didn't want him to go. Not tomorrow, not Monday, not ever. But of course he would. She had been foolish to allow herself to pretend, as she had for the last few hours, that he was hers.

Without answering, Will sat down on the couch beside her. Picking up her hand, he held it in both of his, running his thumb over her knuckles. His gaze was intent. He took a deep breath.

"Hell," he said, "I'm trying to ask you to marry me."

Molly stared at him, dumbfounded.

"What?" she squeaked.

"You heard me." The red spread to the tips of his ears.

"You're *proposing*?"

"Yes." His voice was gruff.

Molly looked at him, at the hard handsome face and strong neck and broad shoulders, at the long-fingered bronze-skinned hands holding her own pale one, at the short blond hair and intent blue eyes.

"Yes," she said, throwing her arms around his neck. "Yes, yes, yes, yes, yes!"

"Hooray!" That particular yell came from Sam, but all four of her siblings burst into the room, shouting and clapping.

Will, in the act of kissing her, lifted his head. "I told you guys I needed privacy for this," he growled.

"Hey, man, we gave you privacy," Mike said, grinning. "And she said yes!"

"I knew she would," Ashley chimed in, her face pink with excitement. Sitting with her arms looped around Will's neck and his arms around her waist, Molly grinned at her sister.

"It's not over," Will said. "Go to bed."

"But Molly said yes!" Susan came to stand beside them, looking enraptured. Clad in a pale blue nightgown with a ruffle around the throat and hem, Susan was so excited she couldn't stand still.

Sam was right behind Susan. "Do you *have* to kiss

when you get engaged?" he asked, sounding revolted as he eyed the entwined pair.

"That's the whole point, stupid," Mike said, nudging him. "They want to kiss. Or they wouldn't want to get married."

"Gross," Sam said, shaking his head.

"Would you *please* go to bed?" Will ground out.

"Come on, people," Ashley said, putting one hand on Susan's shoulder and the other on Sam's, "Now that we know the outcome, let's leave them alone."

"Thank you, Ashley," Will said.

"Good night, guys," Molly called after them, smiling, as Ashley herded the twins from the room and Mike trailed after them. When they were gone, she looked up at Will.

"I'm kind of a package deal," she said apologetically.

"I know." He grinned at her. "That's why I asked them what they thought about the idea first. They were all for it."

"You *asked* them?"

"Today at the hospital. They knew I was going to pop the question tonight. How do you think I got them to go to bed after the movie?"

"They like you," Molly said, smiling at him. "*I* like you."

"You *like* me?" Will asked.

"No," Molly corrected herself. "I love you. Truly. Madly. Deeply."

"I love you too," Will said, and kissed her again.

56

November 20, 1995

It was Monday. Will spent most of the day tying up loose ends. He had come to the conclusion that moving his new family to Chicago was a bad idea. The kids had already experienced enough upheaval in their young lives to last them a lifetime, and picturing Mike in the big city with its accompanying temptations was enough to make him shudder. He would sell his house in Chicago, buy a new one down here, and start a new life to go with it.

Accordingly, when he called in he told Hallum that he was going to put in for a transfer to the Lexington office.

Hallum greeted his announcement with a hoot of laughter.

"Elly May landed you, did she?" he asked over the phone. "The office was taking bets about whether she would."

"Something like that," Will answered, refusing to sound annoyed. If he did, he knew he'd be kidded for the rest of his life.

"Matthews is retiring at the end of January," Hallum continued. "With me to recommend you, I think you can be pretty sure of getting his job."

It was that easy. Will was promised a promotion to go with his new family and his new life, and vowed to develop a liking for the smell of manure if it killed him.

He was just getting into his car with Molly that afternoon when a Federal Express truck pulled into the driveway. They were on their way to pick up the kids from school, after which all six of them were going to troop down to the county courthouse to apply for the marriage license. The ceremony itself would be performed the following Saturday. Kevin, Will's parents, and Debbie's parents would be flying down on Thursday, and the list of friends and neighbors Molly wanted to invite made Will shake his head.

But hey, a man only got married twice.

Will accepted the manila envelope from the FedEx driver, turning it over in his hands. It was from the Chicago office, and it contained a note and a tape.

The note said simply "Congratulations!" above the scrawled signatures of his fellow agents.

The tape was more of a mystery. *Play me* was written on its white casing in pencil. Will eyed it suspiciously as he got into the car.

"What is it?" Molly asked, smiling at him.

"I have no idea. I'm not even sure I want to know." He kissed her mouth, turned on the ignition, and inserted the tape into the tape deck.

A song blared out. Will listened to the Bureau's finest bellowing cheerfully off-key, and began to laugh.

Green acres is the place to be /
Farm living is the life for me /
Land juttin' out so far and wide /
Keep Chicago, just give me that countryside!

Special Preview
from the Karen Robards title

HEARTBREAKER

Now available from Dell

Her butt hurt.

Lynn Nelson stifled a groan and rubbed the offending body part with both hands. Not that the impromptu massage did much good. The ache did not abate.

Realizing how peculiar her actions must look, Lynn dropped her hands and cast an embarrassed glance around to see if anyone was watching. Her fellow vacationers—a group of twenty fourteen- and fifteen-year-old girls, two teachers, and two other parent chaperons like herself—all seemed to be going merrily about the business of setting up camp for the night. Nary a watcher in sight. Nor a fellow butt-rubber, either.

Did they all have buns of steel?

Apparently. No one else seemed to be walking around as if they'd had a corncob shoved up where the sun don't shine. No one else even limped.

"Did you find what was bothering him yet?" The speaker was a wiry, twenty-something pony wrangler whose name Lynn thought was Tim. Dressed in jeans, boots, and a cowboy hat, Tim looked every inch at home on the range. Which, Lynn had already guessed, was the idea.

"Not yet." Lynn cast a loathing look at the cause of her misery—a shaggy mountain pony named Hero—and retrieved the metal pick from the ground where she had stuck it moments before while she attended to more pressing needs. Grabbing the beast around the foreleg as Tim had shown her earlier, Lynn tried to pry a muddy hoof off the ground.

What must have been a thousand pounds of sweaty, stinky horse leaned companionably against her. Its rotten-grass breath whooshed past her cheek.

Pee-yuu. Lynn remembered why she hated horses.

"Get off, you," she muttered, shoving the animal with her shoulder, and was rewarded by a soft nicker and even more of its weight.

Though she pulled with all her strength, the hoof didn't budge.

"Here." Grinning, Tim moved to help her, picking up the hoof with no trouble at all and handing it to her.

"Thanks." If her tone was sour, Lynn couldn't help it. She felt sour. And sore.

Bent almost double, straddling a hairy, muddy animal leg, Lynn once again stabbed her pick into the mud- (she hoped) packed hoof that was clamped between her knees.

Hero leaned against her. Lynn contemplated horseicide.

"Dig in there a little deeper and I bet you'll find a rock," Tim said.

You'll learn to take care of your own horse, the brochure advertising the trip had promised.

Remembering, Lynn thought, whoopee.

Another dig, and the mess in the hoof popped free.

A rock, as predicted, packed in with a dark substance too malodorous to be mud. Yuck.

"Good job." Tim gave her an approving pat (or maybe whack was a better word) on the shoulder. Losing her balance, Lynn staggered backward, dropping both hoof and pick. The pony stomped its foot, snorted loudly, and turned its head to look at her. If the animal had been human, Lynn would have sworn it snickered.

"Oh, sorry," Tim said, *his* amusement obvious as he retrieved the pick. "We'll make a horsewoman out of you yet, you'll see."

"I can't wait."

"Here, give him this and he'll love you forever."

"Lucky me." Under Tim's supervision, Lynn clumsily fastened a feed bag around Hero's head. The pony twitched its ears at her, and began to eat.

"Now pat him," Tim directed. Patting was not Lynn's first choice of things to do to the mangy beast, but she swallowed her less civilized impulses and complied. Hero's hairy hide felt rough beneath her hand. Turning it palm up, she looked down in distaste at the dirt and the reddish-brown hairs left clinging to her fingers.

"Good job." With a nod Tim moved on down the line of the tied string of ponies.

Dismissed at last, Lynn pushed her fist hard against the aching small of her back and tried not to dwell on the fact that this was only the second day of a ten-day-long wilderness "vacation." And tried not to rub her butt again, either.

What had possessed her to come?

Rory, Lynn acknowledged, tottering toward one of the small camp fires that was supposed to provide protection from the no-see-ums. (Hah!) Her fourteen-year-old daughter had not asked her to be part of this freshman-class trip. On the contrary, Rory had groaned when Lynn told her she had volunteered. But Lynn felt Rory needed her. And she needed time with Rory, to shore up a relationship that lately felt as if it were coming apart at the seams.

Anyway, the promotional literature advertising the trip had made it seem educational, fun, and the experience of a lifetime, all rolled up together in one all-inclusive package deal.

So she had taken two weeks off from work—her first real vacation in three years—and here she was, on the side of some godforsaken mountain in the High Wilderness area of Utah's Uinta Range, tagging along on a teenage girl's horseback-riding fantasy trip.

The question was, was she having fun yet?

The answer was an emphatic "no!"

Lynn collapsed on a bale of hay placed near the camp fire for just that purpose, and tried to look on the bright side of things: indulging Rory's love of the outdoors was at least preferable to dealing with her escalating boy-craziness. This trip, the reward for her daughter's sticking out a whole year at Collegiate, an exclusive girls-only academy, had cost the earth, but it was thankfully male-free.

Except for the guides. Six of them, all male. All attractive. Of course. That was the way life worked. She should have expected it.

Just as she should have expected her new riding boots to pinch, her butt to ache, her nose to be sunburned despite lashings of sunscreen and the wide-brimmed cowboy hat she had worn all day, and her skin—even where it didn't show—to feel that it needed a Dustbuster taken to it to remove the grit.

She hated horseback riding.

Lynn shifted position, winced, and rubbed the knuckles of her clenched fists hard against her jean-clad thighs. She felt she was getting charley horses in every muscle she possessed below the waist.

"This might help." The man hunkering down beside her—yes, hunkering was the right word, men really did hunker down in Utah, she had discovered—held out a flattish gold can.

"Doc Grandview's Horse Liniment" was scrawled in black letters across the top. Yeah, right, Lynn thought. When even the salve she was offered looked as if it could have belonged to Wyatt Earp, Lynn's skepticism was aroused. Everything about this trip from the outfitters themselves to the flies that buzzed around the horses' ears would have been right at home in the Old West. Lynn's verdict was, too touristy for words.

"Was I that obvious?" Lynn managed a smile nonetheless, accepting the can and turning it over in her hand. Owen Feldman was part owner, with his younger brother, of Adventure, Inc., the outfitters who had arranged and were guiding the trip. Owen was tall, broad shouldered, and lean hipped, with close-cropped tobacco-brown hair, a craggy, square-jawed face, and baby blues to die for. Maybe a couple of years older than her own age of thirty-five, Owen was, the brochure had promised, a born and bred Utahn, with all the classic Utah virtues including competence, confidence, and utter reliability—a real cowboy.

Two days into the trip, Lynn had already figured out that she hated cowboys. Especially phony ones. Every time the Feldmans and their crew swung into the saddle, she half expected to hear a hidden orchestra strike up the theme song from *Bonanza*.

Rory, though, was eating it up. She had already

pointed Owen out as a potential playmate for Mom. As for herself, Rory said, she preferred the younger brother, Jess.

The memory made Lynn frown. Where *was* Rory? And where was Jess?

"Lots of people get saddle sore the first day out," Owen said, apparently attributing her grim expression to chagrin at wimping out. "Just rub this on your—affected part—and you'll feel lots better by morning."

"Thanks, I will." Lynn slid the shoe-polish-size can into the pocket of her blaze orange windbreaker—new for the trip, the color chosen to prevent some gung-ho hunter from mistaking her for a moose—and stood up. The insides of her knees screamed a protest. Her butt ached. The backs of her thighs throbbed. Trying not to wince at the pain, Lynn glanced around the camp. "Have you seen Rory? Or your brother?"

Owen smiled, the tanned skin around his eyes crinkling just the way the tanned skin around a cowboy's eyes was supposed to crinkle, and stood up too. He topped her five-foot-two by almost a foot. Central casting couldn't have chosen better, Lynn reflected dryly.

"Rory's your daughter, right? The little blonde? She and a couple of the other girls wanted to learn how to cast. Jess volunteered to demonstrate before chow."

"Oh, great." Lynn couldn't help the tartness of her tone. While Owen obviously had no problem with his brother taking a gaggle of impressionable young girls off somewhere alone, Lynn did. Jess Feldman was not cut from the same leather as his older brother. *Utterly reliable* didn't even begin to apply. "Which way did they go?"

She reached for a humorous tone and didn't quite make it. Owen's gaze sharpened.

"Come on. I'll show you," he said.

"I don't want to take you away from anything you need to be doing." Though there was a grain of truth in her answer, the larger reality was that Lynn was simply not comfortable accepting even such small favors from anyone. She had been alone for so long, battling her way through the world so that she and Rory could have something better than the nothing with which they had started, that she had grown to like it that way. Never depend on anyone, was her motto.

Especially fake cowboys.

"Bob and Ernst are on chow detail. Tim is seeing to the horses. There's nothing I need to be doing at the moment." Owen smiled at her. "Come on."

Lynn returned his smile reluctantly, but fell into step beside him as he headed through the campsite toward the thick lodgepole forest that climbed the steep slope on the other side of the clearing. Towering pines had shed enough needles over the decades to make the ground soft underfoot, as if, Lynn thought, she were walking on a thick carpet.

Most of the girls sat together in a semicircle on burlap sacks thrown on the ground, singing. Pat Greer and Debbie Stapleton, the other mother chaperons, glanced up from their self-appointed task of leading the impromptu sing-along to watch as Lynn passed by with Owen.

". . . and if another bottle should fall, there'll be eighty-seven bottles of milk on the wall. . . ."

Milk.

It was all Lynn could do not to gag. The determinedly cheerful and even more determinedly G-rated warble made her want to barf. Pat and Debbie were Tipper Gore clones: they would never permit their young charges to sing about anything as age-inappropriate as bottles of beer.

Lynn *liked* beer. If there had been one available, she would have chugalugged it on the spot just to annoy her fellow mothers.

Because they were annoying her: their cheerfulness, their nosiness, their perfect-motherness.

Lynn could feel the weight of their combined gazes stabbing her in the back as she walked past. Stylish suburban matrons comfortably married to successful men, Pat and Debbie seemed to harbor an instinctive distrust of her. As a single working mother who lived on coffee and cigarettes and had a high-profile, demanding job, Lynn supposed they considered her from a different species than themselves.

And she supposed, withsome reluctance, that maybe they were right.

"You have any other children?" Owen asked as he stopped to hold a branch aside so that she could enter the woods ahead of him.

"Rory's it." Lynn strove to lighten her mood as well as her tone as she stepped past him onto a well-worn trail. It was dark and gloomy under the trees, and ten degrees cooler. Moss covered everything, from the rocks to the tree trunks to the path. The smell was damp, like somebody's basement. "My one chick."

"She looks like you. I would have known her for your daughter anywhere."

Lynn walked smack into a nearly invisible spiderweb suspended across the path. Shuddering, she wiped the clammy threads from her face and kept going.

"She does, doesn't she?" Concentrating on responding intelligently to Owen, Lynn tried not to think about the spider (she hated spiders!) that went with the web. Rory and she did look alike. Both of them had blond hair—though Lynn admittedly gave nature a hand in keeping her chin-length shag bright—pale complexions, and large, innocent-looking blue eyes. Both were less than tall (she despised the word *short*), their lack of stature compensated for by slim builds. The difference was that for the last several years Lynn had had to work hard to keep her weight down, while for Rory such slenderness was still effortless. "Poor child."

"I wouldn't say that." Owen was behind her. Lynn couldn't see his expression, but his tone told her that he admired her looks. Lynn made a face. She hoped he wasn't going to hit on her. Ruggedly handsome or not, he was going to be disappointed if he did. She had no interest in a vacation fling, and no fantasies about bedding a faux cowboy.

"Do you have any children?" Lynn asked, for something to say. The path sloped upward, away from the rocky plateau where they would spend the night. Roots and the protruding edges of buried stones made it necessary to watch where she put her feet. Ahead, Lynn could hear the splash of tumbling water. Cracklings and rustlings and chirpings from living things about which she refused to speculate were nearer at hand.

"Nope." Owen sounded as if he smiled suddenly, although as he was walking behind her Lynn couldn't be sure. "No wife, either. My brother says I'm not a keeper. Once they get to know me, women end up throwing me back."

Lynn was surprised into glancing around. "Surely you're not as bad as all that."

Owen's eyes twinkled at her. "That's what *I* think. But Jess was pretty positive."

Lynn walked on. There was something about that rueful smile that made her wary. It was too charming, almost practiced. Part of the shtick. He might very well be lying to her. For all she knew, the rat could be married with a dozen kids.

Not that she cared whether Owen Feldman was married or not. But it was irritating to think that he might think she was dumb enough to succumb to a smile, blue eyes, and a cowboy hat. She had her faults, but stupid wasn't one of them.

A sudden bright shimmer of light ahead drew Lynn's attention. Through a frame of swaying branches, sunlight bounced off the surface of silvery water. As she walked toward the light, her view broadened to take in a wide stream, a slash of sunny sky, and the brown and green wall of the forest climbing the mountain on the other side of the stream. A well-fed muskrat sat up on a smooth-surfaced gray rock rising from the middle of the current, whiskers quivering as it stared at something the humans could not see. As Lynn watched, it dove beneath the surface with scarcely a ripple, its sleek brown body disappearing from view.

Enchanted at the display, Lynn stepped out from beneath the overhanging foliage into a scene of breath-stealing beauty. A wide darkish green creek flowed over smooth stones toward a rocky staircase some fifty yards away. There it tumbled about twelve feet in a noisy, misty froth of white before continuing its quiet journey down the mountain. Perched on boulders overlooking the waterfall were two slender, jeans-clad teenage girls. A third, blond and petite and laughing, was thigh-deep in the center of the stream just above the waterfall, legs braced apart, blue T-shirted back resting securely against the white T-shirted chest of a tawny-maned, bronze-skinned pretty-boy.

Rory and Jess Feldman. Lynn's eyes narrowed. Despite all appearances to the contrary—she was a hair taller than Lynn now and her childish wiriness had recently been augmented by budding curves—Rory was still a child at fourteen. A boy-crazy child.

Jess Feldman, on the other hand, was no boy. He had to be at least thirty. And, unbelievably, the no-good so-and-so had his arms around Rory.